# "I would aid you," Wolfram vowed in a soft murmur.

Genevieve's lips parted, then she seemed to abruptly recall something less than pleasant. She pulled herself up stiffly and pushed away from him.

"You?" she demanded scornfully, and her tone stung. *"You* would aid me? What kind of poor joke is this?"

"I said I would aid you because I would," he repeated stubbornly.

Genevieve tossed her chin. "As if I would willingly accept the aid of one who cold-bloodedly murdered my own brother," she spat.

To hear the words fall from her lips was no small shock, but Wolfram schooled himself not to turn away. "Well can I understand your anger," he began, though in truth he was destined to say no more.

"You do not even deny it!" she cried. Fury snapped unbridled in Genevieve's eyes, and with a sudden burst of strength, she pushed him away!

Dear Reader,

Claire Delacroix began her Unicorn Trilogy with *Unicorn Bride*, the story that introduced the de Pereilles, a family whose sons bear the mark—and the curse—of the ancient kings of France. With *Unicorn Vengeance*, this talented author brings us another tale of destiny and intrigue, with the story of Genevieve, a young noblewoman determined to bring her brother's murderer to justice. Don't miss this exciting medieval tale.

Miranda Jarrett continues to entertain audiences with her stories of the Sparhawks of Rhode Island. *The Sparhawk Bride* is a delightful adventure about an illegitimate son, raised to be an instrument of revenge, who kidnaps a favorite Sparhawk daughter right from under her parents' nose.

*Heart of the Hawk*, the second book of recent March Madness author Elizabeth Mayne, is a heart-wrenching medieval story of a woman who refuses to marry without love and a man who has vowed to never love again. And *Forever and a Day* is Mary McBride's sequel to her bittersweet Western romance, *The Fourth of Forever*. You'll enjoy it even if you missed the first book.

Whatever your taste in historical reading, we hope Harlequin Historicals will keep you coming back for more. Please keep a lookout for all four titles, available wherever books are sold.

Sincerely,

Tracy Farrell
Senior Editor

Please address questions and book requests to:
Harlequin Reader Service
U.S.: 3010 Walden Ave., P.O. Box 1325, Buffalo, NY 14269
Canadian: P.O. Box 609, Fort Erie, Ont. L2A 5X3

# CLAIRE DELACROIX

# Unicorn Vengeance

## Harlequin Books

TORONTO • NEW YORK • LONDON
AMSTERDAM • PARIS • SYDNEY • HAMBURG
STOCKHOLM • ATHENS • TOKYO • MILAN
MADRID • WARSAW • BUDAPEST • AUCKLAND

ISBN 0-373-28893-X

UNICORN VENGEANCE

**Books by Claire Delacroix**

Harlequin Historicals

*Romance of the Rose #166
Honeyed Lies #209
†Unicorn Bride #223
*The Sorceress #235
*Roarke's Folly #250
†Pearl Beyond Price #264
The Magician's Quest #281
†Unicorn Vengeance #293

*The Rose Trilogy
†Unicorn Trilogy

---

## CLAIRE DELACROIX

An avid traveler and student of history, Claire Delacroix can be found at home when she has a deadline, amid the usual jumble of books, knitting needles and potted herbs.

For Konstantin,
who invariably knows the score before I do

# *Prologue*

A sword age, a wind age, a wolf age.
No longer is there mercy among men.
      —*The Sybil's Prophecy,* circa 1000 A.D.

*Montsalvat—August 1307*

To think that idealism could dictate one's end.

Wolfram watched his victim's breathing slow until it stopped. He waited patiently for the next breath without really expecting it. When it did not come, he reached calmly to check the dead man's pulse.

There was none.

Wolfram permitted himself a curt nod of satisfaction in a job well done and exhaled shakily.

It had been almost too easy, though this task could never be easy enough for him. Indeed, Wolfram had expected a king of kings to have better personal security and that his task would be more arduous. He spared a glance to the hall surrounding him, listening to the labored breathing of those slumbering with rising disgust.

A useless lot were these. The military man within him curled his lip at such behavior. They were all asleep, he observed, scanning the room once more to confirm the truth of that.

Not a single witness. Wolfram could hardly have planned it better. Unfortunate 'twas for this ambitious lordling that he had not shown better judgment in selecting those around him.

Truly Alzeu de Pereille had brought this upon himself with his loose tongue and his poor security. Only too quick had he been to identify himself and spill his tale for Wolfram, despite the fact that he knew naught of Wolfram and that all his retinue slept drunkenly about him.

'Twas beyond belief that a man could be so foolish. Now that his dreaded task was behind him, Wolfram released the breath he had not known he was holding and scanned the hall with new eyes.

He noted the disrepair of the stone walls and the flagstones in the floor that needed refitting. The sight recalled the impression of faded glory he had had on first entering the stables and hall of this old château. One might have expected more of a man of such apparent ambition, Wolfram thought wryly. He tugged on his gloves with economical gestures.

But then one would think that a man of power would realize that this drunken wastrel had offered no real threat to anyone. Wolfram could not imagine why he had been ordered here. But orders he had, and their very existence showed the dreamer Alzeu de Pereille to be a marked man. Should Wolfram have failed, another would have followed fast on his heels and Alzeu would have seen but a few more sunrises before meeting his Maker.

Wolfram considered the dead man once again and shook his head disparagingly in recollection of his fanciful tales. The lost king returning to stake his claim. The nonsense this man had spouted before the poison took effect was quite astounding.

Even more remarkable was the fact that Alzeu had apparently believed every word of it. This drunken wretch had truly believed that he was the culmination of a line of kings destined to rule by divine right. Incredible. Like something out of the old *chansons* it was, though everyone knew those days of chivalrous knights and magical maidens were long gone.

If indeed they had ever existed. Aye, Alzeu had but used such whimsy to his own ends.

Indeed, Wolfram had been remiss in feeling the slightest twinge of pity for this man, for this was one who twisted the dreams of others to his own benefit. Alzeu had been an opportunist, no more than that, and Wolfram wondered how many had been swayed into aiding him by the purely romantic appeal of his claim.

'Twas revolting that a man could use others thus, and mayhap 'twas that offense that had earned Alzeu de Pereille his due.

It mattered naught. Wolfram had fulfilled his orders, as usual, and had not another task ahead of him as yet. Truly, he would take his time in ambling back to Paris, for he did not look forward to the granting of another task. He would earn his keep in this way, for he had no other choice, but he would not hasten to gain another commission.

Suddenly he recalled Alzeu's claim of a mark and eyed the corpse with curiosity. Could it be true? Should he check?

But nay. Wolfram resolutely stifled the impulse to look for his victim's reputed birthmark. If it existed, it was probably as false as his claim to the throne. Whimsy 'twas. No more than that. Wolfram snorted once to himself and spared another appraising glance over the hall before he stalked toward the stables on quick, quiet feet.

Had he heard something stir? Wolfram hesitated on the threshold, his heart in his mouth, and looked back over his shoulder with a frown. But nay, all was still. The keep was too silent for there to be another awake within it. He shook himself deliberately to shed the fanciful notion.

Truly, this place could addle a man's wits. The fog shrouding the bailey and the stillness filling the keep troubled him more than he might have expected. Practical he was beyond all else, and generally immune to such fanciful

notions as divinely appointed kings returning to rule all of
Christendom. 'Twas the fog alone that gave the tale any
credence. Wolfram turned to leave, determined to put some
distance between himself and enchanted Montsalvat this
very night.

The gatekeeper had not even seen his face, Wolfram realized with sudden pleasure. 'Twas a job well done, despite
his earlier reservations, if he did say so himself.


Nay! It could not be thus!

Genevieve blinked, then peered around the corner once
more. She knew not precisely what transpired below, but
liked it naught. Alzeu still lay as motionless as he had when
first she looked. Red wine spread lethargically from the
spilled goblet to cover the plank of the table and drip onto
the rushed floor.

The stranger bent over Alzeu and touched his throat.
Genevieve huddled into the shadows and watched him as
well as she could, instinctively distrusting him and his presence. He waited a long moment, almost as though he listened, then finally nodded with curt satisfaction. Not one
of the unsavory crew of mercenaries Alzeu had hired was
this one, for he was neatly groomed. Genevieve's heart faltered with uncertainty. The stranger's hand dropped away,
and he surveyed Alzeu with a dispassionate eye.

Something had happened to Alzeu! And unless Genevieve knew less of the world than she thought she did, this
man was responsible. He glanced up, and she caught her
breath as she ducked back around the corner and closed her
eyes. Her heart pounded in her ears, and Genevieve prayed
he had not seen her.

Where had this man come from? The gate was barred,
and no one could arrive so late. That he must have gained
entry so late fed her doubts.

Surely she would have remembered such a man had he
been amongst them earlier. She could not restrain herself
from taking another peek around the corner, not daring to

breathe even when she saw that he was completely unaware of her presence. He flicked a glance around the hall and donned his gloves with ease as he stared down at Alzeu.

With considerably more than her usual interest in the other gender, Genevieve noted his attributes. Tall of stature he was, broad-shouldered and well wrought. He was distinctively fair in coloring, more fair than any she had seen afore.

Nay, Genevieve would well have recalled this one. His hair was thick and straight but so light of hue that it seemed to have no color at all. He moved with a deft grace that fascinated her, each motion accomplished with a minimum of effort and with an economy of movement.

Genevieve guessed that he did not act impulsively—that was a trait that consistently drew her into difficulties—and she was immediately envious.

He glanced up to scan the hall, and she caught her breath at the pallor of his eyes. Of the lightest gray they were, and she was reminded of the cold gaze of a wolf. His nose was straight, his cheekbones were high, his jaw was square and determined. His features might have been called handsome if his expression had not been harshly forbidding.

Well it seemed that he had judged Alzeu and found him wanting. Genevieve shivered despite herself at her impression. Instinctively she felt protective of her only sibling and glanced uneasily to his inert form.

What had the stranger done? Or was Alzeu merely asleep?

She eyed the stranger as he donned his helmet, unwilling to confront him before she knew precisely what had passed. Though 'twas clear he meant to leave and she might have no opportunity to challenge him. Genevieve toyed with the idea of challenging him, but hesitated in the shadows.

For if he had wrought any evil, who would defend her here? Genevieve fidgeted indecisively. She alone remained awake, and even should they have awakened, this sorry lot of mercenaries would merely have rolled over to continue their dreams.

'Twas best to wait until she knew the fullness of the tale.

The stranger glanced up suddenly, as though he sensed her presence, and Genevieve's heart skipped a beat. He might see her! Then what would be her fate? She danced back into the shadows, wincing at the cold imprint of stone through her sheer chemise. She flattened her hands against the stone and pressed herself backward, as though she would render herself so small as to be invisible.

She dared not breathe, and all the while she cursed herself for standing and staring. 'Twas unlike her to be so curious, though no time was there now to make sense of her response. Genevieve strained her ears, certain she would hear sounds of pursuit at any instant.

Naught but silence carried to her ears.

Just when she thought she could remain still no longer, she heard soft footsteps on the stone. They receded, one measured step at a time.

He was leaving. Genevieve sagged against the wall in her relief. Hoofbeats did she hear an eternity later, then silence filled the hall once more.

He was gone.

No sooner had the thought filtered into Genevieve's mind than she was around the corner and down the stairs.

"Alzeu!"

He was too still. Genevieve saw it instantly and liked it naught. 'Twas unnatural. She skidded to a halt beside her brother and touched his hand but it fell limply from his side. She touched his grizzled cheek gently, but he responded naught, even when she patted him more forcefully.

"Alzeu!" she cried in desperation, but he slept on. She gave his cheek a resounding slap, knocking the overturned chalice with her elbow and sending it rolling across the board. It dropped out of sight, landing on the rushed floor with a subdued thump and leaving a ruddy trail of wine.

With shaking fingers, Genevieve touched the spot on her brother's neck where the stranger had touched him.

Naught. Her eyes widened in shock and disbelief.

Nay! She must be wrong! Was his flesh cooler than it should be? She touched a tentative finger to her own throat and felt the pounding of her heart echo beneath her fingertip.

Alzeu's heart was still.

Nay! Anything but this! Naught had they but each other—he could not be gone!

"Alzeu! Awake! Do not leave me!" Genevieve frantically tried to revive her brother, the sense growing within her that 'twas futile.

Alzeu merely lolled back on the bench, his form threatening to topple to the floor.

'Twas unthinkable that Genevieve should be left alone. Alzeu could not be gone. He had promised to find her a spouse. He had promised that they would be safe here. He had promised her the security and stability of a new life. Genevieve's vision glazed with tears, and she shook Alzeu, knowing in her heart that he would not awaken.

But Alzeu was departed and Genevieve had naught.

Tears rose to choke her, and she turned to glare at the portal to the courtyard. This stranger had done this. Somehow, in some way, he had stolen Alzeu's heartbeat and, with that, taken the last of her family away from her and the last vestige of her hope. He had stolen Genevieve's only dream as surely as if he had ripped it from her breast.

'Twas his fault alone, and in that instant, Genevieve loathed the fair stranger with every fiber of her being.

But how had he taken Alzeu's life? Was he a sorcerer? An assassin? No wound did Alzeu sport that Genevieve could see, and she frowned for a moment. She stared at the floor as she thought, and her gaze lit suddenly on the toppled chalice.

Her heart went still. It could not be.

On impulse, Genevieve dug the bloodstone from Alzeu's pocket. In good intent had she given him this token, but he had been fool enough to neglect to use it. Too bold he had been with his declarations, too ready had he been to reveal his lineage to any who might listen. Filled with fear that bravado had been her brother's undoing, Genevieve kissed the stone before casting it into the spilled wine.

The stone immediately turned black.

Alzeu had been poisoned. Genevieve's lips set in a thin line of determination, and her eyes narrowed. Well enough did she know who had wielded that poison. There could be only one responsible.

And Genevieve de Pereille would see that he paid the price.

Who might have prompted his hand? Too fair was the stranger for these parts and she wondered what distant soul had seen fit to ensure her brother's demise. Genevieve frowned at the bloodstone, struggling to think clearly before grief overwhelmed her. Their lineage granted them divine right to rule. Surely Alzeu had not dreamed . . . ?

It mattered naught what Alzeu had dreamed. Genevieve knew her brother to have had more sense than that. Bold he was with his tongue, but naught else. Someone, though, had feared he nurtured the dream of his legacy.

And such a dream could be a threat only to someone in Paris. It had happened before and Genevieve's confidence in her idea grew with the recollection. Fourteen years in the hills and the loss of both parents had Genevieve to show for such zeal from the crown.

Now the last of her family had been stolen away, as well.

Well it seemed that she might find the blond stranger making a path to Paris to deliver news of his success. Genevieve's lips set stubbornly, and she squared her shoulders.

And well might that stranger be surprised to find the score was not settled as yet.

# Chapter One

'Twas weeks before she reached her goal.

Genevieve's coin was gone when she stumbled through the gates of Paris, despite her care with it. The horse she had sold in the last town before Paris, yet the beast had not fetched much coin. She had walked the last distance and her shoes were now riddled with holes. The only thing of value she carried was her lute, but to part with it was out of the question, regardless of her hunger.

The lute contained her very soul. Indeed, it always had.

But Paris. 'Twas beyond any expectation. Despite her exhaustion, Genevieve was revolted by its sprawl, its occupants and its stench. 'Twas huge beyond compare. Impossible 'twas to discern any pattern in the city's layout, the veritable rabbit warren of streets confusing her almost as soon as she entered the gates.

It overwhelmed her every sense.

And the press of people was enough to drive her mad. Never had she guessed there could be so many souls in all of Christendom, let alone within the confines of one city's walls. They pressed against her from every side, the casual touch of strangers flooding her with panic. 'Twas confusing beyond compare for one raised in a small company, and Genevieve was disoriented in a span of time that might have been embarrassing, had there been anyone she knew to note that fact.

'Twas only as she gazed in confusion at seemingly endless yet unfamiliar walls and gates, towers and portals, that the resolve that had doggedly carried her this far faltered. How would she find Alzeu's murderer in this place? Had she launched herself on a futile chase?

Never had she dreamed that Paris, or indeed any place at all, could be so large. She saw now that she had been a fool to imagine Paris as no more crowded than Montsalvat, where one might readily recognize all who dwelt within its walls. Indeed, she had never known any place larger and had not considered the matter overmuch.

Paris went on forever, each square much like the last, each street as filthy as the one before. Doubt and disappointment flooded Genevieve's heart as she ambled closer to the heart of the city, for indeed she had little certainty that Alzeu's killer had come here at all.

Or he could have come and gone in the time it had taken her to travel thus far.

Well it seemed that impulsiveness might have steered her false yet again. Genevieve might have come all this way for naught. Despair welled up within her, the smell of fresh bread doing naught to lift her spirits. Her belly growled, and she spared it a consoling pat, for that was likely all it would get this day.

"A bit of silver for a song!" cried a voice unexpectedly.

Genevieve's was not the only head to turn, though her eyes widened when the slender man began to sing and the bustling crowd not only made space for him, but paused to listen. People smiled to each other and listened to his *chanson* as he stood with hands clasped before him and sang. Genevieve endured the press of alien bodies, some washed, some more odorous than she might have thought possible, to indulge her curiosity.

This, too, was new to her, but she intuitively guessed it might have import for her and eyed the man who had cried out with avid curiosity.

The minstrel appeared young at first glimpse, though his face was tanned and his shoulders were broader than those of a boy. His voice was remarkably clear and true. Despite his unkempt state, his features beamed with pride in his abilities as the song unfurled from his lips. Well could Genevieve understand, for she felt much the same satisfaction when she played her lute.

The minstrel's hair was a most uncommon orange color and hung long. His garb was shabby, but despite the oddity of his appearance, he summoned a most charming smile for the onlookers. Genevieve suspected he had no hearth himself to which he might return this night and she felt a curious kinship with him, for all his unfamiliarity.

Still his voice was beautiful. She could not readily decipher the tale, for his words flowed too swiftly for her. Mayhap he spoke another tongue, though it seemed that Genevieve alone did not understand. The onlookers were enthralled, and many appeared to be struck dumb by his tale.

Genevieve noted but one disturbance, and she glanced up at the interruption to find a tall man, distinguished of carriage and silver of mane, pushing his way through the assembly. His manner was that of a man of import, his concern with naught but his own interest. The red cross of the Temple blazed across the breast of his white tabard. A small retinue awaited him on the periphery of the crowd, and a proud silver destrier was held at the ready for his return. Genevieve knew he must be a high ranking officer in the Order of the Templars.

His gaze was avid as he watched the minstrel, and well it seemed that he hung on every word, as though he would devour the tale. The crowd left a minute space around this older Templar, and she wondered briefly at his station, that he should be of repute among the people.

Then the minstrel raised his voice and she forgot all else. When he sustained the last note with a flourish and took a deep bow that had clearly been practiced, more than one silver denier struck the ground before him. Genevieve gasped, her gaze greedy as she tried to count the coins before he collected them all.

She might have spoken to the minstrel, had she not glimpsed the cold avarice in his eyes as he scrambled for his coins. The change of expression surprised her and she realized, rather late, that his charm had been but a cloak readily donned for his audience.

Genevieve turned away with the rest of the crowd now returning to their various occupations even as she tried to make sense of what she had seen. The Templar strode back to his party and swung into his saddle, his brow drawn in a frown as he gave his spurs to his beast.

Silver for a song, indeed, Genevieve mused. The idea had merit in itself, even if the singer's character was less wholesome than she might have hoped. Genevieve could not sing, but she had her lute. She tapped its round belly speculatively as she walked.

Mayhap it could earn her enough to fill her own belly. The possibility fairly made her dizzy. 'Twas true she had a quest to fulfill here, but with her belly hollow, she could not consider what to do with any skill.

First Genevieve had to eat.

She had but to find a spot in which to settle and play. One well trafficked, where she might be readily seen. Flushed with excitement, Genevieve wound her way through the streets, selecting and discarding locations with lightning speed.

Quite suddenly, she came into a square that was dominated by a high tower opposite. Indeed the tower was taller than any she had yet seen, and she gaped at it for a long moment before she saw the walls that rose high around it.

Some establishment of repute was clearly trapped within those walls, which surrounded a goodly number of buildings in addition to the tower. A moat encircled the walls, much to Genevieve's surprise, for they were within Paris itself. This solidly built edifice looked more to be a structure one might find isolated in the wilderness.

'Twas busy here, despite the imposing walls, yet she could find refuge from passing feet against a far wall. 'Twould suit her purpose well, she decided with an assessing eye. The gate stood opposite and people flowed through it in both directions. Noble people, by their garb. Wealthy people. Mayhap kindly folk were within.

Mayhap she might readily earn a meal. Her heart overflowing with optimism, Genevieve found a sheltered spot in plain view. She unwrapped the lute from its protective blanket and examined it carefully for any sign of damage gained in its travels. Genevieve knew full well that she was but delaying the moment she was coming to dread as fears multiplied in her mind.

What if no one listened? What if they did not hold the lute in regard here in the north? Her examining fingers found no new blemish on the instrument, whose surface she knew as well as her own skin, though they moved with a quickness that revealed her agitation.

The lute was fine. Genevieve breathed a sigh of relief and sat down carefully on her cloak. She swallowed nervously as the crowd brushed past her and wondered whether she was being foolish.

Even if they did not stop or listen, playing would soothe her spirits. It always had. And Paris unsettled her with its noise and activity. That conviction alone made her choice.

Blind to all around her, Genevieve bent over the instrument and coaxed a tune from its reluctant strings. Mute it had been for too many days, and for an instant she feared that she might have lost her touch.

But nay. Genevieve closed her eyes as she smiled at the rising sound, reassured by its familiar beauty. She imagined the wind at Montsalvat, the way it tore through her hair as she stood on the high walls, and her fingers took on a grace that eluded them in all other facets of her life.

Naught did she hear but the music, and indeed, it wound its very magic into her soul. It tempted her smile to broaden, it recalled the craggy hills around her home, it reminded her of the taste of the salt in the wind. It caressed her, it was the lover she had never known.

The music was everything, just as it always had been. When she played, naught else mattered in her world. Though indeed Genevieve wrought the sound herself, 'twas as separate from her as though she but released it from its prison.

She was lost in a spell of her own making before half a dozen heartbeats had passed. Alzeu and his murderer were forgotten. Genevieve rocked as the lute sang its haunting tune, her fingers plucking at the familiar strings to coax sweeter and yet sweeter sounds from them.

'Twas this she had been born to do, and naught else could trouble her when she played.

The familiar stench of Paris beckoned Wolfram across the last few miles. He spied the walls of the city that came closest to home for him these days with no small measure of relief. Its pungency assaulted him as he rode beneath the gate and he inhaled deeply of its welcome odor, glad to be within the city's embrace once more. A sense of urgency assailed him, as it always did when he first entered the city's gates, and that old desire to be secure within the heavy walls of the Temple itself set his heels digging into his tired beast's side.

'Twas there alone that he was safe, fed and clothed, secure from the fear of pursuit. 'Twas for that sense of safety alone that he did what he did and fulfilled his orders.

Indeed, there was naught else he could do to earn his place within those walls.

Mere moments passed before Wolfram spied the great double donjon of the Temple towering over the walls of the Ville Neuve du Temple, as solidly reassuring as anything he had ever known. He permitted himself a silent sigh of relief.

Safe again.

A pair of brother knights in full habit rode out from the gate as Wolfram approached. Their appearance, so different from his own, served to give Wolfram his usual pang of jealousy, though he stifled it with a speed born of habit. No right had Wolfram to wear the distinctive white habit of the Order, with its blazing red cross. He was not knighted, a legacy of his illegitimate past, though he had wanted to be knighted with every fiber of his being as long as he could recall.

Still, he had joined the chivalric Order that possessed his dreams, though he had been welcome only as a sergeant.

As 'twas, he could not risk donning even the plain brown mantle of a sergeant brother for fear his presence might be noted. Dressed like any other traveler he was, for 'twas part of his task to blend into the secular world. He checked about himself, though he knew what he would find before he ever looked.

None appeared to have even noted his presence.

Wolfram stood out in no crowd. Anonymity was the key not only to Wolfram's success, but also to his very survival.

'Twas no more than his due to be alone, though increasingly he found that burden difficult to bear. Aging he was, and the solitude of his life chafed within him more and more with each passing day.

Wolfram's gaze rose reluctantly to the gates of that place he called home. His vow to obey had Wolfram granted, and he supposed he was no more lonely than anyone else within this world. Traffic passed through the gates, those sworn to the Templars readily distinguishable from their secular guests.

A twinge of dissatisfaction coursed unexpectedly through Wolfram that he could not openly confess his allegiance. 'Twas an irony of his task that outside the Temple he disappeared into the populace, but here, in the place that came closest to his home, Wolfram appeared as an outsider.

He blended into the crowd everywhere but belonged no-where. The thought had not occurred to Wolfram before and he found it did not sit comfortably. Like the wolf he was named for was he, he realized, for his life was solitary above all else. He belonged nowhere and none belonged with him. His loyalty was to the Order alone.

Wolfram shook the whimsy that clung to his mind like Montsalvat's fog. A cluster of travelers approached the Temple gates from the other direction, their steeds clearly tired after a day of riding, their riders spattered with mud and no less tired themselves. Neither mud nor muted garb could conceal that these were nobles, for their posture and their retinue revealed their ilk. 'Twas clear they made for the haven of the Temple, as well. No doubt had Wolfram that 'twas the reputed safety of the Temple that beckoned them, and indeed they could well afford to pay the price.

He wondered whether they owed any coin to the house. Only the Master knew for certain, but Wolfram would not have been surprised. Mayhap 'twould have been more per-tinent to consider how much they owed to the house. He al-lowed them to enter the gate before him, holding his steed to one side as their retainers passed into the sheltered court-yard.

'Twas then the snare was unexpectedly cast about him.

The plaintive sounds of a lute played with consummate skill carried to Wolfram's ears as he paused outside the fa-miliar gates.

A lute. The very sound prompted him to close his eyes against a rush of recollection. He swallowed hard, then glanced over his shoulder, seeking out the sound.

'Twas only when the travelers had passed that he spotted the woman sitting on the far side of the square before the Temple gates. She bent over the instrument, oblivious of all around her as she picked out an enchanting tune.

Well it seemed that once he permitted himself to listen, Wolfram could not turn away. The tune was haunting. It wound into his ears and teased him with a memory just beyond reach. The music taunted him to listen, to halt the merest instant longer, that he might recall some forgotten golden moment. His steed flicked his ears, but seemed disinclined to move, as well.

The pair lingered there for a long moment, simply feeding on the heady richness of the sound.

The sky shaded to the indigo of twilight, a last ruddy blush from the sun tinging the western horizon above the buildings. A bite was there in the air, a tinge of autumn and the winter yet to come that prompted one to shiver. Yet Wolfram was oblivious of all, so transfixed was he by the music.

When the woman bent lower and he saw the tangle of ebony hair tumble from her hood, he could not have kept himself from dismounting. Her hair gleamed with the rich luster of silk from the Orient in the fading light, and he wondered how 'twould feel against his fingers. The music lured Wolfram closer and tempted him to look at a woman for the first time in his days.

And look he did. So different was she from the rough men with whom he spent his life, and Wolfram's gaze devoured her daintiness. Her bones were delicate and her flesh was fairer and clearly of a finer ilk than his own. She was petite, the breadth of her shoulders much smaller than that of even the boys squired to the Order, and Wolfram was stuck by how like a gentle bird she was.

A gentle bird who sang with the sweet voice of a lute.

And that hair. Never had he seen the like. It poured from her hood and spilled over her shoulders, concealing her face, her arm, part of the lute. Like a dark river 'twas, and it moved and glistened in the fading light as though it could not be restrained. Never had Wolfram believed hair could be of such abundance, such gloss, such a color. Indeed, it seemed to have a life of its own, the way it moved as she played. 'Twas irrational, this compelling urge to finger those dark strands, but the music swept all doubts from Wolfram's mind.

To approach her would bring him closer to that magical
sound, no small thing, though Wolfram would not try to
fathom why the music moved him so. The woman did not
even look up as he approached, and he watched her fingers
dance across the strings, feeling himself a voyeur though
indeed she played in a public place.

'Twas the nicker of a horse alone that interrupted her
thoughts. Genevieve glanced up like a startled doe, surprised to find the square fallen into darkness. She shivered
in the chill of the evening, freezing in place when she realized that a man stood silently before her.

Silhouetted against the twilight sky he was, and so still
that she wondered if indeed he was real. The bustle of the
crowd had faded away, leaving him alone before her, his
horse just behind. Genevieve knew he watched her, though
she could not discern his features in the shadows. The scent
of countless evening meals rode above the scent of Paris itself, and Genevieve could not look away.

Something unnerving there was about his stare. Indeed,
the hairs on the back of her neck prickled beneath its intensity, and Genevieve could not have urged her fingers to stir
for any price.

It seemed that all of Paris held its breath and waited.

Suddenly the man stepped forward and into a chance ray
of light. The fairness of his flaxen hair surprised her, but she
dismissed her heart's whimsical lurch out of hand. Many
blondes there must be in the north, she reasoned, though her
pulse began to pound in her ears with uncharacteristic vigor.
He fumbled in his tabard, then glanced up.

Genevieve gasped to find his eyes were palest gray. Pale
eyes, pale hair. Indeed, his very face was etched indelibly
within her mind.

'Twas him! 'Twas the very man she sought who stood
before her!

Well it seemed that Genevieve's mind froze motionless at
the shock. Then it began to gallop. What was he doing here?

Did she but dream, or had she miraculously guessed aright and found him? Against all odds it seemed, yet despite her blinking in disbelief, his solid figure remained before her. Genevieve barely heard the tinkle of the coin hitting the cobblestones as she fought to make sense of the evidence before her eyes.

The numbness of shock was abruptly replaced by the fear of not knowing how to proceed. Indeed, she had scarce dared to believe she might ever lay eyes upon him. What should she do? What should she say? Naught came instantly to mind, and Genevieve struggled to decide how to handle a situation she had thought herself hopeless to engineer. Well had she despaired of ever seeing this man again, but now he stood directly before her.

And she was too dumbfounded to even speak. Genevieve fancied that he almost smiled, as though he understood her predicament, before he turned away. Impossible 'twas, yet she could not completely stifle her fear that those pale eyes had seen the secret pledge buried deep within her.

Turned away! Too late her mind made sense of what she saw.

Nay! Genevieve could not let him leave! He was astride his horse and through the gates opposite before she managed to rise to her feet. Too much 'twas to imagine that she might lay eyes upon him again! An opportunity spun of gold had Dame Fortune granted Genevieve, but she had done naught of merit with the gift!

"Sir! I would speak with you a moment!" she cried, but to no avail. Either the stranger did not hear her or he chose to ignore her, for he rode away undeterred.

Where was he going? How would she find him again? Genevieve ran in pursuit. By the time she reached the gates opposite, he had disappeared into the grip of the twisted streets within. As she strained to catch up with him, a portly man stepped squarely into her path and blocked her way.

"What is your business within the Temple?" the gate-keeper demanded tersely. Genevieve might have brushed past him, but the man would not be evaded. She danced to one side and the other impatiently, but still he persistently blocked her path, a frown darkening his brow.

"I must speak to that man!" she insisted wildly. The keeper folded his arms across his chest.

"I cannot let you pass without knowing your business here," he maintained stonily. Genevieve sighed with frustration and peered over the man's shoulder, only to find that her quarry had melted into the shadows within the gates as surely as though she had not seen him at all.

"Is it not enough that I would speak with that one?" she asked, knowing the answer all the while. Genevieve strained her ears but heard naught even of his horse's hooves. The keeper shook his head and impatience flooded through her.

"Why did you let *him* pass without challenge?" she demanded in annoyance.

"His business I know," the keeper said flatly.

Genevieve regarded the man in shock. Alzeu's killer was known within the Temple? But he wore no mark of the Order. Genevieve's mind raced as she recalled every rumor she had heard about the mysterious knights.

The Templars were widely rumored to have a deft hand with poison. She saw the blackened bloodstone again in her mind's eye and wondered how many of those rumors were indeed truth. Had someone hired the Templars to dispatch Alzeu? But why? Genevieve eyed the keeper, but he did not confide in her further.

"Now, what of yours?" he demanded.

Hers? Her business here. What business could she possibly have within the Temple? Something Genevieve had to contrive afore her quarry was lost within. Indeed she could not trust to chance that she might encounter him again.

Suddenly Genevieve recalled the business that the Temple conducted openly and that all knew. Bankers the Templars were to all of Christendom, and that fact might well be turned to her advantage.

"A deposit I come to claim," Genevieve lied with a boldness that she hoped might be mistaken for confidence. The keeper's lips twisted wryly and her heart sank.

"Aye?" he asked archly and clearly disbelievingly. "Then you should have no trouble showing me your receipt."

Curse the man! Genevieve had no receipt, and well did she know she could not even forge one. Too late she recalled that the Templars were known for encoding their receipts that counterfeits might not be readily made. She patted her pockets and feigned surprise that naught crinkled.

"'Twas here ere I left," she mused. The skeptical keeper braced his hands on his hips.

"Not within your lute, mayhap?" he suggested slyly. Genevieve slanted him a hostile glance. "You come not to claim a deposit," he informed her solemnly. "Well have I seen and heard you play your lute all this day. No passage will I grant you, for readily enough can I see that you mean to pursue that man within. Well you should know that traffic with women is forbidden by the Rule. Plague me no more with your tales and I will not see that you are removed from begging so close to the Temple gates."

'Twas a threat with which Genevieve could not argue. She opened her mouth, but closed it again, knowing full well that she could not make a case in her own favor.

Curse the keeper, for he was right. And Genevieve could not risk losing her spot at any price, especially so soon after seeing Alzeu's killer again.

Never mind knowing that he lingered within the walls of the Temple. She endeavored to peek over the keeper one last time before she turned away, but that man scowled deeply and disapprovingly.

"Wearing my patience thin, you are," the gatekeeper growled. "I bade you leave this gate. Obey me now ere I have you removed."

"But—"

"Nay! No argument have you that will stay my hand!" the keeper declared with impatience in his tone. "No vagabonds do I let pass, and neither will I permit you to enter the Temple! Away with you!"

Genevieve eyed him for but an instant before she saw the fullness of his intent. No access would she have here on this day. She sighed, frowned and turned reluctantly away, feeling that she had failed Alzeu beyond belief.


The coin had not been his to grant.

The knowledge burned within Wolfram, and he felt the back of his neck heat at his realization. Naught had he to call his own—all he carried was the property of the Temple, held communally for the benefit of all. But a few coins was he granted on each excursion, in case of unforeseen difficulties. Each time he spent one, he had been compelled to supply a rigorous accounting to the Master.

Curse the impulse that had sent that coin flying from his fingers! No acceptable explanation had he for its absence and none could he give. That he had granted alms would do naught but earn him a reprimand. Alms were granted by the house on Tuesday morns and calculated as a percentage of the week's revenues.

No right had Wolfram to independently grant alms. To tell the truth would gain him naught.

But he could lie.

The very thought was shocking for its very traitorousness. To lie to the Master was a crime of the worst order, and Wolfram could barely countenance that he had even conceived of doing so. Never had he lied. Never had he even conceived of lying. Never had he broken the Rule, and he could make no explanation of why such a thought would occur to him now.

The fog of Montsalvat might well have addled his wits, but 'twas the song of the lute that undermined all he knew. He should never have paused to listen.

And he should never have granted to her a coin that was not his own.

Wolfram could not tell the truth about what he had done and he could not lie. 'Twas a predicament of the first order. He scowled as he rode his horse into the stables and dismounted.

He could retrieve the coin.

Wolfram paused in the shadows and considered the wisdom of that option. Indeed, he knew not why he had even granted the lutenist the coin in the first place, he thought with annoyance. Had he been logical, he would never have created this difficulty for himself.

Although no sweeter sound was there to Wolfram than that of the lute. 'Twas only here in the shadows of the stables that he admitted that he had near forgotten that fact. No other music was there that could coax free the distant memories tidily packed away in his mind.

He had locked those memories safely away at the mere age of four, for the sake of his sanity. He would not unleash them now and threaten all that he had gained. He would not, though he was sorely tempted.

Wolfram felt naught, he reminded himself sternly. He believed naught. He trusted none but the Master. These were his own rules. 'Twas this resolve alone that had kept him sane. He would not toss away all he had gained for the stirring sounds of a lute, or even a fetching lutenist.

Yet the lute's music showed neither restraint nor respect for Wolfram's own desires. It threatened to slide the bolts and set those tender memories free once more. He had let the music wend its way into his ears for but a heartbeat before it held him powerless within its silken grip.

A mistake it had been to lend an ear, and he would be a fool to listen again.

But when the lutenist had looked up, the shock in her wide green eyes had broken the spell she was weaving. Even now, Wolfram sobered when he recalled the flash of fear that had lit those remarkable eyes when she first discerned his features. Cold fingers grasped his gut and he shuffled his feet as though he could dislodge their grip.

'Twas almost as though she had seen his secret in that one glimpse. He had felt naked, vulnerable, bare to the elements as he never had before. Every terror he had ever had of discovery had flooded through him in a blinding flash. For an instant, he had been certain that she knew what and who he was, and the exposure he always dreaded had held him captive in its viselike grip.

'Twas then Wolfram had impulsively cast her the coin. A penance? An appreciation of her skill with the lute? An offering born of the sheer delicacy of her and the certainty that she would have to find some shelter? 'Twas all that and more that had prompted Wolfram's hand, though now the gesture made little sense.

Whimsy, he scoffed. What had he hoped to gain? 'Twas impossible that she could know what he did. Impossible. And even if she knew, by some fantastic twist of fate, who would believe the tale of a lutenist who worked in the street? None of repute. He was seeing threat where there was none and letting his customary fears outside the security of the Temple gates take root where there was no soil.

Clearly 'twas no more than that. A squire took his horse's reins, but Wolfram barely noticed the boy, so lost was he in his thoughts.

'Twas evident he would have to recover the coin. He straightened his shoulders as he walked, telling himself that he was foolish to have any doubts about listening to her music again.

'Twas only music, and naught had he to fear. The problem would be solved, the coin would be safely within his grip again before he had to make an accounting to the Master. None would ever know that Wolfram had erred. 'Twas simple.

Before he could even leave the stable, a clerk granted him the summons to the Master's office. In that dread moment, Wolfram was certain that that esteemed man must have guessed what he had done. He felt his color rise guiltily and forced his pulse to resume its normal pace.

Impossible 'twas that the Master could know. Impossible, but the wedge of doubt within Wolfram could not be dislodged.

The pale-eyed stranger had disappeared so completely that Genevieve wondered if indeed she had imagined his presence. Was she not hungry beyond belief? Mayhap her overwrought imagination had conjured him from naught. Mayhap she had not seen him at all. Mayhap the twilight played tricks with her vision.

Mayhap she had been a fool of the worst order to come to Paris. Genevieve confronted the silent square dejectedly as the shadows drew long and cold. The gate creaked behind her as the keeper lowered it against the night and·she strolled dejectedly away.

Naught had changed, and 'twas easy to wonder whether she had conjured him in her mind alone. She shivered suddenly, feeling more solitary than ever she had before.

The sight of the coin reposing on the cobblestones brought her up short. Genevieve straightened carefully, but it moved naught. It glinted in the golden light of the setting sun, and the very sight of it granted her fears a cursory dismissal.

He had been here. But she would not take alms from a killer. Genevieve spun away as disappointment flooded through her.

She had failed to strike the telling blow she had vowed to take. Frustration rose hot and heavy within her breast, and Genevieve fairly stamped her foot. She had seen her enemy and done naught! She had not even learned the man's name! Curse her foolishness! She spun around with the germ of an idea, but the gate was barred and the keeper gone from sight.

Not that that man would have told her anything, she concluded bitterly.

For her indecision, Alzeu's murderer still stalked the streets. Curse her own slow thinking! And in addition, naught had she to show for her attempt to earn some coin. Naught for her belly, naught for shelter on this night when the wind felt fit to bring a flurry of snow. Genevieve shivered again, cursing the threadbare nature of her cloak.

Her gaze dragged unwillingly back to the coin on the cobblestones.

Naught had she but the coin a murderer had cast her way. He alone had seen fit to salute her skill. Genevieve's heart twisted in indecision as she eyed the coin that could be her salvation this night. Wrong 'twould be to take the coin and enjoy the patronage of Alzeu's killer, this she knew without doubt.

As though to challenge that assertion, her belly growled in discontent. Genevieve chewed her lip indecisively. The coin caught the light, as though 'twould deliberately tempt her to pick it up. Dark clouds rolled over the city.

A chill wind frolicked across the roofs and jostled loose shingles. Shutters were slammed shut on a home across the way, and the scent of a freshly kindled fire taunted Genevieve's nostrils. She fancied she could smell roasted meat and readily imagined the scene before many a hearth. 'Twould storm this night, of that she had little doubt.

Genevieve took a step forward, then stopped. 'Twas improper to accept his coin.

But should she leave it, another would undoubtedly pick it up. Well enough she knew that it had been destined for her. A warm dinner 'twould buy, and mayhap modest shelter for this night.

Genevieve looked to one side and the other, as furtively as if she meant to steal boldly from another. Then she darted forward and pounced on the coin, snatching it up and burying it deep in one of her pockets, as though she could not bear to look upon it.

Well it seemed that the coin burned against her flesh.

She glanced around again as though seeking witnesses to her deed and clutched her lute protectively to her chest. No one had glimpsed her betrayal of her family, though indeed knowing the truth within her heart might well be punishment enough. Genevieve gathered up her cloak and glanced back to the gates where he had disappeared without a trace. Those gates were closed against the night, which granted Genevieve an idea.

The stranger could not leave that enclosure this night once the gates were closed. And on the morrow, she would return here at first light, or even before, that she might see him again. Or mayhap the day after. If naught else, he would have to leave the shelter of those walls one day, and Genevieve would be ready.

No matter that the keeper would not let her pass. She would be here, watching and waiting. He would not pass her again without tasting her retaliation! Well would that one regret the day that Genevieve de Pereille found him in Paris.

# Chapter Two

"Ah, our *Italien* returns," the Master commented with his usual slow smile of welcome.

The colloquial reference to his trade never failed to make Wolfram cringe inwardly, but he strove to make no sign of his discomfort. The Master might as well have called him an *empoisonneur* to his face. Much to his annoyance, Wolfram felt his color rise slightly, and felt all too aware of the presence of the esquire who had shown him in.

Next he would be obliged to travel as an astrologer, and any fool would know his task. Had the Master taken leave of his senses to flaunt Wolfram's occupation so openly?

Well it seemed that his encounter with the lutenist had served to make him more sensitive than was his wont. He fidgeted and forced himself to think of other matters.

The esquire was unfamiliar. Though truly that should have been no surprise. But a month past, another had aided the Master of the Temple. It could be naught else but a strategy to constantly change aides, and 'twas a wise one at that, for none toiled here long enough to sense any patterns in the Master's routine. No guest would be recognized or repeat visitors noted by a new assistant. A small safeguard 'twas to ensure no word of what transpired within these offices filtered to the outside world.

'Twas eminently logical, and if naught else, the Master was logical beyond compare. Wolfram respected that. Logical men seldom erred, and he slept better knowing the only one who knew his identity was of the same ilk as himself. He shot the Master a telling glance, disliking that he had made such a fundamental slip before that esquire.

Well it seemed that the Master stifled a smirk.

Wolfram bowed, then straightened to shake the older man's proffered hand. The Master flicked a dismissive finger at the esquire. The young man bowed his head and disappeared, discreetly closing the door behind himself. The Master regarded Wolfram with barely concealed amusement.

"Something troubles you?" he inquired archly.

Wolfram cocked a brow. "I would not presume to comment on your affairs," he said stiffly. The Master chuckled, and Wolfram looked to his superior in alarm.

In but a month, the man had clearly taken leave of his senses.

"Deaf as a post, he is," the Master confided in a devilish whisper. The Master's glittering eyes convinced Wolfram both that his thoughts had been read and that the older man spoke the truth. His ears burned with the knowledge that a jest had been made at his expense, and he took the indicated seat with less than his usual grace.

He cursed the music again that had so addled his wits. How could he have forgotten the Master's wit? All was well here. Wolfram took a deep breath and heard his voice recover its usual tone.

"Of what use is a deaf esquire to you?" he asked with polite curiosity.

"'Tis a great convenience when dealing with those who tend to have loose tongues," the Master confided with reassuringly familiar decorum. "Should I manage to find a deaf esquire who was also mute, I would be the happiest man in Christendom," he added dryly.

Wolfram was surprised enough by the comment that he could not completely quell his snort of laughter. He covered the slip with a discreet cough and looked up to find the Master's expression genial.

"All went well, I assume?" he inquired.

"Better than might have been anticipated," Wolfram acknowledged carefully.

The Master eyed Wolfram for a long moment, as though he sought to identify something different in his manner. Wolfram did not squirm beneath that piercing scrutiny, though his pulse increased with the conviction that the Master could glimpse his innermost thoughts.

Impossible that he could know about the coin. Impossible.

Something flickered in the older man's gaze, and Wolfram was less sure than he might have liked to be. The flame of the candle sputtered in the tallow, and well it seemed that 'twas suddenly uncommonly warm in the office. Wolfram fancied something trickled down his spine, and he counted his pulse in his ears as the silence stretched long between them.

"I trust you will leave me to celebrate alone, as always?" the Master asked finally.

The question caught Wolfram completely off guard. So convinced had he been that an accounting would be demanded on the spot that he blinked dazedly. He gazed uncomprehendingly at the proffered carafe of eau-de-vie for a long moment before realizing what was transpiring.

"Nay. I would join you this time," he said, his voice mercifully more steady than he had feared it would be. The Master shot him another of those piercing glances but refrained from comment as he placed another glass beside the one already on his desk. "A long ride has it been this day," Wolfram added, completely unnecessarily. This time his voice betrayed him in the lie and wavered more than intended.

Curse the lutenist and her nimble fingers.

And her ruddy bowed lips.

That thought stunned Wolfram with its unexpectedness, though the vivid image of those very lips startled him yet more. He had not even realized that he had noticed them, let alone that the sight of them was imprinted on his mind. His chest tightened with the certainty that they would be soft and warm, and he wondered what wicked demon had taken possession of his mind.

Clearly he had best address the matter of the coin as quickly as possible.

He drank the unfamiliar eau-de-vie too quickly to not be surprised by its strength. That the Master chuckled as Wolfram coughed was no consolation. When finally he caught his breath, he fired the older man a hostile glance decidedly beyond the privilege of his station.

"Mayhap 'tis a time to drink like Templars, as the saying goes," the Master jested blithely. Wolfram winced at the fallacious if familiar expression.

The Master, much to Wolfram's confusion, seemed to find the popular saying amusing. He took no heed of Wolfram's less positive response as he drained his own glass. Wolfram waited expectantly for the Master to echo his own flinch at the strength of the liquor, but the other man merely bared his teeth as he swallowed and then exhaled in sharp satisfaction. His gaze was still incisive as it locked once more with Wolfram's.

"More?" he asked brightly.

Mayhap the imbibing of liquor was not as infrequent for the Master as it was for Wolfram. The very idea gave Wolfram pause, and he eyed his superior dubiously. The Master, undeterred, arched a brow high, and Wolfram imagined for the barest instant that that man mocked him.

Ridiculous.

"Nay." Wolfram declined with a hasty frown, unwittingly giving voice to his thoughts. Clearly he was imagining matters that were not there. The Master merely saw fit to celebrate his success at Montsalvat. 'Twas no more than that.

Even if the imbibing of liquor was specifically against the Rule. After all, the Master was free to make exceptions when he saw fit. 'Twas a luxury of his exalted station.

'Twas in the Rule.

Wolfram recalled that the Master had always had a bottle of eau-de-vie at the ready. Although he had always declined to share the toast before this night, he wondered suddenly how often the Master saw fit to imbibe.

Preposterous! Clearly the music of the lute had befuddled his thinking. He gave his head a shake, and the room cavorted before his eyes for a long moment in a slow spiraling dance before settling to rights. This was the Master he sat with, the only man on the face of the earth he saw fit to trust.

Wolfram corrected himself savagely. The only man *worthy* of that trust.

"And what of our petty lordling?" that man inquired conversationally. Though his manner was casual, there was a thread of intense interest underlying the Master's tone. Wolfram watched the Master top up his glass and drain it again, before filling it and replacing the stopper in the bottle. "Was he wealthy and ambitious beyond doubt?"

"Nay." Wolfram shook his head disparagingly. He let the warmth of the liquor relax him and permitted himself to speak freely. The Master was, after all, asking him for information that he alone could supply. "Indeed, I near thought the matter a poor jest at his expense. The village has fallen into ruin for lack of use, and the fortress is a shambles. Long has it been left to crumble, and naught of value was housed within its walls. There was naught to eat and only swill unfit for dogs to drink."

"Ah." Wolfram noted with relief that the Master sipped from this glass. The older man frowned thoughtfully. "But no doubt he had mustered an impressive army?"

"Nay, again," Wolfram supplied with a solid shake of his head. "The company were hired hands, and of the lowest order at that. No doubt have I that they departed with the rising sun.''

"Indeed? Not the sort of men one might want at one's back." The Master snorted with open disdain, and Wolfram could only nod agreement. "Interesting, that is."

"Aye, and a pretty tale he spun for me of his legacy," Wolfram added, feeling that the liquor had betrayed him into speaking more than was his wont. No matter, though. 'Twas the Master alone who listened.

His superior fired him a piercing glance that might have prompted his suspicions, had it come from another. "Indeed?" he asked with a casual air that was clearly feigned. "What manner of tale was this?"

Wolfram shook his head deprecatingly. Incredible 'twas that he knew some tale that the Master did not, and a surge of pride filled him that he might have something of merit to tell. "Well it seemed that Alzeu de Pereille fancied he had a divine right to the throne," he informed the older man, not caring that his skepticism showed.

Surprisingly, the Master did not seem to share his condemnation, though Wolfram was too warm to care.

"Indeed? And he told you freely of this?" he asked carefully.

"Aye," Wolfram agreed easily. "'Twas a high-winded bit of whimsy, to say the least."

The Master traced a circle on his desktop with a fingertip and dropped his gaze to follow that finger's path. "What else did he tell you?" he asked silkily. Wolfram shrugged and frowned as he tried to recall.

"'Twas a tangled tale, and in truth, all I gleaned was his conviction in his divine blood right. The man was besotted when I arrived, and 'twas no small task to make sense of his mutterings. It occurred to me that he might simply be using the gullibility of others to his own advantage."

"I see." The Master smiled an inexplicably secretive smile and leisurely topped up his glass once more as Wolfram's curiosity grew tenfold in expectation. Here lingered a tale he would dearly like to know in truth. The Master made him wait, then finally gestured in dismissal. Wolfram swallowed his disappointment with an effort.

Well it seemed that the time for confidences was not ripe.

Wolfram rose hesitantly, his mind filled with more questions than answers. The Master ignored him, and he abruptly recalled his place. The Master knew best, and obedience was the cornerstone of the Rule. His stomach burning from the unfamiliar liquor, Wolfram did his Master's bidding.

Something nameless prompted him to glance back from the threshold, only to find the Master's lips pursed. The older man held the glass of liquor up so that the candlelight rendered its contents the very shade of liquid gold. Wolfram could not help but wonder what thoughts filled that man's mind.

Whimsy, he snorted impatiently as he turned away. If this 'twas that liquor did to a man's mind, no need had he to taste its heat again.

The next morn dawned a sullen autumn day.

Slate-bellied clouds rolled across a sky of disgruntled blue, and there was a newly vicious bite of winter in the air. The surly mood of the weather was echoed in the expressions of those who listened to the lute's music. Genevieve was disheartened by the lack of coins falling to the cobbles before her.

But hours since he had stood before her, and already Genevieve was beginning to despair that the stranger would ever pass this way again. Both her mood and the weather were echoed in the melancholy tune she plucked. Woefully she admitted that her choice of tune might well be another factor contributing to her meagre earnings.

The daylight had brought a thousand questions to plague her. What would she do if he never passed through those gates again? What if there was another gate to the enclosed Temple? Genevieve dared not risk missing him by scouting around those walls in the daylight, yet once the gates were closed, 'twould be too dark to wander alone.

What if the assassin saw fit to send her to join Alzeu? There was a thought that stilled her heart and made Genevieve's resolve falter. Little enough expertise had she to stave off one such as he, and yet again she marveled at her own audacity.

Curse her own foolish impulsiveness! But what should she do, now that she was in Paris, penniless and far from home?

Indecision plagued her, and Genevieve feared she had made a poor choice in this pursuit. A particularly dark cloud slipped over the sun, and her fingers stilled beneath its cold shadow. Mayhap 'twas time she went home, to face whatever she might find there. Mayhap she had been an idealistic fool to ever think that she could claim vengeance for Alzeu.

'Twas naturally in the darkness of that despairing moment that he came again.

Genevieve knew he was there before she even looked. At first, she dared not believe 'twas so, but she could feel the weight of his gaze upon her as surely as if he had touched her. Her heart skipped a beat, but still she forced her fingers to continue to pluck out the tune while she thought furiously.

He had returned! Here was the second chance she had sought.

But what should she do?

Her pulse leapt in her throat, and Genevieve heard her fingers falter on the strings. Despite all her intent to do so, still she had not devised a plan of any sort. Too late it seemed that she had wasted time worrying about whether this moment would ever come and not what path to pursue if it did. Indeed, she had not thought further than this, and her mind scurried to devise some reasonable course of action.

She felt him draw closer, heard the tread of his boot alone, despite all the other sounds in the square. Her mouth went dry. Feigning ignorance of his presence, Genevieve bent lower over the lute and played, though the tune grew stilted beneath her trembling fingers.

What should she do? What *could* she do? Naught could she say in such a public place, and she could hardly take her vengeance upon this spot. Avenging Alzeu was well and good, but too late Genevieve considered the possible repercussions should she manage to accomplish the deed. Should she take her retaliation publicly, no doubt she would pay for her crime. No taste had Genevieve for languishing in a rat-infested prison for her revenge. There was indeed no need to make her guilt readily clear, but in a public square there would be no escape from observation.

Imperative 'twas that she should find some way to draw the murderer to a secluded corner where neither he nor any other might guess her intent.

Aye. Perfect sense it made, but how to accomplish such a goal? Naught came to mind as she thought furiously, and her tune was drawing to a close. Another tread on the cobbles brought him yet closer, and her fingers quivered in anticipation.

'Twas now or never. Something she must contrive. Genevieve finished her tune with a flourish and took a deep breath before she dared to glance up.

Her gaze immediately locked with one that was pale beyond pale. He stood motionless, watching her like a hunter about to pounce upon his prey. Something else there was in his expression, an intensity she could not fathom, though indeed, the awareness that he watched her alone fired her blood in a most curious way. Genevieve's heart fairly stopped, and suddenly it seemed that the autumn air held less of a bite.

A coin hit the cobbles before her, cast by another onlooker, but Genevieve could not tear her gaze away from his to retrieve it. Trapped she felt. Stalked and cornered, though truly she had thought the reverse to be the case. Had she not sought him out? Was it not she who was the hunter? A shiver crept down her spine as the awareness of what kind of man this was she so boldly eyed, and the hairs stood up at the base of her neck.

Still she could not look away. Though Genevieve felt the crowd of onlookers drift away, she cared naught. The only audience she wanted remained motionless.

So impassive were his features that Genevieve almost fidgeted beneath his perusal. 'Twas as though he were wrought of stone, not flesh and blood, and trepidation made her skin creep. Impossible it seemed that this man could not see to the very recesses of her heart and know the very reason for her presence, though she had breathed a word of it to none.

Could he know? A wave of panic swept over her. And what would he do if he did guess her objective? Genevieve eyed him warily and was reassured naught by what she saw.

'Twas a dangerous man who stood a dozen paces away from her. A man who would not be readily brought down. A man who had killed at least once before. Genevieve felt a niggle of doubt of the wisdom of her path.

Had she truly the skill or the will to fulfill her oath? Genevieve's spirits sank before she caught herself.

He had come back, she reminded herself resolutely. She knew not what had drawn him, but he was here, and that was no small thing. 'Twas a victory of some measure, and an opportunity that could not be overlooked. Genevieve had to ensure that she did not lose him again. Too far away was he for conversation, but as she held his regard, Genevieve sensed he waited for something from her. Why else would he remain?

On impulse, Genevieve smiled.

He straightened abruptly, but did not turn away. Well it seemed to her that his eyes grew brighter, though but a moment sooner she would not have thought that possible. His gaze danced over her face, her hands resting on the silent lute, the barely discernible outline of her crossed legs beneath her faded kirtle, then darted back to her face.

He was surprised. And Genevieve fancied that he was not surprised often. She rather liked that she had managed to unnerve him so in such a short span of time. Well it seemed that the odds had shifted decidedly in her favor. Seemingly of its own volition, her smile broadened, and her lips parted slightly. He stared fixedly but did not move.

A shocking thought assaulted Genevieve with an abruptness that fairly tore the smile from her lips.

What place was more private than bed?

Blood surged hotly through Genevieve's veins at the idea, and she imagined that she flushed scarlet at her audacity. She was suddenly warm beyond compare, though indeed she knew precious little of such matters. Was not her virginity a gift to be cherished by her spouse alone?

Still she could not readily cast the idea aside, particularly given the way the stranger had already responded to her smile. And she had no betrothed who would be bereft.

Truly it might be time to face the reality that she was old to be making a match of any kind. Any man who would have her at the ripe age of nineteen might well not be fussy about details.

Genevieve would have been a fool of the worst order to not realize that this man was attracted to her. Well could she use that fact to her advantage, and 'twas true she might well need every advantage she could muster to emerge victorious from this mission.

And naught said that she would have to make that final sacrifice before accomplishing her goal. Nay, should fortune be on her side, she would not even come close to such a concession. Emboldened by that thought, Genevieve straightened coquettishly and arched her back slightly. His gaze flicked to her breasts and she stifled a surge of victory.

'Twould be almost too easy, she thought.

"I would thank you for your coin the other day," she called encouragingly. He looked momentarily startled before he hastily composed his features. He took a step forward that made Genevieve feel more powerful than she ever had before. Indeed, he stepped willingly into her web.

'Twas truly the perfect strategy.

"Your playing is quite fine," he said carefully. His tone was stiffly formal, and Genevieve thought she detected an accent. Was he a foreigner, then?

What manner of man could take the task he had?

Before a hundred questions could clutter her mind, Genevieve deliberately stifled her curiosity. Predators never showed curiosity about their prey. 'Twould only make the deed more difficult in the end. She swallowed her lingering reservations and forced herself to continue the conversation, that he might come closer.

"Yours was the first coin I earned in Paris," she said in as genial a manner as she could manage.

He took another pair of steps closer but looked away as he slapped his gloves agitatedly against one palm. Well it seemed that he might be uncertain of how to proceed.

Genevieve almost chortled at the sight. Simple as taking a sweet from a child. Indeed, she might well accomplish her task this very day. He cast a glance over her again that made Genevieve suddenly feel so exquisitely feminine that she momentarily lost track of her intent. She forced herself to take a steadying breath and recovered herself.

Until he spoke once more.

"Regrettably, I must ask for its return," he said stiffly.

Genevieve regarded him in shock. She blinked, but he did not look away. Her composure completely lost its footing in the face of this development. Surely she had heard him incorrectly. That coin was long spent.

"I beg your pardon?" she asked breathlessly, feeling markedly less the seductress than she had planned to be.

He cleared his throat and frowned, impaling her with that pale regard so suddenly that it fairly took her breath away. "I must ask for the return of the coin," he repeated. "'Twas not mine to grant."

"But... but, 'tis spent and gone," Genevieve sputtered in protest, hating the hesitancy in her voice. A far cry indeed this was from her plan!

The stranger looked deliberately at the coin that had just been tossed on the cobbles before her. Indignation rolled through Genevieve at his presumption, and she was on her feet in an instant. She swept forward and snatched the coin from the ground before he could lay claim to it, her anger prompting her to wag it beneath his very nose.

"Not yours is this coin, but mine alone!" she declared hotly. He moved naught, though his gaze was bright upon her. "My dinner and board for the night this is, and I will not grant it to you!"

"The coin was not mine to give," he said calmly again, as though she had said naught.

"Well does it seem that you might have considered that before you granted it to me!" Genevieve asserted. A tinge of color stained his neck, and she fancied he gritted his teeth.

"I would have the coin returned," he said tightly.

"Not by me," Genevieve maintained. She tossed her hair back over her shoulder and straightened to her full height. Still she had to lift her chin to stare him in the eye and, had she not been so angered by his audacity, the coldness she found there might have been daunting.

He leaned closer and Genevieve held her breath, though she did not dare look away.

"Give me the coin," he insisted. His hand rose in her peripheral vision, palm up, as though he expected her to meekly drop the requested silver there.

Genevieve slipped her hand into the neck of her kirtle and jammed the coin between her breasts. The way his gaze followed the gesture reminded Genevieve of her original intent and made her bold beyond her wildest dreams.

"Fetch it yourself," she hissed impulsively.

He swallowed and his gaze flicked away. Ha! That had surprised him! When his eyes met hers again, it seemed a flame had been lit there, and Genevieve was tempted to flee from him. But she held her ground, determined to see this matter settled between them.

His gaze was unnaturally steady, and once again she was reminded of the cold stare of a wolf. A wolf on the hunt, a wolf stalking the quarry he would bring down with ease when he was ready to do so. A quarry that he might taunt and tease afore he struck, as surely he would. Naught would stop that wolf from his objective, and Genevieve fancied that little could stop this cold-eyed man. Fear trickled through her with renewed resolve and she wondered what demon fueled her audacious tongue.

But she could not back down now. He had granted her a coin. It had been hers to spend and she had done so. No claim had he on the solitary coin that would ensure her room and board this night.

Still, when he lifted his hand toward her, Genevieve shivered. He touched her wrist and she barely restrained herself from bolting, even as the shock of his intent flooded through her. Would he truly seek out the coin as she had dared him? Did he truly intend to touch her *there?* The heat of his fingertips slid up her arm, but Genevieve could not look away from his simmering regard. Certain she was that his hand shook as his fingers slid over the curve of her shoulder, then his hand rested gently above her heart.

Its frantic pounding would betray her fear, but naught was there that Genevieve could do. Her mouth went dry, her palms became damp, yet still she did not move.

Well it seemed that the stranger had not the will to continue, for he remained motionless before her, his hand cupped over the pulse of her heart. Frozen in time they were, their gazes locked as the autumn wind cavorted around them. Genevieve noted the lines from the sun around his eyes, the faint blond stubble from his beard, the flicker of blue in the myriad grays of his eyes.

There was none but they two in the whole of Paris.

His gaze softened when it fell on her rapidly rising and falling breasts, so close beneath his hand. Genevieve wondered if he thought about the coin secreted there, but when he looked back to her face, she knew he thought of something more earthy.

He desired her. 'Twas burning in his eyes.

The very thought made Genevieve weak in the knees, but she knew with chilling certainty that she must make this moment count. No matter the test to her resolve. A pledge she had to fulfill. This was an opportunity to be exploited in the name of her cause, no more, no less. She could not afford to let the moment pass, for she owed no less to Alzeu. A weakness had this stranger shown her and she would be a fool not to use it to her advantage. There was one good way to do so that she could imagine.

Genevieve gripped the stranger's shoulder, stretched to her toes and pressed her lips against his.

'Twas an inexpert kiss at best, for Genevieve was not experienced in any exchanges other than the sweet embraces one pressed to the cheeks of kin. His lips were firm, yet temptingly soft, and the smell of his skin filled her nostrils in a most intoxicating way.

Yet for all the warmth of his skin, his kiss was cold with all the chilling blueness of winter ice in the mountains. She felt his shock as an immediate echo of her own. He stiffened, then it seemed he sagged toward her as though he, too, was struck by some inexplicable and completely unexpected weakness.

Before her heartbeat had echoed twice, Genevieve sensed the aching loneliness within him. She tasted the sense of betrayal, she felt the scar left by a heartless abandonment long past. She knew his fear as surely as her own and peered into the dark abyss where the pulse of his own humanity should have been.

Emptiness alone echoed there, and 'twas cold beyond cold.

To her complete astonishment, Genevieve felt neither disgust nor dismay, neither revulsion nor hatred. Compassion 'twas that flooded through Genevieve. Compassion in a tide of such magnitude that 'twas fit to unbalance her.

Loneliness had wrought a man who could take another's life. Loneliness and the certainty that none could be trusted. 'Twas that simple, and the truth saddened her beyond compare.

Genevieve closed her eyes dizzily. Gooseflesh rose on her skin, yet she felt feverish. The hand that did not grip the lute tightened on his shoulder before she knew what it was about, and she savored the firmness of his flesh. She wanted to console him. Genevieve wanted to offer this man something he had never had before.

Her heart opened to him in invitation, and she felt the barest vestige of a response flicker to life within him. More she wanted than the gentle press of his lips on hers, and she leaned closer, able to think of naught but granting him refuge from his exile.

And found herself abruptly shoved away.

Genevieve blinked at the sudden change and wavered slightly on her feet, feeling as if she had imbibed too heavily of wine. The stranger stood several paces away and regarded her as though she were a particularly dangerous creature.

"I granted you the coin for your playing alone," he told her with a sneer. "No favor that you might grant in the street will convince me to not retrieve it."

His words stung, and Genevieve caught her breath sharply before she saw the ruddy flush staining his neck. He was embarrassed by his own response. Genevieve eyed him carefully, imagining she detected some acknowledgment of what had passed between them in his expression before he set his lips grimly.

She had not been alone in forgetting herself in that exchange. The very knowledge made something deep within her tingle.

But no matter was that. She belatedly and forcefully reminded herself of her intent. Genevieve's kiss had been intended to draw him into her web, no more than that. Well it
seemed that he had not been as unaffected as he might like
her to believe.

But given her own response, 'twould be safer for her to
resolve matters between them quickly. Too readily might she
succumb to his need again, and 'twas imperative she dispatch him before she slipped again. Genevieve smiled slowly
as she regarded him, knowing full well the invitation that
lingered in her expression.

"Already have you ensured that I am warmed," she
purred, her heart pounding at her own audacity. "Would
you not see to my warmth this night yourself? I might well
be convinced to return your coin."

His eyes widened. His brows drew together in a frown of
disapproval even as his gaze slipped unwillingly over her
form once more. He snorted, though the sound was less indignant than it had been earlier. Genevieve knew the idea
was not without its appeal.

"Street women are all the same." He sneered again.
"Keep the coin. I have no need of anything with the taint of
your kind upon it," he growled disparagingly before he
turned on his heel.

Genevieve caught her breath at the insult. No worse was
it to know that his comment was deserved after her shock-
ingly wanton suggestion. How could she have made such an
invitation? Her cheeks burned at her bold behavior. Stern
words would her grandsire have had for her had he witnessed her deeds this day. She pulled the lute against her
chest as tears rose to blur her vision, though still she could
see him walking away.

But she could not let him leave again! A pledge had she
taken, and petty pride could not stand in the way of keeping her word.

"Wait!" Genevieve cried.

Her words brought the stranger to a halt, though he paused as if surprised before he glanced back with his original impassive expression. Genevieve twisted her fingers together as she sought the words, then finally simply blurted out the first words that came to her lips.

"Will I see you again?"

His eyes narrowed suspiciously, and she immediately knew she had asked the wrong question. Genevieve cursed her tongue for making such a weak and feminine demand.

"Why?" His demand was harsh. Genevieve flushed and could not help but fidget. A far cry was her behavior from that of the seductress she had hoped to be, and dismay flooded through her at her own failure.

Indeed, this plan had been a disaster from the beginning. Her cheeks flamed as she struggled to summon some of her earlier brashness.

"I would like to talk to you again," she said with an attempt to be coy that fell curiously flat. Now there was solid reasoning, she chided herself, hating how her confidence had abandoned her. The stranger snorted in disbelief.

"You would like to know that you would coax another denier from my purse," he accused softly. Genevieve knew her mouth fell agape in shock at that and she glared at him openly.

"Nay! 'Tis not that at all!"

'Twas too much that *he* should accuse *her* of such cold intent! Fury nudged aside her uncertainty and put a vigorous bounce in her step as she stalked after the cold stranger. Something flickered in his silver gaze, but she cared naught for what he might think. Genevieve poked her finger into the air in the direction of his broad chest, determined to set his perception straight.

"How dare you make such a callous assumption about someone you do not even know!" she demanded indignantly. "An honest woman am I, no more, no less, and though I must work for my keep, 'tis not money alone that occupies my thoughts."

Her argument might have gone unvoiced for all the softening she saw in his expression. In fact, his lip curled slightly.

"Spare me your pretty tales," he said dismissively. "All work for their own motivation alone, and well enough do I know it. If 'tis not coin you seek, then 'tis something else you would have from me."

Fear flashed through Genevieve like lightning at that assertion, and she wondered again how much of her motive he had guessed. She prayed that her response had not shown in her eyes and struggled to maintain her outrage.

"'Tis a sorry picture of the world you would paint with such a claim," she retorted. "Impossible is it truly for you to concede that I might wish only to talk to you?"

"Unlikely 'tis at best." He snorted. "But a moment past, 'twas not conversation you pursued." He regarded her for a long moment, his gaze flicking to the coin's repository with undeniable interest.

"Keep the coin," he murmured in a low voice that echoed with a disgust that turned Genevieve cold, "for I have no intent of retrieving it from its sanctuary. But mind you tell no one from whom you gained it."

Genevieve tossed her hair defiantly. "I shall tell whoever I so choose," she asserted brashly.

His eyes flashed silver fire and he closed the space between them again, his voice no more than a growl when he spoke. "You shall tell no one," he insisted vehemently, but Genevieve did not waver beneath the weight of his will. "Or I shall retrieve the coin and see that you say naught to anyone again."

Genevieve had no doubt that he meant what he said. She recalled the cold emptiness within him and shivered in renewed fear.

No surprise 'twas that he could have killed Alzeu. Indeed, this man had a heart of stone, and Genevieve wanted nothing other in this moment than to be quit of him. So, he thought she wanted only his coin? She would show him!

"Do we understand each other, *ma demoiselle?*" he asked silkily.

"Aye, we certainly do," Genevieve muttered. He smiled thinly and turned away.

As soon as his gaze was averted, Genevieve fumbled in her kirtle to retrieve the coin. She flicked it after him so that it hit hard against the back of his neck. He spun in time to see it dance toward the cobbles and hastened to snatch the sliver of silver out of the air.

"Take your wretched coin, and welcome to it." Genevieve tossed the words proudly over her shoulder as she turned away. "No need have I of the patronage of cynics."

Naught did he say, but she knew full well that he stared after her.

He was astonished, Genevieve could feel it. Indeed, she suspected that he knew not what to do, and the awareness of that fed her pride.

Ha! The perfect move had that been! Her confidence burned with a bright flame once more and she dared to let her hips swing provocatively as she returned to her blanket. Not a sound came from behind her, though she could feel his gaze locked upon her.

Genevieve savored a thrill of victory and bent to pack her lute in her blanket as though she had forgotten he was there. In truth, she did not want him to catch the slightest glimpse of her triumphant smile.

Though, of course, there was naught triumphant about having no coin to pay for food and board this night.

# Chapter Three

The coin burned his palm. His lips itched, his heart was hammering in his chest as though he had run a hundred leagues.

Indeed, Wolfram felt far from his logical self.

He closed his eyes in an effort to compose himself as he passed beneath the gates of the Temple. Instead his mind flooded with the recollection of the lutenist's soft breasts pressing against him. Never had he kissed a woman, never had he been so abruptly warm from head to toe, never had he tasted anything so sweet as her lips.

He jammed the coin deep into his pocket in irritation, though it seemed 'twould brand his skin even there.

Had he not what he desired?

*Desire.* There was a word 'twas best not to dwell upon. No place had such a word in the vocabulary of a man pledged to poverty, obedience and chastity.

He had meant to retrieve the coin, Wolfram reminded himself savagely. And he had done so. 'Twas perfectly logical.

Although the jumble of emotions and the curious mix of ideas filling his head were far from logical. Wolfram shook his head, but they stubbornly remained.

He wondered if all of the lutenist's flesh was as soft and sweet as her lips. He cursed himself for not taking the opportunity to discover the texture of her hair before he halted his errant thoughts.

Forbidden were such pleasures of the flesh to him, and he had best recall that fact. Indeed, he had no interest in such matters. None whatsoever.

And he had the coin. No explanation or far-fetched tale would be required for the Master: Wolfram would simply return every silver denier he had been granted. 'Twas perfectly simple.

Why then did he feel so utterly confused?

"You!"

A shout brought Genevieve's head up with a snap. She glanced over her shoulder, but the cold-eyed stranger was gone. An obviously irate man was bearing down on her in his stead, purpose lighting his eye.

Had the stranger summoned the authorities against her? Fear flooded through her before she noted the shabbiness of the man's attire. No official was this, and Genevieve's eyes narrowed in suspicion.

"You!" he repeated angrily, and wagged an indignant finger in her direction.

Genevieve glanced over her shoulder, but she was alone. Clearly the poorly attired man was addressing her. She looked doubtfully back at him and he shook his head.

"Aye, talking to you I am," he growled. Genevieve noted through her surprise that a ragtag band of followers trailed behind the lanky man, hostility etched on their gaunt features. "And well should you have expected it, busking without permission in a square so close to our own."

"I beg your pardon?" Genevieve asked in confusion. The man halted before her, his chest puffed self-righteously. She saw with alarm that the others had closed ranks around her so that she could not evade them. Panic rose in her chest, for they were a disreputable-looking lot and she could not begin to guess their intent.

Trouble it could only be and too late she wished she had not seen fit to dismiss the stranger so soon.

Was that not a foolish thought! What manner of idiot thought that an assassin might provide protection? Clearly her wits were still addled by the shock of Alzeu's demise, or mayhap the shock of her own wanton behavior.

A sane individual knew better than to expect anything of a murderer.

*"I beg your pardon."* One of the women in the group mimicked Genevieve in falsetto as she danced a mincing step. The others chuckled, though that did naught to dissolve their hostility. Genevieve's fear rose another notch.

"You cannot play here without permission," the evident leader asserted boldly. Genevieve looked to him in surprise.

"I was not aware that there was a law—" she began apologetically, but the laughter that erupted from the rest of the ragged band drew her words to a halt.

"A law!" mocked one.

*"I was not aware,"* echoed the woman in her high voice, and Genevieve was reminded suddenly of the difference of her accent. Highborn she sounded in comparison to them and she realized too late that such a trait could readily reveal her origins. Mercifully, they appeared to have concluded that she was taking airs.

"Odo's law, 'tis, and no other."

"But not to be flouted, nonetheless."

Their words revealed the truth. There was no law. At least no law of the city. These ruffians clearly believed that they, or this Odo, had some say over her fate. Genevieve guessed that this was another group of buskers seeking only to interrupt her playing for their own benefit.

Well. No intention had she of easily relinquishing her spot. She planted her feet solidly against the cobblestones, determined to stay put. 'Twas here her quarry was drawn, after all. 'Twas here he knew where to find her, and no doubt had she that he would return again.

'Twas here she would stay until her quest was fulfilled, regardless of what some disreputable and filthy lot of buskers might have to say about it. She could not risk losing her prey now. Genevieve straightened proudly and looked the leader in the eye.

"'Tis here I play and here I will stay," she said firmly. He raised his brows high and folded his arms skeptically across his chest. The others gasped in astonishment at her audacity.

"No permission have you," he objected silkily.

"And of no permission do I have need," Genevieve retorted. "Particularly from the likes of you. 'Tis no one's spot I have taken and no business of yours that I choose to play here."

"Odo thinks differently," warned someone in the tight cluster.

"Aye, Odo will not approve of this tone."

"Who is this Odo?" Genevieve demanded frostily, her voice sounding more brave than she certainly felt.

The group chuckled as one and drew closer in a manner that fed her unease. They were all around her, pressing so close on every side that she could not have taken a step in any direction. Genevieve's trepidation redoubled. Had she been a fool to so quickly dissent with them? Indeed, they were numerous, and too late she saw that they had fought more foes than one to survive. A mean and hungry lot they were, and she swallowed nervously.

"Aha!" crowed a woman's voice victoriously. "A blanket just like this is what I have been needing on these cold nights." The blanket Genevieve had been seated on, *her* blanket, was waved aloft.

"My blanket that is, and none other!" she cried. The woman danced a few steps away as though she would make off with her prize. They could not steal from her! 'Twas wrong! Genevieve tried to push her way through the crowd to no avail. "'Tis mine!" she cried again when 'twas clear they did not mean to let her pass.

"And what of this lovely thick cloak?" Persistent fingers plucked at Genevieve's hood. She spun on her heel, but new fingers took up the task. They grasped at the wool from every side, and she could not manage to escape their tormenting grip, no matter how she turned and twisted. Panic reared within her, and she feared suddenly that she could not take a breath freely, for they pressed too tightly against her.

'Twas too much to be touched by all of them at once, so close in the wake of the revelation of the emptiness dwelling within the stranger. Their bitterness filtered into her, and as she tasted their anger, she knew she would not escape this encounter unscathed.

"And shoes!" cried another. "Long indeed has it been since I had a pair of shoes as good as these!"

Immediately, hands set to tugging at Genevieve's worn shoes, and beleaguered as she was from every side, her fright could no longer be contained. She flailed at her attackers, but so numerous were they that she budged none. Cruel laughter rang in her ears and grasping hands tugged her hair. No escape was there! Despair and an overwhelming sense of failure assailed her when one shoe was wrenched from her foot.

"Nay!" she shouted, but the shoe was passed from hand to hand and immediately beyond her reach.

"Aha! A perfect fit!" A woman in a tattered blue kirtle danced across the square, showing her new footwear to advantage before diving back into the cluster. "Grant me its mate!" she shouted. Genevieve stamped and turned, but there were too many fingers grappling for her shoe to be avoided. Hungry they had been, and cold for long nights, beaten and abused all their lives. The horror of their experiences left her feeling yet more vulnerable to their irrepressible anger.

And well it seemed that she would bear the brunt of their hostility. Hearing their thoughts and feeling their destitution was no consolation when 'twas she they attacked.

"Aha!" The cloak was torn from Genevieve's shoulders, and a man swung it over his own with all the grace of a highborn noble. He struck a pose, and the others, at least those not involved in removing Genevieve's second shoe, applauded.

"Most distinguished."

"As though 'twas made for you."

"Well you look to the manor born."

The second shoe was ripped from Genevieve's foot, and she nearly lost her balance in the process. She swatted at the laughing attackers to no avail. The woman wearing her shoes and man wearing her cloak began a cavorting dance around the square. A bourgeois couple, evidently taking an evening stroll, paused on the far side of the square, and Genevieve immediately appealed to them.

"Help me!" she cried. "I am being robbed of all I own!"

The couple spoke quietly to each other, then tossed a coin toward the ragtag group. Nay! They thought this but a performance!

To Genevieve's disbelief, they smiled, waved and strolled away, blithely leaving Genevieve to her fate. Three of her attackers dived on the coin and scrabbled for possession.

"Ooh... A lovely warm kirtle," cooed another fingering Genevieve's garments.

They would strip her naked! Genevieve bolted at the thought in the hope of preserving some scrap of her raiment. She lunged against the tight crowd in a bid for freedom, and to her astonishment, they parted to let her pass.

Before Genevieve could consider their reason, someone stuck out a foot. Too late 'twas to avoid the obstacle, and though she stepped high, the foot was raised to ensure she tripped. Genevieve fell facefirst toward the cobbles, and her heart skipped a beat in that timeless instant of her falling.

Her grip must well have loosened on the neck of her lute in her fear, though she had clutched it resolutely so far. 'Twas torn from her grasp in a heartbeat.

"Nay! Take not my lute!" Genevieve shrieked. Something ground as she hit the road, but she rolled immediately to her hip.

Naught could she see but her attackers fleeing from the far side of the square.

They had taken her lute! She could not lose her lute at any cost! Genevieve shoved herself to her feet and hobbled in pursuit, her heart pounding in her ears with fear that she would lose sight of them.

What should she do if she lost her beloved lute?

Sleep eluded Wolfram that night as it never had before.

His lips burned.

The other brothers slumbered on either side of him in the dormitory, and he listened to their snores even as he lay restlessly in the darkness. The single lamp sent a flickering light to play against the ceiling, and though that sight usually soothed him, on this night it but reminded him of the inferno within him. He had run cool water over his lips, he had pressed his lips with his fingertips, he had ignored their burning, but naught made a difference.

Branded he was with the touch of a woman, and certain Wolfram was that any who looked at him could see the truth.

Against the Rule 'twas to have any converse with women, except one's mother and sisters, let alone to embrace them. He had broken the Rule for the first time since he had pledged to adhere to it, and the knowledge chafed at his uneasy conscience.

Still worse, he had enjoyed the transgression. Wolfram fidgeted minutely on his hard pallet, but that fact could not be avoided. He could not move restlessly lest he attract the attention of the others, but neither could he lie still. He could not be revealed. His desire could not be guessed. His blankets itched as they never had before and Wolfram longed to rip his sensible long shirt from his back.

Never had he been plagued with sleeplessness.

But never had he broken the Rule.

He could confess and be fined, he *should* confess and do penance, but Wolfram knew 'twould matter naught. Confession and even penance would not ease this burning. Truly the woman had tempted him deliberately, certainly she had initiated the embrace, but he had wanted her to do so. There was no escape from that. And lecherous thoughts were no less damning than lecherous actions.

Indeed, he wanted her even now. The admission did naught to ease his mind.

Mayhap 'twas penance enough to endure this self-inflicted torture. Wolfram's body recalled the lutenist's kiss with unprecedented enthusiasm, though he had repeatedly tried to quell its response. He had but to think of her dark tangle of hair, or picture those startling green eyes, or see the delicacy of her hands darting across the lute strings.

Or worse, hear the echo of her music in his mind.

He tried to regulate his breathing and slow his pulse, endeavored to lull his body into sleep, all to no avail. The snores of the others troubled him, well it seemed that his blanket tormented him, and the dormitory was too cold. But moments later, 'twas too warm, or his dinner troubled his innards, though Wolfram knew 'twas all an excuse.

He wondered where she was.

Wolfram writhed inwardly with the guilty certainty that she had no pallet this night, and all because of his insistence on retrieving that coin. Not his fault was it that she was without a hearth, but still Wolfram could not dismiss the sense that she paid overmuch for his folly.

Indeed, he could have lied to the Master.

No consolation was it that that thought came too late to his aid.

Less consolation was it that he considered a lie to the Master to be a reasonable solution. Truly his resolve was slipping these days, and he could not imagine the source of that.

Nay. Wolfram knew precisely the source, though he refused to even give it voice in his mind.

Though Genevieve quickly lost sight of her attackers, still she could hear them cavorting ahead of her. She doggedly followed the sound of their voices through the darkening streets despite the ache in her ankle.

Surprisingly, though she moved not at her usual speed, they drew no farther ahead of her. Had Genevieve not known better, she might have believed that they kept a constant distance before her that she might indeed follow them to their lair. Nonsense that was, for surely they wanted only her lute. 'Twas clear the instrument alone had more value than all their meager garments and possessions collectively might fetch.

If they sold her lute, how would she purchase it again or acquire another? How would she earn coin that she might eat? How would she lure the stranger closer? 'Twas clear the music drew him, and without that, Genevieve had naught on her side.

Too cruel 'twas to have tasted a modicum of success only to have everything stolen away. Already Genevieve felt bereft without the instrument that she had played for as long as she could remember. Well it seemed that the chill of the night troubled her more than before, and she felt suddenly vulnerable in this great, strange city.

She wished suddenly that she had never left the familiarity of home. She must recover the lute. Voices laughed harshly ahead, and when she saw the flicker of light playing on the stone walls, Genevieve dashed into the square without thinking. Fire! To sell her lute was one thing; to destroy it quite another!

A band of beggars applauded as she burst into the square. The unexpected welcome brought Genevieve up short, and she halted to stare at them.

Her lute was nowhere to be seen.

Otherworldly they appeared in the orange glow cast by flaming torches, especially as the applause fell silent. Their faces were dirty, their clothing was worn and torn, their features were gaunt. She readily spotted the man in her cloak and the woman in her shoes, though their dance halted as they watched her with the others. 'Twas clear the band that had attacked her were but part of the whole, for Genevieve could not even guess how many stood in the flickering light.

A man in the center drew something from behind his back, a coy smile playing over his lips. As soon as Genevieve spotted the lute, she gasped, and well it seemed that he turned the instrument slightly in acknowledgment of the sound.

Tall he was and no less lanky than the one who had addressed her, though his hair was an uncommon orange shade. Long 'twas and fell past his shoulders, the torchlight making it look to be a river of flame. His expression was sardonic at best, but the hands that held her lute were long of finger and gentle with their burden.

Genevieve recognized him as the one she had heard singing some days past. Fear rose in her chest as she recalled the gleam of avarice that had lit his eyes and she wondered whether he coveted her lute. 'Twas a fine one, for her grandfather had seen fit to fetch her the best. As she watched those long hands slide over the rose engraved on the lute's face, she knew a fear stronger than any she had ever experienced.

"I have come to fetch what is mine," she declared with bravado, determined to retrieve the lute at all costs.

The man with her lute smiled. The others chuckled.

"Naught is yours but what is on your back, and even that we may take, should we so desire," he said confidently. Genevieve's chin rose high.

"Wrong you are," she told him, her tone challenging. "The lute is mine, as is the cloak, blanket and shoes you stole from me. I would have them returned immediately."

The crowd laughed to themselves, the man with her cloak pirouetting that the others might admire his new acquisition.

"I say you are wrong," the leader said smoothly. "And I am Odo. What I say is so."

"But what you say here is wrong," Genevieve asserted stubbornly. "My possessions were stolen from me and I would have them returned. No right have any of you to what I have earned."

"You played without permission," Odo claimed. "Your possessions are forfeit for your crime."

"Crime?" Genevieve demanded. "No crime have I committed. I but played my lute to earn a few coins that I might eat."

"Surrender the coin or we shall keep your belongings as ours," said Odo. Genevieve gaped at him. Surely he did not intend to keep her lute? No right had he to it.

But she had no coin. The only one she had earned this day she had cast at the stranger. And the coin the stranger had granted her the day before had been spent on food and lodging the night before.

"But 'tis spent," she admitted weakly. The assembly gasped with mock horror and clicked their tongues chidingly. Odo grinned.

"Well have I been needing a new lute," he said, and gave the strings a savage pluck. It seemed to Genevieve that her precious lute cried out for mercy with the plaintive sound and she sprang forward.

"Nay! You must not abuse it so!" She halted just before Odo when he granted her a chilling glance. Too far had she gone, and well she knew it, though 'twas too late to change that. The crowd's manner became watchful and expectant. "It must be coaxed, gently," Genevieve said in a much milder tone. Odo arched a skeptical brow.

"You can play?" he demanded archly. Genevieve saw the glint of interest in his eye and dared to be bold.

"Only when I have my lute," she asserted. Several on-lookers gasped at her audacity, but Odo very slowly smiled. 'Twas not a pretty smile, for something about it told Genevieve that he was interested in her ability solely for his own ends, but nonetheless, it reassured her.

Abruptly he shoved the lute in her direction.

"Then play," he commanded.

Genevieve barely noted his startling change of manner. Naught could she see but the lute. She grasped it the instant 'twas offered and clasped it close. She ran her hands over it, finding no damage, and heaved a sigh of relief at the discovery before she remembered his order. She looked up to find every hostile eye upon her, swallowed carefully and began to play.


When finally sleep came to Wolfram that night, 'twas an agitated slumber that would leave him more exhausted than he had been before. His lips yet burned, his body strained, he twisted beneath the tangled embrace of a blanket that had never troubled him before.

And then Wolfram heard the hoofbeats.

He was in a fortress, standing in the bailey, watching transfixed as the wind rising from the sea shredded the fog before him. The fog reminded him of Montsalvat and he wondered if 'twas that keep that haunted him. No way had he of knowing, for even when the fog cleared, it revealed a fortress he could not have recognized. Montsalvat had remained hidden from him throughout that night.

In his mind's eye, Wolfram saw a high keep looming above him, its summit still lost in the fog, and ancient walls stretching away to either side to similarly disappear into the mist. Thunder echoed in the distance, and the dark sky suddenly held the portent of a storm. The air was thick and heavy, and Wolfram knew the rain was coming.

Light hoofbeats echoed again in the eerie silence and he turned in place, seeking out the sound. To his surprise, he stood alone with no horse and naught but the garments upon his back.

The keep was abandoned and so was he.

A beast whinnied, and he turned to find a small goat running toward him. Its coat was startlingly white against the unexpectedly verdant green of the grass in the bailey. It lifted its head as it drew near and held his gaze with otherworldly yellow eyes in a manner distinctly alien to most domestic creatures. Wolfram fancied its gaze was knowing, and he took a step back, certain the beast had read his very thoughts.

Impossible that a creature could understand what he had done.

The beast came closer, and he saw that it had but one horn. An opalescent spire twined from its forehead, and when the lightning flashed, that horn caught the light.

A unicorn's horn. An elixir for poison. 'Twas a message for him alone. Suddenly Wolfram was certain the beast knew his secret occupation and that the gleam in its eyes was far from friendly.

It lunged after him and, like a shameless coward, he ran from the truth.

Lightning rent the sky, the flash nearly blinding. The crack of its impact lifted Wolfram to his toes and made the hair rise all over his flesh. He shivered as the sky rumbled and knew relief, even in his dream, that he was safe.

No pursuing hoofbeats did Wolfram hear. Trepidation replaced relief in a heartbeat.

He dared to glance back, only to find the unicorn lying dead on the grass just steps behind him. Wolfram caught his breath in surprise.

Beside the fallen creature knelt a woman, a woman Wolfram knew had not been there before. Whence had she come, so swiftly and silently? She bent low as though stricken by sorrow at the creature's demise, and her hair obscured her features.

Wolfram noted the ebony color of that hair and its wavy nature. He swallowed in recognition, barely having time to brace himself before she glanced up and impaled him with those green eyes.

Wolfram felt that his feet suddenly took root and he was fixed to the spot. Too late he saw that his tormentress was nude and marveled that he could have missed that salient fact for any interval, however short. Her skin was such an even, creamy hue that he longed to touch her. His body responded as he might have expected, though still he could not tear his gaze away from her perfection. His lips burned with renewed vigor, as if daring him to recall her embrace.

When she lifted her hand as though in offering to him, his eyes widened in shock at the bloody ruby resting in her palm. Wolfram glanced unwillingly to the dead beast, knowing all the while what he would see, yet hoping he would not..

His heart sank at the evidence before him. She had retrieved the red carbuncle from the base of the creature's horn. All the old tales Wolfram had heard flooded into his mind as he stared incredulously at the stone.

'Twas a gemstone reputed to reveal the presence of poison.

That she offered the gem to him was not a sign that could be missed. Too readily did he recall his first impression that she knew who and what he was. Was she the knowing unicorn? Was she the one who would reveal him? Did she hold his fate in her graceful hands as surely as she cradled that ruby? Wolfram's fear of being discovered redoubled at the awareness that another whose motives he did not know could reveal him, but he could not keep himself from meeting her gaze once more.

Her eyes were filled with hatred.

Something went cold within Wolfram, and his gut twisted at the unexpected change. She stood deliberately, her gaze unwavering, her expression resolute, and the unicorn's blood ran freely from the stone in her hand. Still he could not deny her beauty or his own cursed desire for the soft fullness of her form.

He could think of naught but having her, even now. Those ruddy lips that he longed to taste again parted and suddenly he feared that she would voice an accusation he did not want to hear.

His vows he had broken! The Rule he had denied! This woman he had tasted, his very life he had betrayed. And she would turn against him and despise him. She would reveal him; she would betray him as he had been betrayed once before. Too much 'twas, too much to bear beside the burden of guilt he already willingly bore.

Wolfram wrenched his neck to turn away from her and awakened with a snap.

His eyes flew open and he stared uncomprehendingly at the ceiling of the dormitory for long moments. The lamp's golden light danced across the fitted stone; his brethren snored contentedly around him, untroubled by dreams. His heart pounded like thunder and he willed his pulse to slow its erratic pace. He felt as though he had run several leagues without pause. A cold trickle of sweat wound its way down his back and still his body was taut from his vision of the lute player.

When his heart had calmed, Wolfram closed his eyes and forced himself to exhale slowly. He licked his lips and cursed their tingling.

Only too easy 'twas to recall. When last had he been so distracted? When last had he dreamed? When last had he broken the Rule?

Never. And Wolfram liked the change not. 'Twas clear he could not afford to listen to her lute's music again.

Yet even as he lay and his determination grew resolute, it seemed that a lilting tune carried faintly to his ears from the streets outside the Temple. Wolfram squeezed his eyes tightly closed and clapped his hands over his ears as he rolled toward the wall, but still the insidious tune tempted and tormented him.

Well it seemed that there was no escape from either the music or his own traitorous thoughts.

And 'twas she alone who knew he had broken the Rule. 'Twas she alone who could reveal him. Helpless Wolfram felt, caught in a web not of his own making, though he knew his conclusion was inescapable.

He held his position because he was perfectly trustworthy. Too much was there to lose by revealing his error. No intention had Wolfram of confessing his lapse, and 'twas true that a more damning penance would he grant himself than any chaplain might give him. Which led to a single terrifying and exhilarating conclusion.

A promise had he to extract from the lutenist that she would not reveal him. Wolfram caught his breath at the bold skip his pulse took.

'Twas only logical that he knot every loose end and ensure his own security. Logical, naught else. 'Twas perfectly logical for a man to protect himself.

There was naught else at work here. No anticipation was there of seeing the lutenist herself, only of seeing this matter resolved. No trepidation had he of hearing her music again, no fear had he of seeing her gleaming tresses unbound over her shoulder, no danger was there of being tempted to touch her again.

Naught else but logic was at the root of this plan. 'Twas that alone that demanded he not leave the matter be.

Despite the burning of his lips.

Genevieve knew not how much time had passed when Odo placed his hand upon her shoulder. Lost in the mists wrought by her own music she was, and she jumped at the weight of his hand. As though she had been wakened from a dream, her gaze lifted to his features, and she was surprised to find the sardonic curl of his lip vanished. Genevieve glanced to the others and noted their demeanor similarly softened.

"I would have you play with me," Odo said firmly.

"No desire have I to play with another," Genevieve retorted. Odo's eyes narrowed, and he moved so quickly that Genevieve did not anticipate his intent. In a heartbeat, her lute was again within his grasp and frustration rose hot within her.

"I say you will play with me," he repeated. Genevieve held his steely gaze for a long moment, knowing all the while that she would never change this one's mind.

"I would have my possessions returned," Genevieve insisted. Odo smiled an unencouraging smile.

"You will have the lute back, you mean," he said in a dangerously low voice. Genevieve nodded agreement.

"And my garments," she added. Odo pursed his lips and she feared suddenly that she had pushed him too far. If only her lute did not have to pay the price for her audacity! Genevieve eyed the instrument as inconspicuously as she could and wondered how she might retrieve it.

What if the pale-eyed stranger returned to the other square while she was away?

The very thought struck fear through Genevieve. He might think her gone! He might not return again! She could not afford to linger here!

"I must have my lute returned immediately," Genevieve said stiffly. The woman who had mimicked her before did so again, but neither Genevieve nor Odo spared the woman a glance.

"You mean to return there," Odo said. Genevieve but nodded. "Well can you imagine that I cannot risk permitting any provincial who happens along to busk in my streets," he added silkily. Genevieve shivered as he struck a vicious chord on the lute.

"Aye, well enough can I see that," she agreed, her gaze unwavering from her pride and joy. "Half of my earnings will I grant you from this point forward," she offered rashly. Odo chuckled under his breath.

"Half?" he demanded. "Nay, I will have it all. You will play with me, and busk with me for your lute has a sweet enough voice that we shall earn thrice as much together."

Genevieve took a deep breath. "I must play by the Temple gates."

"Nay." Odo swept aside her insistence with a casualness that turned Genevieve's innards cold. "Better places are there—" he began, but got no further.

"Nay!" Genevieve cried in dismay. She grasped Odo's arm, realizing only when all the others fell silent the magnitude of what she had done. All eyes fell on her hand, but she did not release his grimy sleeve. Genevieve met Odo's gaze stubbornly. "This alone must I insist upon," she said in a determined voice. "I *must* play there."

Apparently surprised by her vehemence, Odo eyed her for a long moment. He shook off her grip and took a step backward. "Aye," he agreed in a tone that Genevieve did not trust. "Aye, you may play there. And you will grant me half of whatever you earn there." He paused, and Genevieve released her breath slowly in relief before Odo suddenly closed the space between them again.

"And you will play with me whenever I bid you to," he added in a growl.

"Only there," Genevieve replied, her heart sinking when Odo immediately shook his head.

"The venue will be wherever I dictate."

"Nay! I cannot!" Genevieve protested. Odo held her lute high and waved it slightly.

"Then you shall not have your lute," he threatened.

"Nay! You cannot do this! 'Tis unfair!"

"Unfair?" Odo demanded with an arched brow. "*Naught* is unfair in Odo's domain. All is as Odo decrees, and you had best learn that simple fact."

Genevieve's gaze flicked across the features of those avidly watching this exchange and knew he spoke the truth. A lump rose in her throat, and she feared what he might do to her lute should she push him any further. No outside au-

thority was there who would intervene in this matter. They
were of the streets and left to their own rule. She had best
make her peace with Odo lest she lose the lute forever.

Indeed, she had no other option.

"Aye," she conceded, her voice flat with resignation.
"Half of what I earn, and well will I play with you when you
request it."

"And one other condition to be named later," Odo added
brightly.

Genevieve's mouth fell open in surprise and her gaze flew
to his in outrage. Before she could utter a word, Odo smiled
a confident smile and turned his considering eye on the lute
once more.

"'Twould burn well, would you not say?" he asked a
companion conversationally. Genevieve gasped.

"And one other condition," she agreed wildly. The group
chuckled and nudged each other in a manner that did
naught to ease her foreboding, and then Odo returned her
lute with a flourish.

"Until later, then," he said gallantly. He spun on his heel
with all the grace of a courtier and snapped his fingers at his
motley troupe. "Return the lady's garments, if you will. 'Tis
not fitting to steal from our own kind."

Their own kind. Genevieve glanced again at the circle of
leering faces and stifled a shiver. Never had she thought
herself to be among this kind, but naught was there she
could do about the matter now.

"Share the bread with the wench and make space for her
to sleep with us," Odo ordered, much to Genevieve's surprise. He turned to her and smiled, as though he well
guessed her response. "I would not have any ill befall our
newest member," he added in a low voice that made Genevieve shiver.

She was no better than a beggar, and soon she would undoubtedly be filthy and tattered enough to blend readily with

Odo's troupe. Truly it seemed that she had erred beyond belief in pursuing this foolish quest.

Well did she hope that Alzeu appreciated the sacrifices she was making to avenge his name.

# Chapter Four

"**I** would have your word of honor."

The terse words interrupted Genevieve's reverie with a jolt and her fingers stopped dead on the strings of the lute. The instrument fell painfully silent after a discordant rumble, but she barely noticed as she found herself snared by an increasingly familiar pale regard.

He had returned. And she had heard naught of his approach. Genevieve's mouth went suddenly dry.

"I beg your pardon?" she asked, her voice uncommonly hoarse. Although she blinked, the blond stranger still stood stock-still just a pace before her, bathed in the wan light of the midday sun. Genevieve's pulse thudded in her ears and she wondered what conclusions he had come to about her.

Though indeed it seemed that there was no censure in his gaze. Annoyance and irritation, to be sure, but no censure.

Painful 'twas to look up at him from this angle and the sunlight made her squint, but Genevieve would not leap to her feet as though she had been waiting impatiently for his appearance.

Even if she had been.

"I would have your word of honor that you not tell any other of what transpired here yesterday," he insisted with his stiff formality. Genevieve frowned as she cast her mind over her recollection of the encounter and could not understand what led to his request.

"Already did I return your coin," she said cautiously, recalling how he had said 'twas not his to grant. The abrupt way he shook his head told her she had made the wrong choice, and she pushed to her feet in confusion, endeavoring to make certain her movements were leisurely. She lifted her gaze lazily to meet his, as though she were indifferent to his presence.

Never could she afford to let him see that she was shaking like a spring leaf inside, though she knew not whether 'twas fear or something else that lay at the root of her response.

"Not that." He bit the words out. "The other."

Genevieve tilted her head as she regarded him, the tinge of red on his neck sparking her curiosity. *The other.* She looked to his eyes again, but, surprisingly, he could not hold her regard. Apparently the stonework directly over her right shoulder was considerably more fascinating.

'Twas that alone that brought the answer to her in a flash of understanding.

The kiss! He was troubled about the kiss.

Aha! She had disturbed him! He *was* attracted to her. A thrill of victory rolled through Genevieve, and she knew in that moment that her plan was fated to succeed.

She smiled and he grew visibly more agitated. Indeed, she wondered if he would suddenly bolt and run. Her smile broadened when he shuffled one foot hesitantly, though still he refused to so much as glance her way.

'Twas clear he had been unable to avoid coming back. Mayhap this absence had been more difficult for him than for her. The very idea encouraged Genevieve as naught else had before, so much so that she momentarily forgot his demand.

Privacy was what she needed to see the matter through. She leaned toward him and felt a surge of satisfaction when his nostrils flared at her movement. So close she was to seeing her quest fulfilled! Genevieve walked her fingers up his somber-hued tabard with an audacity that might have astounded herself under any other circumstance.

"Mayhap 'tis our embrace you recall," she whispered in the closest approximation of a seductive tone that she could manage. Truth be told, 'twas more breathy than anything else, and another might have thought her having difficulty drawing air into her lungs. Her heart pounded at her boldness, and Genevieve carefully schooled her hand not to shake as she wondered whether she would in truth be able to take vengeance on a cold mercenary such as this. Surely such a man would see directly through her facade. Surely those pale eyes guessed her every intent.

The man before her fired her a look ferocious enough to turn her to stone.

"*Naught* do I recall of any such nonsense," he snapped. "And I would have your assurance that you, too, have forgotten the matter."

Naught? How could she have misinterpreted him? Genevieve was so astonished by his vehement tone that she forgot to play the temptress. She gaped at him, thinking the way his eyes blazed was uncalled-for under the circumstances. Indeed, had the kiss been exchanged with anyone other than this stranger, she might well have found it pleasant enough to be favorably inclined toward him.

As though he feared what *she* might do—an idea that might have been amusing under another circumstance—he backed suddenly away. Genevieve regarded the chasm between them with dismay, uncertain how she would tempt him should he persist in keeping them physically apart. Well it seemed that proximity alone troubled him.

Her plan was not working at all. Genevieve's heart sank to her toes and she suddenly felt as adept as a fumbling toddler. Why had she even commenced such a ploy? Surely she was ill equipped to see it through to its end.

"I do not understand your meaning," she confessed with a frown, not knowing what else to say other than the truth. The man snorted with ill-concealed disgust.

"Naught is there to understand. Nor indeed is there anything worth recalling. I know not why I even bothered to speak to you about a matter that is so trifling as to be without import."

That statement captured Genevieve's attention. 'Twas true that if he believed what he said, it made absolutely no sense that he had even bothered to come this day. Genevieve assessed the man before her carefully once again and noticed that his breathing seemed rather hasty for the situation.

He endeavored to deceive her!

But to what end? It had not been a foul or even a forgettable kiss that she had bestowed upon this man. She could not imagine what game this one played, though she loathed what he had said.

How dare he insist that her kiss was perfectly forgettable? 'Twas an insult of the highest order and one that Genevieve *knew* was a lie. Had she not felt how shaken and distressed he was?

How dare he lie to her? She *knew*.

And he knew she knew.

Genevieve drew herself up to her full height and glared directly into his disconcertingly pale gaze. "Why then did you return, if not because that embrace was memorable?" she demanded haughtily. "No more of your coin do I have, for you saw to that. Surely you did not come out of concern for my welfare? 'Tis clear enough you are a man with a stone for a heart."

He visibly gritted his teeth. "For your vow alone did I come."

"What vow might that be?" Genevieve asked archly, certain she would do all within her power to deny him a favor of any kind. Well it seemed that he noted her determination, for his eyes narrowed and his gaze bored into hers. When he spoke, his voice was low and echoed with a resolve that made Genevieve shiver in dread.

"I will have your vow that you will tell *none* of that embrace. But between you and I 'twas, and it shall be as if it never came to pass," he growled.

Deny it? His insistence made Genevieve feel the fool for ever allowing herself that instant of compassion for him. This man deserved naught of her compassion and he certainly deserved *naught* else beyond the bite of Alzeu's dagger.

If they had been in a less public place this moment, she could readily have fulfilled her pledge. With nary a second thought would she have left his cold carcass to rot. The man was beneath contempt.

Certainly to grant such a man her word was beyond possible.

Genevieve sniffed and lifted her chin. "And if I refuse?" she asked blithely. His eyes flashed in warning, but too late did Genevieve respond. Her lute was within his grasp in a heartbeat, and she lunged after it, but to no avail.

"Then your lute shall pay the price," he declared.

He might have said more, but Genevieve was well tired of having her most precious possession threatened if she did not adhere to another's plans.

"Thief!" she shouted as loud as she was able. She pointed an accusing finger at her assailant and let her voice rise hysterically. "Thief! This thief has stolen my lute! Help me! Someone help me to regain my property!"

Quite naturally, no one leapt to the assistance of a street musician, but a number of passersby stopped to gape. 'Twas enough for Genevieve's purposes, for the pale-eyed stranger seemed quite unnerved by the attention. He glanced about himself in evident dismay as she shouted, that ruddy cloud rising slowly to suffuse his neck. When he glanced to Genevieve again, he took a half step back, as if startled by what he saw in her eyes.

His uncertainty was all the fuel she needed to press on. If attention troubled him, she was well suited to see him troubled indeed.

"Grant me the return of my lute," Genevieve demanded in a loud, resolute voice. His lips set, and fury flashed through her with renewed vigor at the certainty that he meant to do no such thing.

'Twas beyond belief that one should deprive her of her brother's companionship and her lute both. This man had an audacity that showed no bounds, and well did Genevieve intend to set his thinking straight before she dispatched him to the other side.

'Twas no less than such a man deserved.

"*Return to me my lute!*" Genevieve shouted furiously. She snatched at the instrument, but the stranger lifted it out of her way.

She swore in a most unladylike fashion and cursed his height thoroughly before kicking him in the shin with all her might. He swore himself with a savagery Genevieve would never have expected, and leapt backward, obviously completely surprised by her attack. A new light gleamed in his gaze as he regarded her in much the manner one might regard a rabid and unpredictable dog.

The lute he slipped deliberately behind his back, and Genevieve's blood boiled anew.

He could not take this from her!

"Stop this thief from stealing my lute!" she cried. Though his ears burned crimson, he showed no inclination to grant her request, nor did any of those avidly watching the proceedings.

"Grant to me your word," he demanded in a low voice. No intent had Genevieve of fulfilling his request, especially now. She tossed her hair defiantly and knew he guessed her resolve.

When Genevieve lunged in pursuit, the stranger stepped back with annoying ease. Genevieve attacked again, but he consistently kept a trio of steps between them, seemingly with a minimum of effort. One of the onlookers twittered with laughter, and Genevieve's ears burned. Certain he was making her look like an imbecile, Genevieve stopped and propped her hands on her hips to glare at him.

"Too much have you stolen from me already for this outrage to be tolerated," she muttered through gritted teeth.

He looked momentarily confused, and Genevieve realized too late that she had made a fatal slip. Her heart sank to her toes, but she did not dare relinquish her ground. He leaned closer, his eyes blazing with intensity and his breath fanning her cheek.

"What have I stolen from you?" he asked silkily. Genevieve's mind scrambled in pursuit of a plausible response until she contrived one that actually brightened her smile.

"Kisses," she asserted boldly. He inhaled sharply and retreated as though he would flee her very words. Genevieve stalked him across the square as he stepped yet further back.

Ha! This was more the way she had planned it! More than one way was there to gain what she desired. He wanted none to know what had transpired? Well, Genevieve would tell them all. She snatched at the lute and harried him from either side, determined to pursue him until her lute was safely in her own hands again.

"Kisses," she repeated with relish. "Shall I tell them all about your kisses," she whispered for the stranger's ears alone, "or will you return my lute?"

His color deepened but his lips set with a determination that to Genevieve's mind did not bode well for her success. She watched his fingers tighten around the neck of the lute, and her heart sank.

"You would do naught of the kind," he muttered. "You will give me your word instead." Ha! Unlikely indeed was that! 'Twas true he was embarrassed, but Genevieve could well see that the matter grew worse instead of better. Embarrassed or not, he would not be compelled to do her bidding.

And neither would she feel compelled to do his!

Anger rippled through Genevieve again. Too much did he ask of her. Keep the embrace a secret? Never! Genevieve could not imagine why the matter should be of import, but she would deny him what he asked, simply because he had demanded it thus.

And he had virtually dared her to tell all. Well, he would gain more than he had bargained for from that!

"Kisses!" Genevieve shouted to the few onlookers and flung out her arms dramatically. "Took advantage of me, he did. This man," she declared boldly as she pointed directly at the glowering man who held her lute, "this man kissed me fit to curl my toes, just yesterday. Now he returns not only to deny me, but to steal away my very livelihood, as well!"

Indeed, she could almost feel the stranger cringe, but still Genevieve pressed on relentlessly. He threatened her pride and her lute—no mercy would she show him. Genevieve turned to a woman who watched with particular attention and summoned her almost certainly sympathetic ear with a friendly wave.

"My kisses does he steal, and now he would deny not only me, but the very sweetness of our embrace!"

"Men are all alike, love," the woman counselled with a sad shake of her head. Another tut-tutted under her breath, and Genevieve appealed to her.

"Is it not beyond cruel that he would take my lute? My lute alone 'tis that lets me go on, my lute alone 'tis that provides my keep. What kind of man would break my heart, then destroy the one thing that might give me the strength to go on?"

Both women fired accusing glances at the pale-eyed stranger. Genevieve granted him an arch glance, only to find his color yet more unnaturally heightened. A set there was to his chin, though, and her resolve faltered slightly at the realization that she had gained herself naught with this display.

She might well have succeeded only in so annoying him that he would not return at all. And such an audience she had attracted that there was no way she could dispatch him now without witness.

Genevieve's stomach twisted that yet again impulse had served her falsely. Never would she learn, and the certainty of that stole the last of her anger away, leaving her empty and silent in the square.

Much to her surprise, the stranger stalked toward her, his gaze relentlessly locked upon hers, and shoved the lute toward her. Genevieve immediately clasped its neck in joyous relief, but he did not release it to her as yet. Genevieve tugged, but his grip was relentless. Reluctantly she met his eyes and found a heat simmering there that made her wonder what she had wrought.

"Do not play here again," he growled. "'Tis clear you are a woman of precarious intellect and cannot be trusted with the most simple of matters."

She had her lute.

Almost.

The very feel of it within her hands restored a measure of Genevieve's spirit. "I shall play wherever I desire," she asserted, with a defiant tilt of her chin.

"Nay," he threatened softly. The way one brow arched and his voice fell low told Genevieve that he meant what he said. "I shall see you arrested if you do."

Arrested? Surely not!

But when Genevieve met the stranger's gaze, she saw the answer there that she dreaded. Not a doubt remained in her mind once she saw his resolve that he would do precisely what he threatened.

But why? She could not fathom a guess, but something had changed when she pressed him. Refusing to grant him that vow and making a spectacle of that refusal had changed his assessment of her in a markedly less positive way.

Genevieve stared at him mutely as the realization of what she had done fell around her. Something she had changed that would not be readily repaired. All because of her own impetuous defiance.

She felt remarkably bereft. Little sense did that make, for she could not even name what she had lost. Still, 'twas impossible to dispel a feeling, near forgotten, of being caught as a child in the midst of some unforgivable transgression and knowing full well that she had erred.

And done so for no good reason. Yet again, her impulsive nature had steered her wrong.

The onlookers dispersed slowly, bored now that there was naught to watch, but Genevieve barely noted their departure. Fool! A chance had she had to fulfill her quest, but now 'twas all gone awry!

Tears blurred her vision at her own failure, and the pale-eyed stranger slipped out of focus. She felt the weight of his stare for a long moment, then he abruptly released the lute and turned away.

Not again! Should he leave this time, he might never return! She could not simply let the matter be. Genevieve snatched at his tunic in desperation, and he glanced back in surprise.

Yet again, she had that curious sense that she could see within his secret heart and she felt his loneliness as surely as she felt the heat of his skin beneath her hand. Its intensity was enough to send one of her tears spilling to her cheek. The ache within him drew her closer, even as she sought to sort out the jumble of emotions he triggered within her. Genevieve was powerless to look away as her compassion rose again to the fore. Indeed, her fingers fanned out to press against his arm as though she might reassure him somehow with such a simple gesture.

She fancied she saw understanding in his gaze, relief perhaps, before his expression abruptly became cold and shuttered. He grasped her by the wrist with strong fingers and might have flung her hand away if Genevieve had not spoken while his hand was folded around hers.

"What is your name?" she whispered urgently. Her voice was as soft as that of a lover in the dark, yet it seemed fitting somehow to be so intimate in this time and place.

Genevieve could permit herself to think no more than that about her response to him.

His gaze dropped to her lips as though he were indecisive, then he frowned and met her gaze again. His lips parted, though no sound broke forth, and she knew that some part of him fought this confidence, just as another insisted upon it. Genevieve opened her lips and leaned toward him. Her breast pressed against his arm and she felt him stiffen as awareness of the source of that pressure dawned upon him. Her nipple hardened of its own accord, and he caught his breath in what might have passed for wonderment.

"Wolfram," he murmured finally, seeming loath to make the admission but powerless to deny her. His eyes danced over her features as though he were just wakening from a dream. "My name is Wolfram."

"Wolfram," Genevieve repeated softly. Heat rose within her as he watched the word fall from her lips.

His grip upon her wrist loosened and he lifted his index finger an increment higher. It hovered before her lip indecisively, and Genevieve knew the battle he fought between temptation and restraint.

Genevieve's heart swelled, and she folded her hand gently around his palm before she knew what she was about. So much broader was his hand than hers, stronger and wider, the skin of a different texture, and she marveled at the contrast. She slid her hand across his skin, and the sensation of the soft tangle of golden hair on the back of his hand drifting across her palm weakened her knees. A caress 'twas, and Genevieve marveled at her own boldness even as she guided his fingertip to rest against her lip.

His finger trembled, but he did not move it away. She watched Wolfram shiver with every fiber of his being at the contact and could not imagine 'twas her touch that affected him so. He inhaled deeply and impaled her with a piercing glance as his finger slipped across her bottom lip. He outlined the shape of her lips with that gently exploring fingertip, and Genevieve closed her eyes in surrender to his touch.

A distant horn sounded abruptly within the walls of the Temple, and it seemed the sound reminded him of something. Wolfram straightened with a snap. He looked at Genevieve's hand on his shoulder, his own hand resting against her lips, as if he knew not how this had come to be. His grip loosened slightly yet still he lifted her hand from him and gently released it.

He did not meet her eyes again before he turned his back to her. Genevieve clasped her lute to her chest and watched mutely as he walked stiffly away. Naught did he say and Genevieve chided herself for hoping otherwise. A hard lump there was in her throat, though she could not fathom a reason why it should be there. Her enemy he was and she should feel naught but relief to be quit of him again.

As long as he returned. Yet Genevieve felt inexplicably powerless as she never had before, and emotions warred within her as to what she should do.

She could not halt his departure. Too shaken was she by his touch and his confession to run in pursuit. Indeed, she imagined she had not even the voice to call out to him.

Wolfram wanted her to leave. Yet Wolfram was lonely beyond anything Genevieve might have imagined before she had sensed his solitude.

She knew not what to do. She felt alone suddenly in his absence, bereft as she had never been before. Vulnerable she felt, yet shaken by the confidence they had shared. A tear rose at the corner of her eye, a tear that slid unhurried and unnoticed down her cheek and splashed upon the fingers gripping the lute.

He had told her his name. How could she possibly leave? But what if he did not return?

'Twas later that day that Wolfram was summoned to the Master's office once more. A relief 'twas to have an excuse to push the lutenist from his mind, though try as he might, he could not banish either her lute's haunting melody or the poignant memories it awakened.

Or the other.

He had felt something when the lutenist kissed him that he did not dare to empower by granting it a name. He cursed himself silently for so readily falling prey to her charms.

And then today, that other sense had been there again, that curious sensation that she knew what he was. The way her eyes had widened when she touched him. Indeed, it seemed that she saw within his very heart.

This time, it had troubled Wolfram even less. Reassuring it had been almost to see some reassurance of his earlier impression. Reassuring it had been to not feel so alone.

He wondered what madness had taken possession of him that he should have confessed to her his name.

He wondered what the Master wanted and feared he knew the truth of it. Business there was to attend to, no doubt, Wolfram reminded himself with forced enthusiasm. Mayhap another commission that would take him far from Paris and that cursed lute. 'Twas that lute that lay at the root of his troubles, for 'twas that lute that had first loosened the locks on his memories of gentler times.

Aye, mayhap another commission would be a blessing instead of a curse. Work a man needed to focus his life. 'Twas the idleness of the past few days that fed this folly and undermined his conviction in choices he had long made and accepted.

The torches mounted on the walls flickered and cast intriguing shadows on the stone that belied the hour. Well might it always be the dead of night within these halls for all the light of the sun that gained access. Now that the evening meal was past, there were not even brethren in the corridors. All were about their chores before compline.

'Twas likely that was why the Master had summoned Wolfram at this time. None would be about to note the incongruity of a sergeant being summoned to the Master's offices.

He gained the outer office without seeing another, though on this eve there was no esquire, deaf or otherwise, in attendance. The room was still, all documents neatly filed away as though no esquire would soon return.

'Twas odd. Never had Wolfram been here unescorted. He shifted his weight uneasily, unable to dismiss the sense that he intruded in a private domain.

Had there been a mistake? Was the Master here? Should he be so bold as to knock on the Master's door? 'Twas ever so slightly ajar, that heavy portal, and Wolfram wondered what to do. 'Twas not his place to disturb the Master, yet he had been summoned.

Since he had been summoned, the Master would want to know that he had arrived. Reassured by the simple logic of his thoughts, Wolfram knocked resolutely on the door.

No one answered his summons, but the door swung slightly inward at the impact of his knock. 'Twas almost as though he were being invited into the office, but Wolfram knew that was but a bit of whimsy.

"Good evening?" he said.

No response carried to his ears.

Wolfram glanced about the deserted outer office, but no esquire appeared from the shadows. Mayhap the Master had fallen ill. He hesitated, then stepped on the threshold of the Master's office. With one fingertip, Wolfram pushed the oaken door open yet wider.

The office was empty, the shadows falling long within.

A small disarray there was on the Master's desk, a scroll left unfurled, the red wax of its seal casually discarded on the blotter. The Master's small round spectacles lay atop the flattened scroll, and his inkwell held one corner down while an empty glass anchored the other. A candle flickered, its long wick indicative that it had not been long lit.

Mayhap 'twas this missive that had called the Master away unexpectedly.

Wolfram knew he had no right to look. He knew he should not even think to steal a glimpse of the parchment, yet the flourish he could discern from the doorway beckoned him closer. Despite his knowledge that this was not his to see, he was sorely tempted to see what the Master had been reading.

Mayhap 'twas another contract. Mayhap *'twas* a matter that concerned him.

That was all the rationalization Wolfram needed. He crossed the threshold in a heartbeat and was peering at the mysterious document before he could reconsider the wisdom of his move.

A genealogy 'twas. Wolfram exhaled shakily and regarded the marvel unfurled before him. A genealogy. The bloodline of some blessed soul. What might he have done to have such a legacy himself? What a great gift 'twas to know whence your own roots sprang. What could Wolfram have been had he but known the identity of his sire? He almost touched the document before he caught himself.

Nay, 'twas not his to either touch or examine.

But a genealogy. Naught else could have tempted him so. Wolfram's fingers itched with the desire to pick up the document, to examine it at his leisure, to run his fingertip over dates and names.

He longed to imagine, however briefly, that such a glorious possession might be his.

Mayhap 'twas the Master's genealogy. Well could Wolfram imagine that that man came from a distinguished lineage. And not unreasonable was it for a humble sergeant to express some curiosity about the heritage of the man who led him onward. Wolfram permitted himself one quick glance and stopped cold when he read the name *Pereille*.

Pereille. A man name of Pereille 'twas whom Wolfram had last dispatched.

Pereille. Wolfram frowned and scanned the parchment with a familiarity born of years of examining similar documents. He found the name *Alzeu* quickly enough, born 1285 he was. Younger than Wolfram might have thought.

A lump rose in Wolfram's throat at the date *1307* recently added beneath Alzeu's name in a slightly different shade of ink.

No doubt could there be. 'Twas this very man he had dispatched. Was it the Master who had added the date? Did the Master keep records of all? Wolfram's gaze lifted to the rolled scrolls piled on the shelves that lined the office walls with new respect and more than an inkling of dread.

Impossible. No one could keep such records.

Wolfram's gaze dropped unwillingly back to the parchment. As he scanned the network of relationships, births and deaths, names of children in generation after generation, he recalled Alzeu's drunken assertion.

The blood of kings. The true vine. The lineage destined to rule all of Christendom.

Fanciful nonsense, to be sure, but had it been true, 'twould have been the lineage of those kings that lay before him. Wolfram traced the network to Alzeu's name once more with a newfound measure of awe and frowned. Regardless of the destiny of the vine, it had been one that ended with this man's demise.

But nay. Another name there was inscribed next to that of Alzeu.

It could not be! The light was so poor that Wolfram had almost missed the inscription, but now he leaned forward to pick out the ink. Something had been spilled here that had darkened the parchment, but still the name could be discerned.

A sister 'twas, a sister of Alzeu's. Just two of them there were, born of Enguerrand, son of Thierry and Kira. Enguerrand had died alarmingly young, Wolfram noted with an almost precognitive sense. As had Enguerrand's wife, one Sibylla. He checked the dates. Not in childbirth had Sibylla been lost.

Wolfram saw the invisible hand of another, like himself, who had travelled south years before on a markedly similar task. Too coincidental 'twas that man and wife both should expire young and in the same year. He let his fingertip slide over the line that showed the children of Enguerrand and Sibylla.

*Alzeu, 1285-1307.*

And *Genevieve, 1287-*

This Genevieve was alive. Wolfram's breath caught in his throat.

The Pereille line was not dispatched, if that had been the objective in removing Alzeu. As he lingered in the Master's office, staring at the evidence before him, Wolfram could not help wondering if there was some truth to Alzeu's tale. Had Alzeu been ordered killed for his aspirations to the crown? Had those aspirations any justification in truth?

And if so, what burden did this Genevieve carry within her veins? 'Twas true that a woman could have made no claim, but this Genevieve could well bear a son one day.

Or was it all so much nonsense, as Wolfram had concluded that long past night in listening to Alzeu? Somehow finding this genealogy here in the Master's office made Wolfram question his own earlier conclusion.

What if Alzeu's conviction had not been nonsense? The thought was almost too much to comprehend. He glanced down at the genealogy again. Would he be dispatched to remove this Genevieve, as well? Something balked within Wolfram at the very idea of raising his hand against a woman, though he supposed that if he was bidden to do so, he would have little enough choice.

A woman. Wolfram gritted his teeth. He could only hope 'twould not come to that. He could only hope that whoever had commissioned the order to remove Alzeu saw no threat from a woman. His gaze dropped to the parchment again and he frowned.

Why was this document here? And why left open to view? Why had the Master summoned him, yet disappeared? Wolfram could not keep himself from wondering whether this document had been responsible for the Master's apparent hasty departure.

But where might the Master have gone?

* * *

Odo watched a cloaked figure slip cautiously toward his little crew. Well that one thought he approached unobserved, but Odo was sharp of eye, even at night and even when an unexpected visitor clung stubbornly to the shadows, as this one did.

Odo sat apart from the group, watching and listening. He had been planning the triumph that ultimately would be his, the inevitable success he had deserved for so long and that he would finally gain with the accompaniment of the lutenist. Never had he heard another play so sweetly, and her music would make the perfect foil for the ballad he had been polishing all these years.

His outlet to long-awaited success 'twould be, and Odo knew it well. This night, while the others dined and the lutenist herself tended her instrument, Odo permitted himself the rare luxury of dreams of future prosperity.

For the first time he dared to imagine playing before the King's own court. Mayhap the sound would be so sweet he would be invited inside! Odo's heart skipped a beat in anticipation.

Mayhap 'twas time he pursued his lifelong dream. Mayhap on the morrow the lutenist would make the first payment of her due.

'Twas then that the flicker of movement caught his eye. No interest had he in the revelry of his companions, and little more interest had he in this visitor. There could be no threat by one to so many, and Odo but watched the approaching man with one wary eye.

The intruder was close before one of the troupe noticed him. 'Twas almost amusing the way old Austorc jumped, his face alight with surprise before he frowned menacingly. The uninvited guest retreated into the protection of the shadows.

"I would speak with the one who sings," he said, his voice a rasp in the darkness. Deliberately did he keep his voice low that it might not be recognized, Odo was certain, and that fact piqued his interest.

"We all sing," Austorc assured him confidently.

The shrouded figure's head shook once firmly. "The one red of hair."

All eyes turned as one to Odo, sitting off to the side. He watched as the visitor picked him out of the shadows and smiled his most charming smile.

"Odo the minstrel is here," Odo said quietly. When the visitor stepped forward, the others made room for him to pass through their midst, their reluctance and suspicion more than evident. Well it seemed that their guest grew agitated, for he moved through the group with quick steps and clutched his hood about his face. Odo could hear his nervous breathing when he paused but two paces before him.

"No harm do I intend you," he said in that same throaty voice. Odo's smile twisted at this evidence that his visitor was aware of the hostility of the group that had closed behind him.

"Indeed?"

"Indeed." The visitor glanced back over his shoulder and leaned closer to Odo, as though he would not have the others hear. Still his face was too shadowed for his features to be discerned. "My master sends me to ask you a question," he whispered.

When the man paused, Odo prompted him. "Aye?" His troupe fidgeted impatiently, their interest in the visitor waning now that they could not hear what he said. Odo heard several of them mumble to each other, and an indifferent trio returned to their meal.

"He asks... he asks where you will busk on the morrow that he might ensure he hears you again." The words fell in a rush from the visitor's tongue and he seemed unnerved when Odo stared at him in astonishment.

Could he have known? Odo had told no one as yet of his good fortune or of his intent, and the timing of this inquiry indeed seemed opportune.

"Who is your master?" Odo demanded in an undertone. The shrouded visitor shook his head hastily.

"This I cannot tell you."

"Is he a man of influence?" Odo asked expectantly.

The visitor shuffled his feet nervously, and his very manner fueled Odo's hopes. To be attended by a man of influence was no small thing. Indeed, if he could but catch the ear of one with connections, he might well have the opportunity to play at the court itself!

"Indeed, I have sworn to reveal naught," the man confessed hesitantly. "But rest assured that the telling of this one thing will well be made worth your while."

Odo's heart leapt a beat, even as he evaluated the visitor's honesty. He stared at the shadows within the hood for a long moment, then leaned forward, determined to take a chance. He could risk no less. Indeed, it seemed the fates smiled upon him this day and opportunity could not be shunned. Odo dropped his voice to a hiss, not in the least interested in letting the rest of his troupe know his intent as yet. "Then tell your master that 'tis in the square before the king's own court where I will sing tomorrow."

Silence greeted Odo's confession and he wondered if the visitor fancied he told a tall tale. No matter who held that space, Odo was determined to stack the odds in his favor, and he would fight with his bare hands for the opportunity to play there on the morrow. Not the only man of note would this man's master be, for all of import passed to and fro through the king's own gates. Odo was no fool in the ways of the world.

"Believe me," Odo added menacingly. The visitor immediately bobbed a bow and backed away.

"I thank you," he murmured, then turned and swept through the remnants of the troupe gathered behind him. The actors and dancers scurried out of his path indignantly, though the cloaked figure ignored their manner and the insults they flung after him.

Odo watched as the man disappeared into the shadows on the far side of the square. He narrowed his eyes against the darkness and saw the man slip down one of the alleyways that led to the Rue du Temple.

Then he was gone from sight. The troupe began to chatter in the stranger's absence, several of them parodying his manner, but Odo ignored them as he strained his ears against the night. He felt the lutenist's gaze questioning upon him, but not ready was he yet to tell her of his plans.

There 'twas. Satisfaction rolled through Odo at the sound he had awaited. Muted hoofbeats. Two horses, unless he missed his guess, and one was a large destrier such as knights and nobles rode.

The man had not lied. That his master had accompanied him here could be no small sign. Odo fairly rubbed his palms together in anticipation. He had best make the most of such fortune, and he smothered a triumphant smile as he planned. No place had he for the other members of his troupe on the morrow, for their talent was of the second order.

There was one, though, whose skill could only emphasize his talent more. And on the morrow, she would grant him but the first of the favors she owed him.

# Chapter Five

When Genevieve felt someone's gaze upon her the next midday, she caught her breath before she glanced up from her lute. It could mean only one thing.

Wolfram had come again. She had not frightened him away for good.

Relief fairly made Genevieve dizzy. Indeed, she had barely slept the night past, so anxious had she been. She had crept away from Odo's little troupe before most of them had awakened, determined to stake out her place here as early as possible lest she miss Wolfram's visit. Impatiently had she watched the sun trace its path, her certainty that Wolfram would not return growing with every passing moment.

But he had come and she was here. Genevieve's lips still tingled, and when she closed her eyes, well it seemed that she could feel the gentle imprint of Wolfram's finger against them. When Genevieve permitted herself to recall that moment, which she had done time and again, a soft warmth unfurled deep within her. She knew not what 'twas or what it meant, but the sensation was pleasurable, to say the least.

Well must it be a sense of satisfaction that her quest might soon be fulfilled.

That thought did not ring clearly even in Genevieve's own mind, but she resolutely ignored the warning. Wolfram was here. 'Twas all that mattered. She took a deep breath that did naught to check the heat rising within her, and glanced up expectantly.

So certain was she 'twould be Wolfram standing silently to one side that she did not at first recognize anyone else when she saw that he was not there. Her heart sank and she scanned the onlookers again for his distinctive tall frame.

But nay. Disappointed beyond expectation that she had erred, Genevieve bent over her lute again to hide her response. Wolfram would come, she reminded herself, and her lips tingled warmly on cue. How could he possibly stay away?

The presence stubbornly remained, as did the persistent sense of being watched. Genevieve flicked another glance over those few assembled to listen. 'Twas only when one did not move away that she eyed him more carefully and realized 'twas Odo who observed her.

That 'twas Odo she would not have guessed without such a study. His hair was combed and trimmed, and his garments were much richer than his usual garb. A different man 'twas who stood watching her from the street musician and king of beggars she had left dozing just hours past. The casual observer might not note the mending in Odo's hose or that the trim on his tunic had frayed slightly, though truly it had been very fine once. Indeed, Odo looked quite the courtier, if slightly down at heel on closer inspection.

His manner had changed, as well, for he carried himself like a courtier. He seemed taller, his shoulders broader, the expression upon his face more refined. Genevieve realized 'twas this that had fooled her more than anything else.

Indeed, 'twas disconcerting to note the change, especially as 'twas clear Odo did not put on airs. 'Twas this that was his true manner, she saw, and one he had kept carefully concealed from all. Only now did Genevieve see the man as he was, and she could not fathom why he had hidden himself away.

Odo smiled charmingly, and Genevieve wondered what he wanted of her. Somehow she guessed it could be naught good.

"'Tis time we played elsewhere," Odo said simply. He stepped forward and offered her his hand that she might rise. Genevieve shook her head as panic flooded through her.

"I cannot leave this place!" Not today, when she was so uncertain whether Wolfram would return! Indeed, she could not risk straying from her usual place for a moment, lest he return and think *her* gone for good.

"But, of course, you will," Odo assured her smoothly.

"Nay. I cannot," Genevieve argued. Should Wolfram return today and conclude that she had abandoned him, then he might never return to this spot again. Genevieve could not hazard such a chance.

To Alzeu she owed that, she reminded herself sternly, but the flicker of heat within her denied her reasoning. Again Genevieve ignored the hint that she deceived herself. She looked deliberately to Odo, determined to persuade him to abandon his idea at all costs. Odo's lips twisted and Genevieve saw that he would not readily let her decline.

"I say we shall play elsewhere this day," he murmured, as though vexed by a slow-witted child. "Now gather your belongings and come with me."

"Nay. I say I shall play here," Genevieve replied stubbornly. Odo's eyes flashed.

"And I say 'tis time we played elsewhere," he maintained with icy calm. "I would make the most of opportunity while we yet can."

Genevieve tossed her hair. "No interest have I in opportunity. Well did I tell you that I wished only to play here unmolested."

Surprise flickered through Odo's irritated expression. "Here?" he demanded with a wrinkled nose. "Surely you jest? You cannot mean to be satisfied playing here on the streets for the remainder of your days."

"Not for the remainder of my days," Genevieve retorted, realizing too late that she had stumbled into revealing too much. Odo stilled suddenly as he regarded her, and his eyes narrowed assessingly.

Curse her impulsive tongue! She had revealed that his portion of her income would not continue indefinitely! Quite natural 'twas that that had captured his interest! Genevieve silently called herself every manner of fool as she determinedly held Odo's regard.

Odo arched a skeptical brow. "How long then?" he asked silkily.

Genevieve lifted her chin, knowing her response would be lacking. Something plausible she must contrive, but her imagination abandoned her in this crucial moment. "For as long as I so desire," she asserted with a boldness she hoped would not be questioned. To confide the truth in Odo was out of the question, yet she wished she could think of some tale that might otherwise explain her slip.

Sadly, naught came to mind.

"Indeed?" he asked, and folded his arms across his chest. "Do you desire to play throughout the cold winter approaching?"

"No business is it of yours what I desire or do not desire to do!"

"Indeed 'tis," Odo affirmed. "Should you be granting me half your coin, I would know whether you can be relied upon for income during the freeze ahead."

So reasonably did he speak that Genevieve was tempted to throw something at his smug smile. And his reminder of her due was less than welcome. 'Twas clearly that contribution that concerned him above all and she, foolishly, had unnecessarily cast doubt on her own reliability. In a desperate attempt to waylay his line of thought, Genevieve fumbled in her pocket for the meager assortment of coins she had gathered that day, divided the earnings and tossed half toward Odo.

He held her defiant gaze while the silver showered about him, then bent and deliberately plucked each coin from the cobbles. To Genevieve's astonishment, he handed them back to her with no small measure of formality.

Indeed, she was sorely confused now. Genevieve regarded Odo with a wariness normally reserved for lunatics. What was his game?

"You shall need them this day for a new kirtle" was all he said.

Ha! Back to that they were again! Well, Genevieve had no intent of accompanying Odo elsewhere, and he had best understand that matter.

"I need no kirtle for no intent have I of accompanying you," she argued hotly.

Odo's lips thinned. "You are not suitably attired," he informed her coldly, his manner paternal once more. "Come along, for there is little enough time for you to acquire a new kirtle before we are due to play."

Genevieve rose to her full height and tipped her chin to glare at Odo. Her oath demanded she remain, and remain she would. "I will play nowhere but here," she asserted boldly. "Here 'tis that I play and here alone. You cannot force me to leave this place!"

Odo leaned forward and his voice dropped to a growl. "I *could* force you to leave this place, and well you know it." Neither his voice nor his regard wavered, and Genevieve was forced to acknowledge an increment of dread rising within her. Well it seemed that this matter was of considerable import to Odo and she realized in that instant precisely how much larger than her he was.

Though that did not mean that she would not try to gain her way. Her own resolve was not small in this matter, either.

"Mayhap you have forgotten our bargain, but I will remind you," Odo snarled afore Genevieve could speak. "Half your coin, your agreement to play with me on demand, and one last condition to be named later. That was our bargain, and 'tis that bargain I invoke to request your companionship this day.''

Genevieve stood her ground. "I will not go."

"Is your word worth naught then?" Odo asked with a sneer. "You pledged to play elsewhere when I so bade, as I recall." Genevieve's color rose hot in her cheeks, but she reminded herself silently of her quest. "Well did I think your word had merit, or I would not have returned to you your lute."

"Odo, I cannot do this thing," she admitted in a low tone. Odo's eyes narrowed, but Genevieve spread her hands in appeal. "I *must* play here on this day of days. I cannot afford to leave this place. On the morrow I will accompany you, or on the morrow after that, but please do not compel me to leave this place on this day."

"Tell me why," Odo demanded. Genevieve shook her head with a haste that made his expression turn harsh again.

"I can confide in no one," Genevieve insisted. Odo made a sound of exasperation.

"Then 'tis an excuse of little import."

"Nay. 'Tis of great import. I cannot begin to tell you—"

Odo interrupted sharply. "But you would not confide in me?"

Genevieve shook her head slowly. Little evidence had she that Odo could be trusted with the weight of such a confession. Genevieve could not take the risk of telling another soul of her pledge.

"Nay. I cannot."

"You *will* not," Odo said accusingly before he continued in a threatening growl. "A promise did you make to me. And I shall hold you to that promise on this day."

"I cannot leave on this day!" Genevieve protested wildly.

"You *will* leave on this day! 'Twas this we agreed and naught else! Gather your belongings, for I bid you play with me, as we had agreed."

"And if I do not?" Genevieve challenged, bracing her feet against the ground stubbornly. Odo eyed her stance and shrugged, though the cold determination in his eyes diminished naught.

"Then you shall play in this city no more."

His threat hung in the air between them, his harsh expression reminding Genevieve that she had naught with which to negotiate. She glanced to the Temple gates in desperation, but no one stirred from within at this moment.

Well it seemed that she had little choice. Was it not better to sacrifice this one day than to lose all days playing in this place? Doubt assailed Genevieve, and she knew not what to do. Should Wolfram not find her here this day, surely he would return on the morrow? Surely she had granted him enough reason to seek her out more than once?

But then, if she had, surely he would have returned already?

Had she failed at this task so soon? What if Wolfram had already turned away from her? What if she did not see him again? A despair welled up within her that might have taken Genevieve by surprise with its intensity had she had time to consider the matter.

In truth, she likely had naught to lose by aiding Odo.

Mayhap 'twas better to leave than to sit here and witness the evidence that Wolfram had no intent to return. Her heart aching, Genevieve fastened her cloak about her neck and folded her blanket over her arm.

"And do not even think of playing badly," Odo threatened darkly. "Should you see fit to jeopardize our performance, both you and your lute will pay the price."


Wolfram lasted no longer than the next midday before he made an excuse that would take him near the Temple gates. 'Twas weak to seek her out again, he was certain of it. Yet he grimly paced the distance regardless of his certainty he should not. Sorely confused he was by the riotous response she launched within him, yet Wolfram could not stay away.

After all, that sense that she knew Wolfram's secret could not be shaken, inexplicable as it was. A threat she might well be to his anonymity. Plus, she had witnessed his breaking the Rule—nay, she had been responsible for his transgression in tempting him to grant her a coin that was not his to give. And she had refused to grant her word that she would not tell of his second transgression—again, her fault—that of embracing a woman. Wolfram's lips thinned at the recollection of how she had flouted his request.

Indeed, an unpredictable woman in possession of his secrets was well worth watching. His desire to see her was purely logical, naught else.

'Twas not logic that had Wolfram straining his ears as he drew near the gates, but he ignored the taunting voice in his mind that made that observation. No music came to him, and this was of greater concern. Fear quickened his pace and he found himself hastening to the gates. What had happened to the lutenist? Surely she could not have left?

A worse possibility was there than that even. Surely she could not have guessed his affiliation with the Order and sought to reveal his secrets? All knew the Templars were forbidden the company of women, let alone their kisses. Should she have guessed he was of them, she might well have conspired to reveal his error.

How angry had she been in truth the day before? Too late, Wolfram wished he had parted with her on better terms. Was it not said that no scorpion's bite could match that of a woman scorned? Had not the lutenist accused him publicly of spurning her? What retaliation might she seek for that imagined transgression?

A new fear blossomed in his mind and Wolfram wondered how she had seen to her own needs these past nights without silver. A cold hand clenched his innards. Why had he left her without coin two nights past? Might she blame him for any misfortune that had befallen her that night he left her without coin? Who knew what manner of trouble could befall a woman alone in the streets of Paris?

Especially one who would kiss a stranger with such incendiary passion. Heat flared within Wolfram at the recollection of her embrace, but he frowned in concentration as he sought her slender form amid the bustling morning crowd.

There.

Relief made him weak in the knees. Wolfram's gaze raked over her, checking every detail, but though she did not play, well enough she seemed.

And she was yet here. Mayhap she waited for him. The very thought fired his blood and curiously fueled his uncertainties.

He should talk to her.

Although now that he stood at the gates with her slender form within sight, Wolfram's resolve faltered. His pulse rose in his ears and his lips tingled anew. What if she kissed him again? What if he could not find the words? What if they argued again? He saw her smile and was certain that she mocked his indecision.

Then he saw the other man.

A red-haired man 'twas who addressed the lutenist, though his garments marked him as one of little repute. She did not turn away, much to Wolfram's disgust, or appear to do anything to dissuade the man's attentions. Wolfram was ashamed to find himself straining to catch the sound of her voice.

Another man. Well it seemed that she did naught to turn that man aside, and the realization did not sit well with Wolfram. Although the matter was naught of his concern, it took little intellect to see the meaning of that. Only too easy 'twas to guess where she might have found shelter the past two nights, even without coin in her pocket.

The man stepped closer to the lutenist and Wolfram turned abruptly away. He could not bear to see whether she saluted this man the same way she had saluted him.

Mayhap she earned her keep with other talents than her lute playing.

Anger burned deep within Wolfram at the very thought. He felt betrayed. Indeed, had she not accused *him* of faithlessness before all, just a day past? The injustice of her words burned within his innards.

A long-familiar feeling 'twas, this betrayal, especially the betrayal of women, and it should not have troubled Wolfram as thoroughly as it did. Well should he have known to expect as much. It stung deep within him, though Wolfram knew in truth that the lutenist had promised him naught.

But she had kissed him. And no passing, casual kiss had it been. He could not conceive that she might kiss another in the same way.

Not that he was interested in the lutenist's kisses. 'Twas only the threat she posed to his own security that concerned him. Naught else.

Wolfram had turned away because he could not bear to watch, though now he itched to see what transpired between the two of them. Conversely, he wanted nothing less than to stalk away and forget the raven-haired lutenist for good.

But well he knew her image would not be readily erased from his mind. Wolfram paused and glanced over his shoulder toward the gates. There *had* been that heart-wrenching moment when she looked into his eyes. He could not erase the shock of the sensation from his mind.

Still Wolfram was certain that she knew what he was and still the exposure terrified him, yet he had to acknowledge that for that brief moment he had not felt so alone.

Not alone.

Much to his surprise, it had not been so dreadful to have another know his dark secret. 'Twas disappointment, then, that lay at the root of his sense of betrayal, Wolfram admitted with no small measure of wonder. Disappointed he was that she either knew naught of his secret in truth or cared not that she knew.

Disappointed. He frowned at the cobblestones. Foolhardy 'twas at best to feel any remorse over the ways of others, and indeed Wolfram could not recall when he last had. He shook himself, telling himself 'twas fitting that such whimsy be halted before it could truly begin.

In future, he had best avoid the music of lutes and the spell they cast. And fortresses shrouded in silently seductive fog. He should forget this lutenist, with her clear green sight and her soft kiss. He should erase the entire incident from his mind.

But a chink there was in the armor of his solitude that could not be denied. She could reveal him. The terrifying thought would not abandon his mind.

Wolfram glanced through the gates in time to see the lutenist leaving the square with the red-haired man. For but an instant he hesitated, before he knew beyond doubt that he could not so readily let the matter be.

An hour later, Wolfram spared an uncertain glance to the darkening winter sky. Sliding past zenith was the sun, and time 'twas that he returned to the Temple, lest his presence be missed at the board. He knew that he could not afford to be missed, but neither could he afford to lose track of the hastening pair before him.

Wolfram would know where the lutenist was destined afore he returned to the Temple.

Diligently had Wolfram tracked them to a bustling street market, confused as to their intent when they did not disappear into a lodging house. Was it possible he had misread the signs? That the lutenist was less than enamored of the other man's companionship was readily seen in her expression, and that very matter piqued Wolfram's curiosity. Where did this pair go?

They lingered so long in one tailor's establishment that he feared they had used another exit, but then the lutenist and her flame-haired companion reappeared. Wolfram emitted a sigh of relief that quickly changed to one of wonder at the transformation in her appearance. Garbed in lushly embroidered red and gold was she, and her hair brushed out to gleam over her shoulders.

But a glimpse had Wolfram of that enticing sight before she threw her cloak about her shoulders and drew her drab hood over all. Clear 'twas that her mood was less than fine, and Wolfram watched the red-haired man take the lutenist's elbow impatiently and lead her on.

Well it seemed that there was a piece to this puzzle that Wolfram had not discerned. He wondered if his first impression had been wrong as he threaded his way through the crowds in pursuit of his swift-footed quarry.

Now, as all hastened home to the allure of their heavy midday meal. The red-haired man headed purposefully toward the king's own court. Those high, smooth walls rose ahead, and still he did not check his pace, the lutenist in tow behind him. Wolfram watched in amazement as the pair were confronted by a gatekeeper, and he paused to watch.

"What business have you here?" The burly guard garbed in azure and gold looked none too welcoming, and Genevieve shrank back, wondering what indeed was Odo's intent.

That man straightened his shoulders and met the guard's gaze with a boldness Genevieve was uncertain was wise. "Come to play for the entertainment of the king's guests are we," he declared.

The guard raised a skeptical brow. "Invited are you?"

"'Twas the recommendation of one who heard me that my voice should grace the court," Odo stated brashly. Genevieve refrained from rolling her eyes, certain a child could have contrived a finer lie or delivered it more believably than Odo had.

"Who might this gentleman have been?" the guard demanded.

"I know not his name," Odo confessed without hesitation. He frowned with an intensity that made Genevieve suddenly wonder whether he told the truth, and rubbed his chin as though struggling to recall. "Jean, I believe he said," he mused. "A tall man was he, with an impressive retinue"

The guard offered naught. Indeed, his eyes narrowed and he folded his arms across his chest, more effectively barring the entrance than he had before. "Jean?" he repeated. "A common enough name is that, and not enough of a guarantee to see you through these—"

He managed no more before Odo let out a hoot of delight. "There!" he cried triumphantly. "There is the man who bade me come here!"

The guard swiveled to follow the direction of Odo's finger. Before Genevieve could take a breath, Odo had grasped her hand and ducked behind the guard on the other side. She felt the guard spin in search of them, but Odo was hauling her into the milling crowd clustered in the courtyard.

"Oy! Halt, you ruffians!" The guard shouted behind them as he realized what they had done, but Odo darted onward with quick feet. The swarm of nobles and their retinues swallowed them up and Genevieve heard the guard curse far behind them as he abandoned the chase.

"Another minstrel, more or less. What be the difference?" His low muttering carried to Genevieve's ears, and she might have enjoyed the moment under other circumstances. As 'twas, she was still sorely vexed by Odo's meddling. Odo flashed her a triumphant smile.

"A big gathering 'tis this day," he said, his eyes gleaming with ambition as he glanced over the assembly. "Well do I think 'twould be poor thinking to waste such an opportunity on playing in the courtyard alone. Dame Fortune walks with us this day, and I would take advantage of her favor."

"Surely you cannot mean to gain the court itself?" Genevieve demanded incredulously. No answer had Odo for her, for he was already approaching a guard at the portal to the hall with a swaggering step, his coin jingling audibly in his pockets.

Genevieve glanced about herself indecisively, but no choice had she, in truth, but to follow.

Wolfram tapped his toe for a moment after watching the lutenist and her companion disappear through the gate as he decided his path.

He had come this far, he reasoned. The woman who held his secrets was up to mischief, of that Wolfram had little doubt.

'Twas only logical that he continue to pursue her.

And should he be forced to stretch the truth a bit to gain admission, 'twas a small price to pay. He reviewed what he had seen and concocted a tale, surprisingly not far from the truth, and deliberately approached the guard whom the lutenist and her companion had so artfully deceived.

"Declare your business," the guard in question said in a booming voice, and granted Wolfram a baleful stare.

"From the Order of the Temple, am I," Wolfram confided in a low voice. He thought he saw a flicker of curiosity in those eyes before the guard's expression closed. Still the man's manner was disgruntled, and Wolfram well aimed to take advantage of that fact.

The guard's eyes glinted with suspicion. "You wear not the cross," he observed coldly. "Nor is your hair shorn in the usual manner." Wolfram shook his head hastily and leaned closer, pleased when the guard followed suit.

"My task is not one that the Order would have any eyes note," he whispered, eyeing the man who blocked his path.

The guard was heavyset, burly enough that he could give any who might desire to enter without permission reason to reconsider. Indeed, it looked as though the man's nose had been broken several times, and his very appearance might be enough to deter most would-be trespassers. Truly the guard did not seem to be a man of exceptional intellect, and well might that be of use to Wolfram.

The guard's brows rose, then his eyes narrowed. "No proof is there of that," he declared suspiciously.

"Aye, and none should there be, if my task is well fulfilled," Wolfram countered boldly. He gambled that this guard might know others who were or had been Templars. Fighting men, Wolfram well knew, tended to keep company with each other. "Ask me anything about the Order," he offered.

The guard's expression became calculating, and Wolfram's heart skipped at the knowledge that he had hit a mark. "My cousin was a Templar and well did he confide in me something few know outside the Order," he said carefully.

Wolfram's heart began to pound in his ears and he hoped he knew the answer to the test he was about to be presented. The burly guard leaned closer and Wolfram could smell his breath.

"How many horses is a knight of the Order entitled to possess?"

Some jest must this be. Wolfram blinked, but the man was completely serious. Surely this was not a creature of high intellect, and he thanked the stars above for blessing him with such fortune. One needed not to even be a member of the Order to know such a mundane fact.

"Three," Wolfram answered—'twas the truth, as any fool knew—and the guard nodded with slow satisfaction.

"Aye," he agreed jovially, and held up three heavy fingers. "Three steeds. Where is your beast?"

"No knight am I, but a sergeant committed to a dangerous task," Wolfram declared, anxious to return the conversation to its original direction before the lutenist disappeared within the maze of this fortress. He nudged the guard, aiming to establish a camaraderie. "Well should you know that those above oft do not appreciate the talents of those in the lower ranks."

The guard's gaze flashed. "Aye, 'tis often the way that those of us most loyal are rewarded least," the guard asserted in a markedly more friendly tone. Wolfram spared a pointed glance through the open gates, and the man jumped in recollection. "Aye, a dangerous task have you. What task might that be?"

Wolfram permitted his gaze to flick from one side to the other, as though reluctant to part with the tale. "A man and woman do I seek," he whispered in a confiding tone, "for reasons which I cannot disclose. Mayhap you have seen them pass this way."

The guard puffed up his chest importantly. "Many men and women have passed this way this day, my friend, and I have seen them all."

"Aye, but on foot were these two, certainly uninvited here." Wolfram watched a tentative light dawn in the guard's eye and knew precisely what he recalled. "The woman carries a lute, the man is red of hair," he continued and the guard's eyes widened.

"Those two did just creep past me!" he declared. Wolfram permitted his own eyes to widen in mock surprise, though indeed he had seen precisely that happen.

"Nay!" he said in apparent shock.

"Aye," the guard affirmed. "No surprise is it to me that they are bent on making trouble." His eyes glinted bright with curiosity. "What is their crime?" he demanded in a whisper.

"Their crime I cannot confide to you." Wolfram dropped his voice. "'Tis a most *private* matter, should you understand my meaning."

"Involving those of rank?" the guard asked, evidently possessed of an appetite for gossip. Wolfram nodded minutely, then tapped his fingertips against his lips. He could say no more.

The guard looked suitably impressed. "Shall I have them hunted down for you? Shall I have them dragged back to the gates in chains?"

"Nay, nay, nay, 'tis a most *delicate* matter," Wolfram said hastily. "But let me pursue them, that we might discover the precise nature of their mischief within these walls."

"No threat is there to the king?" the guard asked heavily. Wolfram immediately shook his head.

"Nay, 'tis a certain nobleman whom they would threaten..." he prevaricated, not knowing precisely how he would explain something that he had yet to conceive.

Incredibly, the guard's expression lit with understanding. "Aye," he declared, pointing a heavy finger in Wolfram's direction. "A 'Jean' they sought within these walls, well did he tell me so!"

"Shhhh!" Wolfram urged in a hiss. He held up one hand and glanced over his shoulder. "Say not the man's name aloud. A secret 'tis of highest import!"

"Aye, aye," the guard agreed in more muted tones. He peered into the courtyard and pointed out a nobleman who was just dismounting to Wolfram. "This man employs my brother. I shall gain you admission in his retinue, but your guarantee must I have that no harm will come to either him or the king."

"What is this man's name?" Wolfram demanded, as though the matter were of great import.

"Guichard."

Wolfram sighed with mock relief and gave the guard a thin smile. "Safe he is then, for he is no Jean. I gladly give you my word."

"I see no minstrel," the Master said testily. He reined in his prancing steed in the courtyard of the king's fortress impatiently and glared at his aide. The boy looked suitably uncomfortable.

"He said he would be here," the aide murmured. The Master arched an eloquent brow and fired a quelling glance at the boy.

"Sure you are that he said 'twas this day?" he demanded archly.

The boy nodded hastily. "Aye, milord. This day, he said."

"Yet he is not here," the Master mused, casting a deliberate eye over the gathered crowd once again before locking gazes with the boy. "Well do I hope that you have not erred," he murmured. The boy leapt from his palfrey's back with admirable speed.

"Nay, milord. I will find him," he said firmly.

"See that you do," the Master answered. His patience was wearing thin, and yet again he regretted not seizing that troublemaking minstrel on the very first day he had heard him. His *chanson* was scandalous nonsense, yet plenty there were who might well believe in it.

And the Master had little interest in any recalling the name of *Pereille*. Well would it suit him if all recollection of that family slipped away without note. So close had he come to claiming their assets for his own that he would not be thwarted again.

Once before, the Master had thought the Pereille gold deposit in the Temple his to claim. The crown had eliminated the threat of Enguerrand and Sibylla and their potential claim to the royal scepter when the Master was yet a brother knight, burning with ambition in a competitive order. He had scarcely believed it when he found the family deposit on the Order's books. It had taken little more than finding a copy of the family's receipt to tempt him.

After all, the Pereille family was no more and had no further need of the funds that could secure his future. It had seemed an innocent enough prank at the time, and one that would hurt no one.

The Master had copied the receipt, presented it and claimed the gold at a chapter far from his own house, where he was not recognized. Then he had ridden back to his own chapter house, terrified by the value of the burden he carried. In an astute move calculated to ensure his own future, he had then donated the gold to the Order, supposedly as a gift from his own family.

The plan had succeeded admirably. Now the Master stood as highest in command of all France, second only to the dictate of the Master of the Temple of Jerusalem.

And now everything the Master had worked for was at risk.

How was he to have known Enguerrand and Sibylla had spawned? How might he have guessed that he had stolen the legacy of a living man? Harmless his ploy had seemed all those years past, though far from harmless would its discovery be now that he held such a prestigious position.

All in all, the revelation six months past that Alzeu de Pereille drew breath had not been a welcome one. Should Alzeu have come to claim the Pereille deposit, it could well have been a matter of embarrassment for the Master of the Paris Temple. All had the Master to lose and, though he knew not Alzeu's intent, the decision to see him worm food had been an easy one.

But a whisper in the ear of the king had it taken to have the signed contract in the Master's own hand. How convenient that Philip le Beau did not rest easily on the throne! To have the Order paid to ensure Alzeu's demise was an irony that only the Master could appreciate.

Yet no sooner had the task been completed than two more unwelcome revelations came to light! Would this family and the Master's single error of judgment ever cease to bring him grief? Not only had that long-lost and thoroughly cursed pair borne not one but *two* children, but this fool minstrel persisted in singing a *chanson* about the family.

And this cursed daughter who survived, this Genevieve, had disappeared from her family fortress on her brother's death. Not a whisper could the Master rouse about her or her location. Indeed, he knew not even what the woman looked like, and the matter did not sit well with him. For all he knew, she could well be staking her family's claim with an official receipt of the Order at any house of the Order in Christendom at this very moment.

'Twas not a thought that encouraged sound sleeping.

Though little enough would it gain the Master even if he did know her whereabouts. Even the power-greedy Philip was not fool enough to be persuaded that a *woman* was a threat to his hegemony. Likely as not, the king would merely wed this Genevieve to one of his family.

But that solution would scarce suffice for the Master's ends. As long as the woman lived, so did the threat that she might make a claim and reveal his single impetuous error.

'Twas enough to age a man before his time.

Truly, the Master's fortune could turn no worse. The last irritant he needed was this minstrel and the possibility that his *chanson* would pique the curiosity of others within the court. He would see this issue resolved in short order, that it plague him no longer. He gritted his teeth and scanned the assembly impatiently yet again for a glimpse of the red-haired minstrel who was supposed to be here.

And this time he would not let that minstrel out of his sight again, at least until that one could sing no longer.

What the Master saw instead made him doubt the evidence before his own eyes. He frowned and looked again, but Wolfram—*Wolfram*, his own empoisonneur—yet stood within the enclave of a nobleman's party.

Wolfram? What was he doing here? And who did he accompany? Surely Wolfram should be within the walls of the Temple, for no permission had the Master granted that he might leave. What was his intent here? The Master's eyes narrowed and he dismounted abruptly, ensuring that he kept well behind the nobleman's group.

As far as the Master knew, Wolfram had never broken the Rule, though his presence here without permission was surely a transgression of the first order. What might drive such a man to break his oath? The Master could not imagine, but he well intended to find out.

# Chapter Six

"Truly you are a monk?"

Wolfram ignored Guichard's daughter and her apparent fascination with him, though not out of any intended rudeness. The fact that his lie had been repeated to this Guichard, believed and circulated throughout the nobleman's entire party made Wolfram decidedly uncomfortable, and he knew not what to say.

Indeed, was it not against the Rule for a man to break his silence at the table?

Though evident 'twas to even the most casual observer that the Rule held no sway in this place. Court 'twas, the court of the very king of France, and the riot of color and activity was enough to make a simple man's head spin.

Clinging to the familiar rigor of the Rule seemed the only sensible course to follow under such unfamiliar circumstances.

What had prompted him to such folly?

The noise of merrymaking was quite different from the slow drone of a single brother reading Scripture, the accompaniment to which Wolfram was accustomed to taking his meals. People garbed in fine attire the like of which Wolfram had never seen talked gaily on all sides, swapped tales, recounted jokes. Verily, the din of the place would unsettle a man's innards. Women laughed, minstrels

warmed their voices, men bellowed. Dogs scurried under-
foot, cutlery clattered on the board.

Wolfram sat carefully on the bench where he had been
directed and endeavored to make sense of it all. The noise
of people was not all that astonished Wolfram. The very
finery surrounding him made him self-conscious. Indeed,
his plain tabard was ridiculously somber in contrast to the
embroidered silks and taffetas, the damask and brocade, the
jewels and seed pearls that greeted him on every side.

Though indeed Wolfram had stepped out of the hallowed protection of the Temple more often than most of his
brethren, still the riches of this hall were a shock. Truly there
were folk who lived amid such wealth? 'Twas difficult to
believe, yet those about him seemed not to question or even
note their surroundings.

'Twas clear he alone was impressed.

The room was flooded with a rich golden light that flattered the coloring of the women and made the finery of all
sparkle. Blazing fires leapt high in fireplaces at either end of
the hall and torches burned merrily from their sconces on
the smoothly fitted stone walls.

Trestle tables there were set up in long rows, enough rows
to fill the very hall to bursting, with one set crosswise upon
a dais at one end. The tables were covered with fine linen,
most embroidered around the periphery, that of the head
table most ornate of all. Wolfram tentatively fingered the
linen cast across the board before him and marveled that
such a fine cloth would be used where it was doomed to be
stained. More sensible 'twas, to his mind, to keep the board
bare, as was the custom of the Temple.

He noted the dazzling mix of cups gracing the tabletops,
every sort of vessel represented, from cobalt-rimmed glasses
to elaborate brass chalices. Too late Wolfram realized he had
not brought his own simple, unembellished cup and spoon.

Of course, he had had no idea that this was his destination.

What was he doing here? Had he lost possession of his mind in pursuing this ebony-haired lutenist? Back at the Temple should he be, partaking of a simple repast with his brethren, not lying audaciously to follow a strange woman into the king's own court.

Truly Wolfram had never lost track of himself so thoroughly before. He began to rise, certain he should leave this place now, while his wits were about him again.

"Be not so coy with me," Guichard's daughter said teasingly. She laid a hand upon Wolfram's thigh and effectively halted his departure. Never had a woman touched him thus, and Wolfram was uncertain quite how to proceed. Was this acceptable behavior? He knew not. Wolfram glanced up to find her sparkling blue eyes close beside him. "Are you truly a monk?" she asked again.

Wolfram swallowed as he reminded himself that silence seemed not to be the order of the board here. Still, he could summon but a single word in response.

Out of his element he was indeed.

"Aye," he said simply. Her eyes widened, and she blinked before fluttering her lashes. Never had Wolfram seen such a display, and he wondered if mayhap a mote had fallen in her eye.

"A monk," she cooed, and a decidedly scheming smile slid over her lips. "Does that mean you cannot be tempted?" she whispered. Her hand moved deliberately up Wolfram's thigh in a most disconcerting way. 'Twas clear he had much to learn about the ways of women, for her behavior made absolutely no sense to him.

She asked if he could be tempted. He frowned and considered the question carefully. Well must she be testing his knowledge of Scripture. Well, the answer was clear enough to even one with as little interest in such matters as Wolfram. Well had he been taught that none were immune to temptation.

"All men can be tempted," he informed her solemnly. To his confusion, she smiled and arched her back toward him, much in the manner of a stretching cat. First a mote in her eye, and now the poor child had a sore back. Evidently her sire had compelled her to ride far this day.

"Your back troubles you?" he asked politely. Guichard's daughter chuckled throatily and slipped her hand yet closer to his groin. Well did Wolfram wish she might restrain herself from such familiarity, for he certainly was not accustomed to being touched thus.

Though he imagined it might be considered rude to protest.

" 'Tis not my back that plagues me," she whispered intently, "but rather an itch that needs tending."

"Ah." Wolfram knew not quite how to respond. Had it been one of his brethren who confided such a need, he certainly would have offered his aid in the task. Naught more troubling was there than an itch one could not reach oneself. Wolfram feared he knew not this lady well enough to make such an offer, and he knew not what to do. Certainly he had no wish to offend the daughter of his benefactor.

"Mayhap you could assist me," she asked in an unnaturally low and throaty tone. Had she an illness in her throat, as well? Truly the child was unnaturally plagued by tests of her endurance.

Clearly her words indicated that the lady was unlikely to be offended by familiarity. As though to reinforce that conclusion, her hand stole beneath the hem of Wolfram's tabard and landed unexpectedly on a part of him none had touched but himself in years. He jolted backward in surprise at her unexpected caress and nearly tipped the bench in the process.

Though now a distance was measured between himself and Guichard's unfathomable daughter, he earned only the lady's light laughter for his trouble. Wolfram eyed her warily, not in the least reassured when that knowing smile curved her lips once more.

"Shy, are you, then?" she asked huskily. "Well can I adjust to that."

Before she could move, a foppish nobleman from this Guichard's extensive retinue stretched a leg over the bench between her and Wolfram and dropped to a seat.

"Alys!" he declared. "You did indeed save me a place, despite your claim." He settled on the bench, and Wolfram permitted himself a sigh of relief. He was little certain of what Guichard's daughter intended, but grateful he was that he need not waste his time evading her any longer.

'Twas clear the woman was possessed by a strange madness that Wolfram had no time to decipher. Here he was, and should he wish to discover the lutenist's intent, he had best be about his task. He cast a glance over the hall, seeking a minstrel red of hair.

And found him but a moment later.

With an achingly familiar lutenist close on his heels.

The room fell silent for Wolfram. His heart stopped, his mouth went dry, his palms grew damp. The sight of the lutenist readily summoned the recollection of the sweet lips pressed against his, the scent of her, the softness of her. His body responded with unheralded enthusiasm, and he was glad that they were seated against the shadows of the wall near the rear of the hall, where none were likely to note his condition.

No one was there in the hall but the lutenist for Wolfram's eyes. He greedily drank in the sight of her, stunned by the ferocity that raged through him when she granted the red-haired minstrel a smile.

Radiant she looked, garbed in that gold-and-red kirtle, the firelight bringing out the blue glints in her ebony hair. Those curls tumbled over her shoulders in joyous disarray, her lips seemed more red, her eyes yet more vividly green.

Wolfram could not tear his gaze away. Well it seemed that she moved with an ease foreign to him, that this place did not overwhelm her as it did him. Though her garments were finer than those he had yet seen her wear, her movements were as fluid and gracious as ever. He watched avidly as the lutenist and her companion made their way to the gallery of musicians at the rear of the hall.

'Twas not far from the table where Wolfram was seated, though he had to crane his neck to see the woman he wished to see to the exclusion of all others. When the remainder of Guichard's party joined them, Wolfram deliberately slid to the very end of the bench to make room, that he might have the closest possible proximity to the lutenist.

No awareness had she of his presence, and once again Wolfram felt the voyeur. She settled in place and tuned her lute with a concentration that left one believing she was aware of naught else in the hall.

A fanfare sounded, and all rose to their feet as conversation came to an abrupt halt. Wolfram was quick to understand what was transpiring and joined the company afore any tardiness could show his unfamiliarity with such matters. The king himself swept into the hall in attire so resplendent as to put all others' garb to shame.

Philip strode to the center of the table at the front of the hall and gazed over the gathering with no small measure of satisfaction. His retinue followed him and fanned out silently on his either side. He seated himself at the head table with a flourish so innate 'twas beyond training, and lifted his gaze expectantly.

His guests seated themselves hastily and a muted hum of conversation resumed. The king's cupbearer brought to him the first draft of wine, the house steward sprinkled the fine dust of what Wolfram guessed was reputedly ground unicorn horn into the chalice.

Wolfram glanced down to the table to hide his scorn at the futility of the practice. Naught he had seen could detect a poison of his making, though to no one could he reveal his pride in that fact. Let the king believe what he would. Should the commission have been granted, Wolfram could even have engineered his demise.

Unicorn horn. Just as in his dream.

The very thought sent Wolfram's gaze slipping to the lutenist, who watched the proceedings with bright green eyes, her lute evidently primed for her performance. Pages slipped through the ranks of the gathered guests, filling each chalice, glass and cup with red wine. Once again, Wolfram was aware of his omission.

"Have you no service?" The whisper in his ear sent color rising over his neck.

"Inadvertently forgotten 'twas," he murmured with embarrassment. The page tut-tutted, but a snap of his fingers brought another with an unembellished pewter cup remarkably similar to Wolfram's own.

"Have you a spoon?" the page demanded archly. Wolfram was compelled to shake his head.

"Naught but my knife," he confessed. The page inhaled sharply in disapproval and sent the other scurrying for spoon, bowl and linen.

He spared Wolfram a cold look evidently reserved for buffoons who inexplicably found themselves hosted at the king's own board. That the truth was no less only made the unspoken accusation more cutting. Wolfram grasped his filled cup and sipped gratefully of the wine, his gaze slipping, seemingly of its own accord, to the lutenist once more.

Still she sat patiently and, though she observed the goings-on of the court with some interest, 'twas clear she had yet to spy him. Wolfram was not quite certain whether he wished she would do so or not.

Fetching she was, to be sure, and his heart contracted at the sweetness of her bowed and ruddy lips. Lips he had tasted, not once but twice. Suddenly it seemed the hall was significantly warmer than it had been when they arrived.

The lutenist but blinked once when one of the king's retinue snapped his fingers in the musicians' direction. Her red-haired companion whispered something to her that made her nod nervously, then rose to his feet. His movement recalled Wolfram to both his senses and his task, and he leaned forward slightly, intent on hearing what that man might say.

Another fanfare clapped the man's mouth closed when Wolfram thought he might have begun. A procession came from the kitchens on that trumpet's cue, the entire retinue led by a beaming, portly man whom Wolfram assumed to be the cook himself. That man ushered in a pair of help-mates bearing a platter on which a roast boar reposed. The savory smell of the meat was fit to tempt the hunger of any man.

The boar was followed by another, then a hind, seven pheasants, three swans, a positive flock of chickens. Custards and *blanquemangers,* beans in butter, eels in cream sauce, the variety of food was astonishing to Wolfram. Indeed, he had thought himself well fed at the Temple to rely upon meat thrice a week and wine daily. When he traveled about, 'twas evident that most were lucky to see meat once a week, bread and cheese daily comprising most of their diet, yet here there was little else.

Platters were passed down the tables once the king had partaken of a particular dish. Thick trenchers of bread were sliced and placed before each guest, and meat was heaped thereupon. As the passing of food sparked a general mumble of conversation, fingers were snapped once again at the musicians and the red-haired man opened his mouth again.

The lutenist struck a chord that melted everything within Wolfram and the food before him was forgotten. Indeed, he was hard-pressed to attend the verse at all, so disarmed was he by the enchanting sounds of her lute. Overwhelmed was he by the unfamiliar extravagance of the setting, and well it seemed the music took advantage of his vulnerability. It slipped through the chinks in his facade and wound its way around his heart with a dexterity that left him breathless.

Indeed, it seemed she played solely for him. That realization alone prompted Wolfram to recall another who had played solely for him. One whom he had loved with all his heart and soul.

One whom he had lost.

One whom he could not afford to forget. Yet neither could he risk unleashing whatever the recollection of her might bring. He resolutely closed his mind and gritted his teeth as he glared at his loaded trencher.

When the red-haired man began to sing, the clarity and resonance of his voice was surprising. For one who looked to have lived a hard life, there was a sweetness there that Wolfram would not have expected. Truly, his talent was not small.

"A tale would I recount to you, a tale of fidelity and bravery, a tale of love gained and lost, a tale of one knight who rose above the temptations of this earth to capture paradise for his own," Odo sang as Genevieve plucked an accompanying tune from her lute. Never would she have expected that to play in the king's court was his intent. Despite her annoyance with him and her fear that she might miss Wolfram's return, Genevieve had to acknowledge a grudging admiration for Odo's ability to gain his desire.

Would that she were better at fulfilling her own oath.

"'Tis the tale of one Parzival I would share with you," Odo continued. "'Twas long ago, yet not so far away, that this tale first drew breath, and I would bid all to heed its simple message. Though indeed this knight's path was less than true, still he gained that great reward that not a few among us might seek. An intent truth had he, when all was said and done, and like unto a ruby set in base brass, the setting of his deeds cannot steal from the beauty of the pure stone of his heart. Well might there be lessons within the telling to light the path for many another, and I humbly present my own poor representation of his tale for that alone."

The court was rich beyond Genevieve's experience, and she permitted her mind to wander as Odo sang. In truth, she supposed she was fortunate to catch a glimpse of this life, but still she chafed with impatience to return to her square.

"And so it was that Parzival, knighted as he had desired, set out in search of his own fortune.

"He found adventure, as you might imagine, and rather more quickly than even he might have hoped. Soon he came to a fortress on the coast so beleaguered by troops that no ship had been able to put into port. The people were starving, yet Parzival's offer to grant them aid if they but admitted him gained him their meager hospitality.

"Not the least of these people was their queen, and Parzival lost his heart when first he saw her. Even as gaunt as she was, her beauty shone forth for all to see. Virtuous she was, noble and gracious, and 'twas clear to Parzival that she was not only as pure as a maiden should be, but true of heart, such that her people adored her.

"That night the queen came to Parzival in no more than a silk shift and tears on her cheeks. He could not bear to see her so unhappy and begged she tell him her tale of woe. Condwiramirs was her name, and she alone held sway over the territories of her sire. She lay with Parzival, chastely I might add for those of you plagued by lecherous thoughts, and confided in him.

"Well it seemed that one Clamide saw fit to assault her fortress and swore to do so until the lady wed him or sent a knight who won a duel against him. No wish had Condwiramirs to wed Clamide, for he was said to be cruel, yet every champion she sent against him left not the field alive. Her subjects were suffering for her choice, yet 'twas their resolve alone that she not grant herself to the cruelty of Clamide that gave her strength to continue. Her determination was faltering at last, though, and she admitted to Parzival her deepest fear.

"Parzival took the lady in his arms and swore to her that he would ride to joust with Clamide on the morrow. Reassured then by his promise, she slept nestled in his arms, and Parzival fancied 'twas the first time she had slept so peacefully in many a moon.

"Neither will I plague you with the long tale of their duel, for Parzival, good to his word, rode out at dawn, yet did not return before the sun pushed its face into the sky again. All the day and all the night these two knights did battle, and the duel was not easily won. Yet 'twas Parzival who eventually rode from the field victorious, to the cheers of the lady's subjects and the happy tears of the lady herself.

"And on that next day, by some divinely ordained coincidence, a pair of ships rode into the harbor, their sails white against the sky and their holds laden with foodstuffs. Enough there was for all to eat their fill, and in that happy moment, the queen Condwiramirs took Parzival as her spouse, her lord and king. Such a celebration then ensued, the like of which I cannot begin to describe to you. Suffice it to say that the couple were happy, they reigned with great justice and their lands prospered."

Here Genevieve thought that Odo would surely be finished, and she began to wind up her tune, only to earn a frown from her companion. He raised his voice again and she stifled a sigh, wishing he would be quick about his *chanson*.

Well it seemed that Odo intended to make his moment of glory stretch on as long as possible, regardless of Genevieve's desires to the contrary.

She wondered if Wolfram had already visited the square and thought her gone.

"Then, one day, Parzival chose to leave his wife for a time to visit his mother and seek his fortune again. He was young enough and yet naive enough to not appreciate fully the gifts that had come so readily to his hand."

Something about the minstrel's manner when he uttered these lines captured Genevieve's attention. She glanced up, well aware of the weight of another's gaze, and was astounded to meet the calm silver regard of Wolfram.

Her breath caught in her throat. Genevieve blinked in disbelief, yet still he remained, garbed simply as always, yet inexplicably taking a meal here in the king's court.

What was he doing here? Even as she wondered, her pulse leapt to pound in her ears. They stared at each other for a long moment. Naught did his expression reveal to her and Genevieve finally could no longer bear to hold his regard. She bent over her lute again with a hammering heart, hoping she appeared as though she had forgotten his presence.

Her trembling fingers gave away the truth and Genevieve prayed that he could not see their shaking. Why was he here? What strange manner of coincidence could have brought Wolfram here on the very day that she played here, even without her having known so in advance? Well did that seem to defy the odds, especially as he was clearly not one of the courtiers commonly called to court.

Indeed, it could be no coincidence.

He must have followed them.

Rage tripped through Genevieve that Wolfram would have the audacity to pursue her in such a manner. Who did the man think he was? How dare he follow her? 'Twas she who led this hunt, and no other! Genevieve's fingers plucked the strings of her lute with a new savagery as anger rolled through her.

"Came Parzival to a fortress," sang Odo, and Genevieve wished heartily that the cursed man would finish his *chanson*. "A fortress highly buttressed with curtain walls as smooth as the finest silk. And though he marveled at the workmanship of this chateau, still Parzival was bold enough to request admission and young enough to be unsurprised when 'twas granted without delay. Indeed, the very lady of the fortress—Repanse de Schoye was her name—sent to him her own cloak to wear, yet he marveled naught at this, thinking it no less than his due.

"In due time, Parzival was taken before the lord of this noble fortress, one Anfortas, known to all and sundry—but not to Parzival—as the Fisher King. This man reposed on a divan of cloth of gold, and though 'twas evident he was in great pain, Parzival asked no question of him, nor extended his sympathy. A great wonder was shown to him that night, but Parzival appreciated it naught, in his youthful ignorance. I cannot tell you enough of the folly of his error, for in the fortress of the Fisher King, Parzival was shown the True Grail.''

A rustle rippled over the guests in the king's hall, and Wolfram was certain the mention of the Grail had prompted the curiosity of more than one. Not alone was he in listening anymore, and he pushed his trencher aside, intent on catching every word.

''After that night of merrymaking, and retiring late to a sumptuous room, Parzival awoke to find himself abandoned in a forest of barren thorns. Cold he was, for the air was chill, yet no branch could he break with which to kindle a flame to warm himself. He wandered aimlessly, aching in his heart, with neither steed nor squire to console him, let alone the warm hearth and hospitality of the Fisher King. Even the cloak of the Lady Repanse de Schoye had abandoned him, and he wondered if he had dreamed.

''Finally, he saw a flicker of light and hastened forward to find an old man hunched over a flame. Of no mind was the ancient one to share the heat until Parzival prostrated himself and begged for his compassion. Parzival's lips were blue with the cold, and well it seemed the old man could not deny him once he saw that evidence. A deal they struck that Parzival should but listen to a tale, for he had naught else with which to pay for the old one's hospitality.

''And so the aged man began the tale of one feckless fool, name of Parzival, who knew not the merit of what he had. Parzival's eyes widened in surprise at this, but he had not revealed his identity and he dared not do so now, lest the man cease his tale.

''Well it seemed that this Parzival had the exceptional gift of having been called to serve the Grail itself, though he had proven himself unworthy of the task in word and deed. Thrice had he erred, and his errors were thus—he had failed to show sympathy for the wounded Fisher King or offer that man aid in any way, he had killed one of his own kin, through ignorance to be sure and with provocation, but Ither the Red Knight had been blood of his own blood nonetheless, and such a travesty could not be overlooked, and finally he had abandoned his mother and left her to die of grief while he sought his fortune.

"As you can well imagine, these revelations made Parzival's head spin, yet the old man was not finished with his tale as yet. It seemed this Parzival of whom he had heard tell had had the good fortune to gain access to the fortress where the Grail itself was secreted, but had appreciated it not. So filled with vainglory and pride this Parzival was that his heart had not been open to the marvel laid before him."

Genevieve's ears pricked at the mention of the Grail, but she ignored the shiver of dread that tripped along her spine. 'Twas but a fanciful tale Odo spun. Soon enough 'twould end, and she could return to her square, tell Wolfram precisely what she thought of his underhanded pursuit and finish her task here in Paris. 'Twould be easy to take her due with such anger rolling through her veins.

"For none other than Anfortas, the old man told, held possession of the Grail. This fool Parzival had been in the presence of the greatest mystery of Christendom and seen it naught. The fortress Parzival had visited, the fortress known as Munsalvaesche, was the keep of the Grail."

Munsalvaesche. Montsalvat. Genevieve stiffened but resolutely stared at her fingers. Odo could not know the truth. No one left alive knew the truth but she, Genevieve, was certain of it.

It could harm naught to let him continue his song. Why interrupt and draw attention to herself to no gain?

"Though Anfortas guarded the Grail, 'twas his sister, Repanse de Schoye, alone that the Grail permitted to bear its weight." Genevieve fired a quelling glance at Odo, the mention of "sister" coming too close to the truth for her taste. Odo blithely sang on. "And surrounded by Templars the Grail is, for it has summoned them to the task.

"Sworn to the preservation and protection of this great mystery are the Templars alone and, in exchange, its wisdom sustains them and grants them strength beyond any other. No small thing is this, the old man maintained, but there is yet more. The Templars guard the family of Anfortas, as well, a family name of Pereille, because the family of Anfortas alone is granted the responsibility of bearing the Grail. And marked are those within the family, marked with a curious birthmark in the shape of the cross itself."

Genevieve gasped aloud to hear the truth spoken so boldly in the king's own court, before hundreds of his courtiers. What manner of idiot was this Odo?

"Long have the family of the Grail kept its legacy bright, and the Grail sustains them beyond all else," the minstrel asserted as he continued his *chanson*. "Without the slavery of peasants and laborers, their larder is full of divers foods beyond our imagining. Without the benedictions of clergy, their hearts are filled with a love of God beyond our belief."

Had Wolfram not noted the absence of a peasantry at Montsalvat? When he heard the words, he realized there had been no clergy there, either. What *had* sustained those troops? His heart began to pound in his ears.

Could Alzeu's claims have had some root in truth?

Little doubt was there that Wolfram did not attend the tale alone. A murmur tripped through the assembly, and well it seemed that the sounds of merrymaking fell curiously silent. All eyes turned to the minstrel and impatiently awaited his next words. Even those at the head table listened, their hands poised in midair as they forgot the tender morsels they brought to their lips. Outrage registered on the lutenist's lovely visage, and Wolfram imagined that she was not alone in having doubts about the veracity of this tale.

"Great power does the Grail grant to the family who tend it, for they are gifted with the divine right to rule. This is the legacy of the Grail. Kings they throne and dethrone from their remote and unassailable fortress, by dictate of the Grail.''

A ripple of disapproval rolled through the assembly, and Wolfram barely noted that the king himself rose to his feet with a frown.

Yet the minstrel continued undeterred.

''And those of the family, those pledged to the service of the Grail, move among us all. Their men wed in secrecy, sworn to reveal their legacy to none, their women wed openly and bring the heritage of the Grail to bless other families. When a child is born of these matches, this child is summoned to serve the Grail. Thus had Parzival been summoned, though his lineage alone was not enough. Well had he to prove himself worthy of the gift awaiting him.''

To Wolfram's astonishment, the lutenist stopped playing and glared at her companion.

''Stupid fool,'' she hissed in outrage, though doubtless her voice carried farther than she intended. ''Would you see all of us dead?''

*Us?*

To his credit, the minstrel looked as dumbfounded as Wolfram felt. The tone of the room changed subtly, a rustle of curiosity rippled through the ranks of those who had attended the *chanson,* and well it seemed there was markedly less activity in the hall.

''Of what do you speak?'' he murmured to the lutenist in an undertone rife with anger and confusion. His words, too, carried to other ears, doubtless because of the unnatural quiet in the hall.

''Of what do *you* speak?'' the lutenist retorted sharply, her emerald eyes flashing furiously. ''Who granted you the right to share the tale of my family with any who would care to listen?'' She shoved to her feet and jabbed one fingertip in the astounded minstrel's chest. ''No right have you to tell this tale, no right have you to jeopardize the safety of a family you do not even know!''

The king's fist hit the board, and his voice rose in a roar that demanded attention. "What family would you say he jeopardizes?" he demanded regally. The lutenist spun, her anger not abandoning her at this interruption.

"*My* family!" she declared hotly. "The family of Pereille. I am Genevieve de Pereille!"

Genevieve de Pereille!

The assembly gasped as one, but Wolfram could recall only one thing. He had seen that name on the genealogy in the Master's office. 'Twas she!

The collective gasp seemed to recall the lutenist to her senses. She glanced about herself, as though she had just realized where she stood and what she had said, and all the color drained from her face.

Genevieve de Pereille. Wolfram recalled the parchment unfurled on the Master's desk and knew the Temple might be seeking this woman. Her location might be sought even now for a waiting commission from a nameless client.

Surely 'twas that knowledge alone that prompted his desire to see her free of this place. Any fool knew that crown and Temple did not see eye-to-eye on many matters, and should Genevieve be imprisoned here, the Temple might well be unable to fulfill a contract.

Surely 'twas Wolfram's pledge to serve the Order first.

Impulsively Wolfram darted forward.

"Guards!" roared the king from the dais.

"Guards!" cried the assembly in echo of his order. The guests rose to their feet, pressing closer to Genevieve, that they might catch a better glimpse of her, but Wolfram shoved his way impatiently through their midst.

As he pushed closer, Wolfram saw that fear had paralyzed Genevieve and that she knew not what to do or where to turn. A space there was around her, for all feared to touch her. The minstrel who had accompanied her had fallen back against the wall, his face a mask of astonishment. Clearly he had thought his tale no more than that. Wolfram stepped boldly into the space beside the lutenist, and her gaze lifted to his with all the shock of a startled doe's.

" 'Tis true?'' he demanded in a hoarse undertone. She shivered and closed her eyes, gathering her lute close before her. When she met his gaze again, there were tears in those glittering green eyes.

"Aye," she admitted reluctantly, the words barely given voice. " 'Tis all true.'' Sincerity echoed in her tone, for all its softness, and Wolfram knew she spoke the truth. He thrust his hand immediately toward her.

"Then come," he said flatly. "I vow I will see you safe."

Safe? Surely that was overstating his intent. But the relief dawning in those green eyes dismissed Wolfram's qualms.

Without hesitation, Genevieve put her slender hand within his. No time had Wolfram to consider the marvel that she trusted him or the tentative warmth spreading within him now that he held her tiny hand securely within his own.

It mattered naught to him if she was relieved, for 'twas to the Master alone he would grant her custody. Naught more was there behind his action than that. His conscience pricked, but Wolfram could spare it no time now.

"Give way!" cried the guards, and the crowd muttered as they parted reluctantly.

Genevieve gasped in sudden understanding of their plight, and she gripped his fingers more tightly. Wolfram squeezed her hand in reassurance, then they turned as one and ran.

# *Chapter Seven*

Genevieve felt the difference the instant she touched him.

A tentative warmth there was dawning within the cold cavern of Wolfram's soul, and Genevieve knew then that she had not misplaced her trust. Help her he would to the best of his ability, and little doubt had she that his ability was greater than her own.

They leapt of one accord toward the exit, the cries of the king's guard rising behind them. Genevieve's heart pounded, but Wolfram faltered naught. He dived through the tiny door at the back of the gallery, hauling her behind him when her footsteps failed to keep pace with his own.

In a corridor they were. Abandoned 'twas, and the ends bent away, so that its path was not clear in either direction. The sounds of pursuit carried from the gallery behind them and Genevieve's pulse raced in fear. Musicians swore as they endeavored to be obstructions and thereby protect one of their own. A sour key was struck, something cracked, a man cursed. Genevieve's heart tore at the knowledge that some instrument had paid the price of her folly, but Wolfram was oblivious.

He lifted his nose to the air, then turned crisply to the right. When he broke into a run, Genevieve did her utmost to keep up. They slipped around a corner in the very nick of time. Footsteps broke into the corridor behind them. Genevieve caught her breath in certainty that they would be found out, but Wolfram merely fired her a quelling glance.

Silence was imperative. She understood his meaning at once and struggled to make her footfalls as light as possible.

A great staircase curved away before them and Wolfram took the stairs three at a time. When Genevieve slipped and bumped her lute on a granite stair, the instrument released a muted yet distinctive thump.

She winced, but Wolfram said naught. He lifted the lute from her grasp without ceremony, and for the first time in all her days, Genevieve permitted another to carry her pride and joy.

No time had she to reflect upon this instinctive trust, though, for they were charging down the stairs at breakneck speed. Only now could Genevieve smell the stables below, and only then did she realize what Wolfram had sought when he sniffed the air high above them.

They burst out into a courtyard Genevieve had not seen afore. A pair of guards jumped in surprise at their abrupt arrival, but Wolfram heeded them naught. By the time they had recovered from their surprise, Wolfram and Genevieve were out of their reach. Wolfram ran full out across the cobbled courtyard. Genevieve thought to fight him for his folly in fleeing so openly.

Then she saw the great gaping maw of the gate. The spiked portcullis yet hung high, though she had only noted it when the cry rang out from far above

"Close the gate!"

Genevieve gasped as a guard separated himself from the shadow thrown by the wall. Ahead of them he was, and he evidently spied them, for he lunged for the gatehouse. Wolfram muttered something Genevieve fancied was uncomplimentary. Well it seemed he ran faster, and she regretted that she hindered his escape.

So she ran.

The rope holding the portcullis creaked all too soon. Genevieve's heart pounded fit to burst and she could not imagine they could clear the gate in time. Though she knew not what waited in store for them here, readily enough could she guess 'twas not good. The spikes descended slowly, though well Genevieve knew they could be let fall with a vengeance if the keeper so desired.

Wolfram surged forward with a sudden burst of speed. 'Twas too late and Genevieve knew it, but still she ran with all her might. Their footsteps pounded on the cobblestones, their breath rasped in her ears. The gate was close, the portcullis yet higher than Wolfram's head. Their pursuers gained the courtyard in a clatter far behind and bellowed. Genevieve did not dare to look back.

"Close the gates!" came the shout from behind.

"Aye, Captain!" responded the gatekeeper.

"Nay!" Genevieve cried. She heard the ratchet spin as the rope was released in full. Her heart sank with certainty that they were trapped within and doomed to some undoubtedly painful demise.

Wolfram swore and dived.

Genevieve was jerked forward, her hand held fast in his. She saw his intent and mimicked him as well as she was able. The lute within his grasp scraped along the cobbles and Genevieve cringed at the sound, even as the flesh was ripped from her palm and knee. The portcullis whistled overhead, and for a terrifying instant Genevieve glanced up to see those spikes descending directly upon her.

Her heart stopped, but she could do naught else but watch the gate fall.

Wolfram yanked her hand and she rolled. The spikes but impaled the hem of her fine new kirtle as they buried themselves in their iron receptacles with a resonant clang. The ground vibrated and Genevieve shook like a new leaf, but Wolfram granted her no time to reflect. He hauled her to her feet and her kirtle tore before he began to run anew.

Well did Genevieve think her very lungs would burst, and she thought to beg for clemency. She wanted to scream at him to slow his pace, but had not the breath for the task.

Then she heard the rope creak as the portcullis was raised again, and she knew they were not safe yet. Men shouted from within the courtyard behind. The unexpected baying of hunting dogs fairly paralyzed her with fear before that same fear gave new vigor to her step.

They were on the run in truth. With no one to help them. Panic flooded through Genevieve. Where would they run? Where would they hide? Where in this pitiless city might they find sanctuary from the king himself?

Wolfram seemed to have no doubt of his destination. He ran with a purposeful resolve that reassured Genevieve. Though she could not guess his specific intent, she knew he fostered no doubt at all. A destination had he in mind, one whose security he doubted not, and Genevieve permitted herself to trust his judgment.

Indeed, she had precious little choice.

He cut an unerring path through the city's silent streets when Genevieve was forced to acknowledge she would have been lost long before. She dared not protest his breakneck pace, for well it seemed their very lives stood at stake.

Her mind could make little sense of its certainty that she had been lucky to cross paths with Wolfram again. That this man who had dispatched her own brother would save her hide made little sense, and she feared for an instant that he intended to betray her to some other dastardly fate.

Though if that was his intent, she had little enough time at this moment to fret about it. For now, she put one foot afore the other as fast as she was able.

The barking of those dogs echoing through the streets behind them was enough to chill her blood. Genevieve's heart pounded in her ears and she felt her palms go damp. Was this how the hind felt in the woods when noblemen set to the chase? Indeed, she knew not if she would ever manage to catch her breath again.

They burst abruptly into a square, and Genevieve realized with astonishment that 'twas the gates of the Temple itself that stood open before her. Here 'twas she played, though indeed those days seemed longer past than they were.

And here business progressed as 'twould any other midafternoon during the week. Carts were hauled through the gates ahead, women chatted, children dodged cartwheels and horses. Indeed, the baying of the hunting hounds was distant enough to almost be ignored.

Dread flooded through Genevieve at the distant sound, though, for she knew well enough that she would be denied access to this establishment. Had she not tried to gain entry before, to no avail? And where else might she go? If this was Wolfram's sanctuary, 'twas one she could not share.

Only too well could she imagine those dogs tearing into her flesh. She tugged at Wolfram's hand, but his grip merely tightened around her.

"I cannot go here," she cried in despair. He fired her a glance of such intensity that she almost wished she had held her tongue.

"Nowhere else have you to seek sanctuary," he informed her tightly. Genevieve was forced to acknowledge that he spoke the truth, though that reality was far from comforting.

"But I cannot enter the Temple," she argued.

Wolfram looked away, his profile stern, and his words were bitten out tersely.

"Pull up your hood—I shall contrive some tale," he bade her tersely. "Say naught."

To her astonishment, 'twas as simple as that. A large group approached the gate, and Wolfram slid into the shadow beside the cart on the far side of the keeper. He placed Genevieve's lute atop the mélange of goods atop the cart. Nary a word did he spare for the driver, who noted him not, though the woman who walked at the back of the cart watched Wolfram avidly.

Wolfram lifted a bale from the cart and dropped it on Genevieve's shoulders. Her eyes widened at the weight of the burden, and the woman behind chuckled unkindly, though still she said naught.

Wolfram darted her a sharp glance, then stepped away.

"Keep your pace lively," the older woman whispered warningly when Genevieve attempted to turn to see where he had gone. "'Tis the only way you shall gain admittance unnoted."

Genevieve glanced to the woman, distrusting the gleam in her eye. "You will say naught?" she asked in an undertone.

The woman smiled, though her expression was hard. "Not the first time would it be that a young, pretty woman was slipped into a monastery," she confided. "And not the first time will it be that I have been compensated for aiding in such a task."

Genevieve turned back to the road, the woman's certainty in her lack of morals making her ears burn. Two pieces of silver jingled in Genevieve's pocket, and well she knew the destination of those pieces now. Little doubt had she that the woman had heard their distinctive jingle, as well.

Far behind them, dogs barked in anticipation of catching their prey. Genevieve's pace quickened as a shiver tripped over her skin. She felt Wolfram's presence slip away and heard him exchange some pleasantry with the keeper on the far side of the cart as she passed beneath the gates of her salvation. The woman chuckled in anticipation of her prize.

Genevieve supposed sanctuary was well worth such a paltry sum.

The Master cursed under his breath at the sight of the dogs far ahead of him. Too long had it taken him to retrieve his steed in the confusion that had filled the king's stables, and now he feared he had missed his opportunity.

Genevieve de Pereille! The very woman he sought had been right afore his eyes. What was more, the ever-loyal Wolfram had unexpectedly aided her escape. How that sergeant had known the Master's own objectives, he could not guess, but he praised the day he had seen fit to accept the oath from Wolfram's lips.

If only the guards did not capture him before he reached the gates of the Temple.

The Master spurred his horse onward and took a dizzying sequence of side alleys to circumvent the hunt. As 'twas, he burst into the square opposite the Temple mere heartbeats before the first dog.

Several large parties were passing through the gates of the Temple.

"Brother Michel!" the Master cried, relieved to see that sergeant come out of the keeper's hut with a questioning expression on his features.

The Master hauled his destrier to a halt and glared imperiously down at the man. "Has Brother Wolfram returned?"

"But moments past, milord," the keeper responded quickly. "Indeed, he cannot be more than a hundred paces from here by now—"

"Close the gates!" roared the Master. Naught would be his advantage should Philip's troops gain admission to the Temple. 'Twas true their secular power did not extend within these walls, but once their larger forces invaded, there would be little effective argument the Master could make.

"Lift the drawbridge and bar the way to all who might enter!" He snapped his fingers impatiently when Brother Michel did not move, and the keeper sprung to life.

The keeper bobbed a bow and set immediately to his task, his assistant drawing up the bridge over the moat just as the first of the dogs approached the gate. The beast leapt after the lifting bridge and fell into the moat with a resounding splash. The entire baying pack was close on his heels, but the

Master watched the bridge strain toward the late-afternoon sky with satisfaction.

'Twas too late. The Temple gates were secure. The dogs lined the opposing shore and barked loudly in frustration while the bridge leisurely rose to its vertical position.

The Master of the Temple watched the riders approach, yet held his ground. He turned his mount to confront them proudly, knowing the sight he made on his white destrier with his cloak lifting in the autumn wind. The red cross of the Order blazed upon his white tabard, and his chin was high.

The drawbridge settled into its closed vertical position, the ropes ceased to creak. Both gate and portcullis were barred against intruders. The hounds barked as they raced back and forth in renewed frenzy with the arrival of their masters. Burly men shouted futilely for the release of the bridge. The Master smiled. The water in the moat was blessedly high this autumn, and the outer walls of the Ville Neuve were as smooth as glass.

The fortress of the Temple was impenetrable.

And well should it be, for the Temple stood outside the jurisdiction of all authority, of hierarchies both secular and ecclesiastical. 'Twas right and good and the Master had no qualms about exercising his authority.

Answerable solely to the Master of the Temple of Jerusalem was the Master of the Temple of Paris, and thence responsible to the Pope alone. No other held sway over his choices and to no other would he bow in deference.

But a little time did he need to solve this particular problem. The last threat to his security was secreted within the walls of his own domain. Brought to him she had been by the most loyal of his sergeants, and she would be dispatched, quietly, mayhap by that same sergeant, afore any could put together the pieces of the puzzle.

The Master's future would be secure once more. He would open the gates when all was resolved.

And none could compel him to open them sooner.

His eyes narrowed as a man unmistakably garbed rode into the square opposite, the chilly wind tossing his fair hair into disarray. Displeased he looked, his mood revealed by his gesture even from afar, and the Master smiled at the sign as the hounds bayed at his very gates.

Answerable to *none* in France was the Master of the Temple.

Not even to Philip le Beau, king of all France. And well did Philip know the truth of it, though he liked it naught. Had the Order not defied him openly in the past? Openly and brashly, but naught was there any could do. Denied entry to the Order Philip had been but three months past, and though the king had been near to fury at the slight, no retaliation had there been.

Indeed, there could be none. Papal orders, issued time and again, protected the autonomy of the Templars. Not a hand could any king lift against the Master of the Temple. 'Twas decreed repeatedly by Rome. And the repository of the treasury of the king within the Temple's own vaults added a modicum of additional security. None other had the resources to handle the financial demands of a court the size of Philip's, though it likely irked Philip's pride to have his house funds secured by those who slighted his will. The very thought filled the Master of the Paris Temple with a satisfaction well earned.

Truly, he and his brethren deserved no less than to protect all of Christendom, unmolested by the partialities of petty rulers. Little understanding had self-absorbed men like Philip of the greater obligation before them. No less than the saving of every soul in Christendom was the responsibility of the Order's leaders and the retrieval from infidel hands of that land held most holy.

But kings overlooked such duties in the pursuit of material gain. And popes had responded accordingly, that the most important task in Christendom not be left unfulfilled.

To be sure, the Templars guarded their own material gains and were sure to collect their tithes in a timely fashion. But for a greater good was this destined, a nobler end than the expanding wardrobe and extensive household needs of a vain man.

Jerusalem awaited the Templars. And one day they would return to that fair city triumphant, to claim its hallowed ground for Christendom. God above could permit naught else, though man below would need extensive resources to accomplish the task. The Templar treasuries, the bounty of their estates, the men sworn to the Order's service, these would form the backbone of the force destined to reclaim that most sacred central jewel stolen from the crown of Christendom.

"The gates remained barred at my word," the Master informed the keeper tersely. That man nodded his understanding and returned his attention to his post with a sharpness that did his training proud.

No finer league of men was there than the Order's own. The Master basked in a glow of pride for an instant, then turned his back deliberately on the king, knowing full well his departure would be seen and noted.

As he walked away, his pace as leisurely as if he were a man with naught on his mind, the Master heard Philip's shout and permitted himself another slow smile.

Wolfram led Genevieve through the twisting streets of the Ville Neuve at breakneck pace, and her thoughts jumped ahead almost as quickly.

This was Alzeu's killer. And Genevieve had foolishly accompanied him, though she knew not where they were destined.

Yet worse, Wolfram now knew her identity, as well. He might well guess her intent to see Alzeu vindicated and strike before she could. Well she knew the man was experienced beyond her in such matters.

For the first time, Genevieve realized the fullness of her folly in so boldly declaring her identity. She would be hard-pressed indeed to see her way clear of this muddle, and her heart began to pound in trepidation.

Indeed, for all she knew, those who had ordered Alzeu dead might well see an advantage to her own demise.

Genevieve's gratitude dissolved in the cold lump of fear that took up residence in her belly. Yet again, impulsiveness had steered her false. When would she ever learn? Not a soul did she know within these walls, and indeed, Genevieve knew not whether she could even leave the Ville Neuve without Wolfram's aid.

Her last two silver deniers had she granted to the woman with the cart. Now she was penniless and within the power of the man who had dispatched her brother. Even Odo's companionship looked a brighter option at this point in time.

Mayhap Genevieve had made a slight error of judgment in trusting an assassin.

They ducked through a labyrinth of alleyways and skidded around a corner, no sounds of pursuit carrying to Genevieve's ears. A man stepped out of the shadows and she gasped, her hand falling of habit to the hilt of her dagger. 'Twas just a young man on some errand for his master, and he spared her and her companion no more than a passing glance.

Genevieve breathed a sigh of relief, her fingers dancing on the hilt of the blade. The touch of cold steel beneath her hand reminded her suddenly of her quest and her gaze darted to the intent man beside her.

She had sworn to kill him.

And she had best see her way about the task quickly, lest she lose the chance.

He glanced over his shoulder, as though seeking any behind them, but the narrow alley was abandoned. Straw was cast on either side of the way and the smell of mucked-out stables assaulted Genevieve's nostrils. Her pulse thumped in her ears.

They were going into the stables. And if her ears were right, no one else stirred here. Well might this be the opportunity she had awaited.

She would disarm him.

Then she would take Alzeu's vengeance.

Always had Wolfram thought the tales of Grail were fanciful fables, no more and no less. But never before had the name of a real individual been associated with them, at least in his hearing.

And never, certainly, had he held the soft and small hand of that person within his own. Wolfram's heart took a dizzying lurch and he dared to glance over his shoulder to Genevieve as they reached the doorway of the stables where he thought she might well hide.

She smiled sunnily and his heart missed a beat. Wolfram was suddenly certain there was not enough air in all of Paris to fill his lungs.

He checked the street with markedly less than his usual finesse. Curse this woman for the way she addled his wits! Mercifully, no one was about. Indeed, the smell of cooking on the wind and the sound of crockery revealed the common folk to be planning their evening repast. The golden sunlight basked the cobblestones in its bright glow and the sound of the dogs faded into the wind far behind them.

Well it seemed that their flight might have been no more than illusion.

But 'twas not. Still endangered were they. Fear pricked within Wolfram, and he wordlessly tugged Genevieve into the darkness of the stables. 'Twas warm, the air redolent of the sweet leavings of the horses. He slid the door closed behind them and the darkness enveloped them like a black cloak.

She moved closer to him and instantly Wolfram regretted his choice.

The scent of the fresh hay stored above pricked at his nostrils, mingling with the other earthy smells of the stables, but even that was not enough to hide the soft musk of her scent. Dark 'twas, and intimate beyond compare. Wolfram's heart pounded yet faster as Genevieve moved a step closer to him. He fancied the fullness of her breast brushed against his arm and wondered what had possessed him to bring her here.

Alone they were in the darkness. Alone in the privacy of this warm and welcoming place. Wolfram swallowed with difficulty and wondered what madness had taken possession of his mind.

Although he had told himself that he helped Genevieve escape because the Master might well be seeking her out, here in the darkness, the truth was not so easily evaded. He had helped Genevieve because he would not see ill befall her.

The Master's intent mattered naught, in truth, and that realization troubled Wolfram beyond compare. When had he ever acted in the specific interests of an individual? Always for the Order had he lived, not even for himself, and the very idea that he had pursued a path strictly to see this woman safe was beyond belief.

Her breast pressed more fully against his arm and his body responded with enthusiasm. Mayhap 'twas not so far beyond belief as he might like to think.

Had Genevieve compelled him to break the Rule yet again? Too much 'twas that she tempted him with lustful thoughts, too much that he had foolishly granted her a coin not his to give without a second thought, too much that he had been plagued by unfitting dreams. For the first time in his life, Wolfram had responded intuitively on this day, plunging into the king's court in pursuit, a lie quick to fall from his lips, with nary a thought to either the Order or the Rule.

He heard the soft rhythm of her breathing too close at hand and his mouth went dry. Waiting for his cue she was, and Wolfram fancied he could feel the weight of her gaze upon him.

He recalled the sweet press of her lips against his and inhaled sharply.

Nay! He did naught to betray the Order! Odo maintained the Order was pledged to protect Genevieve's family. And Genevieve was the last of that family. Yet more important, she had clearly been endangered. 'Twas the Order's objectives he had aimed to serve by aiding her.

'Twas no more than that. There. Good sense that made indeed.

"Are we to hide here?" she prompted softly.

Well it seemed that her whisper fanned Wolfram's throat with a gentle breeze that launched an army of goose pimples across his flesh. He became aware of the weight of her precious lute within his grip, just as he caught a whiff of her scent. Panic flooded through him at the very thought of being alone here with her.

"Aye," he responded, even more tersely than was usually his manner. "I mean, nay. You alone are to hide here. Upstairs will you hide, where none will see you."

Wolfram thrust the lute toward her in the darkness, managing to put an increment of distance between them in the process. Genevieve caught her breath, as though surprised to find the instrument's smoothness bumping against her. She gripped its neck, her fingers brushing against Wolfram's in the process in a most disconcerting manner, and he stepped hastily away.

The move eased him not. Indeed, he felt the absence of her warmth beside him with an acuteness that did not bode well for his resolve.

"What of you?" she asked gently. It seemed to Wolfram that her voice was lower, softer, more silky in the darkness than he had recalled, and he swallowed nervously.

"I . . . I have a pallet," he muttered. "In the dormitory. 'Tis my place. 'Tis where I sleep."

"And you would leave me alone here?"

Wolfram backed away from that seductive voice and hit the back of his head soundly on a pillar that help up the loft.

He swore, the soft ripple of her laughter doing naught to reassure him. "Alone you must stay," he asserted with what he hoped was unassailable conviction.

Her fingertip landed in the middle of his chest, feather-light and cursedly accurate. Wolfram's heart stopped cold.

"Surely you would not abandon me here?" she whispered, and his pulse began to thunder in his ears.

"Little choice have I," Wolfram confessed stiffly. He endeavored to back up farther, but the cursed pillar obstructed his course.

Her hand flattened against his chest, and he did not dare to breathe. When he felt her toes touch his, Wolfram knew full well that she was too close, just as he knew there was naught he could do about it. Her breasts nudged against him and he closed his eyes, terrified that she would touch him again, yet knowing all the while that he would be terribly disappointed if she did not.

"Will you not return to keep me warm this night?" she purred, and her breath fanned Wolfram's throat.

"Nay, not this night," he said hastily. "'Tis against the Rule to leave the dormitory, though certain I am that you did not know such a thing...."

"Where is the ladder?" she asked with that same gentleness of manner peculiar to females alone. Too long had it been since Wolfram had been accustomed to such a sound, yet the chasm of the years did naught to feed his immunity.

He was possessed suddenly by a vivid image of his mother before the hearth. She laughed, as he readily acknowledged she had done often, her cheeks rosy and her fingers drifting across—

Wolfram would not think it. He would not permit the softness of such memories to invade his mind. He slammed the door within his mind that led to that sweet recollection, knowing full well the horror that would tread quickly upon its seductive heels. Wolfram lifted one hand and resolutely pushed Genevieve, and temptation, away.

"Something troubles you?" she whispered, and indeed, Wolfram could hear the concern in her voice. It wrenched at his heart, and for one fleeting moment, he considered confiding in her.

Then he recalled his place. The business of the Order alone occupied his interest. That the woman should be safe required no confessions from him. Wolfram strode across the stable. "The ladder is here," he fairly snapped, welcoming the rigidity of his customary formality. No need was there to confide in a stranger, no matter how fetching she might be. "You should hide immediately against the possibility of further pursuit."

Genevieve hastened toward him in a manner that made his heart skip as she evidently followed the sound of his voice. What if she had been hastening to him, and not merely safety? The very thought made his knees weaken. Wolfram's eyes were adjusting to the darkness, and he braced himself as her petite shadow drew nearer. She hesitated beside him with her free hand on a ladder rung, but he offered naught.

"Could you hold my lute?" she asked finally. Wolfram gritted his teeth and shook his head but once. He could not afford to touch that instrument again. Its music and the very touch of it undermined his determination to forget the past.

"Nay. 'Tis best that you carry it."

An awkward silence followed his words, making Wolfram wish he could draw back what must have seemed unnecessarily churlish. Genevieve tipped her head back, and he imagined she looked to him with loathing in her gaze.

No matter. Indeed, 'twould probably be easier to deliver her to the Master should they not be amiable.

Would the Master order the same fate for Genevieve as her brother?

The very thought wrenched Wolfram's heart in a manner that was most unfitting. He wished suddenly and desperately that her dispatch might be granted to another, should his suspicion prove correct.

To his further dismay, Genevieve paused unexpectedly on the first rung. Though he could not see more than the pale oval of her face, he knew well that her eyes were even with his and that she gazed at him. The hair on the back of his neck prickled as yet another part of his anatomy rose to the occasion.

"You are indeed most clear-thinking," she whispered. "I would thank you for your aid this day." Before Wolfram could respond or question her intent, Genevieve leaned closer and kissed him full on the lips.

'Twas as if she aimed to feed his burgeoning doubt. Though Wolfram thought as much, he was powerless to move away and deny himself her touch. No fleeting kiss was this, for she pressed herself against him with unprecedented abandon. The sweetness of her scent inundated him and drew him ever closer. The taste of her passion made his head spin, and of naught could he think but Genevieve.

What if he did not tell the Master of her presence? The intoxicating thought flooded through him unexpectedly, and Wolfram was shocked at the magnitude of its appeal.

What if he stayed with Genevieve?

In the span of a heartbeat, his mind conjured the image of Genevieve lying bare in the straw while he worshiped every curve of her soft skin. He wanted to hear her moan, he wanted to feel her wrapped around him. His own passion astounded him with its intensity. Drowning in the softness of her lips, Wolfram was, though there was naught he could do about it.

He gasped in surprise, as much at her boldness as at his own response, and her tongue slipped adroitly between his teeth. Warm pleasure rolled through Wolfram, and his free hand was lodged in the neat indent of her waist before he knew what he was about. Genevieve leaned fully against him, the heated press of her breasts against his chest awakening every fiber of his being with a vengeance. His second hand joined the first without a thought, the way his fingers nearly met on her back making him groan aloud.

Never had he burned like this for a woman. Indeed, never had he had a woman, but Genevieve's touch was intoxicating beyond compare. Well enough could Wolfram understand earthly temptation now as he never had before. He smelled the heat of Genevieve's skin and imagined himself licking the faint patina of exertion from her flesh. He readily pictured her gloriously nude before him as she had been in his dream, or, better yet, beneath him, and his desire raged unchecked.

Wolfram lifted her demandingly against him, his tongue joining the fray to twine sinuously with her own. He cared naught if she felt his desire, indeed he cared for naught but pulling her so close that their very flesh might meld together. Genevieve moaned into his mouth and he felt her nipples harden against his chest. Her tongue danced with his, her teeth nibbled on his lips, she strained against him as though she could never get enough. Everything quickened within Wolfram as she hesitantly slipped one hand into the hair at the nape of his neck. Her tiny fingers caressed him there and he thought he might burst his chausses.

She wrenched her lips away from his and pressed a flurry of kisses against his throat. Wolfram closed his eyes at the sensation and tightened his grip around her waist, loath to let her move even an increment away. Naught was there for Wolfram but the secluded darkness of this stable. Naught was there but the taste and feel of Genevieve in his arms.

"In the loft should we go," she whispered. The flurry of her breath against his ear made Wolfram shiver. The loft. Genevieve. His mind consumed the idea as his fingers explored the graceful arch of her back. He found her nape, his fingers lost in the thickness of her hair, and he slipped his thumb under her chin to angle her lips toward him.

Genevieve sighed with a satisfaction that could not be feigned. Wolfram tightened his grip possessively around her. This woman could be his this night. This woman who enflamed him and drove him to distraction invited him to sample fully the charms with which she had tempted him. Wolfram cared not why.

Indeed, the very promise falling from her soft lips was enough to make him fear to spill his seed.

A horse stamped in its stall somewhere in the darkness, and the abrupt sound recalled Wolfram suddenly to his senses.

What was he thinking? What was he doing? He stared down at the woman locked in his arms, the oath he had pledged to the Order of the Templars ringing in his ears.

What had possessed him to so break the Rule?

Wolfram flung Genevieve from his embrace and cringed inwardly at the sound of her sharp inhalation. He ran one hand through his hair, forcibly recalling that he was pledged to the Order for the remainder of his days.

"What is this you do?" she demanded in mingled outrage and confusion, but Wolfram had not the words to explain.

'Twas imperative he leave this place—and the temptation of this woman—behind. 'Twas imperative he leave these stables immediately.

"Hide yourself," he said tersely, and then he did the only thing a man in his position could safely do.

Wolfram fled.

# Chapter Eight

Genevieve had never expected that he might flee.

She stood in the stable door left open in Wolfram's flight and gaped as he strode hastily away, consternation etched in every line of his figure. Mercifully, she had the sense to at least remain in the shadows as she watched, but to her disappointment, Wolfram did not even glance back before rounding the last corner and fading completely from sight.

Genevieve picked out the location of the ladder before she closed the door, her brow drawing into a thoughtful frown.

Well it seemed that Wolfram was afraid of her.

The thought would have been laughable had he not just disappeared with such haste. Genevieve's lips quirked in an unwilling smile that, once launched, soon spread gleefully across her features.

A hired assassin was afraid of her. Of a lutenist.

Genevieve chuckled. 'Twas ridiculous. She took a few cavorting steps in the direction of the ladder and her shoulders shook with amusement.

And why? Because she had kissed him? Because he had enjoyed that kiss? Foolishness. This man dispatched people with ruthless efficiency, and surely he had naught to fear from anyone on the face of this earth. Surely 'twas Genevieve who should have been afraid that she might taste the bite of his skill.

She halted halfway up the ladder, her laughter stilling when she realized she did not fear him. Surely 'twas naught more than a passing whimsy. Any woman of sense would fear a cold-blooded killer. Genevieve doubtfully glanced over her shoulder to the closed doorway and acknowledged that 'twas somewhat endearing, the way he had panicked.

Her kiss had affected him, this much she knew. She supposed that for a man pledged to a monastic order, that effect might well have promised a threat to his very security. Pledged he must be to poverty, chastity and obedience.

Yet Wolfram had not stayed to take advantage of whatever Genevieve might have offered. Loyal he was to what he had pledged this Order, and some corner of Genevieve's heart had to admire his conviction.

Not only had her opponent a face and a name, 'twas clear he had a heart, as well.

Though indeed, 'twas a heart he kept well hidden.

A ridiculous thought that was! No heart had Wolfram! What whimsy had possessed her mind? Genevieve stubbornly refused to indulge her doubts and resolutely climbed the ladder to the loft. Her brother had this man stolen from her side, and she would do best to recall that fact. No softness did she owe him, and certainly she should not permit his antics to make her laugh.

Nay. Genevieve must harden herself against his appeal. Angry should she be in this moment that her plan had been thwarted. Aye, furiously angry. She folded her arms across her chest once she had gained the loft and endeavored to summon that foul mood—to no avail.

Wolfram had evaded her this day and thwarted the fulfillment of her pledge when 'twas virtually within her grasp. Here had been the perfect opportunity to take her vengeance, but the moment had been stolen from her. Genevieve could well hold that against him, but instead she recalled the warmth his kiss had unfolded within her.

Genevieve schooled herself not to smile in recollection. Wolfram had charmed her, she told herself firmly, and he had done so for naught but his own ends. He had undermined her determination. Truly the man had many crimes for which to answer and Genevieve would do well to recall them all.

Wolfram had spirited her away from the court and certain danger.

Before Genevieve's heart could melt, a thought launched in her mind that triggered her doubts as naught else could have done.

But *why* had he brought her here? Genevieve could not fathom an answer to that, and a cold slither of dread made its way down her back. She hastily reviewed all that Wolfram had said and realized he had made no explanation for this path. Genevieve rose to her feet and stared about herself, uncertain what to do. No clue had he given her of his plans and her fear redoubled at that realization.

Indeed, she knew not when Wolfram intended to return! Genevieve licked her lips and wondered if she was a fool to meekly remain here.

What if Wolfram did not return? Truly he had made no promises.

A sudden ray of light and an accompanying squeak indicated that the stable door swung open. Genevieve knew not what to expect and wondered whether she had summoned Wolfram with her very thoughts.

Mercifully, she held her tongue when impulse might have demanded she hail him.

"Hasten yourself, Brother! I would see these beasts bedded down and not miss my dinner for your tardiness this night!"

'Twas not Wolfram's voice that boomed below. Genevieve's hand flew to her lips in mingled surprise and fear. Did they hunt her even here? What if she was discovered? What would be her fate here? She froze in place as the footsteps of several horses carried to her ears.

"Aye, Brother. 'Twill take but a moment."

But a moment. She had but a moment to endure. Genevieve forced herself to breathe slowly, hoping the sound could not be discerned below over the rattle of the horses' tack being removed. The beasts stamped their feet with welcome vigor and Genevieve crept away from the top of the ladder that she might be well out of view.

What if they came into the loft?

A faint light there was in the loft from a lattice for ventilation under the eaves at one end of the roof. 'Twas adequate to discern her surroundings, and Genevieve stealthily wound her way to a secluded corner far from the ladder. Hay bales aplenty were there stored in the loft, and she was grateful for the concealment they might offer. She crouched behind a particularly high stack and clenched her fists against the dampness of her palms.

"Do you think we have need of another bale?" demanded the younger voice.

Genevieve was certain her heart stopped cold at the very suggestion.

"Leave it this night," advised the elder. "Well do I imagine that dinner is cooling. 'Tis flesh we are to have tonight, and that is a meal better savored warm."

"True enough, Brother," the younger agreed amiably.

Genevieve leaned against the wall when her knees weakened in relief. The door creaked an eternity later, emitting a beam of light before 'twas closed again. Silence descended on the stables and Genevieve dared to release the breath she had been holding.

She was safe. For now.

While the stable was yet deserted, Genevieve found a safe nest for her lute and bedded it down with hasty hands. Determined to hide herself as well as she was able, she wedged herself between the bales of hay in her corner sanctuary. Genevieve pulled some hay across her lap against the chill in the air as she furiously considered what she should do.

* * *

As soon as Wolfram saw the deaf esquire enter the dormitory the next morning, he knew the boy came for him. His fingers fumbled with the customary task of rearranging his bed linens. Surely the Master could not know that Wolfram had secreted Genevieve within the Temple's Ville Neuve. Surely the Master could not have seen the truth, despite the fact that Wolfram had not notified him of Genevieve's presence.

Even though that had been Wolfram's entire justification for bringing the fetching lutenist within the confines of the Temple's walls in the first place.

Of course, that had been before Genevieve kissed him, yet again, with even more passion than the first time. His flesh warmed at the memory and he glanced about himself, certain his brethren would guess the forbidden direction of his thoughts.

With an effort, Wolfram caught himself before his mind recalled more of Genevieve's touch than was fitting here in the dormitory. Throughout the restless night just passed, he had refused to speculate on why he was reluctant to follow his original intent to reveal her immediately. He would not question his impulse now.

At the boy's nod in his direction, though, Wolfram's breath caught.

The Master knew. The Master knew all, and he was about to be chastised for breaking the Rule. The certainty of it filled him with dread.

But how? How could the Master have known? Surely Wolfram saw a threat where there was none, for the Master had no way of knowing Wolfram's secret. None had noted Genevieve's arrival—Wolfram was certain of it—and none had seen him return from the stables.

'Twas likely just another commission. Wolfram forced himself to nod efficiently to the esquire, as though naught troubled him.

Indeed, mayhap he would take this opportunity to tell the Master about Genevieve. Uneasiness welled up within him at the prospect, but Wolfram deliberately pushed the feeling aside. 'Twas right and proper to tell the Master of Genevieve's presence, and naught did he risk by doing so. The Master alone knew what commissions the Order had taken. The Master alone would know what to do. Wolfram deliberately ignored the uncertainty that thought prompted and reminded himself of the fundamental tenet of his life.

The Master alone could be trusted.

The Master was waiting in his office, his gaze bright over his tented fingertips.

"Where is she?" he demanded without preamble.

Wolfram was so surprised by the question that he was momentarily dumbfounded. Surely he could not have been wrong? "Who?" he asked, as though he did not know.

"Who?" The Master arched a silver brow, and his voice dropped to a conspiratorial whisper. "Well enough do you know who I mean," he muttered through gritted teeth. "'Tis Genevieve de Pereille that I seek, and you know where she is."

Wolfram was surprised by the Master's intensity, but endeavored to hide his response. Something in the Master's unexpected manner prompted him to be more evasive than he might have been otherwise, and he impulsively played the fool. "I, milord?" he asked, and the Master's eyes flashed angrily in response.

The older man shoved to his feet and paced around his desk in a flurry of taffeta robes to plant one heavy finger in the middle of Wolfram's chest. Wolfram was surprised to realize for the first time as they stood toe-to-toe that he was slightly taller than his superior.

"Aye, *you*." The Master spat out the words. "With my own eyes did I see you leave the king's court with that Genevieve, and well enough did I hear that you had returned to the Temple. A breach of the Rule 'twas for you to be outside these walls without my specific permission, but I *presumed* that a loyal brother like yourself had done so only to serve a greater good.'' The older man paused, and his eyes narrowed. ''I assumed you intended to fetch that troublemaker here to me.''

Troublemaker? What trouble had Genevieve caused the Master? Wolfram swallowed carefully. 'Twas clear this was a matter of great import to his superior, though Wolfram could not fathom why it might be so. Mayhap, with the Master so impassioned, he might well learn what lay at root here. Was there truth in the minstrel's tale? Did someone aim to eliminate the entire family of Pereille?

And why was Wolfram suddenly so reluctant to reveal Genevieve? Surely he had intended no less when he had brought her here? 'Twas not logical that he should be so confused, yet Wolfram knew not how to escape his uncertainty. Never had he been plagued by indecision before meeting Genevieve!

''No idea had I that you had interest in the matter,'' Wolfram said slowly.

The Master snorted and spun away to pace the width of the room and back. The ferocity of his gaze diminished not a whit in the process. ''No interest? Surely you have not forgotten the identity of the last man you dispatched? Or who sent you on that mission?''

''But well I thought that to be a commission from outside the Order,'' Wolfram argued.

He caught but a glimpse of the Master's cunning smile before that man turned away to pace again. ''Aye, from outside it came.'' The Master paused for a moment, and Wolfram watched him tap his chin with one fingertip, his profiled features thoughtful. That smile quirked the corner of the older man's mouth again. ''But some, as we all know, often need suggestions for their impulses,'' the Master mused.

His words sent a chill through Wolfram, for their low tone suggested that he had not been expected to overhear. Had the Master suggested Alzeu be killed? A shiver of dread raced over Wolfram's flesh. Did the Master himself bear malice toward Genevieve's family?

It could not be. The Master was beyond reproach. Surely 'twas the commission from a nameless client alone that prompted this animosity against Genevieve. The Master must only be interested in fulfilling a contractual obligation.

" 'Tis a pity we knew naught of the sister when you were there," the Master added, with a sharp glance to Wolfram. "The matter could then have been resolved all at once."

Wolfram blinked in astonishment, but the Master's knowing expression changed naught.

"But what is this family's crime?" Wolfram asked, the words slipping from his lips before he could stop them. Impertinence 'twas to question the Master, and thoroughly did Wolfram regret that he had spoken, before the Master smiled sadly.

"Surely you attended the *chanson* yesterday," he prompted as he slid into his seat again. "A fanciful tale 'twas to be sure, but therein lay a germ of the truth. Aspirations to the crown have this family, and their interference cannot be tolerated. 'Tis an upset to the natural order of the world." He paused delicately and tented his fingers together once again. "Our client does not take well to the Pereille family's claims."

"But surely a woman poses no real threat," Wolfram heard himself arguing.

The Master's smile broadened. "Ah," he said smoothly. "One might readily think as much, but in truth, their threat is much more insidious. While a man like Alzeu might openly challenge the throne in his attempt to claim it, a woman will whisper in the ears of her spawn, filling their heads with fanciful notions. Well might it take decades afore the threat rises again, but great damage could be wrought nonetheless. Memories are short, and in the past, this family's intent has been forgotten over the years."

The older man cleared his throat. "Our client would avoid future surprises." The Master tapped one authoritative finger on his desk. "'Tis best the family be completely eliminated now, while the opportunity is within our hands."

"She has committed no crime," Wolfram argued. Contending with the Master? Surely he had lost his wits? No place had he to question the Master's demand.

Yet the Master did not reprimand him. "You seem to have an interest in this situation," he charged quietly. Wolfram could not stop the flush that suffused his neck, and he knew well enough that the Master did not miss his unwilling response.

The Master's gaze grew hard, as did his tone. "No one is innocent, my friend," he said harshly. "Do not imagine this woman to be any different. If naught else, she showed the poor judgment to be born to a cursed family." He paused and eyed Wolfram consideringly. "And you have very little experience of the wicked wiles of women. Do not permit yourself to be deceived by her charms."

"You mean to kill a woman," Wolfram concluded stonily. The even tone of his voice surprised him, for everything within him balked at the Master's conclusions.

"Nay," the Master said, with that same knowing smile. "I mean for *you* to kill a woman." He surveyed Wolfram for a long moment, as though trying to guess the younger man's thoughts. "It is, after all, your particular expertise," he added in a low voice.

Wolfram could not utter a word, not even a mere acceptance of his duty. Dispatch Genevieve. Could he truly do this deed? Well could he imagine that she would not embrace the news of her fate, but he doubted he had the will to fight her.

"Pledged to the Rule are you, Wolfram, and sworn to obey my command," the Master reminded him forcefully, and the words recalled Wolfram to his place. The Master's bidding should be his doing. He had pledged to obey. "I command you to dispatch her from this world."

Even that reminder could not bring agreement to Wolfram's lips. Never had Wolfram dispatched a woman. Never had he dispatched anyone he knew. Surely that must be the reason that everything within him fought to defy the order of the Master of the Temple.

"Further," the Master said tightly, "I would have you fetch the woman here, that I might witness the deed with my own eyes."

Wolfram met the Master's gaze unwillingly. That man smiled and nodded. No choice had Wolfram. His word had he given and this command must he fulfill. He fought against his instincts and managed to nod obeisance.

"Aye, milord," he whispered reluctantly.

The Master's smile broadened. "Be quick about it," he counselled with a snap of his fingers. "My patience—and our client's patience—in this matter is wearing thin."

When Wolfram gained the courtyard outside the main tower of the Temple mere moments later, he noted the shadow trailing behind that was not his own. The very hint that he was no longer trusted was enough to fuel all his doubts—and feed his fledgling defiance.

Wolfram deliberately stepped out of the courtyard in the direction opposite to the stables where Genevieve was hidden, his mind working furiously.

'Twas only natural that he should balk at killing a woman, he told himself fiercely. And even more natural that he should avoid delivering a person to her execution when that person was deemed guilty by merely her birthright.

It mattered naught that his lips burned in recollection of Genevieve's sweet kisses. 'Twas the fact that she was a woman, her innocence and the Master's abrupt removal of his trust that made Wolfram want to aid her.

'Twas naught more than that.

Wolfram was not coming back for her.

By midday, the truth of the matter was inescapable.

Genevieve chewed her bottom lip and desperately tried to decide how to proceed. She was not fool enough to think she might be lucky two days in a row and sneak past the gate-keeper yet again. Nor did she know what awaited her out-side the Temple walls. Was she yet hunted by the guards of the court?

How she wished she was home at Montsalvat! How she wished she had never taken this foolish pledge and had re-mained in that beloved, drafty keep!

Enough of waiting! A wave of homesickness had Gene-vieve shoving stubbornly to her feet. Had she not waited long enough for Wolfram to return? 'Twas clear he had no intention of doing so, and she would not linger here any longer.

He was gone, lost to her in the labyrinth of the Ville Neuve, where she could not follow. Had she not tried to ex-tract a toll for Alzeu's untimely demise? Genevieve sent her most sincere apologies skyward to her brother, knowing full well that she had done her best.

Evidently, her quest was not to be fulfilled. Better 'twas that she return home and leave this unfamiliar place, put her failure firmly behind her and move on. 'Twas not to be.

She refused to consider the import of the chase from the king's court after she had declared her identity. 'Twas only because she and Odo had trespassed. Naught had Gene-vieve to fear for herself, for a woman offered no threat.

And home was safe. That she knew beyond all else.

Genevieve did not permit herself to acknowledge a mod-icum of relief at the abandonment of her quest. Certainly she felt no compassion for Wolfram at all and, had she the opportunity, she would have taken her vengeance without a second thought.

Certainly. Not a doubt was there in her mind.

Genevieve scowled at the direction of her thoughts. She was *not* shirking her responsibilities. Nay. How could she kill a man who did not show his face?

That she had had numerous opportunities to do so reassured her naught.

Wolfram was gone and Genevieve could not pursue him here. 'Twas that simple.

Indeed, if she left, he might well pursue her, granting her another opportunity to fulfill her pledge. The very idea lightened her heart, and Genevieve scooped up her lute, refusing to examine the reasons why such an idea pleased her.

The quest might not be lost, after all. 'Twas that alone that buoyed her spirits.

She was down the ladder and half-way across the hay-strewn floor when the stable door was suddenly cast open. A hooded figure was silhouetted against the morning light. Genevieve gasped, knowing she stood fully in the light and that there was no way she could hide.

"Genevieve!" muttered Wolfram angrily. So shocked was Genevieve by his presence that her knees nearly buckled beneath her. "Fool!" he snapped as he ducked into the shadows of the stable. He darted a glance over his shoulder and shut the door firmly behind him, the last ray of light showing that he tore the hood from his head. He advanced upon her, and Genevieve had trouble forcing air into her lungs.

Another opportunity 'twas, she told herself wildly. Her heart pounded and Genevieve knew 'twas only the promise to yet fulfill her pledge that garnered such a response within her.

Wolfram was back, and relief gave her tongue a new-found audacity.

"Well I thought never to see you again," Genevieve said breathlessly. Wolfram paused directly before her and she tipped her chin back instinctively, as he loomed over her, the shadow of his form discernible against the shadows.

"Surely you did not imagine that I would abandon you here?" he asked. His tone was clipped, and Genevieve wondered why he had glanced over his shoulder so. Her eyes adjusted to the darkness again, and she could make out the frown that marred his fair brow.

Mayhap she had misunderstood. . . .

Nay! She tossed her hair stubbornly, determined to give him the benefit of no doubt. "Naught did you say to me of your intent."

"And naught did you ask, as I recall," Wolfram retorted.

Only too well did Genevieve recall the embrace they had shared instead, and she plunged ahead, certain that discussing that moment of weakness would gain her naught.

"Then what is your intent?" she demanded crossly. "Why did you bring me here?"

To her astonishment, Wolfram's annoyance seemed to desert him. He ran one hand agitatedly through his hair. "In truth, I did not think overmuch about the matter. This place alone could you find sanctuary from the king, that I knew. And well I thought that the Master might seek you. Truly, I thought no further than that."

"The Master? Who is this Master?"

Genevieve felt the weight of Wolfram's gaze upon her. "The Master of the Temple of Paris. 'Tis his will alone that I fulfill."

Instinctively, Genevieve understood the import of Wolfram's words, but she would not reveal to him how much she knew. 'Twas this Master who must have dispatched Wolfram to kill Alzeu.

The fact that this Master might well know of her location in this moment did naught to reassure Genevieve.

"And what might this Master want of me?" she demanded with bravado. "Surely the Templars have no need of a lutenist?"

Wolfram laughed dryly, though the sound was less than lighthearted. "Nay, Genevieve, he desires not a lutenist," he said in a low voice. He cleared his throat, and Genevieve knew to dread his next words. " 'Twas only this very morn that I learned he wishes to see you dead."

Genevieve felt her mouth open, but no sound came forth. She shook her head, shocked to hear her own worst fear so casually uttered. "But, but what have I done to earn his animosity?" she asked weakly.

Genevieve fancied that Wolfram smiled sadly before he shook his head. "'Tis your lineage," he whispered. "No more and no less than that."

Genevieve's mind worked furiously at the news. 'Twas not Alzeu alone that was wished dead, but the entire line of the Pereilles. And she was the last. Even being a woman gained her naught. She blinked back tears and squared her shoulders as she confronted Wolfram.

"And you are here to accompany me to my fate?" she asked coldly.

To her astonishment, Wolfram shook his head. "'Twas why I was sent, but in truth, I cannot do the deed, Genevieve." His voice faltered, but he pressed on. "I would not see you so ill-used."

Genevieve was flattered for an instant before she suspected a trick. Surely the man aimed only to soften her objections with flattery. But nay, he pressed on in much the same vein, his sincere tone inviting her belief, his words falling in haste once his confession was made.

"Breaking the Rule am I, and my pledge to the Order, but this I cannot do. Sooner would I have come to you, but the Master must have suspected my uncertainty, for someone did he set to follow me. This long has it taken me to ensure that I arrived alone."

"What will you do now?" Genevieve asked. Wolfram summoned a vestige of a smile. His hand closed warmly over hers and Genevieve could not halt the resulting surge of the blood in her veins.

"I will see you clear of the Ville Neuve and Paris itself," he vowed solemnly.

Such heartfelt conviction was there in his tone that Genevieve could do naught else but believe him.


Good intentions aside, a closed gate was an obstruction that could not be waylaid.

Wolfram chafed with impatience to find the main gate still barred to traffic. Open should it have been on a weekday such as this, and 'twas no relief to find merchants similarly disgruntled.

"Why is the gate barred?" Genevieve asked in a whisper, and Wolfram shook his head.

"I know not, but 'tis clear we are not the only ones who would prefer otherwise."

A merchant raised his fist and shouted at the impassive keeper, to no avail. Wolfram turned from the donkey they had borrowed from the stables, a donkey whose bulging baskets hid naught but a lute and rags from the stables from curious eyes.

A frown darkened his brow as his gaze raked over his companion. Genevieve's hair had been pulled back tightly and her hood pulled over her head that she might not be readily recognized and dirt smeared across her face. To all appearances, they might have been a couple embarking on a shopping excursion for household miscellany. Her brow puckered with concern, and Wolfram was acutely aware that he was responsible for her welfare.

Was it possible the Master sought to confine them here?

The thought was unexpected and certainly unwelcome, though Wolfram could not discard it for all of that.

Although Wolfram was certainly proving himself to be worthy of distrust. And already had he suspected he had been followed. He eyed the closed gate, disliking his sense that the Master intended to find Genevieve, one way or the other.

Wolfram went cold with the realization that his cooperation might not be required.

"What is it?" Genevieve demanded as she leaned closer, and he knew his features had revealed the shock of his thoughts.

Wolfram shook his head, unwilling to worry her unnecessarily. "Another gate is there," he said tersely instead. "Let us try that way."

He led the donkey through the twisting streets of the Ville Neuve, the cobbled alleys bending gradually around the great tower of the Temple itself, which stood over the town's center. As they worked their way through the twisting streets, a rumble of discontent signaled to Wolfram what they might find at the back gates.

And 'twas precisely as he feared. Those gates, too, stood barred against arrivals and departures. Swarms of indignant townspeople milled before the gates, demanding their opening, but the keeper ignored them all. Wolfram's heart sank with the realization that they were trapped within the Temple's walls with no way to escape.

He could not help but conclude that that was precisely what someone had hoped.

A marked man was Wolfram now, clearly, and he could not risk returning to his pallet. Somewhere must they contrive to hide within the town until they could gain an escape.

"What shall we do now?" Genevieve asked, and Wolfram heard the thread of fear in her voice. Well aware of those pressed about them and knowing there were always ears listening, he slipped one arm over her shoulders and summoned a smile for her.

Genevieve looked at him as though he had lost his mind, but mercifully held her tongue.

"Come, wife," he said with false cheer. "We shall simply have to fetch the flour on another day."

"But—" Genevieve protested, the very hint that she might resist prompting Wolfram to hasten her steps. He tightened his grip about her slender waist and nearly lifted her back in the direction they had come when she did not move.

"Come along, wife," he urged, forcing a measure of conviviality into his tone that he was far from feeling. Curse the woman for hindering his path! Could she not simply follow his lead, that they might escape notice? "Certain I

am that there is enough in the larder for one last meal this
night.''

''Are you quite mad?'' Genevieve demanded in an undertone.

''And if not,'' Wolfram continued in a slightly louder
tone, as though she had said naught, ''I shall endeavor to
find another way to keep you warm.'' He pinched Genevieve's buttocks, fully aware of the interested gazes of others upon them.

Genevieve squeaked in a most satisfactory manner and
slapped indignantly at his hand. To her credit, she bustled
self-righteously in precisely the direction Wolfram wished to
go. Several onlookers chuckled, and one man spared Wolfram an encouraging wink as he hastened in pursuit of
Genevieve.

Wolfram glanced back once to the barred gates, the sight
of a cloaked figure disappearing into the crowd sending his
heart racing. Was that the one who had pursued him earlier? Or was it just another in the crowd? He could not say
and liked the feeling naught.

Without appearing to do so, Wolfram hastened a clearly
seething Genevieve back to the stables. For once, she appeared to have naught to say, and though Wolfram knew it
could not last, he savored the moment while it yet endured.


''Of all the unmitigated nerve!'' Genevieve snapped as
soon as they had stepped into the welcome darkness of the
stables. Had she not known better, she might well have
guessed that Wolfram had deliberately taken a more circu-
itous path back here that her temper might have time to
cool.

A foolhardy hope had that been! None had ever pinched
her buttocks, and unlikely was she indeed to let the matter
pass unnoticed.

Wolfram, however, seemed disinclined to notice her outrage. He peered into the street through the crack of the door
for long moments, holding one finger to Genevieve as an

indication that she should be silent. He then returned the donkey to its stall—firing an intense glance in her direction that ensured her further silence—and fastidiously replaced all the tack they had borrowed. Her lute he carried as he returned to look through the crack again.

Genevieve tapped her toe impatiently and waited for her moment. Surely the man could not imagine that she would countenance such familiarity without comment! Surely he did not imagine that he could avail himself of her charms so readily?

"Wife" had he called her. Genevieve nearly snorted in recollection. Who did this man think he was?

"Upstairs," he bade her with sudden terseness. Genevieve briefly considered defying him before she heard the sound of footfalls in the street outside. Her eyes widened just as Wolfram turned. His lips thinned when he found her yet before him, and he pointed emphatically to the ladder.

Genevieve needed no further reminder. She scrambled to safety as the men's voices grew louder, her hands trembling on the rungs of the ladder. Wolfram followed hot on her heels.

"Hurry," he whispered urgently. Genevieve dived for the back corner and Wolfram followed suit. The two of them collapsed together behind the bales just as a glimmer of light was admitted to the stables. Genevieve was wedged into the corner, Wolfram pressed tightly against her, and she did not dare to breathe.

"Well did I tell you that the donkey was yet here," came a man's bored voice. "Here he is, just as I said, eating his hay just as calm as you please."

"He could well have been out and returned," protested a second voice. It seemed to Genevieve that Wolfram caught his breath, but when she glanced to him, his expression was unreadable, his gaze fixed on the ladder.

"Nonsense. The beast has been here all along. Truly you see trouble where there is none," the first man argued easily.

"What is in the loft?" the second man demanded abruptly.

Genevieve caught her breath and welcomed the weight of Wolfram's arm slipping around her shoulders. She huddled against his strength, certain they would be discovered at any moment.

"Wasting your time are you here," the first man observed. "Full of hay 'tis, so full that there cannot be room for a mouse up there, let alone two people."

They *were* being sought! Genevieve imagined that she could feel the gaze of the skeptical man running over the bales that separated them from his view. Would he discern some minute sign of their passing? Would he climb the ladder to check for himself? She shivered and felt Wolfram's fingers tighten about her shoulder.

"If you say so," he agreed with obvious reluctance. "'Twould be best we not waste any time searching here if there is not room."

The door squeaked, then fell closed. The men's footsteps faded as they walked away from the stables, and Genevieve dared to release her breath.

Naught could she hear but the sound of the animals below, the swishing of their tails, the occasional stamping of their feet, the drone of flies. She permitted herself to relax against the softness of the hay, her earlier anger with Wolfram seeming petty in comparison to the risk they had just had.

Wolfram. Genevieve spared him a glance, realizing too late that the weight of his arm yet rested across her shoulders. Warm he was, and loath though she was to admit it, she felt safe nestled against his side. Genevieve dared to lift her gaze to his and was surprised to find his silver regard fixed upon her.

His lips quirked in a most engaging manner and well it seemed that she suddenly could not catch her breath.

"Are you warm enough, wife?" he whispered teasingly. Genevieve was mortified to feel herself flush. Wolfram watched the color suffuse her cheeks with apparent fascination. She watched as he carefully laid her lute aside, not daring to imagine his intent.

He raised his hand and carefully fitted his palm to the curve of her cheek. Genevieve shivered at his gentle touch. Wolfram gathered her closer and she was powerless to object. His gaze locked with hers and she noted that his head inclined towards hers. Her heart began to hammer, yet no protest came from her traitorous lips.

They but parted in welcome. Genevieve moaned softly as Wolfram's mouth closed demandingly over hers. Her fingers entwined themselves in the thickness of his hair as her eyes drifted closed and she submitted to the passion of his kiss.

It could be naught else but the unexpected possibility of fulfilling her quest, she reasoned wildly as she arched against Wolfram's strength. Had her strategy not been to disarm him with kisses afore taking her vengeance? 'Twas surely no more than the delight that he unsuspectingly aided her plan that melted her bones and made her languid in his embrace.

# Chapter Nine

Wolfram lifted his head, wondering if he would ever get enough of this woman's intoxicating kisses. Light-headed he felt, and 'twas not due to any pressure of this day. Genevieve smiled at up him, her teeth gleaming faintly in the darkness, her expression feeding his desire yet more.

He was warm, basking in the heat of her embrace. Wolfram felt the tension ease from him as he sat with this intoxicating woman nestled in his arms. He realized suddenly how exhausted he was, how little he had slept these past nights, and stifled a smile.

It was tormenting dreams of Genevieve that had kept him awake. Genevieve, who laid her cheek on his shoulder even now. Genevieve, who sent the blood thundering through his veins despite his languor.

Bound together were their paths from this point, and Wolfram could not have said that he was disappointed. He hauled her closer and let his lips close purposefully over hers, savoring her minute gasp when he lifted her into his lap and his hardness collided anew with her curves. Her fingers clenched in his hair, holding him close while her lips ravaged his, then she tore her mouth from his.

She rolled suddenly to her feet and trotted toward the lute he had laid aside. Wolfram could not help but watch the gentle sway of her buttocks as she moved. Indeed, he caught more than a passing glimpse of her ankles when she bent to lift the instrument, as well. He savored the grace of her hands as she carefully nestled the lute in the hay, and his pulse accelerated in anticipation.

No mistaking could there be of her response. Well enough could Wolfram recall Genevieve's ardor of the night before and his certainty that she could have been his.

His. The first glimmer of moonlight shone through the latticed vent at one end of the loft, casting a pattern of faint silver squares on the hay beneath. Jammed with bales was the loft, as the man had said, though they had found a small space to nestle in this one corner.

The thought of her curled up here alone the night before, sleeping where he now sat, prompted a response within him that surprised Wolfram with its intensity. She turned to face him and hesitated just long enough to fire his blood. He was on his feet and before her before he could think to do otherwise.

Wolfram could see the stain of a flush in her cheeks, the green sparkle of her eyes as she glanced up at him. Aye, he would make her moan beneath him this night. He might have touched her, but she stepped nimbly around him and shed her cloak, giving him an enticing view of the slender curves outlined by her fitted kirtle. The padding of the hay was more luxurious than the thickest pallet, and when Genevieve spread her cloak across the hay, Wolfram was certain there could be no finer bed anywhere.

She turned and beckoned him closer with naught but a smile.

Wolfram took but two steps before Genevieve leapt forward and locked her hands around his neck. The imprint of her fingers against his skin fair drove him mad and he hungrily pulled her closer, only to have her tumble backward onto their makeshift bed. Wolfram let himself fall with her and they rolled across her cloak as she laughed.

Then she was beneath him, her eyes wide and glittering like emeralds, her breasts rising and falling with a quickness that fascinated him. Wolfram dared to let one hand cup the fullness of her breast, and Genevieve arched against his hand as she gasped. He felt the nipple strain toward him and closed his eyes at the answering swell of passion within him as he ran one fingertip across its peak cautiously.

Genevieve deterred his audacity naught. She moaned—it was a sound fit to loosen everything within Wolfram—and her eyes were dark with passion when she looked to him again. Wolfram could not have resisted her allure to save his soul. He bent his head and drank of her nectar like a man dying of thirst. Genevieve seemed possessed of a thirst as great as his own, for she drew him closer, her lips moving against his in a frenzy. She writhed beneath him, her breasts rubbing against him bewitchingly. Wolfram heard himself moan as the storm gathered within him.

Inexperienced though he was, he knew well enough what his body yearned for. When Genevieve twisted, her nails digging into his shoulder even through his tunic, he could think of naught but that she wanted that, too.

Well did Wolfram intend to satisfy both their desires this evening.

Mayhap over and over the whole night through.

Instinct guided him on and his hand, seemingly of its own volition, found the hem of her kirtle. Wolfram let the weight of his hand fall on Genevieve's bare calf. He nearly swooned at the softness of its curve and could readily imagine its milky smoothness, but he watched Genevieve carefully for her response. Still he could not believe that she would not rebuff him. She caught her breath and broke their kiss, her gaze wide as she stared up at him.

Then she smiled that lusciously seductive smile and playfully traced the outline of his lips with her fingertip. The light caress launched a languid heat within him and made Wolfram close his eyes like a great cat basking in the sun.

He leaned down and nuzzled Genevieve's neck, kissing her ear and flicking his tongue across the lobe until she gasped with pleasure. Well did he savor the soft sound of her breath against his neck, the way she stiffened in surprise, the way her legs moved restlessly beneath him. He kissed her ear fully, taking the lobe within his mouth, delighting in the moan that broke unwillingly from her lips.

His hand slid over the smoothness of her knee.

When his fingertips encountered the velvety softness of Genevieve's thigh, Wolfram thought he would come undone. Never had he felt anything so soft in all his days. Never had his body responded with such enthusiasm. He could think of naught but the sweetness that waited yet further on for him.

Wolfram slipped to one side and lifted his knee so that its weight slipped between Genevieve's legs. He slipped his other hand into the thick silkiness of her hair and waited, certain his advance would be rebuffed.

Genevieve merely shifted to accommodate him.

Then she arched against him, his hand slid instinctively to support her nape, and she parted her lips, inviting him to kiss her again. When Wolfram's lips closed over hers, Genevieve spread her legs wide beneath her kirtle and his hand slipped right up her thigh.

Wolfram thought he might swoon at the dampness he discovered. Drowning he was in the smell and the taste of this woman, her writhing and arching beneath him fueling his desire beyond belief, the evidence of her own desire fit to send him over the edge. His kiss grew more possessive, he knew, but she seemed to welcome his passion with an equal passion of her own. Wolfram touched her dampness, and she cried out with pleasure, the sound swallowed by his kiss.

Then she rolled him summarily onto his back and Wolfram knew not what she did. But an instant had he to wonder before her fingers were on the lace of his chausses.

"Genevieve, nay!" he whispered, but she heeded him not. The touch of her frenzied fingers enflamed Wolfram yet further, the way she faltered with the lace enough to drive him mad with desire. He wildly endeavored to pull her hands away. Genevieve evaded him, though she gasped just as

Wolfram's already snug chausses tightened yet further. He gasped himself at the restriction.

"Curse the knot!" she muttered with a vehemence that might have been amusing at another time.

To Wolfram's shock and dismay, she bent over and took her teeth to the uncooperative lace.

"Nay!" He choked out the one word, but too soon he could feel the gentle nibbling of her lips, even through the heavy wool of his chausses.

'Twas too much to bear. Wolfram gasped at the wave of pleasure that coursed through him and fell back bonelessly against the hay, helpless to intervene. The dark tangle of Genevieve's hair fell about them like an embracing shadow, and Wolfram found himself uncertain whether he wished her to make haste or prolong this sweet torment.

"Ha!" Genevieve triumphantly pulled the lace from his chausses with a suddenness that astonished Wolfram. Too late, he realized through his haze of pleasure what she did.

But then his chausses were open and her tiny fingers were upon his very flesh.

The shock of her gentle touch undid him. Never had anyone touched him there, and Genevieve's unexpected caress sent a rush through him that abruptly culminated his passion.

Nay! Not so soon! Wolfram felt his seed spill across his stomach in a warm, tingling rush, even as he heard himself moan. Never had he experienced the like and her gentle touch sent him straining for the stars. It was exhilerating— and exhausting.

As he exhaled and closed his eyes in the wake of his release, Wolfram permitted himself to relax totally for the first time in weeks. Safe he was with Genevieve. Safe and at home in her arms. His lack of sleep tormented him and he wanted nothing other than to gather this woman to his side and sleep for a few blissful moments.

Then he would pleasure Genevieve. Wolfram endeavored to pull her close, to make some explanation, but his words fell in an incoherent mumble. He felt Genevieve draw away and imagined she turned away from him in disgust.

What had he done? What had *she* done? Had exhaustion not been slipping over him like a protective cloak, he might well have been embarrassed. Indeed, even in this dazed state, Wolfram knew he would be sorely troubled by this event when he awoke.

But now he could think of naught but sleep. Naught but sleep and the intoxicatingly sweet passion Genevieve offered him.

But a few moments he needed before sampling her charms more fully. Days might they have to secrete themselves here, and his mind readily enumerated ways of passing that time. Wolfram felt himself smile as he rolled over onto his stomach. Genevieve. He smelled her scent on the cloak beneath him, and it mingled with the heady sweetness of the freshly harvested hay to carry him blissfully off to the land of dreams.

Genevieve watched Wolfram with a pounding heart. His eyes drifted closed like a man drugged and his breathing slowed remarkably quickly. Before a dozen heartbeats had passed, he was snoring softly on his stomach. She folded her arms across her chest and regarded him with disgust.

*This* then was what lovemaking was about? Indeed, Genevieve was quite surprised. No fool was she, for livestock had her family always kept, but *this* was a revelation. Goaded by desire and some intuitive sense of purpose, she had desired only to touch the hardness secreted within Wolfram's chausses. Never had she imagined her mere touch would affect him thus.

And this sleeping was something the goats had not seemed inclined to do. Genevieve's lips twisted with dissatisfaction. What of the persistent tingle within *her* that demanded a release she knew not how to gain? Well it seemed that Wolfram had shown little heed for that. It helped little that he looked endearingly tousled or that his hand flexed on the straw as though he would beckon her closer. Genevieve sniffed indignantly. She would not be tempted to abandon her ire, regardless of how his appearance moved her.

Indeed, it seemed this lovemaking was vastly overrated by those who extolled its charms.

Genevieve glared at the man in question, who snored contentedly and undisturbed. She sniffed indignantly again, though none noted her disgust. She fancied that a dog yawned in the stables below, a snuffling canine snore rising to her ears moments later, and a frown worried her brow.

Curse the man! How dare he kiss her as he had? How dare he agitate her so, then fall asleep? She tapped her toe in frustration. What sorcery was it of his that had made her forget her objective? Indeed, she had intended only to disarm him, to waylay his suspicions that she might fulfill her objective. Instead, Wolfram's kisses had emptied her mind of all but a burning need for his touch.

'Twas illogical. 'Twas unfair. Indeed, she might well have granted more to him than his due if he had not fallen asleep. Genevieve chewed her bottom lip for several moments and watched him doze as she considered the worrying possibility of that.

The very idea that she could so readily lose her grasp of her quest prompted the edginess within her to recede slightly and permitted her to think clearly. Almost had he stolen the gift of her virginity from her, as well. Genevieve forced herself to put aside the unexpected wedge of dissatisfaction lodged within her as she counted her blessings.

Had that not been good fortune, that he had fallen asleep? Genevieve ignored the persistent voice of dissent within her. Still a virgin was she, though truly Genevieve felt more warm and flustered than one might consider virginal.

No idea had she had that a man's touch could enflame her so, let alone that this man's touch might do so. Of naught had she been able to think but Wolfram's hands upon her, and in truth the heat of his fingers on her bare flesh had near driven her to distraction.

She had wanted him to touch her privacy with a wantonness that shocked her only now.

She had wanted him to do more than touch her. 'Twas his doing that she had become such a wanton, his fault that she forgot her objectives beneath his tender assault.

Genevieve gritted her teeth, disliking that that accusation did not ring as true as she might have hoped. 'Twas no matter. A quest had she to see done and 'twould put all of this behind her, where it belonged.

Aye. She had best see her task done and be on her way.

Genevieve drew Alzeu's dagger from its scabbard and purposefully leaned over the sleeping Wolfram. One sharp downward stroke and 'twould be done.

Her hand moved naught, and Genevieve scowled at her own weakness. Did he not owe her a debt? Was it not honorable to dispatch one who had stolen her brother and nearly ravished her? She eyed the man responsible for these injustices, and her hand moved naught.

Wolfram's blond hair was tousled like that of a child, and his features were curiously relaxed in repose. Genevieve could smell the heat of his skin, and that sweet longing unfolded within her with a vengeance once more.

She wanted naught in this moment but to curl up next to his warmth. She wanted to awaken with the weight of his arms about her and his lips on hers. She wanted him to dispel this unfamiliar longing within her.

He had killed Alzeu, she reminded herself sternly.

Coldly and without provocation. What she felt was naught but base desire and was not worthy of consideration.

Wolfram's hand curled against her cloak, a gentleness taking command of its strength in sleep. Genevieve recalled only too well those fingers curved around her breast. She shivered at the memory of his fingertip sliding tentatively across her nipple but moments past.

It mattered naught, she told herself crossly, and lifted the blade high. A vow had she taken, and in this moment, she could, she *would,* see it fulfilled.

He had helped her escape the king's wrath. The acknowledgment shook her determination more than Genevieve would have liked. But for Wolfram, she might be trapped in a cold dungeon, fending off rats, or worse. Even if she had run, the dogs would have brought her down had Wolfram not brought her to the Temple's sanctuary.

And he had aided her again here, when the Master of the Temple might have seen her dead.

She owed this killer her life.

Twice over.

Genevieve's grip on the dagger faltered. She remembered that fledgling warmth she had sensed budding deep within Wolfram. It had been that new greenery taken root within the cavernous darkness of his soul that had first prompted her to trust him. 'Twas the recollection of that dawning that stayed her hand even now.

Genevieve knew she could not dispatch Wolfram as coldly as she sought to. He was not a man of stone, at least not any longer, and only too well did she know it.

'Twas his fault she could not fulfill her pledge.

"Curse you!" Genevieve muttered savagely. She cast the dagger against the wall of the stable with all her strength.

It clattered as it fell and the moonlight glinted off the blade, yet Genevieve left it there. Tears flooded her vision and she shoved to her feet to stalk across the loft.

How *dare* Wolfram weaken her resolve? How dare he become a man with a name within her mind? How dare he show himself to be human? How dare he touch her and rouse her passion as it had never been roused before?

Genevieve kicked a bale of hay, in poor temper. How could she fail in this single task? To Alzeu did she owe but one simple deed, but that deed was one she could not fulfill.

A failure she was, a shame to the glory of her lineage, and 'twas the fault of one man alone that she had fallen short. Genevieve spun on her heel and glared at the blissfully sleeping man.

"Curse you!" she said again, her tone low and angry. "How dare you steal this from me? How dare you undermine my resolve? *How dare you?*"

That Wolfram moved not provided absolutely no satisfaction. Indeed, his breathing continued at the same untroubled rate. 'Twas not in the least reassuring for Genevieve to find her skin yet hungry for his touch. All atingle she was, and for naught at all. Genevieve stamped across the loft in sour humor and scooped up her dagger, jamming it deeply into its scabbard.

Wolfram slept like a babe. Curse him and all his kind.

Genevieve fought against the urge to beat him senseless for so agitating her for naught. She should well have been able to plunge the dagger deep into his treacherous heart! A plague on the man! She stalked to his side and grabbed the corner of her cloak. So sharp a tug did she grant the garment that Wolfram shifted bonelessly to the bare floor.

Still did he slumber peacefully. Genevieve cast her cloak about her shoulders and sniffed indignantly when his breathing remained undisturbed.

Foul man. She would see that he *never* touched her again.

Wolfram, for his part, maintained the rate of his breathing with care as he struggled to make sense of Genevieve's actions.

The unsheathing of the blade had nudged him out of his dozing slumber with an instinct born of years of living under the fear of being discovered. No sense had he been able to make of the sound, even when he felt Genevieve poised over him and knew it could be no one else.

His gentle lover intended to kill him? Why?

Genevieve de Pereille, he recalled suddenly. Sister of Alzeu de Pereille, whom Wolfram himself had dispatched.

Well it seemed that the lady knew his role in that. His heart beat in a frenzy at the knowledge that he had been discovered and that his worst nightmare had come to pass. Certain he was that his agitation was audible, and he fought to control his response.

Safety lay in remaining undetected. She thought him asleep. He must appear asleep, that he might gain time to think.

What would he do? How could he defend himself against a woman?

Confused him mightily had Genevieve, for Wolfram knew she could not have feigned her response to his touch. Aye, without this abrupt change of manner, he might have concluded that the woman held him in some regard.

Yet she seemed intent on plunging a dagger into his heart. Wolfram felt the blade dangle above him as surely as if he saw it, and marveled at her change of mood. Well it seemed that he could not form a coherent thought, his body responding of its own accord to her proximity. Cursed woman! He schooled his breathing carefully as he desperately struggled to consider his options, certain she would not be fooled.

Somehow, incredibly, it seemed that Wolfram managed to deceive her that he yet slept.

Had Genevieve but lowered the knife, he would have snatched it from her grip with lightning speed. This he knew beyond doubt, though less certain was he that he would have turned it against her own treacherous heart.

Much less that he could have finished the task.

That Genevieve was unable to do the deed was a relief unexpected under the circumstance. Fortunate for him 'twas that she stepped away when she did, for Wolfram was certain that otherwise she would have seen the bead of sweat that trickled over his brow.

He heard her stalk away to sleep in some other nook of the loft and tried to understand her choice. No sense did it make, though indeed he was grateful for the outcome.

Failing comprehension of that, Wolfram endeavored to decide how to proceed from here but had no better luck with that conundrum. Drove him to distraction Genevieve did, with her music and her very presence, prompting him to recall things he would rather not consider ever again. She undermined his certainty in his chosen role, she tempted him to defy the Rule that dictated the routine of his life, she made him forget his only allegiance with a dexterity that was frightening.

Then she threatened to slaughter him.

Then she changed her mind. The woman was a whirlwind of perplexities. Not reassuring was it in the least that Wolfram was filled with an abrupt and intense desire to spend years sorting out her convoluted thinking.

He wished fervently that she was gone and temptation banished from his life. But an instant later, he hoped he would never see her walk away from him.

Illogical 'twas, and emotional undoubtedly, yet Wolfram, who prided himself on feeling naught under any circumstance, felt a tangle of emotions in this woman's presence that he would do well to ever unravel. He fancied her absence would not dispel whatever witchery she had cast over him, and that thought, surprisingly, did not strike terror into his heart.

A puzzle was Genevieve de Pereille, and a puzzle Wolfram was condemned to share quarters with for the time being. He considered feigning an awakening, that he might beckon her back to sleep with him, and cursed himself for playing the fool.

He would do well to recall that the woman had considered killing him as he slept.

Wolfram stifled a sigh and rolled over in his mock sleep. He opened his eyes now that Genevieve could not see him and stared at the wall in frustration. He would summon his resolve. He would close those doors within his mind that Genevieve persisted in prying open and lock them securely against her. He would see her safe, but grant her naught more of himself.

He certainly would not let his emotions become any more entangled than they already were. Dispassionate efficiency had served him well all these years, and he would be a fool to abandon its merits in any measure.

Sadly, Wolfram was less convinced of his ability to keep Genevieve at arm's length than he would have preferred himself to be. 'Twas an irrational and entirely unwelcome change. He thought of her hand upon him and closed his eyes weakly.

Mayhap Dame Fortune would see fit to smile on him.

Mayhap Genevieve would see fit to touch him again. Or, better, she might permit him to touch her again. The very idea nearly made Wolfram swoon with pleasure, and though he scolded himself for the inappropriateness of his thought, he could do naught to dismiss it from his errant mind.

Genevieve de Pereille was indeed dangerous company, and he would be well advised to ignore her charms in future.

If indeed he could manage the task.


'Twas with the dawn of the thirteenth of October, a Friday, in the year 1307, that the seneschals of the king of France tore open their orders as instructed. Sealed those orders were and delivered from the court of the king himself, though none knew their content before that morn.

The seneschals read the command, then gathered troops and horses to set out and do the king's bidding. Though some might have questioned the curious nature of the demand, still they followed it, for 'twas by dictate of the king and not to be questioned by a mere seneschal.

Accordingly, those seneschals began to arrest and imprison all knights within the length and breadth of France sworn to the Order of the Poor Brothers of the Temple of Solomon.

* * *

Wolfram heard the ruckus in the street below.

"This you cannot do!"

"What travesty is this?"

Wolfram rolled over and opened one eye, surprised that the loft was barely tinged with pink. Cold the air was with the fullness of the pending winter in the morning's bite. He shivered before the sounds of argument grew louder and dismissed any thought of slumbering a little more.

"Lies you told, all lies! But coming through the gate were you to parley, and thence only a few were to come!"

The gate had been opened?

Wolfram sat up abruptly, the sight of Genevieve bringing him up short. He froze in place and eyed her uneasily as the recollection of what had happened the night before flooded through him. She slept at the other end of the loft, seated and leaning awkwardly against a bale of hay. The glorious tangle of her dark hair spilled over her shoulder, the tendrils enfolding the smooth curve of her breast.

Wolfram swallowed carefully as he straightened. It had all been well enough until he lost control, he thought with a pang of self-accusation. What must she think of him? What would she say? 'Twas clear enough she could not bear the thought of even sleeping near him.

What would he say to her when she awakened? Wolfram certainly intended to say naught of what he had done—or *not* done—and indeed, he could not imagine how one might broach the subject.

What if Genevieve had no such reservations?

"What travesty is this?" The dissatisfied rumble of a crowd rose to Wolfram's ears and recalled him to himself. He knew he could delay no longer with musings about Genevieve.

A sense of urgency filled him at the sound of the mass of people outside. Wolfram unfolded silently to rise to his feet. He prided himself on sparing only one covert glance to the sleeping Genevieve as he crept toward the ladder.

Well could it be that something of import was happening. Aye. His duty 'twas to investigate. And should the gate be open, he might well be able to see Genevieve safely away.

Wolfram could not imagine that 'twas so, but 'twas as good an excuse as any to avoid meeting Genevieve's eyes when she awakened. Surely someone erred in saying the gate was open. Wolfram crept down the ladder, realizing too late that someone might be in the stables and note his descent.

Curse Genevieve for making him forget his usual caution! He had not even thought to check! Though 'twas too late to matter, he scanned the shadows of the stables.

To Wolfram's relief, no one was about. Though that was distinctly strange, he shoved the oddity of it from his mind and hastened through the stables, hesitating just inside the stable door to watch what transpired outside.

So great a commotion was there in the street that 'twas difficult to perceive what was what. Knights on horseback in the king's own colors rode amid a crowd of loudly protesting residents. Several merchants whom Wolfram recognized had drawn blades to take contest with liveried men he did not know.

To his complete astonishment, the knights of the Order who were in the street, readily identifiable by their white habits, did not draw their blades. They stood to one side, a row of stalwart sergeants standing defensively between the Templar knights and the king's knights.

The expression on every face was mutinous.

What was this?

"You cannot do this thing!" shouted a sergeant far to Wolfram's right. All glances swiveled in his direction and he waved a fist in the air, his face ruddy with anger. The crowd rumbled agreement. "'Tis not the place of the king to do this, whatever the charge!" A chorus of enthusiastic *Ayes* erupted from the press of people and they edged closer to the king's knights, their manner hostile.

A knight garbed in azure and gold whose mount was nearest the sergeant smoothly unsheathed his blade and deftly dropped the tip to rest against the sergeant's throat. All fell silent as they watched. The sergeant swallowed carefully, though his defiant gaze did not waver.

"We can and we will," the knight asserted calmly.

"Against the edict of Rome 'tis," growled the sergeant.

The knight smiled coldly. "As is heresy, last I heard," he observed curtly. The crowd of onlookers gasped and turned as one to the Templar knights. Those knights looked as stunned by the charge as the crowd. "Charged to arrest and imprison all knights of the Order of the Temple are we on this day. An official edict from the Crown 'tis, and 'twould be best for all if you people saw fit to go about your usual business. No need is there to interfere, lest you *accidentally* bear the price."

The crowd murmured to themselves in dissatisfaction, but little doubt had they or Wolfram that the threat was real. They parted reluctantly to grant a path to the Templar knights, uncertainty clouding their brows at the charge leveled against the Order. The king's knight's destrier picked a path across the distance, its nostrils flaring agitatedly. The Templar knights moved not a muscle.

"Heresy?" one asked archly. "Well had I thought that was the domain of the ecclesiastical courts, not the king's courts."

The king's knight smiled again with strained politeness. "The king but puts his forces at the disposition of the Pope, for he has not the wherewithal to arrest so many at once."

"Nor has he the wherewithal to stand against Philip," muttered someone in the crowd. The king's knight spun, but could not identify the heckler in the sea of silently mutinous faces.

"You cannot hold us," growled another Templar knight.

The king's knight shrugged. "It matters not. On this day, we are charged to arrest you." He granted the half dozen Templar knights before him a wary eye. "One would hope that you might come along quietly, so as not to endanger those about you," he murmured silkily. The knights exchanged a glance, then stepped forward as one.

"We will come without protest," said the first that had spoken.

"And you will grant to me your weapons," added the king's knight. The crowd gasped its indignation, as did Wolfram. The knight glanced over his shoulder with an uneasiness that showed his awareness of the numbers of those around him. "I must insist," he added testily.

"Men of honor are we," the Templar knight argued in a reasonable tone. "Our pledge will we give that we will not draw weapons against you unless provoked."

The king's knight shook his head. " 'Twill not suffice. Your weapons, if you please."

The tone of the exchange altered dramatically at that demand. Glances met and held across the crowd and suddenly it seemed the air was cooler, the threat to these knights that much more suspect. Wolfram feared for his brethren in that instant, even knowing that no one held sway over them but the Master and the Pope himself.

Yet they were being arrested like common criminals. Rounded up as one rounds up livestock for the slaughter. The image could not be dislodged from Wolfram's mind.

"Back for compline will we be," the Templar knight assured his companions with a confidence Wolfram was not sure he was feeling. The Templar unbuckled his sword and presented it to the king's knight with no outward sign of hesitation. His shoulders were squared and his carriage was proud as he walked into the circle of those sent to arrest him.

His companions hesitated but a heartbeat before they followed suit. Wolfram's mouth went dry. No good portent could it be to see Templar knights imprisoned.

The crowd murmured with dissatisfaction to each other as the knights were led away. Wolfram strained his ears and heard the sounds of protest elsewhere in the Ville Neuve. Over a hundred knights there were within these walls, and he wondered abruptly how many of those the king intended to incarcerate.

He pulled his cloak about himself and stepped inconspicuously into the curious and disgruntled crowd that trailed behind the retreating party of knights. Toward the gates they rode, their destriers held in check that the walking Templar knights could keep pace. Wolfram's heart clenched as they passed the smaller streets that fed into the main avenue and more Templar knights were brought into the fold. He glimpsed the familiar faces of sergeants in the ranks of the crowd, their expressions mingling despair and anger.

'Twas when they stood before the gates of the very Temple itself that he saw a scene he would never forget in all his days.

Fully eighty Templar knights stood within the circle of the mounted king's knights. The king's knights waited expectantly, the watching crowd shuffling restlessly, as they knew not what they might see.

The sight of the Master himself being led from the Temple on foot brought a simultaneous gasp of outrage from the crowd. The treasurer followed on his heels, and several other senior officers whom Wolfram did not recognize directly. The king's knights moved their horses, that the barrier betwixt Templars and crowd would be unassailable, as fury burned hot in Wolfram's chest.

What was this travesty of the Order's position? How dared Philip do this thing? He leapt onto a stoop, that he might better see the Master's fate, and in that instant his superior glanced up. Well it seemed to Wolfram that their gazes met for one endless moment and his heart lurched to a halt.

Then the Master glanced down, before any could guess to whom he had looked. Wolfram clung to the wall in disbelief as the king's knights rode through the open gate and escorted every Templar knight they had found to the hospitality of the king's own prison.

# Chapter Ten

Genevieve braced herself to meet Wolfram's gaze before she opened her eyes.

But for naught. He was gone.

She propped herself up and gazed carefully about the loft, but there was no sign of him at all. Genevieve frowned and shoved to her feet. She stalked the narrow space between the bales that ran the width of the loft, convinced he played some sort of poor joke upon her.

But nay. She was alone with her lute.

Of all the brass cheek! The truth brought Genevieve's temper to the fore once more. She folded her arms about herself and scowled at the floor. First the man weakened her will with persuasive kisses, then he disappeared! Not a doubt had Genevieve that 'twas Wolfram's fault alone that she had been unable to fulfill her sworn quest, and she silently, roundly cursed his sorry hide.

Wherever it might happen to be.

Truth be told, it had been a relief to not find him here, as she had fully intended to slip away from him this day and this made her task easier. But still his choice irked her pride. No right had *he* to be the one to leave her behind! How could she leave someone who was not here? Indeed, what point was there? The man would never know how she despised him for foiling her plans!

Genevieve scooped up her lute in poor temper and made to leave. So annoyed was she that she lost her footing on the third rung down and was compelled to snatch at the ladder. Her motion set the cursedly unsteady apparatus swaying and she could do naught but close her eyes and pray.

Left it this way apurpose had he, Genevieve was certain of it. She gritted her teeth with resolve. If ever she had the misfortune to lay eyes on Wolfram again, he would sorely regret the day he had set himself to cross her!

Genevieve gained the stable floor with an ungraceful thud and an accompanying flurry of her lavish kirtle and chemise. She spared the ill-used garment a glance and shook her head at the dirt upon it. A peek over her shoulder revealed that the swatch torn from the hem by the portcullis was more obvious than she might have hoped. Indeed, she was doomed to flash a goodly bit of ankle when she walked, but there was naught for it.

The only way Genevieve could make her feelings clear was to leave before Wolfram came back.

If indeed, he had any intention of returning at all.

Genevieve cast her cloak about her shoulders, jabbed her chin into the air and sailed out into the street. Yet, despite her anger, she could not quite believe that Wolfram would simply abandon her. Not when he had pledged to help her. 'Twas not enough doubt to change her intent, to be sure. But put a spring in her step it did to think that he was likely not gone for good. Indeed, the man would know the full depth of her ire when he returned to find her gone without a trace, and that gave her no small measure of satisfaction.

Her bold move would almost certainly not go unnoticed.

But where would she go? Genevieve's bold step faltered and she looked about the street, realizing the odd atmosphere for the first time. Something was amiss. People stood in small clusters, whispering to each other in a most unusual manner. 'Twas true that Genevieve had heard some commotion earlier this morn, but after tossing and turning for the better part of the night, even the burning of the stables themselves would likely not have stirred her from her eventual slumber.

No matter what troubled these folk. Genevieve tossed her hair. What happened in the Ville Neuve had naught to do with her anymore. She was leaving Paris.

Of course, there was the matter that the Master had sought her out that she might meet the same fate as Alzeu. Genevieve's footsteps faltered and she glanced about herself, but the townspeople in the Ville Neuve seemed too occupied with their own business to have noticed her.

In truth, she had heard that tale from Wolfram alone, and now she wondered if there was truth in it. Might he have deceived her purely to ensure they spent the night together? Tales had she heard of the desires of men. Genevieve chewed her lip in indecision, until the disinterested manner of both sergeants and townsfolk in her presence finally reassured her.

Wolfram had lied to her. Another deed 'twas that she could hold against him. Genevieve lifted her chin and walked briskly toward the Temple gates as she hastily planned. She would not be surprised if the barring of the gates had been no more than a coincidence. Indeed, it only made sense to seek out the truth for herself.

Foul man. How dare he think she was a woman of such meager virtue?

Her quest had failed, but Genevieve would fault herself no more for that. She had tried but had been weaker than she might have hoped. 'Twas no more than weakness that had stayed her hand.

Now she would go home. 'Twas as simple as that. Genevieve would return to Montsalvat and build that secure future she had desired above all else. Truly, Montsalvat was too far for any, even the king, to pursue a mere woman. The more Genevieve reflected upon it, the more she doubted she would be endangered at home.

If perchance Wolfram *had* spoken the truth, 'twas only her presence in Paris that might prompt such action. Montsalvat was too distant to merit the trouble.

And it was home. She would raise goats and plant a garden and play her lute and mayhap, if she was fortunate beyond compare, some eligible suitor would rap on her gates. Mayhap even, one day, Genevieve would be able to rebuild the fortress of her forebears to its earlier majesty.

'Twas enough of a dream to merit going home, even if Genevieve knew how little chance she had of making it all come true. She hugged her lute closer and hastened to the gates.

Mayhap she could be home before the full bite of winter was in the wind.

What she would do in that isolated fortress in the dead of winter, with nary a stick for kindling or a grain of wheat in the cellars, she did not permit herself to think.

Wolfram crept into the dormitory with practiced stealth. He glanced carefully to the left and the right, but none was about.

Indeed, the Temple was quiet beyond compare. But that suited his purpose well enough. He furtively made his way to his own bed but hesitated when he gained its side.

What if they were gone? The very thought was chilling, for who knew what horror could be wrought if they fell into the wrong hands?

No personal possessions had any member of the Order, but a concession had been made to Wolfram because of his particular skill. He strained his ears before bending to extract his treasure, but heard naught.

Hastily he bent and shoved his hand into the midst of his straw pallet. His fingers encountered glass vials, one, two, three.

They were yet here. Wolfram's breath caught in relief even as his hand folded around the vials of poison. He pulled out his hand, shoved the vials into his tunic, turned smartly and marched out of the dormitory, his heart pounding in his ears all the while.

There was naught else to keep him here.

A panic had settled within him when he saw the Master taken away. Mayhap it had been when the Master's gaze met his—Wolfram could not have said. He knew only that 'twas imperative to put distance between himself and this place. Only the knights had they arrested, but Wolfram would have had to be slower of intellect than he was not to see that the frenzy could spread.

He could not even imagine what price his own head might bring, should he have the misfortune to be identified. An assassin who could no longer move invisibly was disposable indeed. And too many secrets did he know, not the least of which was the names of those he had dispatched. Wolfram was at risk, and that alone could prompt him to break one of the fundamental tenets of the Rule.

A brother remained in the house unless told to do otherwise. 'Twas basic to the Rule, and though Wolfram acknowledged the magnitude of what he did, still he walked onward. Poverty and chastity were major vows, but obedience was the greatest of them all. Obedience and stability walked hand in hand; obedience and stability were the cornerstones of any successful monastic order like the Templars.

But nary a doubt was there in Wolfram's mind. He might not have been granted permission to leave the Temple in Paris, but leave it Wolfram would.

'Twas his own hide at stake. He could not afford to be revealed. Was he to survive, he had to leave. Quickly, immediately, alone. His mind filled with purpose, Wolfram made to leave the Temple alone while he yet could.

Until a stray thought brought him up short.

But two knew his secret. But two could reveal him. One enjoyed the hospitality of the king. And one he had vowed to see to safety. Genevieve knew his secret, as well, and already had she proven herself untrustworthy.

Wolfram hesitated on the threshold.

Aye, he had pledged to aid her, but that had been afore she tried to kill him, he argued silently with himself. And he had seen her safely to sanctuary when otherwise she would not have escaped the king's court. Surely he owed her no more than that?

Wolfram shook the misgivings out of his head and began to walk away. The woman had tried to dispatch him from this earth. No matter if she had succeeded or failed, her intent to dispatch him surely voided any earlier agreement betwixt them.

But that persistent voice within his mind would not let the matter be. Would he not have done the same as Genevieve had he known one of his own brethren to have been brought to an early demise by the hand of a stranger?

Wolfram's resolve faltered. He could not say he would, but neither could he say that he would not. 'Twas not reassuring in the least that he could not readily dismiss a possible similarity betwixt himself and Genevieve.

She alone could reveal him. That fact was unquestionable and was enough to send him in the direction of the stables. Well it seemed that he was not quit of this woman and her schemes just yet.

Tranquillity greeted him within the stables and Wolfram permitted himself a sigh of relief. Still there was not so much as a stable hand here. Dust motes danced in the golden autumn sunbeam that slanted through the doorway, the brightness of the sunlight making the shadows beyond appear yet darker. A horse snorted, another stamped, flies droned, a friendly hound came with tail wagging to sniff Wolfram's chausses. He ignored them all and made purposefully for the ladder.

On the second rung, Wolfram realized that not a sound was there from above, not so much as the whisper of a woman softly sleeping. 'Twas too still in the loft. His breath caught in his throat and for an instant Wolfram feared that something had befallen Genevieve in the short time he had been gone.

It could not be! Not here in the peaceful bower of the stable. Busy had the king's men been, too busy with Templar knights to trouble themselves with a lutenist.

The explanation comforted him naught. Never should he have left her alone! Had they not been hunted just a day past? Wolfram bounded up the ladder and burst into the stillness of the loft.

Naught was there. He stared about himself, incredulous. He spun on his heel, as if he thought to startle something or someone hiding just behind him.

To no avail. Naught was here but the sunlight gleaming through the lattice of the vent and turning the hay to spun gold.

Genevieve was gone.

But where had she gone?

"Genevieve!"

There she was! The woman Wolfram pursued ran across the square far ahead of him. Wolfram rode through the Temple gates just in time to see a man leap forward from the shadows to grasp her arms.

"Genevieve!" Wolfram bellowed in relief, not caring for the moment who heard his cry. None would threaten her when he was so close! He dug his heels into his horse's side as the man gripping her arms gave her a savage shake. Endangered Genevieve was! And 'twas the fault of none but Wolfram. Never should he have left her alone, even for those few moments this morn.

Had he had the chance to consider his response, Wolfram might have thought himself relieved to have found her, as ridiculous as that thought might have been.

'Twas simply his duty that called him to task, naught else.

Genevieve jumped in a most satisfactory manner at his bellow. She spun, her eyes widening in such shock that Wolfram fancied he could see their vivid green. Relieved she was to see him, clearly, and that realization fairly made Wolfram dizzy.

No time was there for her gratitude now, though, for 'twas high time he and Genevieve were safely away from the villains of Paris.

Wolfram bent low as he bore down upon the pair. The man leapt out of the way, but Genevieve seemed too surprised to move. Wolfram slowed the horse but an increment as he swept alongside. The villain swore to see his plans foiled as Wolfram scooped Genevieve up into the saddle before him with a deft grace he had never known he possessed. Her lute bounced harmlessly against the horse's side, and he was proud that even it had been rescued unscathed. The man's cries of distress rang in Wolfram's ears as he bore Genevieve away, but he spurred his horse onward.

Like some hero from an old *chanson* was he, Wolfram thought with a smug smile. Well satisfied was he with his accomplishment of his goal, indeed. Wolfram glanced down to the delicate maid before him, well expecting some token of her gratitude.

'Twas only then he realized that Genevieve's eyes were flashing with something that looked markedly more like anger than gratitude.

"Imbecile!" she hissed through her teeth, and swatted him across the shoulder.

The blow was surprisingly hard and nearly unbalanced him. Wolfram regarded her with no small shock of his own as her eyes narrowed dangerously. 'Twas clear the woman's wits were addled, and he tightened his grip around her, that she not lose her seat.

"Unhand me, you barbarian," she spat furiously. Wolfram pulled back slightly and granted her a wary eye.

"Mayhap you did not notice that I have just saved you from a dastardly fate," he observed with all the calm he could muster. Genevieve snorted.

"Hardly that," she snapped.

"You would not deny that that villain intended to abscond with you?" Wolfram demanded archly, his pride pricked that she refused to see the dashing sweep of his bravery. Genevieve, to his dismay, made a sound of deprecation under her breath.

"'Twas *Odo* you saved me from, you imbecile," she retorted. "Odo, the minstrel," she added at sight of Wolfram's blank expression.

Odo? Wolfram blinked as Genevieve's tirade continued unabated.

"Mayhap you could confide in me what particular odious fate you imagined a *minstrel* might have planned for me?"

Odo?

Wolfram reined in the horse and glanced back over his shoulder doubtfully. A heartily disgruntled man with decidedly red hair glared after them, his hands propped on his hips. The minstrel had had red hair, Wolfram acknowledged belatedly, and well enough did this man resemble him.

He even sported the same garb. Wolfram swallowed slowly and glanced back to Genevieve, a hearty seed of doubt planted in his mind.

Her openly skeptical expression prompted that seed to grow a root.

"Well I thought that he threatened you," he offered tentatively. Genevieve rolled her eyes scornfully, and that budding plant unfurled a leaf.

"Oh, indeed," she replied. "Aye, you could likely tell as much by the way we stood, discussing matters like civilized beings."

Wolfram was forced to admit belatedly that there had been little suspicious about their pose. Belatedly he admitted that the man *could* have simply grasped Genevieve's arm in greeting.

The seed unfurled another great green leaf and strained for the sunlight. In fact, he supposed there had been naught at all to prompt his response. 'Twas not a revelation that sat well, and Wolfram felt his neck heat.

He had been terribly wrong, and embarrassment rolled through him too late to affect a difference. Impulsive he had been beyond compare. How could he have not even looked at the man? How could he have barged ahead in a most impetuous manner, he who always carefully considered every move first?

Anger rose within him as he met the judgmental gaze of the woman seated afore him.

'Twas *Genevieve* who had done this to him. 'Twas fear for Genevieve that had prompted his hand. Indeed, the woman fairly made his innards writhe. She unleashed his passions, she poked in secret corners of his mind, she provoked his emotions. She was dangerously unsettling and precariously attractive and ... and ...

And Wolfram would do anything within his power to see her safe. The very thought stilled everything within him, until the only rational explanation for such erratic behavior spilled into his thinking.

His task 'twas to fulfill the pledge he had given her to see her safe. Aye, Wolfram had dashed in only to fulfill his responsibilities. No more than that. 'Twas not that he had cast his usual manner aside—nay, never that—only that some situations required urgency.

Even if urgency oft led to error. He fidgeted in the saddle beneath Genevieve's scathing gaze.

"And well you were mistaken in your conclusions," Genevieve retorted unnecessarily. "I believe you owe Odo and me an apology."

An apology? For attempting to fulfill his task? Never!

Genevieve must have seen the mutiny in his eyes, for she pushed with sudden impatience at the grip of Wolfram's hand on her waist. "Let me down," she demanded.

"No reason is there for you to dismount," Wolfram protested. "'Tis only reasonable, after all, that a lady ride—"

He got no farther than that, for Genevieve seemed quite determined to wriggle against him in a most disconcerting manner. His voice faded to naught as he stared down at her twisting hips. Only too aware was Wolfram that she sat directly in his lap, though indeed he had thought little of the matter until this very moment.

Genevieve glanced up in confusion, and her gaze was snared by his. Marvel spread slowly through Wolfram as he held her clear green gaze. Marvel that this woman alone knew who and what he was, yet she did not scorn his company completely. His secret, it seemed, was safe with her, and he saw the confirmation of that in her eyes. She could reveal him, but he saw in her expression no judgment at all.

Did this mean he could trust this intoxicating woman?

Wolfram caught his breath in mingled admiration and vulnerability. His body responded of its own will in a manner that could be mistaken for naught else. God's blood, but this woman plagued his resolve!

Indeed, Genevieve seemed not to have mistaken his response, for she halted her squirming abruptly. Recollection of the previous night flooded through him, and Wolfram knew not what to say. His neck heated as certainty filled him that Genevieve was watching the color rise in his face with that unwavering scrutiny.

Then she shook her head and abruptly pushed at his hand anew.

"Let me go," she muttered forcefully. "Naught have you and I to say to each other at this late date."

"What do you mean?" Wolfram demanded in surprise. She glanced up to him again, and he fancied the set of her lips softened momentarily at his evident dismay.

"Make no mistake," Genevieve said with a terseness that her eyes belied. "Well do I appreciate your aid last eve, but this morn my path lies in another direction."

"What direction is that?"

"Naught of your business are my affairs," she declared, but Wolfram could not let the matter lie.

"Where do you go? Tell me, that I might aid you."

Genevieve dropped her gaze, and Wolfram knew she intended to be evasive. "'Tis a direction in which I must go alone," she said. So sharp was the gaze he bent upon her that it seemed she was obligated to meet his regard once more.

"I would aid you," he vowed in a soft murmur. Genevieve's lips parted, then she seemed to abruptly recall something less than pleasant. She pulled herself up stiffly and pushed away from him.

"You?" she demanded scornfully, and her tone stung. "*You* would aid me? What kind of poor joke is this?"

"I said I would aid you because I would," Wolfram repeated stubbornly.

Genevieve tossed her chin. "As if I would willingly accept the aid of one who cold-bloodedly murdered my own brother."

To hear the words fall from her lips was no small shock, but Wolfram schooled himself not to turn away. "Well can I understand your anger," he began, though in truth he was destined to say no more.

"You do not even deny it!" she cried. Fury snapped unbridled in Genevieve's eyes, and with a sudden burst of strength, she pushed him away and leapt from the horse. Wolfram snatched at her to no avail, the way she winced when she landed making him wince in sympathy.

But no interest had Genevieve in his sympathy.

"You!" she shouted as she wagged one finger up at him. "*You* stole away the last of my family, yet you calmly expect me to accept your aid. What manner of idiot do you fancy me to be?" The color rose in her cheeks and her voice grew louder, yet Genevieve granted Wolfram no reprieve.

"How could you imagine that I could sleep easily with *you* standing guard over me? Ha! A fine jest that is! As likely as not you would slip something foul into my wine one day and leave me to expire!" Genevieve swung her lute around viciously as she turned and stalked toward an Odo who clearly listened avidly. Wolfram felt his face heat, but he dared not open his mouth to defend himself.

What defense had he, after all? The lady called him to task for a deed he had committed in truth.

"Well, no fool am I." Genevieve turned back to Wolfram and jabbed a finger through the air toward him. "Whoever 'tis that you might be! No interest have I in *your* assistance. Odo will help me instead." With that, Genevieve turned and stalked away. That she limped slightly as she walked did naught to dissipate Wolfram's certainty in her anger.

*Odo?* Surely that man was at the root of Genevieve's predicament!

"You would instead employ the aid of a minstrel when all the king's court hunts you?" Wilfram forced himself to ask mildly. Genevieve fired a glance of such loathing over her shoulder that Wolfram nearly flinched.

"I suppose you find yourself better outfitted to aid me?" she demanded, her contrary opinion evident enough to leave Wolfram's ears burning.

No small thing was it for her to insult his talents, however angry she might be. He *could* aid her more effectively than Odo, and well had he thought she had the wits enough to know it. Sparks were struck within him and anger lit with a dull glow. Wolfram urged the horse to stroll in pursuit of her as he forced himself to compose a telling argument.

Not that she would appreciate the effort. Well it seemed the woman made judgments and decisions with an impulsiveness that made him cringe. Solid logic she would not recognize should she trip over it on the street.

"Aye," he retorted sharply. "Aye, I do know myself to be better equipped to aid you, and well should you."

"Aye," Genevieve observed sourly. "A killer is the kind of man of whom I have dire need in this moment."

"A song, no matter how fetching, will gain you little if the king's hounds set their teeth in your hide," Wolfram snapped. "You might well be pleased to see something die at my hand in that circumstance. Could your minstrel stomach the task?" Genevieve flicked him a glance filled with more fear than she likely wanted him to see. "Could your minstrel have seen you to safe haven these last two nights?"

"At least I could sleep through the night assured that morning would not find a dagger in my back," she snapped in return. Wolfram cocked a brow high.

"Well had I thought the dagger was your weapon of choice," he accused softly.

Genevieve's eyes flew wide and she gasped as she turned to confront him. The color drained from her face as she evidently saw that Wolfram knew the fullness of what she had intended to do.

"Mayhap we have something in common, after all," Wolfram purred, enjoying that he had the upper hand, for the moment at least. Well enough he knew it would not last, and when Genevieve inhaled sharply and bolted, he was prepared to give pursuit.

"I cannot travel with you." She tossed the words hastily over her shoulder as she ran, but Wolfram was not finished with their discussion as yet. Blessed stubborn, Genevieve was, but Wolfram knew his determination would outweigh her own.

He was right and he knew it. He aimed not to cease arguing until she knew it, as well. Curse the woman for being so determined to ignore what he said!

"You cannot travel without me and survive," Wolfram observed as he dug his heels into his horse's side. The beast cantered after Genevieve as she tried to hasten toward Odo.

"I can and I will," she declared as he rode alongside. Her breath came in short spurts and she shot him a glance ripe with fury.

"And where would you go?" Wolfram inquired mildly.

"Home." Genevieve bit the word out viciously.

"Montsalvat? A choice of meager appeal, in truth," he commented.

That captured her attention fully. Genevieve halted abruptly and clutched her lute close with one arm while she propped the other hand on her hip to confront him. Wolfram pulled the reins and the horse stepped sideways at the abrupt change of pace, tossing its head once or twice before it settled.

Once again they confronted each other, and the air crackled with tension. Odo was close enough to hear their words now, and Wolfram hoped that man would throw his argument on the side of good sense. Who knew what whimsy a minstrel might find compelling? Well it seemed that this lutenist was determined to cling to a path of little merit.

"Why?" Her demand hung in the air between them.

"But think upon it, Genevieve," Wolfram urged, leaning forward. "'Tis the first place they will seek you out."

She lifted her chin stubbornly and he knew she would argue the point. "Nay, they will not. 'Tis too far."

Wolfram snorted. "Aye, 'twas clearly too far to send me," he commented dryly.

"'Tis not such a leap of intellect to connect Munsalvaesche with Montsalvat," Odo added.

Genevieve looked between both men with evident frustration, her expression slowly changing to dismay. Her color rose angrily and she fired a hostile glance in Odo's direction. "'Tis all your fault, if they would seek me out now," she accused.

Odo arched a skeptical brow and folded his arms across his chest. "Aye, 'twas I who demanded you declare your identity before all," he commented.

"No risk was there in that, surely," Genevieve protested. "I am but a woman and no threat to any man's power."

"But young enough to bear spawn to an ambitious man," Odo declared flatly.

Genevieve's eyes widened and she turned to Wolfram.

"I do not think they will leave the matter be," he said gently when she seemed to be waiting for his conclusions. "Accept my aid in this."

His last words went unheard as Odo interjected. "You should have known better than to come to Paris and draw attention to yourself," that man accused. Genevieve gasped but Odo merely shrugged. Wolfram saw rage light her eyes before she turned and savagely punched the minstrel in the belly.

"Fool! Addle-pated idiot! How dare you sing of my family in the king's own court and jeopardize everything! How dare you reveal me that I cannot return home! How dare you meddle with my life! How dare you steal everything away from me that I have known!"

"I thought it but a tale!" Odo cried as he tried to defend himself. Only the fact that Genevieve resolutely held her lute out of the fray, leaving her with but one hand to attack, granted the minstrel any chance at all. Wolfram leapt from his saddle to aid.

"A dangerous thread of truth there is in all of it!" Genevieve insisted. "How could you do this to me? How could you risk everything for naught?"

"I knew not who you were!" Odo declared. Wolfram captured Genevieve's arms and trapped her back against his chest. She struggled futilely, then took refuge in spitting on the minstrel.

"No excuse is that! Have you no idea what has been risked?" Wolfram felt a wet splash of tears on his hands but he knew she would welcome naught of any comfort he might try to grant her.

"All is revealed," Genevieve whispered tearfully, and it seemed that her resolve crumpled in acknowledgement of the truth. Her anger was spent, but Wolfram felt the knave for having to tell her the truth. The two men's gazes met helplessly as she sagged against Wolfram. "But where else might I go?" she asked through her tears, her voice so quiet that she might be asking herself.

"We cannot linger here," Odo said carefully.

Genevieve flicked a venomous glance in his direction. "Thanks to you," she charged, with some vestige of her former anger. "Though why you speak of 'we' I cannot fathom. Do not imagine that I would have anything to do with either of you at this point."

"You have little choice, should you desire to leave Paris alive," Wolfram observed in an undertone. Genevieve stiffened against him, and he watched her chin rise defiantly.

"Even I am hard-pressed to believe my best option lies with a murderer," she snapped.

"I for one do not mean to stay here," Odo said with an evenness that Wolfram imagined cost him dearly. What was his intent? Wolfram narrowed his eyes skeptically, though the way Odo met his gaze again was reassuring.

"Nor do I," Wolfram agreed. Though Genevieve's expression was mutinous, well did he know that she listened avidly to their planning.

"It seems that my little troupe has an engagement elsewhere," Odo murmured.

Ah. There was an idea with appeal. "They will be watching the city gates," Wolfram observed cautiously.

Odo smiled a thin smile, but his intent gaze never wavered from Wolfram's. "No one takes note of actors and acrobats," he said quietly. "Come join my troupe. We will leave the city, though I know not where we might head."

Genevieve granted Odo a venomous glance. "And why should I accept *your* aid?" she demanded.

Odo shrugged, though his gaze burned bright. "'Tis clear a debt is owed from me to you. Among my kind such things are not taken lightly."

'Twas enough reassurance for Wolfram, though he well knew Genevieve still harbored doubts.

"We should go to Metz," Wolfram offered impulsively. Both of his companions glanced to him in surprise, but he looked only to Odo. "The Templar knights have been arrested within all of France. 'Tis over the closest border and in the opposite direction of Montsalvat." And a place of memories for him, but neither of them needed to know that.

"I like your thinking well," Odo agreed.

Genevieve spared an arch glance in Wolfram's direction. "Mayhap you should simply return to your Ville Neuve," she suggested coldly. Wolfram shook his head.

"I cannot return there," he said flatly.

"All of us are marked," Odo confirmed. "Logical it seems in truth to venture forth together now that our destinies are entwined. 'Twas only luck alone that saw me escape the court unscathed and I would not tempt fate by remaining overlong in Paris."

"Think whatsoever you will," Genevieve commented frostily, "but no intention have I of venturing anywhere with either or both of you."

"Do not be a fool, Genevieve," Odo muttered.

Genevieve tossed her hair and stepped quickly out of Wolfram's grip, the very image of the impetuousness of the fair sex. "I will take my chances alone," she asserted with bravado.

"No chance have you alone," Wolfram argued flatly. "'Tis as simple as that. Should you choose to live, you must make your way with us."

Genevieve's eyes snapped. "I will do no such thing."

"A promise did you make to me," Odo said in a low tone that told Wolfram the other man knew he had Genevieve cornered. She regarded the minstrel warily, her manner doing naught to dismiss Wolfram's suspicions.

"You would not," she murmured threateningly. Odo merely nodded, clearly well pleased with himself.

"I will and I do," he asserted boldly, and his expression became more assessing than Wolfram had yet seen it. "One condition to be named later did you promise me, that you might play where you chose. This condition I name as your accompanying our party to Metz."

"You cannot do this thing," Genevieve murmured angrily.

Odo cocked a brow. "I do this thing for your own welfare alone," he maintained.

"I will not," Genevieve argued. Odo's gaze flicked to Wolfram, but he had already stepped behind Genevieve again. Should she defy them, 'twas good to know they were both so bent on seeing her safe, one way or the other. He would toss her over the back of his horse to see her away from Paris, if need be.

"Yet again, I am compelled to ask you if your word is worth naught," Odo said silkily. Genevieve swallowed carefully and glanced from side to side as if seeking some escape.

Genevieve looked as though she might have said something else, but Wolfram reached down and firmly captured her hand within his. Soft 'twas and he closed his fingers resolutely around it, as though to show her somehow that he intended to let naught happen to her.

To his astonishment, the tension seemed to filter out of her at that contact.

"To Metz and no farther," she stated weakly. Odo nodded.

"Then shall we be even," he agreed. Genevieve was not so resolved to their will that she refrained from a sardonic snort.

"I should think we would be markedly more than even," she muttered. Too relieved was Wolfram that she had finally agreed to take offense at her tone.

"We shall have to sell the horse," he said, forcing himself to think of practical matters. Odo spared the beast an assessing glance and nodded.

"Aye, too fine is he for our kind. Attention we do not need, and the coin will be of aid. Well might it be long before we can busk again." Odo glanced to the clear blue of the sky, and Wolfram scowled at the lateness of the hour.

When the two men's gazes met again, they nodded as of one accord.

"We should make haste," Wolfram said. Odo nodded again and set a quick pace toward the far side of the square. Wolfram kept Genevieve's hand firmly trapped within his own as he led the horse in Odo's wake, surprised that she seemed to have naught more to say.

Well did he expect that that might change once they were safely outside the city walls. Indeed, he more than expected it—he dreaded as much.

# Chapter Eleven

Just after a chilly gray November dawn, in a dark corner of the château on the Île de la Cité, a bargain was struck.

The Master of the Temple of Paris was awakened by the sound of a key turning in the lock of the cell he had occupied these two weeks. The room was yet shadowed and filled with the dampness of the night, but the import of that sound could not be mistaken.

Visitors. His heart leapt, his defiant mood not in the least improved by his incarceration in the company of rats. Loudly had he cried for justice in the early days, vehemently had he demanded the summoning of ecclesiastical authorities, stridently had he demanded to be released as a man of honor on his own recognizance.

His demands had fallen on deaf ears.

Mayhap until now.

The Master shoved to a sitting position and straightened his belted, plain linen tunic just as the door swung open. A bevy of brightly burning lanterns were shoved into the room so hastily that he blinked at the unexpected light. Wicks were left long, the lamps crowded together on the table close afore him so that he was forced to squint at their brightness.

Well he knew this trick, for he had used it oft himself when he wished to keep his identity unknown. The Master narrowed his eyes and peered through the light as best as he was able. He detected a guard on either side of him, most assuredly to keep him from bolting. The dancing flames effectively deterred him from leaping forward and the solidity of the stone wall behind him severely limited his options for movement.

He thought he detected a tall shrouded figure sweeping into the room and taking his place behind the bright flames. Just out of sight his interviewer was, and the Master grudgingly acknowledged that man's experience.

"Something have you that we desire" came a muffled voice, evidently pitched low, that the Master might not identify it.

Immediately he thought of the Temple treasury, and resolve grew hard within him. Never would he reveal its whereabouts to the crown. Never under any terms. Property of the Order alone were those riches, and the Master would surrender their guardianship to none but the Master of the Temple of Jerusalem himself.

And then only if that man was as determined to keep them to the Order as he.

Certain he knew what was at root, the Master remained stubbornly silent.

"Well do we understand that you wish to be released on your own recognizance," the voice continued unhurriedly. "And as a man of honor, we well know that your pledge to remain within the Ville Neuve is a reliable one. But we would have something in exchange. A proof of your good will, shall we say."

When it seemed some response was awaited, the Master nodded understanding warily. Truly Philip ventured too far this time. Surely the Pope would slap him down and call him to order. Surely this affront could not pass unchallenged.

But two weeks had passed and the Master had heard naught from Rome. He wondered in this dark moment whether the Pope was as firmly held under Philip's thumb as he had long suspected.

If so, that boded naught good for the Order.

"But two requests have we, and well it seems to me that they are so insignificant as to be laughable. A trinket of your loyalty, if you will. Surely this can be construed as no more than a formality between men who understand each other."

The Master braced himself for the worst with that disclaimer, but deliberately kept his expression benign. If ever he saw release from these walls, he would personally ensure that Philip sorely regretted this travesty.

"A woman there is with whom we would speak," the voice continued reasonably. The Master was so astonished at this that he doubted he was entirely successful in concealing his surprise. His visitor's next words confirmed as much. "Aye, well might you scoff at such an objective, for 'tis but a whimsy of the crown. The king wishes but to offer his hospitality to the lady that he might have converse with her."

The Master raised a brow. Little doubt had he that he could venture a solid guess as to who this woman might be. And he heartily doubted that converse was within Philip's goals. "Hospitality the likes of mine?" he asked skeptically, and was rewarded with a low chuckle.

"The technicalities mean little at this date, and indeed I myself do not know precisely the king's intent. It matters naught to you and me, in truth."

A fool the Master had been to trust the word of the party sent to the gates that morn. Stormed the gates, the king's knights had, that first party doing naught but seizing the gatekeeper, that the drawbridge might not be raised against them. Had they not done so, the woman might yet be within the walls of the Ville Neuve.

As might the Master have been all these days. The Master gritted his teeth yet again in recollection, knowing full well 'twas too late to effect a change.

"Who might this mysterious woman be?" he asked mildly.

"Genevieve de Pereille is she. The daughter of a petty provincial lord," his visitor supplied dismissively. Aye, she was that, the Master thought, though that lord had paid heavily for his petty provinciality. Surely these men were not such fools as to imagine that *he,* the Master of the Temple of Paris, could not divine their game?

'Twas their own meddling that had freed that very woman from the Master's secure grip and sent her who knew where.

Although the Master well fancied that even if he knew not where Genevieve might be, then he likely knew with whom she kept company.

There was an expectant silence, but the Master revealed naught of the direction of his thoughts.

"Ah…" His visitor chuckled under his breath. "Well do I see that you would know the fullness of the offer afore you decide. The second condition is nearly as paltry as the first, as you will see, so your reservations are for naught. A small request 'tis, really." He hesitated, and the Master knew that this was the meat of the matter, and not likely to be small at all.

"A man have you within your ranks, an *Italien* of the finest order whom the king would like to welcome within the ranks of his own employ."

The Master's heart lurched at this news. Philip desired to know Wolfram's identity. Did he truly mean to employ Wolfram as an assassin? Or could the Master be betraying Wolfram to his death? Indeed Wolfram knew overmuch about Philip's commissions.

'Twas tempting to betray Wolfram thus, for the responsibility for whatever fate befell him could not be laid square at the Master's door. Well enough did he know that this conversation would be known to have occurred by few and acknowledged to have occurred by still fewer.

He should put up a pretense of objection, he decided.

"This I cannot do," the Master said firmly. "The man's pledge is to the Order and no right has any man to come betwixt a man and his vow."

"We see no reason to break the man's vow," his opponent countered smoothly. "He may continue to live in whatever fashion he desires as long as he makes his home within the court."

"Nay," the Master argued. " 'Tis in the Rule that a Templar brother must reside within the walls of a Temple alone. He must live with his brethren."

"We must insist," the visitor hissed.

"Revealed he would be and of no use to you," the Master argued. He fancied the man on the other side of the flames smiled and knew they intended no good for Wolfram.

But did it matter to him, in truth? What were they prepared to offer him, the Master, in exchange?

"Certain am I that you can be convinced of our resolve," the visitor purred. The Master intuitively understood the threat.

"And if I agree?" he demanded tightly.

"Then you and six knights of your choice will be released on your own word." The visitor's words were clipped and efficient. "Those who remain in custody will be granted finer quarters until this matter is resolved."

Six. That would see the officers of the Temple released and mayhap one or two more. The Master pursed his lips, knowing full well that he could orchestrate the release of the rest better from within the Ville Neuve.

For if this arrest had been carried out throughout France as he had been told, his first loyalty had to be to those knights in custody. 'Twas his office, after all.

Still had the Master a few tricks up his sleeve.

"Naught can I engineer from here," he complained testily, and sensed relief coursing through the man opposite. So, they had not been as certain of his response as they might have liked. The Master's resolve grew, and a germ of his old audacity took root within him. "Indeed, I shall have to go myself to fetch these two."

"A man can we spare who confesses an interest in this situation," the visitor acknowledged.

"No interest have I in delegating a task of such import to me personally to one of your inept aides," the Master argued.

The visitor hesitated, but the Master smelled his uncertainty. This concession he had to gain, for Wolfram might well not return to Paris. Ever.

And the Master suspected his visitor knew he had little choice but to accept the terms.

The visitor paced the width of the cell and back afore he decided. The Master's palms grew damp but he gave away naught of his concern in his posture. The air virtually crackled in the small room, and the Master fancied he was not the only one holding his very breath.

"My word is yours," the visitor conceded tersely. He spun on his heel, and the Master sighed with relief as he saw the hem of a cloak flutter against the scant light of the corridor outside. The lamps flickered from the breeze, then were summarily gathered up and the Master was left alone in the cold gray light of his cell.

He would have his release and his vengeance. An errant sergeant would he curtail and an annoying risk would he eliminate, all at the behest of the crown. Naught would be traced to the Master himself.

And still there was the matter of the Treasury, he recalled victoriously. Should Philip aim to deceive him, the Master had yet another advantage on his side.

Only a matter of time 'twas afore the crown's representatives completed their counting and discovered no more than the crown's own funds secreted in the Paris Temple's vaults. Indeed, the Templars did store and administer the king's own funds, but readily enough could the Master guess that Philip would have hoped to grasp all of the Templars' own resource in his seizure of the Temple and the Ville Neuve.

But a single slip of the tongue weeks past had it taken to prompt the Master's suspicions. And that had been enough to see one of Philip's purposes thwarted. Nigh on a month

ago, the Master had transferred the Temple's own wealth
elsewhere, covertly and in easy stages, though not even torture would drag a destination from his lips. The ships had
left the Templar port of Le Havre fully a fortnight past.

Though 'twould be long afore he admitted even that
much, if ever he did. The Master permitted himself a thin
smile of satisfaction at a match well played.

Nay, the Master of the Paris Temple was not without aces
to play in this game. 'Twas clear that neither Philip, Wolfram nor this Genevieve understood the manner of opponent they had engaged.


'Twas in a good-size town three weeks after leaving Paris
that they found the Temple razed to the ground.

The troupe had walked hard every day, putting as many
leagues behind them as possible at Odo and Wolfram's insistence. Genevieve's anger had sustained her for the first
few days, but then it had started to ebb away, leaving her
more tired than afore. Still they pressed on. Food became
sparse and coin nonexistent. Conversation was surly and
brusque, and tempers were short.

Genevieve knew she was not alone in glancing periodi-
cally over her shoulder for signs of pursuit. The solid walls
of the town ahead had prompted new hope to stir within her
heart. 'Twas true they were still within the realm of the
French king, but mayhap this town was far enough from
Paris that they could busk. A warm meal would go far toward restoring the camaraderie within the troupe. And there
had, after all, been no evidence that they were being followed. Mayhap they had truly slipped through the net.

The burned shell of the Temple, however, was a brutal
reminder of the proximity of Paris. The troupe halted as one
to stare at the wreckage. They had heard rumors that the
Templar knights had been arrested throughout France, but
'twas still a shock to see the remains of such a brutal response.

Genevieve watched Wolfram step silently away from the mute group. He hesitated before the charred ruins and she saw his gaze dance uncomprehendingly over what remained.

Well it seemed that he was struck numb by the sight and could make no sense of it. Wolfram's hands clenched and unclenched but once, and though that was the only move he made, it reminded Genevieve forcefully of the compassion that had flooded her when first she touched him. She ached to go to him, even after all that had passed between them, but hesitated with the fear that he would turn her aside.

"Good sir, tell me if you will, what has happened here?" Odo hailed a shopkeeper bustling past with a cheerful air. The man wiped his brow and slanted a telling glance to the remains. Genevieve followed his glance and found her gaze snared by Wolfram's stillness yet again.

For one of the Order, this must be a chilling sight. Genevieve's heart wrenched sympathetically, though she doubted he would welcome any consolation from her. Truly all the cards were on the table betwixt them now, and she had not as yet the fortitude to risk being spurned.

But a man was he, she thought suddenly, and no less human than any other, regardless of the task he had fulfilled.

"The Temple 'tis, or mayhap I should say 'twas the Temple," the shopkeeper supplied gruffly. "Set to blaze 'twas, in the night after the arrests."

"The arrests of the knights of the Temple?" Odo asked, though indeed they all knew the answer. The shopkeeper nodded tersely and Genevieve fancied a shiver tripped across Wolfram's broad shoulders at the reminder.

"Aye. A sorry bit of business that was, but the seneschal would hear no protest. Orders from the king's own hand, he said, and naught was there to do but fulfill them."

"But they burned the Temple, as well?" Odo asked with politely expressed surprise. Genevieve was startled when the shopkeeper shook his burly head.

"Nay, 'twas not the seneschal responsible for that," he said. "'Twas some of the boys down at the tavern that night. Got to talking, they did, about the treasury of the Temple. How I hear it, the more ale in their bellies, the more convinced were they that they should claim its contents for themselves, seeing as the days of the Order were about to come to an end. 'Twas a cache of coin, after all, to which they had contributed through their tithes, and they saw it as no more than their due to reclaim it."

"And they burned the Temple for it?" Odo demanded with less well concealed incredulity. The shopkeeper shook his head once more, as though he too found the very idea dismaying.

"Nay, 'twas not like that. Seems as they sauntered on down to the Temple in the wee hours, but the sergeant at the gate did not see fit to admit them. A right-thinking man was he, to my mind, seeing as they were in such a state, but they threatened him and somehow a flint was struck. In the muddle that followed, the flame ended up somehow in the straw strewn about the Temple courtyard." The keeper spared the ruins a sad glance. "'Twas gone afore anyone was roused to douse the flames. Two days did it burn afore the rain washed out the last."

"And the 'boys' responsible?" Odo asked.

The shopkeeper's lips twisted wryly and he sighed once afore responding. "Seems as the seneschal was too busy to meddle in the affairs of the townsfolk that day, and now none can recall precisely who was where and when."

"So they escaped unscathed?" Genevieve interjected indignantly, unable to hold her tongue any longer. She knew not whence her anger issued, but it mattered naught, even if 'twas from sympathy for Wolfram's plight that she was outraged. Such a travesty of justice was inexcusable! The Order was esteemed, 'twas respected, 'twas under the jurisdiction of the Pope alone. Beyond belief 'twas that such an establishment could be razed by a mob.

The shopkeeper raised bushy eyebrows as he regarded her, his gaze steady. "Well it seems that that will be the way of it," he admitted softly.

An awkward silence settled over the troupe as they stared once more at the charred Temple, this recent revelation making the sight all the more horrifying.

"And the sergeant at the gate?" Wolfram asked hoarsely, his voice sounding curiously distant. In that instant, any vestige of doubt about his allegiance to the Order was swept from Genevieve's mind. Something about Wolfram's tone revealed him to her, and she knew full well that he was one of the brethren of the Order. And she guessed that his rank had been sergeant. Her heart twisted for him, but he kept his back to them all.

The shopkeeper slanted him an assessing glance, but Wolfram did not turn to face them. "I know not exactly," he confessed heavily, and Genevieve dreaded his next words. "Bodies there were found within once the flames had done their damage, and whispers there were of some of the men of the house fleeing town with naught but was on their backs."

This time Genevieve knew she did not imagine the shudder that swept over Wolfram's tall frame. Still it seemed that he could not turn away from the wreckage. The light faded around them and the perfectly typical evening quiet possessing the town seemed suddenly rather ominous. A few stray dry leaves scuttled down the street as the troupe watched Wolfram warily.

He moved not, though his companions grew restive.

The shopkeeper cleared his throat abruptly and seemed to look at the troupe for the first time. "Minstrels, are you?" he asked conversationally, with no hint of censure in his tone.

"Aye, that we are, and well in need of a suitable venue this night," Odo answered promptly. Genevieve ignored the purposeful undercurrent to his words, her entire being focused on Wolfram.

Alone he looked.

"Verily?" the shopkeeper asked, his words so remote to Genevieve that they might have come from another world. "A tavern have I, just down the way, and well would I welcome your entertainment this night. Naught can I offer you when all is said and done but a place afore the hearth, a hot bowl of soup and mayhap a bit of silver from the patrons."

The troupe twittered in excitement at the promise of shelter from the elements and Odo sketched a deep bow.

"Deeply honored would we be, sir, and well can you expect a fine show for your generosity."

The shopkeeper's eyes gleamed with mingled pride and pleasure. "Aye, a good while it has been since we have had the luck of entertainment. Hurry along, would you, for the night is growing cold. Just on the left 'tis, you cannot miss it."

Odo nodded gratefully, and several of the members of the troupe called their thanks to the shopkeeper as he bustled away in the indicated direction. Some of the troupe skipped in his wake, some sauntered, Odo hesitated after taking a few steps to glance back to Wolfram and Genevieve. Plump white flakes of snow began to drift out of the deep indigo sky above, though Wolfram did not yet move.

Again, Genevieve was struck by how solitary he looked, his posture not unlike that of a lost child who knows none search for him. He said naught. Still he stood proudly, but there was an air of defeat about him that had not been there afore.

'Twas Genevieve who finally stepped forward to stand by his side. She waved Odo away and that man turned after the troupe with but a nod. Wolfram glanced not in her direction, even when she stood but a handspan away from him, but she knew full well that he was aware of her presence even so. She hesitated but a heartbeat, then reached down and folded his hand within hers. His fingers trembled, and she gripped his hand yet tighter as the weight of his pain rolled through her.

Aye, he was hurting sorely indeed. Genevieve did not dare close her eyes and surrender to the torment swirling within him, lest it overwhelm her and leave her naught with which to reassure him.

"'Tis gone," he whispered hoarsely. His voice was flat and toneless, tinged with disbelief and no small measure of defeat. "'Tis all gone."

"The Order will rebuild it, surely?" Genevieve asked, forcing a false brightness into her voice. Wolfram shook his head slowly, and when he turned to her, she knew not whether the pain in his eyes or the tears glistening there surprised her more.

"Nay," he whispered unevenly.

"What rank do you hold?" she asked quietly. Wolfram's gaze drifted over the ruins once more.

"A sergeant am I," he admitted. "But now the Order to which I am pledged is gone."

Genevieve could not begin to imagine what such a passing might mean to him. A lone tear spilled over his cheek and splashed onto their entwined hands, leaving Genevieve aching with the rawness of his pain. All that he knew and relied upon had been swept away, though she could not imagine that such a powerful Order would not rise again from the ashes.

She reached up and laid one hand against his cheek. Wolfram glanced down to her, and she longed in that instant to gather him close. "'Twill be fine in the end," she murmured, unable to restrain herself from pressing a single kiss to his cheek. To her astonishment, he did not turn away. "Come with us to find some shelter this night. You will see that all will look brighter in the morn." Genevieve gave his hand a little tug, and he turned after her to follow her to the troupe.

Something altered in his manner when he looked away from the ruins, and Genevieve knew the very moment that the change occurred. He stood taller suddenly, as though long years of discipline had suddenly been recalled to him, and his grip grew firmer before he released her hand.

Genevieve thought he meant to stand alone, but 'twas not to be, for he folded her elbow into his resolute grip. Escorted her like a lady nobly born he did, and with that Genevieve knew he appreciated her few words, though she doubted he would ever say as much.

"My pledge to you yet stands," he murmured to her as they gained the entry to the tavern. Genevieve looked to him in surprise at his resolute tone, and his eyes burned with determination. "I vowed to see you safe. That the Order is gone changes naught, for I am a man of my word."

"Aye," Genevieve agreed weakly, unable to fathom his insistence. Though Wolfram might well be certain the Templars were doomed to fade from this earth, she was not in the least convinced that they would fail to triumph again.

Yet if he insisted on seeing her safe in the interim, she supposed she had no cause for complaint. 'Twas the least the man owed her, after all, though even that reasoning could not explain the curious way her stomach lurched when his gaze locked with hers. She stared up at him and fancied he smiled slightly. He opened the tavern door with a flourish she might have thought uncharacteristic, releasing a warm bevy of scents before ushering her into the tavern's redolent shadows.

Until Metz, then, she would enjoy his protection. She still held a dream of returning home somehow or in some way, but undoubtedly Genevieve would return there alone. She pushed her doubts aside and stepped into the welcoming warmth of the tavern.

Until Metz.

'Twas late that night afore Genevieve played, the tumblers having astounded the patrons, a mute conjurer having prompted chuckles from many a merry mouth and even Odo's clear voice having been heard. The crowd had thinned when Genevieve lifted her lute into her lap and bent over it to play.

All night she had sat pressed against Wolfram, and for the first time since the loss of her grandparents a year past, Genevieve had not felt so alone. Warm he was, the rumble of his rare chuckle enough to produce her own smile. The past meant naught to her this night—they were but two amid a troupe of twenty, all bent upon the same path. Wolfram hurt, and Genevieve knew that she had consoled him.

What threat was there after all to consoling a man pledged to a monastic order? Naught had she to risk by following her impulse, for no ill-begotten ideas could such a man have of her intent. And no doubt had Genevieve that as soon as they gained Metz, both Wolfram and Odo would abandon this curious conviction that they were safer together.

She would be alone then, as she never had been alone before, for she would not even have the drunken companionship of Alzeu. On this night, Genevieve could not chastise herself for counting her blessings, such as they were.

The music she summoned from her lute, as always, bore evidence of all these thoughts and feelings. It swirled with a richness Genevieve had never yet found. Though she heard the patrons fall silent in wonder, she could do naught but savor the fruit of her own hands, even as she marveled at its beauty.

She closed her eyes and rocked with the rhythm, letting the music take the tune where it would, her fingers naught but a means for it to gain its voice. The tune was cajoling, it soothed and eased, it spoke of gentle compassion and understanding, it uplifted and induced each and every one present to savor the sweetness of this night.

'Twas only after considerable time that Genevieve realized she played for Wolfram.

Her eyes opened and she looked to him before she could check her response, her fingers faltering not a whit on the strings. He gazed at her with a fixedness that made her heart skip a beat. In that enchanted moment, it seemed there was naught but the two of them in this smoky and crowded tavern.

The music surged forth as if to invite him closer, and his eyes blazed in the shadows with an intensity that made Genevieve shiver. Still she could not turn away. In some refuge of her mind, she knew this night would not pass without incident, yet she welcomed the revelation wholeheartedly. A glimmer there was within Wolfram's eyes that he had not permitted her to see before. Indeed Genevieve wondered whether any had glimpsed this flicker of longing within him.

A heat she found in the silver she had long thought cold, and Genevieve knew that the tentative dawning she had sensed within him had blossomed yet further. Wolfram's fettered heart had been unleashed, and with that knowledge, her own heart leapt in response.

Genevieve wanted to console him. She wanted there to be just the two of them this night. She wanted this moment when their gazes locked and all else faded to naught to endure as long as she could make it so.

Alone Genevieve would be within a matter of weeks. Pledged to his Order for life was Wolfram. And should their paths be destined to part, as Genevieve knew they must be, then she would have the passion of one more kiss to call her own.

She did not fool herself that Wolfram would ever abandon his vows for her, nor did she even expect him to return her regard. She but wanted to taste him again, to feel his lips pressed against hers, to feel the thump of his heart beneath her fingertips. So lost was she in the mists wrought by her own music that she did not think to question the fervor with which she wanted that kiss.

Wolfram was powerless against the allure of the lute that night.

Indeed, he had hoped Genevieve would not play, even as he wanted naught else, his emotions warring throughout the evening with unprecedented vigor. When Odo nodded and she picked up the lute lovingly, it had been almost a relief to have the matter resolved.

But then the sweetness had unfolded from her fingertips. The music made Wolfram ache as it never had before, but he could not even protest its invasion. Recollections were unleashed with an abandon he could not check.

'Twas the shock of seeing a Temple desecrated that had undone him. Faith had Wolfram nurtured all the way from Paris, even after seeing his brethren arrested. Faith had he cultivated within himself that the Order would rise up and survive this miscarriage of justice. Certainty had he built within himself that the king's misguided rule would be overturned, that the Pope would arrive triumphant and the Templars would ride again.

The burning of this Temple completely dismissed his conviction. Should both populace and king scorn the Order and the papacy not intervene, then the Order itself could not survive. The papacy's silence would condemn even those Temples outside France to fade away, as well. Other kings would act similarly once they knew no repercussion would come from Rome. 'Twas only a matter of time.

Everything to which Wolfram was pledged was gone. The conclusion was inescapable. It might well take some time for every structure to crumble, but no longer could he deny the truth before him.

No more Rule was there to guide Wolfram's life. No longer was he beholden to the will of the Master. No longer was his obedience expected or required. No more boundaries and restrictions were there upon him. Yet no more security was there, either. No more had Wolfram the certainty of three meals a day and meat thrice a week. No longer could he be sure of garments to warm his back and a horse beneath him when required.

The shock of change was simultaneously invigorating and terrifying. Wolfram knew not what he would do, where he would go, how he would earn his own keep. Should he pledge himself to another Order? Should he stay within the comfort of this troupe? He knew not, and indeed, the possibilities were so endless as to be impossible to count.

And the music did naught to soothe his thinking. It roused yet more emotion and, as a man used to making decisions dispassionately, Wolfram found the influx to be near overwhelming. He closed his eyes to the sting of smoke and dared himself to look within. He heard the pulse of his own heart in the forefront of the lute's siren's call and felt the heat of the blood coursing through his veins.

Alive he was, despite all the storms he had weathered in this life. A survivor he was, unlike the unfortunate sergeant in this town and mayhap those he had left behind. Wolfram was alive and unfettered, and that realization sent a curious feckless joy coursing through him.

He was alive! Wolfram recalled with sudden fierceness the sweet splendor of Genevieve's kiss. No more was the touch of a woman forbidden to him.

And something there was of this world he had not tasted. An act there was that was life-affirming beyond all else, and Wolfram had yet to claim that experience for his own. He burned for it now, as he never had before. Something there was that a man could not savor alone, and now, freed of his vows as he was and invigorated with the glory of life, Wolfram was free to sample of that feast.

He opened his eyes to find Genevieve's gaze upon him. Her eyes were wide and his breath caught at the certainty that he saw that same desire reflected there. His pulse quickened with the promise of her eyes.

Aye, this night Wolfram would know the fullness of mating. He imagined how Genevieve would writhe beneath him and his body responded with a vigor fit to make him dizzy. Genevieve flushed, as though she guessed his very thoughts, but she did not look away. Wolfram grinned, despite himself.

Aye, this night would well be one to remember, and a fitting start to his new life.

# Chapter Twelve

It seemed to Wolfram that the patrons would never leave.

He was restless, impatient with their dallying, even though he could well understand the appeal of Genevieve's playing. The music of the lute bolstered his resolve and lifted his spirits, convincing him as he watched her delicate fingers dance across the strings that his choice was both right and good.

Genevieve would be his this night. The very thought thickened him beyond belief, and he fidgeted impatiently.

Then, finally, the last of them filtered out into the night. There was a slight fluster of activity as those members of the troupe who had not already dozed off before the hearth found places to sleep.

"A garret is there, as well, that none is using this night," the keeper informed Odo. Clearly that man was well pleased with the benefit the troupe had brought his business on this wintry night. "'Tis cold up there, yet welcome you are to its privacy."

That word struck a welcome chord within Wolfram, and he fired a glance fraught with significance in Odo's direction. Odo caught his gaze and lifted a brow, though he asked naught afore he accepted. He nodded almost imperceptibly, and Wolfram knew in that instant that the loft would be his alone.

His and Genevieve's.

Wolfram turned to her again, watching hungrily as she loosened the lute's taut strings, as was her habit. Her fingers danced over the instrument in a fleeting caress, and he imagined her small hands fluttering across his skin in much the same manner. Wolfram swallowed carefully just as Genevieve glanced up and their gazes collided.

He could not look away. Neither could he take a breath.

Genevieve appeared struck motionless, as well. Her lips parted slightly, her eyes widened in some measure of surprise, but she did not move away. Wolfram's heart hammered in his ears and he dared to take a bold step forward.

Genevieve's gaze never wavered.

Blind to those few still around him, Wolfram took another step, then another, each easier than the last, until he stood directly before her. Genevieve stared up at him mutely, the soft expression in her eyes enough to set his very flesh to burning.

Would she truly permit this familiarity? What if she spurned him? What if she turned aside? What if she had no desire to mate with him?

He recalled the sweet press of her lips on his, and an increasingly familiar ache was launched within him at the very promise of tasting her once more. Stunned by his own audacity and knowing he was on unfamiliar ground, Wolfram inhaled sharply and dared to offer Genevieve his hand.

To his complete astonishment, she smiled. Then she slipped her hand into his and rose to her feet so that they stood toe-to-toe. Wolfram did not dare to breathe. He froze in place, uncertain what she intended to do.

Genevieve stretched to her toes, laid her other hand flat on his chest and brushed her lips across his. Wolfram was certain his heart stopped. She pulled back slightly to eye his response, and he imagined she saw the wonder in his eyes, for she smiled affectionately.

Then she cupped his jaw in her delicate little hands, leaned against him so that he was certain he could feel her beaded nipples and kissed him full on the lips.

She agreed! The tavern spun giddily about Wolfram at the realization. He knew not how she had guessed his intent, but he cared naught.

Blood rushed in his ears, and he closed his eyes, his entire world focused on the tempting softness of Genevieve. Wolfram's hands found the neat indent of her waist and he lifted her against him, willing her to understand that 'twas no small thing he desired of her. He wanted her to feel his arousal and harbor no doubts of his intent.

Wolfram inclined his head slightly, that he might sample her more fully, and Genevieve opened her mouth to his in surrender. Her fingers tangled in his hair and she moaned gently beneath his embrace, the smothered sound making desire roar unchecked within him.

She desired him! Wolfram lifted Genevieve yet higher and cradled her against his chest as his kiss deepened. He wanted to sample every bit of her flesh, he wanted to know her body as well as he knew his own, he wanted to be intimate with her as he had never been with another being in his life. He wanted to share and be shared, he wanted to explore and be explored, and in that heady instant, he wanted to take a lifetime to discover all of her.

Wolfram nuzzled her neck, loving the way she gasped against his throat, everything masculine within him savoring how she strained against him. His woman she would be this night. He burrowed his nose beneath the neckline of her kirtle and smelled the intoxicatingly feminine scent of her skin, and his passion redoubled.

The fire crackled and Wolfram abruptly recalled their circumstances. He reluctantly lifted his lips from Genevieve's, his heart thumping at the way she collapsed dreamily against him. Slowly she opened her eyes, and he caught his breath when she smiled up at him as though he was the only man in the world.

Privacy they needed in this moment of moments.

"The garret," Wolfram whispered. She hesitated and he feared for a heartbeat that she would decline, but then she impaled him with that emerald regard. A thrill ran through him when Genevieve smiled a secretive smile and nodded hastily.

"Aye," she breathed, and he could not believe that Dame Fortune would smile so upon him. Too much 'twas that they should be of one accord in this matter. He took her hand, still disbelieving, but she took her lute in the other hand matter-of-factly and accompanied him without protest.

The weight of her hand in his filled Wolfram with a protective pride, an urge to see her safe and warm, to see her cherished this night that she might recall the memory with favor. This night he would leave Genevieve with naught to regret.

Though his ears burned at the teasing catcalls that followed them, Wolfram did not look back.

When they gained the second floor, naught but the slow breathing of the sleeping patrons filled Wolfram's ears. The cool darkness enfolded them in its embrace, and he regretted not bringing a lantern. He found the second set of stairs with his hand, their span much narrower than those from the first floor, and led Genevieve to their sanctuary.

'Twas cold in truth here, as the keeper had warned, for the shutters on the small windows at either end of the loft were poorly fitted. The ethereal light from the falling snow filtered around their edges and granted enough light to see shadows and silhouettes. The roof was steeply pitched, and the air was redolent with the scent of the fresh wooden casks stacked to either side.

Wolfram could smell the hops from the beer stored within them as his awareness of the woman behind him redoubled. Uncertainty assailed him now that they were alone once more. Only under the ridgepole itself could he stand, and he straightened there, turning to confront Genevieve.

She eyed him for a long moment, then her gaze flicked away and back. "Blankets there are here," she murmured quietly as though fearing to awaken someone.

Her voice wavered slightly, that minuscule sign of her own uncertainty the only reassurance Wolfram needed. He could well enough be strong for her—in fact, he owed her naught less in this moment.

He reached down and lifted her lute from her grasp, surprised yet again at how readily she released it to him. Wolfram laid the instrument carefully aside atop the casks and tucked the warmth of Genevieve against his side.

She resisted not at all. One arm around her shoulders, he touched her chin with the fingertips of his other hand and tilted her face to his. She watched him, the very sight of her trust flooding him with awe. Wolfram brushed one fingertip across the petal-softness of her lips, and Genevieve's lashes fluttered closed even as she released a ragged little sigh.

She desired him. Wolfram needed naught else to restore his confidence.

"Come to bed, Genevieve," he whispered. She opened her eyes languidly, and her unexpectedly intense green gaze locked with his once more.

"Aye, Wolfram," she murmured, a heat burgeoning in her expression as she scanned his features and evidently found something she sought there. "If you will come with me."

Wolfram smiled. "'Tis too cold this night to leave a lady to sleep alone," he answered. Genevieve smiled in return, her smile a curious mingling of shyness and audacity that made his heart pound in his ears.

"Well did I suspect you were a gentleman," she breathed. Wolfram chuckled despite himself and pulled her closer.

"I would not disappoint, milady," he promised against her lips.

"Nay." Her hands slipped around his neck, their feather-light touch making Wolfram shiver deep inside.

He lifted her against his chest and kissed her gently, reassuringly, with all the wonder he felt for her and the possibility of this night. She responded with an ardor unexpected that fired his own desire anew. Naught could he think of but Genevieve.

Wolfram carried her to the blankets laid atop a pallet, his fingers urging her laces open before they even reached the wool. Genevieve confounded him by nibbling on his ear in a most disconcerting manner, her hands roving over him hungrily. Now that she had surrendered to the moment, well it seemed that she would embrace it with vigor. The very idea launched Wolfram's desire yet higher.

The side laces on her kirtle gave way unexpectedly and he pushed the garment over her shoulders with ease. Her loose chemise followed suit with lightning speed, and the sight of her creamy flesh was enough to make him burst his chausses. Wolfram caught his breath as he hesitated and ran one hand cautiously over the warm satin of her shoulder. So soft she was, so delicate, and his resolve faltered slightly.

What if he should hurt her? As if sensing his uncertainty, Genevieve slipped into his lap, her hands locking around his neck with a fervor that reminded Wolfram unaccountably of her strength.

"I want you," she whispered, her breath tickling his ear. Wolfram glanced down at her, reassured by her smile. "I want to *know,*" she added emphatically. So parallel was her desire to his own that Wolfram could not deny her. That she was a virgin like him made the moment all the more special, yet less intimidating, for they both would be feeling their way.

"As do I," he murmured. Before she could respond, Wolfram placed his hands on her shoulders and nudged her kirtle and chemise further. She moved not, so as not to hinder him though he felt her quiver within his grip. The garments slipped lower with agonizing speed, revealing her upper arms, the ripe curve of her breast. The chemise caught on the pert peaks of her breasts. Wolfram swallowed slowly, then reached out to lift the cloth and reveal the dusky nipples beneath.

Hard they were, and contracted tightly, like two dark raspberries. She caught her breath as the cold air impacted them, and he watched the responding motion of her breasts with fascination. Wolfram bracketed Genevieve's ribs with his hands, marveling at how large his hands looked upon her milky flesh, and urged the garments to her waist. Genevieve pulled her wrists free, and when Wolfram hesitated, she met his eyes steadily and placed her hands on his.

Their fingers entwined, Genevieve deliberately rose to her knees. She pushed down, and together they eased the garments over her hips to reveal her creamy perfection to Wolfram's hungry gaze. She was smooth and supple, unblemished and as perfect as some ancient pagan goddess born fully with the dawn. Wolfram slid his hands wonderingly over her warmth, that juncture at the top of her thighs, with its tangle of dark hair, tempting him with the promise of what would come.

He pulled her closer, and Genevieve tumbled willingly into his lap, her hair spilling about them in a dark cloud. Their lips met seemingly of their own accord and locked together. He dared to touch his tongue to hers, and Genevieve arched toward him with another of those delicious moans that were his to swallow. Emboldened by her response, Wolfram slipped his fingers up her thigh. The tangle of wiry hair presented no barrier to his exploring fingers, and Genevieve parted her legs in invitation.

Wolfram needed no further urging. His fingers slipped into that secret sanctuary, everything surging within him at the slick dampness he found there. Genevieve cried out with pleasure, and Wolfram felt suddenly as powerful and invincible as a young god himself.

He caressed her and she writhed. Fascinated with her response to him, he explored her soft contours and noted what seemed to please her best. He tickled and cajoled as he watched her squirm with pleasure. This he could give her. This they could share. He bent to nuzzle her ear, and the flurry of his breath sent her shivering.

Undaunted, Wolfram laved her earlobe with the tip of his tongue. Genevieve gasped. He tasted the soft skin under her jaw. She arched her neck back to grant him access, even as she moaned. He slipped his arm beneath her and let his hand close around the weight of her breast. Wolfram had to close his eyes at the flood of tenderness let loose within him as he cradled her weight against him.

Never had he imagined he was missing so much. This marvel of a woman was his to love this night. He feared in that instant that he dreamed, but Genevieve's tongue darted daringly into his mouth and proved his fears groundless. His fingers and thumb kneaded the beaded point of her nipple, his other hand echoing the movement to gently lock around the pearl between her thighs.

Genevieve cried out.

She moved in a frenzy as his fingers danced, and Wolfram knew the heat built within her as it had built within him that long-past night. He wanted her to feel that burst of sensation, he wanted to be the one to cast her over the edge as she had cast him. His mind filled with the memory of the weight of her hand falling upon him and the resulting tingle that had shot through him.

He wanted to give her that this night. And he would.

"Wolfram," she whispered. She grasped at his shoulders, her fingers digging into his flesh even through his shirt.

"Follow it," he counseled quietly, not certain where the words came from. "Safe you are with me." A glow lit in her magnificent eyes at that, and she locked her arms trustingly around his neck. The feel of her tongue in his ear was enough to send Wolfram bursting from his chausses. Her small hands tore desperately at his clothes even as she quivered beneath his touch.

"Wolfram, I want to feel your skin," she murmured urgently, but he would grant her no quarter. He slipped one finger into her and her eyes widened abruptly, her hands falling still within his shirt. A quiver shook her from head to toe and her body clenched around his finger with a strength that made Wolfram dizzy. He hauled her close and kissed her with savage intensity, but she met him touch for touch, quaking with her release all the while.

When her shivers had passed, Genevieve reached purposefully for the lace on Wolfram's chausses. He felt himself engorge yet further, but watched powerlessly as her nimble fingers made short work of the binding. She tugged at his tabard and shirt impatiently and spared him a glance so filled with frustration that had he not been so enflamed, he might well have laughed.

"I want you nude," she whispered fervently. The ardor burning in her gaze had Wolfram complying with nary another thought. He cast aside the tabard and shirt, hauled off his boots and chausses with economical movements.

Wolfram had not even the chance to return to the makeshift bed afore Genevieve attacked him. Her bare breasts were against his chest, her arms were around his neck, the unfathomable softness of her stomach was pressed against his arousal. She rolled her hips against him and kissed him with abandon.

Wolfram was nearly lost. He locked his hands around her waist and they fell together to the pallet once more. Dizzy he was with the scent of her skin and the taste of her lips, but Genevieve wriggled atop him. Her knees were on either side of his chest before he could question her move. Then her warm dampness was atop his arousal and he could think of naught but having her.

Wolfram cupped Genevieve's buttocks in his hands and lifted her that he might slide within her. The collision with her tender spot left her gasping and she collapsed against him long enough for him to roll her to her back. Her eyes flew open as her knees locked around his waist, and Wolfram knew in that moment that she would match his passion.

The very thought sent him surging into her velvet heat. Genevieve writhed in a manner fit to drive him mad with desire. Hot she was, soft and tight, and when she moved, he was certain he had never felt such pleasure in his life. The pulse quickened within him, even as he hoped he could prolong this ecstatic moment.

When Genevieve's eyes met his with mischievous sensuality, Wolfram wondered how he had ever imagined he could resist this woman. She speared her fingers though his hair and hauled his head down for a heart-stopping kiss, and Wolfram knew he could last no longer.

He captured her delicate hands within his and stretched her out long beneath him. She locked her ankles behind his waist and arched to meet his thrusts. The heat that could not be denied rose unchecked within him. Wolfram locked his lips over hers in a demanding kiss and swallowed her cry of release in the same moment that Genevieve swallowed his own.

'Twas much later, when Genevieve rolled away from him sleepily, that the scales were ruthlessly torn away from his eyes and Wolfram saw the magnitude of his error.

Genevieve's hair fell away from her shoulder in a dark cascade, revealing to Wolfram's entranced gaze a port-wine birthmark. He blinked, but the mark remained. Graced one delicate shoulder blade it did, and its very shape sent a chill through his heart.

'Twas a cross. A cross over her heart. Wolfram propped himself up on one elbow to check, but his vision had told no lies.

'Twas the mark of the guardians of the Grail.

Wolfram's mouth went dry. Any doubt he might have harbored about the truth of Odo's tale deserted him in the span of a single heartbeat. Convinced his eyes must be deceiving him, he leaned closer and peered at the mark. He ran his fingertips across it, and Genevieve purred sleepily. No counterfeit was this.

Genevieve was the last guardian of the Grail. Could this mean that all else Odo had declared was true? Wolfram frowned as he chased the fragments of the chanson through his mind. Had Odo not declared the Templars to be guardians of the family? Wolfram had granted little credence to the idea when first he heard it, but as he eyed Genevieve's mark, he wondered if that was true, as well.

He stared at her sleep-washed visage in wonder. If 'twas true, 'twas a travesty fit to strike horror into his heart that he, a Templar, had been the one to dispatch Alzeu.

Yet that was not the worst of it. Wolfram inhaled sharply. To err out of ignorance was one matter, but passion had led Wolfram down a dark path that had led to betraying Genevieve a second time.

Genevieve's virginity had Wolfram stolen in search of the satisfaction of his own base desire. Surely he could not have erred more deeply than this had he tried. He had betrayed the Order and its pledge yet again. Indeed, he was losing count of the incidences of his own faithlessness.

Such a knave as he should not be permitted to draw breath. Clearly his word—nay, worse, his oath—was worth naught these days.

'Twas this he had to show for permitting the spell of the lute's tune to unlock the secret recesses of his heart. Long had he lived without the luxury of emotion, and too late Wolfram wished he had not turned his back upon that path.

Some stirring of tender feelings had prompted him to a betrayal that could not be brushed aside. He cursed the moment that he chose to ignore the lesson his life had already taught him. Naught was there of merit in tender feelings, and in the predawn greyness Wolfram decided he had best cling tenaciously to that belief for the rest of his days.

Genevieve awoke to fine clear sunlight spilling through the sole window in the loft. The air was warm, the light as crystalline and bright as it could only be when the ground was covered with fresh snow. No doubt had she that the sky was a delicately hued blue and that the air was crisp-edged with cold. The weight of Wolfram's arm was locked around her waist and the scent of his skin deluged her senses. Genevieve snuggled deeper beneath the coverlet with satisfaction and curled against Wolfram's warmth, more than content with the state of her world.

She opened her eyes and watched the light glint off his fair hair, realizing only when she met his eyes that he, too, was awake.

"I meant only to keep you warm," he said with unnecessary haste. He stirred, but Genevieve had no intent of letting him move away. She smiled and locked her arms around his neck, her smile widening when he caught his breath at the press of her breasts against him. She pressed a kiss to his stubble-roughened cheek, loving the abrasion of his chest hair against her nipples. It seemed he stiffened, as though he might abandon the bed, but no place had shyness betwixt the two of them now.

'Twas when her lips brushed his jaw that Genevieve suddenly realized why she had not been able to plunge the dagger into Wolfram's heart.

"I love you," she whispered in awe.

But one platinum moment had she to recognize and savor the unexpected truth before Wolfram abruptly shoved her away. Gone from her side he was in a flash and hauling on his chausses purposefully.

"I said that I loved you," Genevieve repeated slowly, stunned into silence by the glance of loathing Wolfram fired in her direction.

"I *heard* well enough what you said," he muttered.

Indeed, this was hardly the response Genevieve had expected from her confession. She swallowed her disappointment, certain there must be some small misunderstanding at work. Mayhap he feared she meant to make him break his vows.

Determined to give Wolfram the benefit of the doubt, Genevieve sat up in their rumpled bed. Suddenly shy despite all that had passed between them, she carefully held the linens over her bare breasts and was acutely aware of the tangle of her hair hanging down her back.

"And naught have you to say in return?" she prompted with a feigned casual air. Wolfram shot her another of those ferocious glances, then tugged his shirt over his shoulders.

"I do not love you, if those are the words you seek from me," he said tersely.

Genevieve caught her breath as his barb hit its mark, but Wolfram had already turned away in pursuit of his boots. Her mouth went dry, but Genevieve knew she could not let the matter be. His explanation did she need to hear, regardless of how deep the wound might cut.

"Why then did you couple with me?" she forced herself to ask.

Wolfram shot her a wry glance. "Because your form tempts me," he said cuttingly. Genevieve knew he must be able to see the blood draining from her face. "Because I wanted you and you wanted me. Because 'twas an experience I wanted to taste."

Nay. He lied, she thought wildly. None could feign the wonder that had lit Wolfram's eyes when he touched her the night afore. None could pretend as skillfully as that, for Genevieve knew 'twas more than the pleasure of the flesh that had made him moan against her throat.

But still his denial stung.

Genevieve licked her lips cautiously before she spoke. "So, you have no regard for me at all?" she asked, astonished that she could sound so calm.

Wolfram snorted with disgust. "No idea have I why you must complicate something simple with a confession that means naught."

"Naught?" Genevieve asked, her anger rising slowly to the fore. "How can you say such a thing? 'Tis love that is the gift making our time together so sweet, whether you would acknowledge the truth or not."

"Nay, Genevieve," Wolfram corrected in a low voice that told her he was serious beyond measure. "'Tis pleasure alone that makes your flesh sing with mine." As if to demonstrate his point, he leaned down and ran one hand over her skin. Despite her determination to resist him, Gene-vieve was powerless to keep herself from arching toward the weight of his fingers.

"You see?" he demanded with a triumphant air that made shame rise within her. "Animals and men both please their mates in this way, but men alone would sully the simplicity of it all with a confession of love. Make no mistake—'tis love that prompts the scorpion's sting, not that rouses the heat beneath your skin. A false sweetness love promises, for 'tis dishonest in nature, and wise is the man or woman who avoids its trap."

The man protested too strongly to be believed. Genevieve propped herself up on her elbows and regarded Wolfram skeptically as he tugged on his boots. Truly these words could not be falling from the lips of the man who had just loved her with such abandon.

She refused to believe it.

"Wolfram, you cannot have known of love if you believe thus," she whispered in a low voice.

But Wolfram's laugh was harsh, and Genevieve liked not the sardonic twist of his lips.

"Of love I know more than I would like to," he said acidly. Genevieve left the bed and went to his side as she regarded him quizzically. No sense did his assertion make. Although Genevieve had intended to touch Wolfram, once she was beside him and felt the anger emanating from him, she could not. She clutched the blanket to her chest and leaned closer.

"How can you speak thus?" she asked. "I love you and I share myself with you because of that." She reached out tentatively and, when he did not move away, ran one hand over his shoulder.

'Twas then Genevieve felt the lingering chill within him. No longer did she question this insight she seemed to have of his thoughts when she touched him, for natural it seemed to Genevieve that there should be such a link betwixt herself and the man she loved. Hurt Wolfram had been, and well she could feel that that scar yet troubled him. That was at root here, and no more than that. He feared to be hurt again.

Well enough could she understand his resistance then, and she was certain 'twas just a resistance to admitting the truth.

"Tell me the tale of it, Wolfram," Genevieve whispered urgently. No other way was there to dismiss his fears than to talk about them. Mayhap if Wolfram told her, Genevieve would better understand the nature of his fears. He looked startled at the very idea, and Genevieve pressed herself against him, that she might encourage his confidence.

"Tell me your tale of love and I shall tell you mine," she suggested impulsively. "And in the end, we shall decide together which tale speaks of the stronger truth."

Wolfram held her gaze for a long moment, the expression in his silver eyes inscrutable.

"You do not want to hear my tale," he said accusingly, though she heard the waver of uncertainty in his tone.

"Aye, I do," she assured him solemnly. He held her gaze silently for a long moment, then cleared his throat and glanced away with a frown. He took a step away from her, but Genevieve was content to grant him his distance in exchange for the truth.

"'Tis your lute that starts the trouble," Wolfram began haltingly, though his voice seemed to warm quickly to the confession once it was begun. "For it recalls me to my childhood and the sweet cocoon of what my mother called her love." He paused again and glanced to her skeptically, but Genevieve nodded emphatically.

"Tell me," she urged. Wolfram propped his hands on his hips and stared at the floor.

"No fleeting golden moment were those years, for my mother was sweet of disposition, gentle and kind, and she lavished her attention upon me. 'Twas she who played the lute, though I fancy her skill was not as great as yours, still she loved the music and played with a passion that could not

be denied.'' He swallowed, the gesture making Genevieve
ache with the price this confession extorted from him.

''Loved her I did, with all my heart and soul.'' Wolfram
cleared his throat. Genevieve knew she did not imagine the
tear that glinted in his eye. When she might have touched
him, he moved farther out of her range, though whether by
accident or design, she could not say.

''So implicitly did I trust my mother, that never did I
doubt her intent that cold night that she took my hand in
hers and led me into town. Late 'twas and the windows were
shuttered against the night, a light flurry of snow falling on
the silent streets. Yet never did I even question the oddity of
our being out at such an hour.

''She took me to the tower where the bell tolled the hours
and took my hands in hers. Tears there were in her eyes, and
I could think of naught but doing as she bade me, that she
might not cry. She had to leave for a time, but I was to wait
in this place for her. Should a man open the door, I was instructed to give to him the lump of salt she entrusted me
with. My mother bade me behave and I vowed fervently to
do so, never dreaming the import of what she did that night.
She kissed my cheeks, and not only the softness of her flesh
brushed against mine, but the damp trickle of her tears.

''And so I stood, cradling the precious lump of salt in my
hands and watched my mother stride away in the falling
snow. She turned a corner but never looked back. Then I
was alone.''

Wolfram looked down at his hands, and Genevieve
imagined some vestige of that frightened boy yet lingered in
his troubled frown. She longed to touch him, though she
knew he would tolerate naught from her in this moment.

Indeed, it seemed he had been ill-used.

''What of your sire?'' she prompted quietly, certain there
had to be a ray of hope somewhere within the tale. Wolfram fired her a glance that spoke volumes.

''Never did I know him,'' he confessed thickly, and Genevieve heard the echo of his shame. A bastard had Wol-

fram been, and she ached to ease the pain of his heritage. He avoided her gaze, though, and cleared the thickness in his throat once more before he continued.

"Eventually a man did open the door behind me, though I was chilled through to the bone by that time. 'Twas dark as pitch above, the snow glowing faintly with its own light as it fell and drifted about me, the cold working its way right to my bones. I offered him the salt as bidden and he took the lump solemnly. His eyes were kind, I well recall, and his face etched with more wrinkles than I had ever imagined skin might sport. He laid one hand on my head and led me into the monastery.

"For 'twas at the monastery my mother abandoned me that night. With naught but a lump of salt and nary a farewell, she entrusted me to their care forevermore. Well do I recall telling the trio of old monks who bathed me and fed me warm soup that I but awaited my mother. Still can I see the look they exchanged, those three, at my youthful confidence. 'Twas in that moment that I knew deep within my soul that my mother would never return.

"I waited, though, determined to ignore the truth that resonated within me. I waited, and for a time I pined. I watched and listened like some lapdog deprived of its owner's companionship. She never came. Fanciful stories I composed, as children are wont to do, that she had been abducted by troublemakers and her return delayed, that the monastery moved mysteriously during the night, that none who left its gates might find it twice, that she lay ill somewhere crying plaintively for me."

Wolfram paused and his lips thinned to a grim line. "But all the time I knew that she was gone." He blinked away what might have been a solitary tear and his voice became suddenly more purposeful.

"Years passed and even the most stubborn corner of my mind was forced to admit that she had never intended to return. The monks offered me the opportunity to be a novice and potentially join their ranks. Not all oblates stayed and certainly not all abandoned there were invited to do so. A home I had with the monks, and though 'twas humble, 'twas the only home I had. Naught of love did anyone promise or expect, no whimsy was spun to tug at one's heartstrings. Poverty, chastity, obedience and hard work were a small price to pay for a life I could understand and terms I could accept. 'Twas there I stayed until I requested admission to the Order of the Templars.''

Silence reigned between them as Genevieve absorbed what he had said, then she lifted her gaze to meet Wolfram's. '' 'Twas then you barricaded your heart against all.'' He flushed at her softly spoken accusation, but shook his head all the same.

''Nay, 'twas long before that I knew its urgings could not be trusted,'' he said with a vehemence that disturbed her. '' 'Twas on that stoop, when I felt the cold ease into my bones and the salt crumble in my hand, that I knew I had been ill-used. Alone we all are, Genevieve, alone we arrive in this world and alone we depart. 'Tis best to rely on oneself, for 'tis only a matter of time before another will show betrayal.''

Genevieve's mouth dropped open in surprise. ''Surely you cannot believe that I would betray you?'' she asked in astonishment. Wolfram did not appear shaken by the question, which did naught to reassure her. He returned her regard for a long, silent moment, then his gaze danced over her features as though he assessed her very soul.

'' 'Tis only a matter of time,'' he murmured. His eyes met hers again and he shook his head, as if she were a fool not to see the truth so evidently displayed.

Genevieve bounded to her feet and snatched her chemise and kirtle from the floor. She hauled the garments viciously over her head, yet Wolfram moved naught to pursue her. Tears rose to blur her vision that he should think so little of her, but she spun angrily to confront him.

''Naught do you know of what is right and true in this world,'' she told him hotly. ''*I love you!* No small thing is this, but naught does it mean when I tell you so. A boor you are of the worst order, and a knave, to insult me with your certainty that I would betray the man I love."

"Indeed?" Wolfram asked mildly, but the avidity of his gaze revealed his intensity. He folded his arms across his bare chest and arched a brow high. "You do not believe that you would betray me under any circumstance? That you would never choose your welfare over my own? That you would never make a choice to my detriment? Illogical that would be, Genevieve."

"Aye, illogical 'twould be, but that is the price of love," Genevieve snapped in return. "Illogical 'tis that I love you at all. Of course I would not betray you, not under any circumstance. 'Tis rude beyond compare of you to even imagine such a thing, let alone openly accuse me of it."

Her tears threatened to spill, but still she would not back down from him. "How could you poison this night for me?" she demanded urgently. "My virginity did I grant you, and that gift I did give out of love alone. How can you turn my love aside?" This last was more a wail than an entreaty, yet Genevieve saw she had stirred Wolfram naught.

He regarded her solemnly, then glanced down at his hands.

"What if you had to choose between your lute and me, Genevieve?" he asked silkily. "What if you could have but one or the other by your side? Which would you choose?"

The answer Genevieve wanted to grant Wolfram rose swift and sure to her lips, but then she met his questioning gaze and her response froze within her throat. The truth she owed him, not some easy promise that might not be kept, and once she paused to consider the matter, the choice was less readily made.

Her lute had always been her life. Mad she would go without it, yet Wolfram gave her a strength she could find nowhere else.

She could afford to be without neither of them.

Wolfram's steady silver gaze revealed his awareness of her quandary, and in that moment, Genevieve hated his perceptiveness with all her heart and soul. "Never shall I have to choose!" she cried in frustration. Wolfram—curse him—smiled, though his smile might well have been mistaken for a grimace of pain.

"You see?" he asked under his breath.

Genevieve could not bear to look at him. She could not tolerate being in the same room with his bitterness. Impossible he was! Unthinkable that she would ever have to choose!

And, curse him, he was right.

"Indeed I see, as only a deceiver in his own right could show me the truth." She spat the words out, wanting only to hurt him as he had hurt her. Wolfram clenched his lips, but did not block her course, so Genevieve plunged onward. "No need is there to ask whether you would betray me for some objective of your own, for already have I seen the work of your hand. Did you not strike my only brother dead?"

Wolfram sighed and crossed his arms over his chest, his expression wary. "Had it not been me, it would have been another who dispatched Alzeu. A fool he was for talking so brashly of his intent, and I, at least, saw him pass quickly and without pain."

"Oho!" Genevieve cried. "So, I should be *grateful* to you for your mastery of your despicable task!" She spat on the floorboards directly before his feet but Wolfram moved naught. "Take that for your skill! 'Tis your own fault that I am destitute and far from home! 'Tis your fault that my only loving kin is gone and your fault that I was revealed in Paris! 'Tis your fault that I erred so seriously and granted my heart where 'twas undeserved!"

Her store of accusations depleted, Genevieve glared at the resolutely silent Wolfram. He cleared his throat, but his silver gaze never wavered from hers.

"Naught is there that I can do to repay you for the untimely loss of your maidenhead," he said carefully. His very words muted Genevieve and prompted an awkward lump to rise in her throat. Certain she was that she would not like whatever 'twas he would say next. "But you may indeed rest assured that my hand is pledged to ensuring your welfare."

The words cut more deeply than Genevieve might have imagined possible, even though she had expected them. Wolfram cared naught for her, and he was telling her clearly. Their night that she had thought so wondrous meant naught to him.

Genevieve had been a fool. Yet again her impulsiveness had led her astray.

"More do I want from you than your protection," she said. Tears rose to blur her vision, though she fought against them stubbornly. Through the mist of her tears, she saw Wolfram shake his head firmly.

"My pledge is all I will grant you," he said, so evenly that she loathed the very sight of him. Impossible 'twas to reconcile this dispassionate warrior with the man who had coaxed her to such heights of pleasure just hours before.

"Nay!" Genevieve cried, as angry with herself for her misplaced loyalty as with Wolfram. "Then I will have naught from you at all!"

Genevieve spun on her heel and stalked from the room before Wolfram could say anything else. She stamped down the stairs, a pain launched within her when he did not even bother to give pursuit.

It helped naught that his words had changed little of her feelings.

Still she loved Wolfram. Still she ached to show him that her love would not betray his heart. Wolfram was closed to her, resistant, though indeed she prayed he might hold her in high regard within some secret corner of his own heart.

But Genevieve knew any dreams she harbored might be for naught, for she suspected that Wolfram would never change his mind. Hurt he had been, and still he bled from that old wound. Naught could she say to repair the damage.

She dashed at her falling tears with clumsy fingers. Yet still she loved him. That was the worst of it. Even knowing the truth could not sway her heart. Her longing rose in her throat as though it might choke her, and Genevieve could not imagine how she would live without Wolfram at her side. Come to depend upon him she had, as well as to love him, though all that meant naught to a man with his heart locked safely away.

She could not stop loving him, yet she could not reach him. Tears of powerlessness flowed unchecked down Genevieve's cheeks with the realization.

She had abandoned her heart to the care of a man who wanted it naught.

And there was naught that she could do to retrieve it.

# *Chapter Thirteen*

Genevieve ignored Wolfram for the next fortnight as the troupe traveled east again.

The cursed man appeared to be completely untroubled by her anger with him. Truly, her displeasure did naught to dissuade him from his pledged task. He remained stoic and steadfast by her side and seemed to take her avoidance of even the most mundane discussion perfectly in stride. He was close by her side at all times; she awoke and fell asleep with Wolfram in close proximity. His hand dropped to his dagger when they entered a new town, and when they did busk again, a local man was soon convinced to abandon any ideas he might have gained in watching Genevieve with unswerving interest.

Indeed, had she not known better, Genevieve might have mistaken Wolfram for a superbly trained hound.

No balm was it to her wounded pride that he clung tenaciously to the letter of his pledge to her. More from Wolfram she wanted and more she was clearly not to have. Her guardian and protector he seemed satisfied to be, and naught had he touched her since that night.

'Twas enough to make Genevieve grind her teeth in frustration. Indeed, had she had the strength for the task, she might cheerfully have wrung the man's neck with her bare hands. Denying the link between them, he was, and she longed to shout at him until he heard the truth.

But Wolfram had closed all avenues to his heart. Once again, he was the dispassionate mercenary whom she had spied leaning over her brother, and Genevieve despaired of ever seeing that tender side of him again.

And when Odo announced late one afternoon that the town on the horizon was Metz, a panic came to life deep within Genevieve. She glanced to Wolfram only to find his features impassive and his attention fixed on the approaching city walls.

To Metz he had suggested they travel. To Metz alone had she agreed to accompany him. Now that they were arrived, what was his plan? Did he intend to leave Genevieve to her own resources? Truly she had hoped to breach the defenses around his heart before this time. Metz stood just ahead and Genevieve, yet again, had not succeeded.

She knew not his intent and, to her dismay, the possibility of parting ways with Wolfram here troubled her so deeply that she could not hide her pain. No consolation was the certainty that her opinion mattered naught in this matter. Whatever Wolfram would do, she was convinced he would do, regardless of her feelings.

Unable to stop herself, Genevieve reached out and touched his arm. His gaze dropped to her hand as though he could not understand her gesture, his silver gaze fathomless when his eyes finally lifted to meet hers.

'Twas clear she had breached some unspoken agreement betwixt them. He would not even tolerate her touch.

Genevieve found herself murmuring an apology as her hand fell away. She averted her gaze as sorrow welled up fit to choke her, and eyed the city walls ahead. Metz. 'Twas here she would be abandoned to her own fate. Suddenly the air seemed much colder than it had just moments before, as the promise of the future Genevieve had nursed for a fortnight finally expired within the secret enclave of her heart.

Never had she felt so alone in all of her days.

* * *

'Twas the cold of the stone floor that awakened Wolfram the morning after their arrival in Metz.

Their first night here had been a successful one, and well it seemed that the troupe's skills had been highly appreciated by the tavern's patrons. Wolfram, having been granted the task of collecting all contributions, had been mildly surprised by the generosity of these folk as he counted the coin.

Mayhap they could play for a while here afore being forced to choose their next move. Wolfram certainly had no idea how or where to proceed from here. His plan had been solely to reach Metz, a town beyond the long reach of Philip, and he supposed he had not imagined they would make it. Certainly he had thought no farther than this.

Certainly he had not considered the import of his own roots in this town.

With a muffled groan, Wolfram rolled over to greet the chill of the winter morning and discovered that Odo had apparently planned farther than he.

The tavern was deserted.

Wolfram shoved to his knees in astonishment, relief flooding through him when he spied Genevieve. She slept curled in a ball like a small cat, her arm cradling her precious lute close to her belly. Evidently she was as unaware of the others' departure as he, and yet again, Wolfram was assailed by a curious sense of kinship with this woman.

But the fact remained that the troupe had vanished without a trace. Vaguely Wolfram had assumed that Genevieve would continue to travel safely with the troupe, though this changed matters. He scowled at the stone floor, knowing full well that he could not abandon Genevieve to find her own way.

Wolfram wondered unexpectedly if this might not have been part of Odo's plan. Suddenly the knowing looks that man had granted him over the past fortnight made an eerie sense, and Wolfram was seized by a need to prove his suspicions wrong.

The proprietor's cheery whistle carried to Wolfram's ears from the kitchen beyond. He pushed purposefully to his feet and ran one hand through his hair. Surely that man would know the way of things.

"The others?" The keeper asked with an arched brow. Wolfram nodded, but the man did not even look up from kneading the bread. The kitchen was warm and flooded with harsh winter sunlight, the smell of yeast making Wolfram's stomach churn hungrily. "Aye, gone they are, and that is a fact."

"Have you any idea where they went?" Wolfram asked. The stout man fired him a pointed glance filled with wariness of the world and its ways.

"Well it seems to me that you would know that yourself, should they desire your company," he remarked shrewdly. Wolfram shrugged and struggled to contrive some excuse. He struck what he hoped was a confidential manner.

"Truth be told, we have argued over Odo's awakening me after a late night afore," Wolfram said in a low companionable voice. He leaned on the table and managed to summon an easy smile for the watchful keeper. "Well do I imagine that Odo plays a jest upon me in return," he added. "A great trickster is Odo."

The keeper eyed him for a long moment, then turned back to his bread. "Mayhap 'tis so," he conceded, and Wolfram expected the truth to fall from his lips. "But in all honesty, I know not where they went. Left they did, quick as rabbits diving for cover." He shrugged, as if unable or uninterested in fathoming the thinking of actors and minstrels. "A pity in truth, for they turned fair coin for me last eve."

"But naught did they say of their destination?" Wolfram persisted. The man shook his head.

"Nay," he admitted, then snapped his floury fingers. "This there is," he declared in sudden recollection. The keeper dug in the pocket of his apron and retrieved a small sack, his fingers leaving traces of flour on the suede.

"Left it for you, that Odo did," he said and tossed the sack at Wolfram. "The tall fair one, he said, the one as says naught but watches all. I reckon that would be you." Wolfram caught it, and it jingled with the impact. His heart sank with this new evidence that Odo had indeed intended to leave him behind.

"And when did they leave?" he asked, expecting little in response.

"Oh, not long past now," the keeper said without hesitation. He cocked a finger at Wolfram, his thoughts clearly lagging behind the younger man's. "Well might you catch them afore they part the gates, you know, for they do but open them with the dawn. And after last night's snow, the gatekeeper might well be late in gaining their free passage."

A possibility 'twas, only, but a welcome one at that.

"I thank you for your aid," Wolfram said hastily. Mayhap he could yet catch Odo and dismiss his suspicions. Mayhap Odo had other intentions for Genevieve than to leave her in Wolfram's care. He dashed out into the frigid morning air.

The cold in his lungs awakened Wolfram in truth and made him consider his path indecisively for an instant. Genevieve slept behind, alone in the deserted tavern. Should Wolfram awaken her, they might well be too late. But should he find Odo, surely that man could be convinced to return for Genevieve. Or Wolfram could fetch her and catch up to Odo once his path was known.

Aye, he had little heart for stirring Genevieve from her slumber so early. His mind made up, Wolfram dashed down the street in pursuit of the troupe he had traveled with for near a month.

"Good morning, Genevieve de Pereille."

Genevieve stirred restlessly at the unfamiliar low voice so

close to her ear and frowned as she hesitated on the periphery of sleep.

"Rouse yourself, Mademoiselle de Pereille, for far have we to go this day."

Something was not right. The certainty troubled Genevieve and coaxed her to reluctantly awaken. She shivered as the chill of the morning air impressed itself upon her senses and rolled over, wincing at the ache in her bones.

She should have insisted on finding a pallet. The floor was no place for sleeping, even if one was as exhausted as she had been the night before. Indeed, she had become increasingly tired of late as Wolfram retreated further within his protective shell.

Genevieve sighed and forced her eyes open to greet the dawn.

The first thing she saw was an older man kneeling beside her. He smiled when her eyes opened and Genevieve scooted backward in shock.

She blinked, but the man and his confident smile remained. Her eyes widened and she frowned, certain this man could not be the officer of the Temple she had seen all those days past in Paris when she first heard Odo sing.

He arched a silver brow, and the dread that fired through Genevieve in response fed her unease. Only too well did she recall Wolfram's certainty that the Master of the Temple of Paris aimed to see her dead, and to have an officer of that same Temple before her seemed less than a positive portent.

The second thing Genevieve saw was that she was completely alone to face her new companion. The tavern was deserted. Her breath caught in her throat and she turned dazedly back to the man, sure she did not imagine the way his smile widened. Predatory he looked, and Genevieve liked it naught. She squirmed backward until she hit the wall and lifted her lute before her as though 'twould protect her from whatever his intent might be.

Her heart sank as the truth became clear to her. They had all left her alone to fend for herself. Curse Odo and Wolfram! They had not even had the audacity to say farewell.

Mayhap it mattered that little to them that they left her behind. Genevieve swallowed and blinked back her tears.

"Good morning," the man purred as he stood up. "You are Genevieve de Pereille, are you not?"

"Who desires to know?" Genevieve demanded by way of greeting, hating how uneven her voice sounded. Too much 'twas that a person should have to face so many surprises on awakening.

"Come to fetch you to the king's own court am I," the suave older man confided, and settled himself before her with ease. The pair of wolfhounds lingering behind him settled on their haunches as he relaxed, their eyes yet bright.

"Me?" she repeated in surprise.

The man before her nodded confidently. "Aye, you. Well it seems that Philip himself was intrigued by your skill with the lute."

The man lied, and Genevieve knew it well. Naught good could the king himself want with a provincial lutenist like herself.

"I ask you again for your name," Genevieve said tightly. The man smiled thinly, his bright gaze landing upon her once more.

"My name is not of import, though my post commands respect from men everywhere," he said with no small measure of pride. "Master of the Temple of Paris am I, confidant of kings and leader of bold knights." When Genevieve failed to appear impressed, he glanced about the tavern as though fearing to be overheard and leaned closer as he dropped his voice. "And a mercy 'tis that I arrived in time. Do you not know that that tall fair one you travel with, the Templar, is charged with ensuring your demise?"

"Nay," Genevieve insisted hotly. "Aided me, he did, when I might have been endangered. Were it not for his assistance, I should not have made it this far."

"Indeed? And how far have you made it? Little trouble did I have in finding you, and clever enough are you to see that that cannot be good fortune alone." The Master leaned yet closer, and his breath fanned Genevieve's cheek even as her eyes widened in disbelief. "Have you considered whether your benefactor might have been merely gaining your trust? Easier 'tis to lead one astray who trusts you implicitly."

Doubt hovered on the periphery of Genevieve's mind. Was this why Wolfram refused to open himself to her? Did he intend to betray her in the end? Did the Master of the Temple speak the truth? Instinctively Genevieve distrusted this one, but still his argument was persuasive.

The Master leaned closer. "Do you in truth believe that you can trust a man who so readily breaks his word?" he whispered. Genevieve's eyes widened and the Master nodded knowingly. "Aye, cast aside his oath to the Order like so much worthless chattel has this one, and I, for one, would be cautious in extending to him my trust."

Genevieve was not certain what to think. Everything Wolfram had told her was being twisted by the Master and she was not awake enough as yet to think clearly.

'Twas evident the Master intended to press his advantage. His eyes narrowed as he raised a confidential finger and his voice dropped once more to that intimate tone. "I do not mean to shock you, but your brother's demise was not a natural one. Did you know, Genevieve, that the same man who aids you now is the one who murdered Alzeu?"

Genevieve swallowed but did not respond. She eyed the Master carefully as he warmed to his tale.

"An assassin, he is," he continued, his eyes gleaming with a sincerity she might have trusted had she known less of the matter. "As soon as I heard the whisper that this foul man intended to dispatch you, as well, I rode out in pursuit." His words fell more quickly as he warmed to his theme. "Mercifully, the dogs found the trail despite the snow, for it seems I have found you in the very nick of time. We must escape from this tavern afore he returns to fulfill his scheme. Evident 'tis that he has finally shaken that troupe of minstrels with some far-fetched tale and will return to do his worst."

The Master pushed to his feet and offered Genevieve his hand imperiously. She stared at his fingers for a moment and frowned.

Genevieve supposed a woman of sense would choose the path that would ensure her own safety. Her companions had abandoned her. 'Twas clear Wolfram had not only spurned her but left her to her own resources. She eyed the Master, and his lips drew into a hard line at her indecision.

Genevieve had always followed impulse and could do no less now.

"I do not believe you," she whispered, and the Master's eyes turned cold.

"It matters naught what you believe," he declared. His hand fell to the hilt of his dagger and he snapped his fingers imperiously. Too late Genevieve considered the possibility that he was not alone. The stamp of heavy feet outside the tavern shadowed her heart with dread.

"The king is expecting you," he said with a thread of steel in his tone. "My patience wears thin, Genevieve de Pereille."

Still Genevieve refused to take his hand to rise, and the Master's brow darkened. The door to the courtyard opened, emitting the cold fingers of the winter wind and a dozen grim-faced men-at-arms. Genevieve's heart skipped a beat.

Where was Wolfram?

Wolfram was gone, she reminded herself savagely. Had that man not declared that he cared naught for her? The recollection of his denial stung and fortified Genevieve's will as naught else could.

Alone she was, and upon no one could she rely but herself.

Genevieve looked back to the Master in time to see him smile thinly. "Surely you are not a foolish woman," he whispered.

Nay, Genevieve had never been a fool. And well it seemed that she had no choice in this matter. She lifted her chin and accepted the Master's aid in rising, knowing that she alone could see herself free of this situation.

The troupe was gone.

Wolfram stood at the gate of the city and stared off into the distance. He squinted against the glare of the fresh snow, but not a sign of movement could he see on the entire visible rippling length of the road.

Odo was gone.

"Did a group of people leave by this gate this morn?" he asked the gatekeeper. The man glanced in Wolfram's direction, his features creasing into a grin as he waggled one finger at him.

"One of those were you with the foreign minstrels at Heinrich's last night, are you not?" he demanded genially. Wolfram nodded and the man nodded appreciatively. "Aye, a fine show that was, the like of which we have not seen in these parts of late." The man appeared to lose himself in recollection of the night before, and Wolfram cleared his throat pointedly.

"Did the troupe pass this way this morn?" he asked again. The man glanced up with a start and smiled encouragingly.

"Aye, that they did. Lively a group as you could hope to see, to be so wide awake as to beat me to the gates this morn."

"Do you know where they went?"

The man appeared surprised by the question. "Nay. None of my business 'tis where one goes when they leave. I but assumed they went to another town to busk."

"Where does this road lead?" Wolfram demanded impatiently.

The man shrugged. "To Nancy. Is that not the way of these types, to move continually?" The man slapped his forehead in an exaggerated parody of recollection. "But indeed, why do I ask you such a thing? Are they not your friends? Surely you know best where 'tis they are headed.''

"Nay, I know not.'' Wolfram admitted heavily.

"Stole from you, did they?'' the keeper asked with enthusiastic relish.

Wolfram regarded him with thinly veiled horror. "Nay. Fine people are they.''

The keeper *tsk*ed under his breath and leaned close to whisper confidentially. "One hears tales, you know, about these traveling types, and well did my mother teach me never to trust a man whose door you could not find two nights in a row.'' The gatekeeper regarded Wolfram brightly, as though expecting to be entrusted with a bold secret at any moment. Wolfram held his regard for a long moment, having no idea what to say, and finally simply turned away.

"I thank you for your aid,'' he said flatly. The gatekeeper, undeterred, granted him a cheerful wave. Wolfram was not surprised to catch a last glimpse of the man peering down a narrow alley with avid curiosity.

He stalked back in the direction of the tavern, letting his sour mood take the reins. Never had he imagined that Odo would part paths with him and Genevieve with nary a word. Wolfram scowled and kicked aside the fresh dusting of snow as the purse of coins jingled discordantly within his pocket.

The keeper of the tavern might know more about Odo's departure than he realized. Experience had shown that that man's memory oft needed some prompting. Truly there was nowhere else Wolfram could turn. He strode purposefully back to the tavern, knowing all the while the certainty that he would soon see Genevieve again could not be what was buoying his step.

But when Wolfram reached the tavern long moments later, Genevieve was gone.

He searched the common room, but not a sign of her was there remaining. When he noted that her lute was gone, his heart stilled with trepidation.

"Where is the lady who slept at the hearth?" he demanded of the keeper, who was still in the kitchen. That man looked up with surprise.

"Sleeping she was when last I looked," he said, his blank expression all the assurance Wolfram needed that the man told the truth.

"And no one else came while I was gone?" he asked.

The keeper shrugged as he rolled another batch of dough into round loaves. "The lord there was who sought a room, but none other."

"A lord?" Wolfram's throat caught in his chest. The keeper nodded amiably.

"Aye," he agreed with a wave. "One of those types filled with their own import was he, with his staff and his dogs. Last night he was here, but I had not a room for him and his men on account of the space taken up by your little troupe."

Wolfram's mouth went dry. Surely 'twas just coincidence that someone had stopped in last night after their arrival. Surely his past had made him too suspicious of every turn of events. "And you told him as much?" he inquired mildly.

The keeper grinned. "Aye, for well I guessed his purse was well lined. Indeed, I thought he might stop for a tankard of ale and attend their skills, for he seemed truly interested to hear the news, but he merely popped his head into the common room for a moment afore he left."

Too much did that sound like the behavior of a man on a trail for Wolfram's taste. Surely he was seeing fault where there was none, but he could not let the matter be.

"Had he an accent, perchance?" he asked. The keeper wagged a finger at him good-naturedly.

"Oho! With your aid, I recall more than I thought," he said with an enthusiastic nod. "Aye, an accent he had, and 'twas a Parisian one, unless I miss my guess. Hasty speakers are that lot, yet very crisp in their speech. Enough of them have I had passing through here to know my business in that. Exacting folk, they are, frustrating no end in their certainty that they alone know what is what—''

Wolfram leaned across the table and interrupted the keeper, willing the man to discredit his unruly thoughts. "Do you recall his features?" he demanded abruptly.

"Oh, aye." The keeper rolled his eyes and missed not a beat in his chat. "A handsome man he was, for all his somber mood, and, despite his age, he stood straight and tall. Silver of mane and imperious of manner was that one, and had me doing his bidding afore I thought twice. Made me glad my sisters are off at the convent this winter to take their lessons, it did, for this one would stir trouble without a doubt."

Wolfram was immediately put in mind of the Master of the Temple. He felt the color drain from his face, but the keeper seemed to notice naught. Surely that man could not have pursued him this far? To have broken his oath to the house was no small thing, but to have the Master himself give chase was far beyond typical.

Or, more ominously and infinitely more likely, did the Master intend to complete unfinished business with Genevieve?

Had Wolfram not seen that very man arrested in Paris? Surely the Master could not have gained freedom *and* lent chase this far? Surely that was unlikely at best?

But Genevieve was gone. That much was beyond dispute. Wherever she had gone, she had chosen to leave Wolfram and that he could not deny.

Genevieve had abandoned him. That he had feared—nay, *anticipated*—the very same did naught to reassure him, and he stood in the kitchen of the tavern with the smell of fresh bread filling his lungs even as emptiness filled his heart. Bereft he was in that moment, alone as he had been all of his life.

But this time, the pain was more than Wolfram thought he could bear.

Had he erred in refusing to trust Genevieve? Too late to matter, the possibility tempted him, and he wondered if he could have done anything different from the way he had.

Genevieve was gone. And Wolfram was alone once again. Though this time, he had not the security of the Order to regiment his days.

He had naught at all to call his own. Well it seemed that he had not appreciated what lay within his grasp until 'twas gone, though the revelation came too late to reassure him at all.


The lute summoned Wolfram as he wandered blindly that night.

He heard the faint whisperings of its music wafting to his ears through the deserted streets of Metz. He knew not whether the strains of the tune were real or imagined, but he fancied they would lead him directly to Genevieve.

Whimsy it was, and Wolfram knew it. For the first time in his days, solitude was barren and empty for him, and he marveled at the change. He jingled Odo's coins in his pocket as he paced the snow-dusted streets of Metz and considered the lure of the tune yet again.

Whimsy indeed, but what else had he? Nowhere was there for him to go, and pursuit of a fetching tune was as worthy a goal as anything else. Wolfram turned and followed the sound as intently as a hound bent on tracking a scent. His footsteps carried him up one twisted street and down another, past a bakery, a butcher's, a cloth merchant's, a candlemaker's.

And brought him to a halt before a modest tavern.

The music was real here, its muted strains filtering through the frame of the wooden portal to escape into the street. 'Twas not Genevieve's playing, for 'twas less skillful, but still its magic taunted Wolfram with lost memories.

He knew instinctively that he had been summoned here and did not dare to wonder why. Before he questioned his impulse overmuch, Wolfram opened the door and stepped into the warm glow of the tavern.

Deserted 'twas—too late for most of its patrons, evidently. The smell of roast meat lingered in the air and wet rings from crocks of beer marked the trestle tables. Benches were left askew and the fire burned down to embers in the grate.

Wolfram had not realized that he had walked so long.

Yet one occupant of the room was there. 'Twas a woman who sat on a stool afore the hearth and fingered a lute. Older she was, a thick braid of silver cast over her shoulder and glinting in the firelight. Her fingers moved in a manner that suggested a deftness lost with youth, but something there was about her that nudged Wolfram's memory. He stepped fully into the room before he thought, and when the woman looked up, he knew her identity all too well.

Eyes of soft silver met his own, and wonder widened them immediately.

"Wolfram," she whispered, and he caught his breath at the familiarity of her voice.

Wolfram closed his eyes, a primitive urge deep within him telling him to turn tail and run from this tavern as quickly as he was able. And once he would have turned away with nary a second thought. Three moons past, afore the seductive fog of Montsalvat had shown the weaknesses in his defenses, afore Genevieve had stormed his ramparts, afore those walls he had once thought indestructible had tumbled to rubble, he might well have done so.

But now he could not. His dam she was, and there was something he would know of her. Genevieve's abandonment weighed heavily upon his mind, and Wolfram would hear from this woman's lips what 'twas about him that urged those he cared about to desert him.

He needed to know the truth.

"Wolfram," she whispered once more, though there was no question lingering in her tone. Neither of them could pretend any longer that they were not who they were.

"You left me," Wolfram said stonily without moving from the threshold. Still the chill of the night was at his back and he heard, to his own disgust, all the hurt and uncertainty of that long-lost child in his voice.

His mother smiled to herself and dropped her gaze for a moment. Left before him was a woman of such dejection that a voice deep within Wolfram urged him to console her. That he could not do, though he knew not what else to do. He stood silently, motionless in the doorway and waited.

She brushed away what might have been a tear, but then her shoulders straightened so proudly that Wolfram thought he had but imagined any dismay in her expression. She set the lute deliberately aside and stood up, her gaze rising to lock, unwavering, with his. His mouth went dry when she walked toward him, but his own gaze danced over her questioningly.

'Twas her, there could be no doubt in his mind. Smaller she was than he had recalled, and more delicate of bone. A new tracery of lines was there on a visage he remembered smooth and unblemished; a more resolute set was there to a mouth he recalled soft with laughter. When he met her eyes again, he saw that she had traveled far in those intervening years, mayhap farther than he, and that not all she learned had been sweet.

"Aye," she said finally when they stood toe-to-toe. "Aye, I left you, and this I do not deny." Wolfram's heart lurched at her admission and she took a breath as though she sorely needed to steady herself. "Would you not hear the tale?"

The familiarity of the Germanic tongue he had spoken little since she had cast him aside beckoned him closer. A language 'twas that summoned emotion from the depths within him, much as Genevieve's lute had done, for 'twas a tongue that spoke to his ears of that sweet time of his childhood. Wolfram braced himself against its allure, not in the least ready to surrender even the small victory of welcoming his mother's language to her as yet.

"I would know the truth," he said tightly. His mother's nod was so slight as to be imperceptible.

"Then come," she invited tonelessly. She lifted one hand to him, and Wolfram hesitated as he stared at her outstretched fingers. He wanted to know, but she had been the one to betray him. A part of him wanted to concede naught to her, to turn his back and deny her what she asked, though 'twas but a simple thing. A part of him wanted to hurt her in return.

But he knew all the while that such a course would gain him naught. Wolfram steadied the shaking of his fingers, reached out and took his mother's hand.

To his astonishment, her fingers trembled within his grip and a tear glinted on her eyelash before she turned briskly away.

"Cold you are," she said hastily, her back to him as she led him into the tavern. "Come sit by the hearth."

When they were seated on a pair of stools, facing each other warily, the firelight illuminating one side of their faces, they fell silent for a moment that stretched to eternity. Wolfram waited. Well it seemed his mother struggled to find the words as she stared down at her hands. Finally, she swallowed visibly and looked up at him, her expression like one who was seeing him for the first time.

"So like him you are," she murmured wonderingly. "Indeed, I would have known you anywhere." She reached out as though she might touch his face. Wolfram kept his expression impassive, and her gaze faltered slightly from his. Her hand dropped away to twist with its mate in her lap once more.

"Who was my sire?" Wolfram asked bluntly. His mother arched a brow.

"A nobleman he was, his name is not of import." Wolfram wanted to argue that point, but his mother hastened on. Well it seemed that she feared an interruption would silence her confession for good, and the words spilled from her lips in a ceaseless torrent.

"He came to the inn where I was playing in those days, and well enough did I note him from the very first. Tall he was and well-wrought, fair of hair and blue of eye, and confident of his own charm, you can be sure. I knew well his name and his rank and granted him no attention in return, though I was aware of him, for my mother had taught me that naught of merit can come from the nobility.

"And well she knew that those within our family are passionate. We love without reserve, Wolfram, and once our hearts are granted, they cannot be so readily reclaimed. My mother but fretted for my own happiness, for as musicians, we were not considered fit to be wed into the blooded classes. Beware your legacy in this, for love grants no guarantees to those who surrender their hearts. Those there are who think love no more than a game, but always have our kind been deeply loyal, as you will see.

"Well I wished that I could have heeded my mother's advice better than I had, but I was young and this nobleman was determined to win me. Flowers he sent, and gifts, jeweled trinkets, but these were easy to ignore, for we were musicians and had little use for such finery.

"'Twas when he discovered my passion for food that I was lost, for he sent then wine and delicacies such as were far beyond my purse. 'Twas not long before he insisted upon feeding them to me, on carrying me off to the woods for impromptu meals in the grass. Clear did I make my demands from the beginning, and never did he touch me, just as I had dictated. But he charmed me, as only one trained to do so can, and 'twas not long before I regretted making my demands." Wolfram's mother sighed and impaled him with a single glance that spoke eloquently of the pain within her heart before her gaze dropped away again.

"Despite my mother's warnings," she confessed softly, "I fell in love with a nobleman. So far above my station he was that there was naught good that could come of this love." She shrugged almost to herself. "Mayhap part of the appeal in those early days was that our love was stolen away and forbidden. I know not. It matters little, in truth.''

She fell silent, and Wolfram watched the firelight play over features so like those in his memories, yet subtly changed. He wondered whether the years had been kind to her or not and checked the thought harshly.

Had she spared a thought to his welfare on that snowy eve so long past? Why, then, should he consider hers?

But Wolfram recognized that the harsh judgment he had long held against this woman was softening, even as she sat before him. His faded recollections of warmth and love were rekindled by the sight of her features, and Wolfram knew he had Genevieve to blame for this weakening of his resolve.

Genevieve, who had coldly abandoned him, precisely as he had feared she would. That Wolfram had anticipated the loss did naught to mitigate the pain of the knife turning in the wound.

## Chapter Fourteen

"At any rate, I slowly fell in love with this irrepressible young nobleman, so bent was he on earning my approval. I hid my regard for him for a long while, mayhap out of some tardy respect for my mother's advice, but one day I could resist no longer. A stone had he tossed through my window early that spring morn, and I had known immediately that it could be no other than he. He urged me to join him, for he had a surprise, and indeed, the air was so fresh, the hills so verdant, that I could not decline." She stifled a smile of recollection that sent a pang through Wolfram's own heart. "Helped me climb from the window, he did, and laughing under our breath all the while, we fled the town before any awakened.

"The sunrise 'twas he wanted me to see from a particularly secluded and lovely hill. Deer there were there, and birds of so many kinds I could not name them all. Early flowers there were in bloom, crocuses and periwinkle mixed in the young grass, and the dew was thick and cool under our feet. A blanket had he brought, as well as a handsome repast, and we ate our fill, silently watching the sky turn from indigo to pink and thence to gold.

"When the sky tinged blue and our repast was long gone, he requested of me a kiss. In the magic of that morning and with the fullness of love dawning within my heart, I could not decline. And in the end, 'twas that kiss and more I granted him that morn. Indeed, 'twas nigh eventide when I returned to town with regret lodged firmly in my throat.''

Was he the product of this illicit union? Wolfram could barely stifle his shame at the thought. Out of wedlock had he been born, the product of a rake's passion and a maiden's naiveté, but the telling of the tale was less than welcome. His mother cleared her throat and frowned as though she meant to continue, but Wolfram knew not what she might say in addition.

'Twas a sordid enough tale as it stood, and he was not certain he wished to hear more. He made to stand, but his mother's frown deepened. She laid one hand on his arm and looked to him in confusion.

''More there is that you should know,'' she advised in a low tone that brooked no argument. Wolfram found himself sinking back into his seat. ''This may well astonish you as much as it did me, but that nobleman did not disappear from my life. Well I imagined that once he had had his pleasure, he would be gone, and truly my mother would have made that point if she had but guessed my transgression.

''Remarkably, my reticence had proved a purpose, for in courting my submission so ardently, my nobleman confessed to have fallen in love with me, as well. His ardor diminished naught after our mating, and soon 'twas known to all that we belonged to each other alone.'' She shook her head slightly and met Wolfram's gaze steadily. ''Those halcyon days were the happiest of my life, Wolfram, and you must believe that 'twas no small thing to love and be loved by such a man. Everything he was to me and I to him.''

She paused, and the next words fell flat from her lips. ''And so it continued until his family insisted that he wed.''

Wolfram must have made some sound of surprise, for his mother's expression turned grim as she glanced to him again. Instinctively he knew that she was not the one his sire had wed, and he was surprised to feel a trickle of sympathy for her that she had been ill-used.

"Aye," she said softly. "'Twas not I he wed. His family, of course, knew well about me, and mayhap 'twas that union they sought to destroy. The legitimacy of line was paramount, the selection of a mate from acceptable levels of society critical to ensuring the fortitude of the family. Or so they said. He argued with them, to no avail. The arrangements had been made, the dowry paid, the bride en route to his family château even as he first learned the news. He threatened to flee, they called upon his honor, and being the kind of man he was, he could not deny them.

"He learned the truth on the eve of his own nuptials, and as soon as it could be contrived, he fled to me that night. 'Twas late and we held each other close, secreted in my garret room, and whispered that my mother might not suspect anything amiss. I wept, and though he tried to console me, there was naught in truth either of us could say or do. He vowed to keep me as his mistress, but we both knew it could not be. Our last night together 'twould be, and once we realized that, we pledged to make love yet once more afore we turned away. A few fleeting hours of passion 'twould be, a tribute and a dirge both, for we well knew that we would never lay eyes upon each other again."

She swallowed carefully and reached across to touch the back of Wolfram's hand. "'Twas that night you were conceived, my son, and I knew it well even as his seed spilled within me. God did I praise weeks later when 'twas clear that you would I have, instead of merely the fleeting mist of memories. A child to hold close to my breast, a child to love, a child to cherish as I grew old without my one true love."

She straightened and blinked back the gleam of tears, her gaze snared now by the dancing flames, her manner purposeful. "I left the town before 'twas evident that I carried the fruit of his seed, and left all those I knew, that I might not bring shame to them. No desire had I to see my beloved's bride, no need had I to learn whether he became accustomed to his fate over time. I refused to let the knife be turned in the wound. Naught did I have but you, my wits and my lute, and though I ached with my loss, it seemed for a while that it might be enough.

"Born you were one autumn when the wind rattled the chimney. A finer and plumper babe has never been seen on this earth, and from the beginning you were hale and hearty. Made me smile again, you did, and thence to laugh, a sound I had thought never to hear fall from my own lips. A humble living did I make, but steady work did I find in a tavern where the keeper was kindly and granted us a room beneath the roof. 'Twas warm and we were well fed and I fancy happiness did we find together." She flicked a glance to Wolfram as though seeking confirmation of his agreement, but he could not treasure her sweet reminiscing while the specter of what lingered ahead loomed large in his mind.

"Until you saw fit to desert me," he charged flatly. She flushed and looked back to the fire. Her hands twisted in her lap again, but Wolfram was not prepared to grant her any respite. He waited impassively for what could only be a meager explanation.

"He came for me," she admitted finally, in a voice so small as to be virtually inaudible. "You were but four. Well can you imagine my shock to find him standing in the corner of this tavern years after he had first watched me in the same manner many leagues away. A sadness there was in his eyes, a hunger from which I could not turn away. He talked to me, he told me of his undying passion, his misery in his marriage. Indeed, so great was his dismay that his wife had agreed to permit me to live within their home and openly be his mistress.

"Her sole condition was that I never bear to him a child." She licked her lips nervously. "I knew not what to do. 'Twas evident he knew naught of you, but his fierce expression when he told me of this condition made me wonder what in truth he might do should I tell him. Well it seemed that he was prepared to let no obstacles come betwixt us, and I feared for your safety should he hear tell of you."

"You chose him over me," Wolfram interjected coldly. "Spare me your pretty tales and but confess the truth." His mother straightened proudly, and Wolfram knew well that he had insulted her, but she held his gaze unswervingly.

"I chose him over you." She bit out the words. "I chose my lover over my child, 'tis true, but at the time, I well imagined that I could somehow tell him of you if I but had more time. Fully did I intend to return for you, for certain was I that he would not deny you." Her eyes clouded with tears as she regarded Wolfram.

"I was wrong," she whispered, and her pain could not be denied.

That his father had denied him was a blow Wolfram had not been expecting. He caught his breath and wished otherwise, but his mother's eyes told him the truth. His sire had not wanted him. She did not look away now, her gaze locked to his as the words spilled from her lips in haste once more.

"You cannot know what a blow 'twas to my regard for the man that he did this thing," she murmured urgently. "Not only did he deny you and refuse to retrieve you, but he forbade me to seek you out. Too late did I see that I had forsaken the one thing that was important to me—too late did I see that I had not appreciated the fullness of what lay within my grasp. I had discarded all for what looked a finer fate, only to have that bright promise fall to tatters around me."

Her lips twisted and her tone became savage. "Never could I look upon him in the same way again," she said tightly. "Never could I reconcile the man I loved with the man who had declined to see his son."

Her mouth worked silently for a moment as she fought for control of her emotions, and Wolfram felt an overwhelming wave of sympathy for her.

For this woman who had abandoned him. 'Twas astonishing that he could feel such compassion for her, even after all that had gone before, and instinctively Wolfram knew that 'twas Genevieve who had awakened this gentler side of his nature.

"But once the moment was past, 'twas as though it had never been," his mother continued tonelessly. "At least to him, it seemed thus. Never was the issue mentioned again, and indeed, we had some happy times together. But a shadow 'twas on my horizon, and I suspect on my horizon alone, for he was completely untroubled by the matter."

She took a deep breath and glanced down to her hands. "I loved him so deeply that there were moments when I forgot his slight."

Wolfram glanced away at that, though he respected her strength in telling to him the truth. His mother's tale began again and he attended her silently. "Though indeed, the life itself was a comfortable one," she admitted, "and I did remain there in his home, for I had given him my pledge in an early moment of weakness that I would remain by his side. Years passed, and ever did I think of you and wonder what had become of you.

"Ashamed I am to admit that in some corner of my soul, 'twas a relief when my lover was wounded in battle and died. Summoned me to his side he did, instead of his lawful wife. I suppose a last token of his regard 'twas to be the one holding his hand when he left this earth, but all I could think as I watched the life flow from him was that I would have been better served if he had never found me in that tavern. A weight was lifted from my back that day, and I knew 'twas beyond time to seek out what I had lost."

She sighed again. "'Twas then I returned to Metz to seek you out, for 'twas here I had entrusted you to the monks. Unhelpful they were at best, and told me only that you had taken vows and moved they knew not where. Alone I was then, as I had never been alone before, and I know not how long I wandered these streets pondering my own folly.

"Fate conspired that I would stumble upon that self-same tavern once more, the one where you and I had passed such happy years. Well did the proprietor remember me, and I realized suddenly how well he had treated me when I was but a perfect stranger to him. Solicitude he showed me again that night, when I was in the deepest despair, and offered to me the same task and room.''

She gestured about herself with one hand, and Wolfram instinctively knew what she would say. '''Tis here I still stay, 'tis here I still play to earn my keep, 'tis here I have awaited you, hoping that one day you would return.''

She lifted one hand and laid it against Wolfram's face, and this time he could not move away. '''Tis here, where we began, that you have found me again.'' Her eyes glazed with tears and Wolfram was shocked to see his own vision blur. Something warm spilled over his cheek. His mother smiled sadly and brushed it away with a warm finger.

''Do not imagine that I did not love you,'' she whispered urgently. ''Light of my life you were, but like some addle-pated fool, I saw not what I had until 'twas gone. My heart and soul would I have given to have you back at my side, but my error was not something so easily undone. I regret but one thing I have done in my life, and that was leaving you on that stoop.''

''With a lump of salt,'' Wolfram said quietly. His mother nodded.

''With a lump of salt,'' she agreed. ''That they would know you were baptized. I was not so foul a mother as to see my own child without the grace of protection.''

Another tear spilled over Wolfram's cheek, and it seemed his mouth was so dry that he could say naught. His mother shook her head, her own tears beginning to fall as she framed his face within her hands. ''Say something to me, my child,'' she begged brokenly when she evidently could guess naught of his thoughts. ''Forgive me if you can. If not, I ask only that you not despise me.''

''Never.'' The word broke from Wolfram's lips with unrestrained fervor, and he saw immediately that his mother had misinterpreted him. Her expression of disbelief was so pained that he could think of naught but reassuring her.

"Never could I despise you," he whispered. Her features fell as she began to cry in earnest, and Wolfram hauled her into his arms with nary a second thought.

"I forgive you, Mother, and wish you had not been so ill-used," he murmured into her hair as she crumpled against him. Strange 'twas to embrace her after so much time, for her scent was achingly familiar, yet their relative sizes had been transposed over the years and 'twas she who was the smaller now.

"I understand now, as I never did afore," Wolfram whispered. "And well you know that I love you, as well." She answered not, but her fingers clutched at his neck as she sobbed openly. Wolfram rocked her in his arms and whispered soothing nonsense to her as a warmth began to glow within him.

'Twas this love he had been denied so many years, and its return near made him dizzy. So much had he lost but it mattered naught, for now 'twas all his again. He pondered the details of his mother's tale and vowed silently to himself to learn from her error.

Wolfram would not let his love slip away from him and lose the only thing he had of value. He could not afford to lose Genevieve, and should the price of keeping her by his side be the submission of his heart, he would well do it. Indeed, his heart yearned for naught else, and he knew in that moment that it mattered not whether he could trust her fully or whether she might ultimately betray him.

He believed he could trust her, and that was all a man could ask of his own heart. Wolfram closed his eyes and hoped fervently that he would be able to find his own Genevieve.

"Melissande?"

Both mother and son glanced up as one to find an older man standing hesitantly in the doorway to the kitchens beyond. His brow was puckered with concern, and a damp dishrag hung in his hand, a stoneware crock in the other.

"Is something amiss?" he asked when neither of them spoke. Wolfram saw his mother smile gently, felt the hand that rose to rest proprietarily on his shoulder, as right as could be.

"Everything is fine, Gunther," she said quietly, paying no mind to the tears staining her cheeks. "I would like you to meet my son." She flicked Wolfram a telling glance as her smile broadened. "Again."

His mother had not abandoned him. The truth came to Wolfram as he shook the older man's hand, and the possibility that followed fairly took his breath away.

Mayhap Genevieve had not abandoned him either.

"I need to find someone," he said urgently to the couple afore him. "A woman who disappeared from the tavern owned by Heinrich this very morn. I know not where she went."

"Important to you, is she?" Wolfram's mother asked quietly, and he could only nod. She smiled and laid a hand on Gunther's arm. The older man cleared his throat.

"I shall fetch my dogs," he said tightly, and Wolfram saw immediately that this was a man who saw matters done. "Old Esquin misses naught of what happens in this town, and the keepers of the gates do I know well. Should your friend be within the walls of Metz or without, rest assured that we shall find her in short order."

By the time the Master found them accommodations in a neighboring small town that night, Genevieve knew full well that she would be hard-pressed to see her way clear of this tangle.

A fool of the first order she had been in accompanying the Master and his men without seeking out Wolfram first. In retrospect, she realized that she knew not whether he had truly left her—indeed, she could give little credence to the Master's insistence that Wolfram intended to dispatch her. Wolfram had had more than ample opportunity to do so, and the fact that he had never lifted a hand against her was a better indication of his intent than this one's self-serving lies.

A fool Genevieve had been to let the sting of Wolfram's rejection guide her decision. The Master's men had enfolded her in their midst so effectively that Genevieve knew she had no hope of escape.

In Metz should she have run. While she had feared there that she had little choice, now she knew that she had no chance.

And the Master was a cunning one, that much could not be denied. No telling was there what he might do if confronted publicly, for Genevieve knew not how much he risked personally in this endeavor. She guessed that it mattered little whether she was returned to Paris alive or dead.

Genevieve wondered if the man had a purpose in leaving her alive thus far. Could there be something the Master desired of her? Surely it could not be intimacy he craved? Genevieve eyed him warily and wondered what she would do if 'twas.

She waited restlessly until they had retired to their rooms, tapping her toe until a leisurely dinner had been served and consumed and the fire had been stoked up. Finally, both men-at-arms and proprietor retired, leaving Genevieve and the Master alone.

The gleam in his eye told Genevieve she had guessed aright to fear him. Her heart leapt to her throat, although she struggled to give no outward sign of her response.

"Now then, Genevieve," the Master began smoothly. "Something I would have from you this night, and well enough do you know what 'tis."

She had been right! Genevieve regarded the older man with shock.

"Why not make this transaction simpler for both of us and simply concede to me the receipt?" the Master continued.

Genevieve blinked in surprise. "The receipt?" she repeated uncomprehendingly.

A fleeting frown danced across the Master's brow. "Aye, the receipt that lies at the root of all this trouble," he confirmed impatiently.

Genevieve frowned in turn, uncertain what he was talking about. "No receipt do I possess," she said cautiously.

The Master's eyes flashed with anger, and he stalked her across the room. "Play no games with me, woman!" he declared. "The receipt your family holds for its deposit in the Temple is what I desire from you, and neither of us will leave this room until 'tis surrendered."

"Deposit?" Genevieve repeated, feeling every inch the fool but knowing naught of what he spoke. "No deposit has my family with the Temple...."

"And a convincing tale you make of that lie," the Master said with a sneer. "Think you that I do not know the truth of it? Spare me your foolish tales and surrender the receipt to me immediately!"

He advanced upon her threateningly, and Genevieve stumbled to her feet. She darted behind the table, feeling more secure with its wooden expanse betwixt herself and this increasingly angry man.

Mayhap she would learn more if she echoed his game.

Genevieve curled her lip scornfully. "Naught will I surrender willingly to the likes of you," she asserted boldly.

The Master's eyes flashed and he lunged toward the table. "Aha! So you admit to having it!" he said. "Well did I know that it existed in truth! Give it to me!" Avarice sharpened his features, and Genevieve cautiously slipped around the table, that the distance between them would be greater.

"Why should I grant something so precious to you?" she demanded.

The Master chuckled. "Surely you do not imagine that I will permit you to collect the deposit? Too much have I to lose from that claim."

"What have you to lose?"

"Oho! Surely you know the truth of it. Usurped your family's claim, I did."

"You did not!" Genevieve declared in shock.

"Aye, long ago 'twas, and I was but young and foolish. No one I thought could be hurt, for your parents were recently demised." The Master's lip curled with scorn as he eyed Genevieve, and he dived around the table abruptly. His hand darted in her direction, but Genevieve anticipated the move and danced out of his range, leaving his fingers to snatch at empty air. "No one could have guessed that those two had spawned," he snarled.

"You 'twas behind my parents' demise."

The Master shook his head hastily at Genevieve's accusation. "Nay, 'twas that nonsense your family tends to spout that saw them dead while they were yet young, for the crown does not take kindly to rival claims." He smiled, though naught warm was there in the expression. "'Twas that tendency, admittedly, that saw the removal of your beloved brother so readily accomplished."

"You saw to Alzeu's demise!"

"Nay, the crown ordered his dispatch," the Master told her with an oily smile. "But 'twas I who whispered the truth of his existence into the appropriate ear. 'Twas smoothly achieved, if indeed I alone must say so."

"But you had not counted upon me," Genevieve guessed.

The Master arched a brow. "Nay. No one, it seemed, had counted upon there being yet another Pereille. But the last of the lot you are, and the last who can threaten my security with the revelation of a receipt."

"Your security?"

"Aye, all is at risk as long as the possibility of that receipt coming to light endures. 'Tis you alone who can reveal that long-ago error of my judgment, 'tis you alone who might jeopardize my position within the Temple."

"Well have I heard that the Temple is gone," Genevieve asserted. She was not prepared for the anger that contorted the Master's features, nor for the way he lunged unexpectedly across the table. He snatched at her wrist, his grip closing viselike about it so that Genevieve knew she could not shake free.

"Never will they fell the Temple," he vowed. "To a divine mission are we appointed, and 'tis only a matter of moments before the righteous come to our aid."

The man was clearly mad. And Genevieve knew naught of a Pereille deposit in the Temple, much less the location of a telling receipt. Well enough could she guess that it had been lost during the years they were in exile, but she was not interested in paying the price.

On impulse, Genevieve jerked her knee skyward.

"Deceitful bitch!" the Master cried, but his grip loosened enough that Genevieve gained her freedom.

Convinced this would be her only chance, she fled across the room. The Master's raspy breathing filled her ears, her heart pounded in her throat. Her hands trembled so that she almost fumbled with the latch on the door. Mercifully, she managed to open it and stumbled out into the dark hallway. The sounds of merrymaking rose from below, and Genevieve dived in the direction she knew the stairs to be.

And collided with a solid wall of purposeful masculinity.

Genevieve's mouth barely had time to go dry before she realized 'twas Wolfram's chest beneath her hands. Her knees threatened to buckle with relief even as his hand snaked around her waist.

"Do not imagine that you will escape me, you feckless bitch," the Master growled behind her. Genevieve made to explain, but the sound of steel on steel summarily halted her words.

Wolfram had a sword. She felt the Master hesitate in the darkness behind her and knew he had heard that distinctive sound, as well.

"Do return to your chambers, milord," Wolfram invited in a tone that brooked no argument. "It well seems we have a matter to discuss."

"You!" the Master declared. "How did you find us?" he demanded boldly, but Genevieve heard the thread of fear in his tone.

"Not the only one are you with hunting dogs," Wolfram asserted. He took Genevieve's hand in his and led her back to the room. When she turned, she saw that the point of the sword he had drawn rested on the throat of the silhouette that was the Master of the Temple of Paris.

Wolfram had ridden in pursuit of her! Her heart sang with the news as relief allowed her thinking to clear. Surely this could be naught but a good sign. Genevieve could feel only resolve emanating from his touch and hoped desperately that his resolve pertained to her in some way.

They entered the room and Wolfram flicked Genevieve a glance. She understood immediately and closed the door behind them, hanging back to watch whatever would unfold betwixt these two men.

To Genevieve's surprise, the Master's features relaxed and he began to chuckle.

"Well I knew that you would follow, Wolfram," he charged gleefully. "And now, two birds have I captured within one cage."

"I think not," Wolfram said firmly. He backed the Master into the table, and that man leaned backward to minimize the impact of the blade. 'Twas sharp, Genevieve saw, for a thin trickle of blood ran from the Master's flesh where the blade touched. His eyes widened and she fancied he felt that solitary trickle.

But the Master's certainty of his position was undaunted. "I think so," he said in a low tone. "Surely you have not failed to note the dozen men who accompany me on this mission? Always had I thought you more observant than that, Wolfram." He tut-tutted under his tongue confidently, but Genevieve saw something in Wolfram's expression that reassured her fears.

He smiled coldly as he released her hand and carefully removed a slender glass vial from his tunic. He tossed it to the Master, who instinctively snatched it out of the air. His brow puckered in a frown.

"'Tis empty," he observed, clearly not understanding the point. Wolfram tossed him another, and the Master shook his head to find it empty as well.

"I do not understand," he confessed carefully, his eyes narrowing as he looked to his opponent.

"I did not fail to note your companions," Wolfram informed his former superior. "Unbeknownst to them, your men participated in a test of sorts." The Master eyed the vials in his hand warily as though he anticipated what Wolfram might say. "The wine of this house is sour," Wolfram confided, "and well disguised the bitterness of this elixir."

Genevieve's eyes widened at the evident import of Wolfram's words, and the Master shivered visibly, his mask of self-assurance slipping visibly.

"You poisoned them," he whispered hoarsely.

Wolfram inclined his head incrementally. "This elixir is very quick of action," he said easily. His hand slipped into his tunic, and the last vial he removed shone, with half its contents remaining. "But some I have saved for you, that you might see its effectiveness yourself."

"You lie!" the Master accused wildly. "Someone will come to my aid! Someone rides from the king in pursuit even now! You cannot manage this deed and escape unscathed!"

Wolfram cleared his throat and arched a knowing brow. "'Tis evident you overestimate the abilities of your allies," he said softly, and all color drained from the Master's face.

He shivered in evident dread, his gaze dropping to the vial and its clear, fluid contents. The Master swallowed visibly. "I swear I will leave you both alone from this point onward," he declared fervently.

Wolfram shook his head slowly. "Time has shown that your word is worth naught," he said flatly. "Too much have you at stake in this matter to leave us be."

The Master eyed the vial warily, and his breath came in uneven spurts. "What manner of elixir is it?" he asked.

Wolfram held the vial to the light, his expression impassive as he turned it. "One concocted to bring death quickly and painlessly," he said. The Master's gaze danced away as though he assessed his options one last time. He seemed to listen but naught carried to their ears. No men-at-arms came in pursuit.

He met Wolfram's gaze squarely.

"Give it here," he said firmly.

Wolfram handed the Master the vial and he removed its stopper warily, the tip of the sword blade hovering a finger's span from his throat. He sniffed the concoction, put the vial to his lips and dropped his head back as he drained its contents.

He eyed Genevieve and Wolfram, the three of them barely drawing breath as they waited expectantly. Genevieve could not believe the poison took so long to take effect, yet in truth, her heart beat mayhap thrice.

Then the Master's eyes rolled upward and he slumped against the table. The vial slipped from his limp fingers and shattered on the floor.

'Twas over. She exhaled shakily as Wolfram lowered his blade and stepped forward to check the pulse at the older man's throat.

"Aha!"

The Master's head snapped up, eyes burning, and his hand darted out to grasp Wolfram's throat. With the grip of a man who knows he has not long, he pinched Wolfram's windpipe and clamped one hand on the back of Wolfram's neck. Genevieve's heart stopped in fear. Wolfram struggled to shake off his opponent to no avail.

The men fell to the floor, Wolfram pounding on the Master with his fists and clawing at the man's fingers. His face grew ruddy beyond compare as he kicked and twisted, but the Master's grip was sure. Genevieve tried to leap into the fray, but the older man could not be shaken from his grip. His breathing grew more labored, but a determination was there in his eyes and Genevieve knew he would not surrender to the poison's call while his opponent yet drew breath.

What could she do? The men rolled and grunted as her gaze danced over the room. The entwined men hit the table and the lamp teetered precariously. Another blow sent the table lurching across the floor. The oil spilled across the wood and the flame leapt hungrily in pursuit.

They would all perish here unless she did something to aid Wolfram!

Suddenly Genevieve spied her lute.

With nary another thought, Genevieve snatched it up. Her heart in her mouth, she stood over the men and awaited her moment. What seemed an eternity was in truth but an instant. The Master rolled to the top, obviously intending to squeeze the last breath from Wolfram as his own features contorted in pain. Genevieve swung hard and cracked the lute hard over the back of the Master's skull. It shattered into a thousand pieces, but the Master crumpled bonelessly beneath the blow.

Wolfram shook off the other man's weight and cleared his throat with an effort. His breathing was raspy, but when Genevieve might have fallen upon him in relief, he pointed to the other side of the room.

The tapestries on the walls were consumed by flames. The bed blazed high, and the fire licked at the wood timbers overhead. Genevieve stared in astonishment that the fire could have spread so quickly, but Wolfram rolled to his feet. He kicked open the shutters over the window, ignoring the flames curling around their base. Genevieve tasted the cold bite of the night in her lungs and felt the strength of Wolfram's arms lock around her for but a moment before he leapt out the window.

They fell and landed with a thud on the thatched roof of the stables. Heat flicked at Genevieve's calves and she glanced down to find her beleaguered kirtle in flames.

"Nay!" she cried. Wolfram rolled her hastily across the roof and the fire was crushed to extinction, but not quickly enough that the roof itself did not catch. The straw was dry, and they were hard-pressed to roll to safety in time.

No sooner did their feet hit the ground than Wolfram left Genevieve. Her hands rose to her mouth as she watched him dash into the burning stables. Too long it took to see the horses run wildly from the smoke-filled interior. A trio of squires accompanied the coughing ostler, and she could not take another breath until Wolfram's own tall silhouette came forth from within. Genevieve fell upon him and he gathered her close as they retreated from the growing heat and watched the stables burn. High above, the window on the Master's room revealed naught but a dancing orange inferno.

'Twas frightening to realize how close they had come to perishing there. Genevieve shivered at the very thought. Well it seemed that Wolfram's thoughts followed Genevieve's own, for he cradled her close against his chest. Already a crowd had gathered to watch the flames, and whisper among themselves at its cause, and Wolfram slipped them unobtrusively into the group.

"You, boy!" the ostler cried to one of the squires. "Hasten yourself into the tavern and see that all are roused! It looks as yet as though only the south end is past saving."

"'Twas milord's chambers!" wailed one squire in distress. Genevieve stiffened, but she dared not look to Wolfram, though she knew he, too, had noted the young boy's words. Well it seemed that Wolfram had missed one from the Master's retinue. "I must awaken him!" The boy might have plunged into the flames, but the ostler held him back with one burly arm.

"But thank the Fates that you were not sleeping at his foot this night," the ostler told the boy. Tears began to run down the squire's young face and he turned to the ostler in distress.

" 'Tis only because the lady was with him this night that he bade me sleep in the stables," he said.

The ostler ruffled the boy's hair. "Aye, some 'lady' she was, I am certain."

"Nay! 'Twas not like that!" the squire declared, outraged that his lord's intent was being mistaken. " 'Twas the Lady Genevieve de Pereille whom he escorted back to Paris. Well do I know that to be the truth, for a tall, fair man came to seek them out. On a mission from the king was the Master of the Temple of Paris."

The ostler smiled sadly and pulled the boy into an affectionate hug as his gaze rose to the crackling orange flames. "Naught is there you can do for any of them now, boy," he counseled. "Mayhap 'tis best you inform the king of his emissary's demise."

The squire straightened at that, as though he found the idea a fitting tribute to his lord. "I will do so, sir," he informed the ostler stiffly. "I will ride forth to Paris this very day."

The import of his words barely settled in Genevieve's mind before Wolfram pulled her to the back of the watchful group.

"Come," he said, offering her his hand. "Since Genevieve de Pereille is dead, no reason is there that you cannot go home." His eyes glowed with some nameless emotion, and Genevieve could not quell a surge of pleasure that he had chosen to accompany her to Montsalvat.

A change had there been betwixt them, and possibilities lingered temptingly on the horizon. Genevieve took his hand as she summoned a shaky smile and knew somehow all would come right, should they but give themselves some time.

She felt the certainty within him that had not been there before and realized that the man before her had reclaimed some lost part of himself since she had met him. Genevieve eyed him curiously, but he revealed naught more as he strode purposefully from the blazing flames.

The odd thought occurred to her that 'twas Wolfram who had risen from the ashes of the Order's destruction to re-create himself, not the Order of the Templars itself.

## Chapter Fifteen

Spring was ripe in the air when Genevieve and Wolfram climbed the long road to Montsalvat. The gates to the old fortress hung open on their hinges, the wind whistled over the high walls. They said naught to each other as they crossed the bailey, and Genevieve wondered if Wolfram saw the same majesty here as she.

Wordlessly she took his hand and led him to the north ramparts that she had climbed long ago with her grandsire. They climbed to the sentry turret and looked out over the rough land falling away from the outer face of the wall, Genevieve's eye picking out the bright green of new growth far below.

"'Tis a good site," Wolfram said finally. Genevieve heard approval of more than the location in his voice and turned to him with a smile.

"Nowhere else in Christendom could be home to me," she confessed. She shivered in the cool caress of the wind and he pulled her close before him so that they both faced out over the hills. Genevieve closed her eyes at the reassuring solidity of Wolfram against her back and knew she had been fortunate indeed to find a man whom she could so rely upon. Too late she had seen that Alzeu had not been worthy of her trust, but well it seemed that she had learned from her error.

When he spoke, his breath teased the hair above her ear. "Long ago, we vowed to tell each other a tale of love," he reminded her in that pensive deep voice she had grown to love. Genevieve glanced up in time to see Wolfram's lips quirk in a smile. "Never did you tell me yours," he prompted. A glimmer in the quicksilver of his eyes tempted her with the possibility that he had yet changed his mind about their future together, and Genevieve caught her breath.

Wolfram but smiled. "Tell me," he urged.

Genevieve turned back to face the hills, momentarily uncertain of what to say. At that time in the garret, she had intended to tell him of the love her parents held for each other. Now she hesitated, but knew she owed him no less than the truth.

But she trusted Wolfram. And at this point, he well deserved the tale, whether he chose to remain with her here or not. Genevieve took a deep breath before she began.

"Once, long ago, a woman arrived in these parts. She came alone and departed from a ship in a port not far from here, her belly round with a child. That she was beautiful gained her little, for whispers there were about her in the region from the very first. Some said she had come from as far as the kingdom of Prester John, some said she was a witch, some said she ran from the charge of murdering her babe's sire. The woman neither confirmed or denied these tales, and but settled in to begin a quiet life.

"The accusers stopped their whispering when a local man began to court the woman, apparently oblivious to the seed of another man rounding her belly. She laughed in the company of her suitor and they were oft seen together in public, such that none were terribly surprised when they announced their nuptials. The man, it seemed, had a remote property that he had inherited and the new couple headed off into the countryside, waving off the objections of any who observed with concern the advanced state of the woman's pregnancy.

"A home did they build on this property, situated as it was at the top of a hill. 'Twas indeed remote, though they loved it that way, and they named it appropriately. Montsalvat was the name they chose, and well do you know the name means none other than 'Wild Mountain.' 'Twas at Montsalvat the woman's child was born. Even as far away as the coast where they had wedded, there were tales told, which were said to have emanated from the midwife, that the babe had a curious birthmark on his chest in the shape of a cross.

"The child was said to have been remarkable, for he had an affinity for small creatures and 'twas said even the birds came to him when he was but an infant. 'Twas rumored he had but to touch an ailing neighbor to see the malady remedied and that the larder of Montsalvat was never bare. When one had the audacity to question the mother on her curious child, she but smiled and said the boy was like his sire. 'Twas all that was ever said of that man and none knew his identity in truth, though over time, the flurry of interest faded away.

"When this child grew to manhood and took a wife, the tales of his birth resurfaced, for the child of that union bore the same curious mark. People knew no more what to make of this than they had afore, though the family was growing to be a respected one in the neighborhood. As the generations passed and the family's fortunes grew, the matter became of less consequence and diminished to the importance of an oddity regarding a local family. The family prospered in the meantime, their reputed skill with healing attributed to knowledge passed quietly from generation to generation.

"Time passed and the radius of territory with which people concerned themselves grew broader. The powers of other families, particularly in the north, grew stronger. At one point, a daughter of the house was requested by a king far in the north. She was sent north with a generous dowry to cement relations for the family elsewhere, as was becoming increasingly common. Children three she bore her lord— three sons, no less—and none was more shocked than those hereabouts when the tale filtered over the hills that the king, his wife and his sons had been slaughtered in the woods while taking a day of leisure together.

"The custodians of the palace were said to have seized the crown and ruled in the place of those divinely chosen for the task, and folks here grumbled at the injustice, though there was naught they could do. The Pereille family grieved the loss of their own openly, until suddenly they withdrew into their own silence.

"Years later 'twas revealed that the youngest son of this northern union had escaped the carnage and somehow made his way south. 'Twas when he arrived that the family turned into itself to shelter him safely. Named Sigisbert, he was, and his existence here was only acknowledged when he mustered troops long years later in an attempt to regain his legacy. He lost that bid but never gave up the fight, retreating here and swearing his own sons to the task of restoring to the family the crown that had been lost.

"And so it has been these years. Efforts to recapture the crown, some more elaborate than others, each and every one resulting in failure. Well do I suppose that Alzeu was the last of his line in hungering after that task." Genevieve fell silent and examined her folded hands.

"What of the woman who first began your line and the sire of that first babe?" Wolfram asked. Genevieve smiled sadly.

"If ever her identity was known, 'twas lost in the mists of time."

"And the Grail?" he asked quietly.

"*San Graal,*" Genevieve said, her gaze unwavering from his as she willed him to understand. "Another rumor lost in time and one of which I know naught, but a curious coincidence has occurred to me that reminds me of a persistent tale told within our family. Consider that should you but move the break betwixt them, the two words become *Sang Raal*.''

''*Sang Raal*. Blood Royal,'' he murmured in wonder.

''Aye,'' Genevieve admitted. ''Long has it been held within our family that our bloodline, from wherever it sprang, bears the duty of kingship within it. Alzeu well believed that he was destined to rule by virtue of his lineage alone.''

Wolfram's gaze brightened, and Genevieve knew he was making the connections. ''And 'tis the sister who alone bears the burden of the Grail,'' he continued. Genevieve nodded and dropped one hand over her belly where her womb was secreted.

'''Tis said that the repository of the family's lineage is the vessel lodged within me.''

Wolfram shook his head in amazement. '''Tis the blood at the root of it all,'' he whispered, as though struggling to make sense of it all. ''Do you believe this tale?''

When Genevieve finally spoke, her voice was harsh. ''The blood it is that carries the lineage to each of us, a lineage that marks our flesh and renders our spawn alone fit to rule all of Christendom. The blood royal, they call it, and tell us 'tis a gift, even when it brings naught but grief to any who pursue the dream.''

''You do not believe these claims.'' 'Twas more a statement than a question from Wolfram. Genevieve shrugged and frowned.

''I believe there is naught to be ashamed of in my lineage,'' she murmured, then lifted her chin to stare blindly out over the hills. ''But my grandsire oft said that his father feared the blood royal had been diluted overmuch, that now it ran too thin to manifest its attributes in each of us who is fruit of the vine. Mayhap 'tis naught now but an old tale fit to regale children."

Wolfram's hands cupped around her shoulders, and Genevieve savored their warm weight. "What attributes might those be?" he asked quietly.

"An ability to heal by merely laying hands upon the ill is one oft recited," Genevieve recounted.

"Mayhap a greater measure of compassion for our fellow creatures than most?" Wolfram demanded.

Genevieve glanced up, uncertain what he meant.

"You did not plunge the blade into my back when you had the chance," he reminded her quietly.

Genevieve shook her head hastily, knowing he gave credit where 'twas not due. "I loved you even then. You had saved my life and shown me kindness."

"And killed your brother," Wolfram observed.

"'Twas the Master's hand that guided your deeds then. I understand that now."

Wolfram shook his head sagely. "It matters not, Genevieve. When first we met, you knew fully who and what I was, yet you did not turn away from me."

"To vengeance was I sworn," she argued, but Wolfram shook his head once more.

"Nay, 'twas more than that at work. 'Twas compassion I saw in your eyes," he said, and his hand rose to stroke her cheek, "and I knew not what to make of it." He leaned closer, and his gaze bored compellingly into hers. "Is it not said that one should love one's enemy rather than seek retaliation?"

Genevieve flushed and might have turned away if Wolfram had let her go. "'Twas naught but weakness," she said to excuse her behavior. "Surely you see virtue where there is none."

"Nay," Wolfram argued. "'Tis you who would mistake strength for weakness."

Genevieve shook her head, still not convinced. "I cannot heal. Right my grandsire was that the blood royal runs too thin for any good effect."

"I would argue that point." To her surprise, Wolfram ran his fingers lightly down her arms to capture her hands within his. She turned slightly, not understanding what game he played, only to have him place her hands over his heart. Genevieve felt the fluid pulse of his heart pound beneath her fingertips even as the heat of his palms trapped her hands there. She met his eyes in confusion, and Wolfram smiled.

"Do you not think you have done as much for me?" he murmured, his tone urgent, for all its low timbre.

"Wolfram," she whispered, and her voice caught in her throat. "No healer am I. Do not be deceived by what you wish to believe."

"Nay? Feel it, Genevieve," Wolfram urged as he flattened her fingers against his chest. "The warmth of a loving heart now beats where once there was the chill of stone. Even I thought naught could be changed, but your sweet love has proved me wrong." Genevieve blinked back her tears as Wolfram urged her closer.

"I can take no credit for this," she protested, wishing all the while that what he said would prove true. "'Twas finding your mother that set your fears to rest alone."

"Nay, Genevieve. I could never have spoken to her, were it not for you." Wolfram's lips grazed her temple and he bent to whisper in her ear. "This heart beats but for you, my own gentle healer, and none can tell me otherwise."

"You have a task with the Order," she argued. "Surely you cannot mean to leave their ranks?"

Wolfram shook his head sadly. "The Order of the Templars, for better or for worse, is no more. One cannot leave something that exists no longer." His lips quirked with unexpected amusement, and Genevieve regarded him with curiosity. "And none too soon, I would say, for it seems that reclaiming some lost part of myself has made me lose my touch in certain matters." He smiled then, openly, though Genevieve was not yet ready to share his confidence in their match.

She pulled back and looked into his eyes, certain she needed to warn him of her own lack of worldly ambition. "No interest have I in pursuing my family's legacy of retrieving the crown," she admitted hastily. "Times have changed, and such a feat is no longer feasible, if indeed it ever was. Do not imagine, Wolfram, that I will commit myself or my children to such a path."

To her astonishment, Wolfram did not turn away. Instead, his arms slipped around her and he regarded her with an indulgent smile. "What then do you desire from this life, my Genevieve?" he asked. The way he said her name made her heart skip a beat, but Genevieve would not grant herself any false promises.

She looked past him to the windswept bailey with its soft new grass. "I would make my home here at Montsalvat," she said quietly. "I would live simply here, raise my children and be safe from the troubles of the world."

"None can make the troubles of the world go away," Wolfram observed matter-of-factly. Genevieve smiled.

"Nay, but I would not invite those woes to my board."

"As Alzeu did," he offered. Genevieve nodded.

"Aye, I would be safe and untroubled."

"Alone?" Wolfram asked, with a lack of curiosity that must be feigned. Genevieve flicked a glance upward to find a twinkle lurking in his eyes. The very sight emboldened her, and she forced a mock sigh.

"I know not who I might coerce to live in such a wild place with me," she said coyly.

"Ah." Wolfram leaned back against the wall and surveyed the bailey. "Mayhap you should consider one who might help you secure that safety you so desire," he suggested with apparent idleness.

"Ah, but the only one who makes me feel safe is you."

There, she had said it. Genevieve held her breath as she waited. Wolfram's lips quirked but he was leisurely in meeting her eyes. When he did, she saw that mischief danced unchecked in those silver depths.

"Well it seems that a proposal might be in order," he purred. Genevieve flushed, and Wolfram chuckled in response. He swung Genevieve so high that she squealed, then let her drop back into his embrace. His features suddenly sobered when she was trapped against his chest, her feet dangling in the air.

"I love you, Genevieve de Pereille," he murmured as his gaze danced over her features. "Will you be my bride, my love and my partner for all my days?"

Genevieve smiled and reached down to frame his strong face within her hands. "Will you be mine?" she whispered hopefully in response. Wolfram smiled broadly then and let her slide down his chest so that their noses were almost touching.

" 'Twould be my utmost pleasure," he whispered. Genevieve's heart thumped in her chest so loudly that she was certain Wolfram could not miss its pounding.

"As 'twould be mine," Genevieve accepted with a shy smile. She caught but a glimpse of the exuberance that lit Wolfram's features before his lips closed over hers purposefully. His hands braced her back and lifted her against him as she locked her arms around his neck and surrendered wholeheartedly to his kiss.

Bride, love and partner. Aye, there was a role she was more than willing to fulfill for this man. Genevieve's heart sang with the certainty that here Wolfram would find the home he had lost and sought all these years. She closed her eyes and let his happiness flood into her, its warmth capturing her heart in an endless embrace.

Genevieve had helped Wolfram to heal and, together, they would seek out the greater mysteries of her legacy. Her blood rose to his touch and she leaned fully against him, her thoughts fading to one as sensation took the reins.

Wolfram was no longer alone.

And neither was Genevieve.

She fancied her grandsire would have been pleased with her choice.

* * * * *

# Harlequin® Historical

## Coming in December from Harlequin Historical

From award-winning author
**Theresa Michaels**

The next book in the saga of the unforgettable Kincaid brothers—

# ONCE AN OUTLAW
## The story of Logan Kincaid

"...an engrossing, not-to-be-missed read."
—*Romantic Times*

"...a delightful, fast-paced, and rip-roaring adventure..." —*Affaire de Coeur*

### Don't miss it!

Available in December wherever Harlequin books are sold.

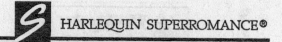

## HARLEQUIN SUPERROMANCE®

a heartwarming trilogy by *Peg Sutherland*

*Meet old friends and new ones on a trip to
Sweetbranch, Alabama—where the most unexpected
things can happen...*

Harlequin Superromance #673 *Double Wedding Ring* (Book 1)

Susan Hovis is suffering from amnesia.

She's also got an overprotective mother and a demanding
physiotherapist. Then there's her college-age daughter—and
Susan also seems to have a young son she can't really
remember. Enter Tag, a man who claims to have been her
teenage lover, and the confusion intensifies.

Soon, everything's in place for a Christmas wedding.
*But whose?*

Don't miss *Double Wedding Ring* in December,
wherever Harlequin books are sold. And watch for
*Addy's Angels* and *Queen of the Dixie Drive-In*
(Books 2 and 3 of Peg Sutherland's trilogy)
this coming January and February!

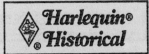

## WOMEN OF THE WEST

Don't miss these adventurous stories by
some of your favorite Western romance authors.

Coming from Harlequin Historical every month.

November 1996
#294—FOREVER AND A DAY
by Mary McBride

December 1995
#298—GERRITY'S BRIDE
by Carolyn Davidson

January 1996
#300—DEVIL'S DARE
by Laurie Grant

February 1996
#305—DIAMOND
by Ruth Langan

March 1996
#310—WESTERN ROSE
by Lynna Banning

April 1996
#314—THE FIRE WITHIN
by Lynda Trent

Don't miss any of our **Women of the West!**

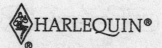

# *Harlequin Romance* ®

## New from Harlequin Romance a very special six-book series by

### MIDNIGHT SONS
### DEBBIE MACOMBER

**The town of Hard Luck, Alaska, needs women!**

The O'Halloran brothers, who run a bush-plane service called Midnight Sons, are heading a campaign to attract women to Hard Luck. *(Location: north of the Arctic Circle. Population: 150—mostly men!)*

"Debbie Macomber's *Midnight Sons* series is a delightful romantic saga. And each book is a powerful, engaging story in its own right. Unforgettable!"

—Linda Lael Miller

### TITLE IN THE MIDNIGHT SONS SERIES:

#3379    BRIDES FOR BROTHERS (available in October 1995)
#3383    THE MARRIAGE RISK (available in November 1995)
#3387    DADDY'S LITTLE HELPER (available in December 1995)
#3395    BECAUSE OF THE BABY (available in February 1996)
#3399    FALLING FOR HIM (available in March 1996)
#3404    ENDING IN MARRIAGE  (available in April 1996)

DMS-1

# HARLEQUIN ⬥ PRESENTS®

### Don't be late for the wedding!

Be sure to make a date in your diary for the happy event—
the sixth in our tantalizing new selection of stories...

### Bonded in matrimony, torn by desire...

#### Coming next month:

### *THE YULETIDE BRIDE* by Mary Lyons
### (Harlequin Presents #1781)

#### From the celebrated author of *Dark and Dangerous*

A Christmas wedding should be the most romantic of
occasions. But when Max asked Amber to be his
Yuletide Bride, romance was the last thing on his mind....
Because all Max really wanted was his daughter, and he
knew that marrying Amber was the only way he'd get
close to their child!

Available in December, wherever Harlequin books are sold.

# HARLEQUIN PRESENTS®

Dark secrets...

forbidden desires...

scandalous discoveries...

an enthralling six-part saga from a bright new talent!

### *HEARTS OF FIRE*
### by Miranda Lee

This exciting family saga is set in the glamorous world of opal dealing in Australia. *HEARTS OF FIRE* unfolds over six books, revealing the passion, scandal, sin and hope that exist between two fabulously rich families. Each novel features its own gripping romance—and you'll also be hooked by the continuing story of Gemma Smith's search for the truth about her real mother, and the priceless Black Opal....

Coming next month:

The story concludes with

### BOOK 6: *Marriage & Miracles*

Gemma's marriage to Nathan couldn't be over! There was so much that was unresolved between them.... And, most importantly, Gemma was still in love with Nathan. She also had an extraspecial secret to share with her husband—she was expecting his baby.

Harlequin Presents: you'll want to know what happens next!

Available in December, wherever Harlequin books are sold.